I0636674

LIGHT
OF THE
DARK
MOON

LIGHT
OF THE
DARK
MOON

BERNETTE SHERMAN

MOUNT HOPE MEDIA

Copyright ©2023 by Bernette Sherman

All rights reserved by Bernette Sherman. No part of this publication may be reproduced or transmitted in any form by any means, electronic or mechanical, including photocopying, or recording (with the exception of unpaid personal use), or by any information storage and retrieval system, without permission in writing from the author. Reviewers may quote brief passages. For permission requests, write to the publisher, addressed "Attention: Permissions Request," using the web address below.

All rights reserved
Published by Mount Hope Media, LLC
Austell, GA
MountHopeMedia.com
BernetteSherman.com

ISBN: 9781954636101

For every person who dares to be brave and stand for what's right.

For my daughter who now seeks her own adventures and my son, who will one day seek his.

YOU MAY ALSO ENJOY
STAR JUMPERS
AN ACCIDENTAL QUEST FOR FREEDOM

BOOKS2READ.COM/STARJUMPERS

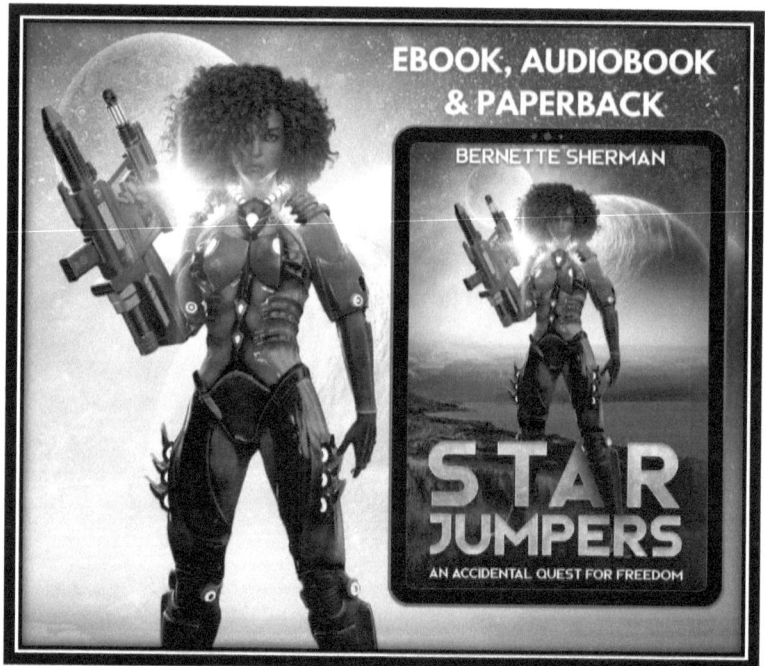

TABLE OF CONTENTS

I

DEMONSTRATION OF MAGIC

Clarod split the swirling, howling smoke, narrowly missing my target. The horned beast whipped its tail and evaporated before my eyes. Then it rematerialized mere steps away, its roar overpowering the wind. Now on the ground, I tried to wrestle away from the outstretched paws that reached for my neck. Moist fur lay heavy against the claws that pulled me toward it.

Above my head, my feet suspended in its clutch. Clarod hung below, gripped with all my strength. I laid my other hand on top, raised myself up along with Clarod, and swung. This time Clarod did not miss. It sliced the flying beast across the arm before it disappeared again, indistinguishable from the smoke.

"Run!" My scream cut through the howling wind as Clarod had done.

Something in the darkness cried back. There was laughter. Somewhere someone, or something, screamed horrifically. I held Clarod tightly, rotating slowly, in search of the sources of the mocking laughter and screams of pain.

The beast, whatever it was, might reform at any moment, resolute in its singular job of protecting itself. I grabbed my pack and slung it over my back before helping my friend stand. They were both heavier due to the energy I'd expended. Nontu ran beside us. Encountering that disappearing beast meant the entrance was near.

Thick smoke still covered the path, making it nearly impenetrable, even with goggles. It was impossible to know if it would gather itself into a solid form.

"There is no time to waste." I divided the space in front of us with Clarod. "Stay close. Don't get separated."

The wind howled and whipped, threatening to tear us away from one another. With arms linked, we marched forward. The light ahead was my sole focus. Then a song only I could hear cut through all the other sounds. An important song, even though I have yet to figure out why.

One born in the season of expecting
Shall walk amongst the other side
And find great power from the well
That only can be found inside

The little girl trilled while she skipped about and played with a beautiful woman in a flowing silver gown. A broad smile crossed the girl's face as she brought the woman a bright yellow flower. The moment the woman's fingers touched the stem, the color faded, and the dull petals crumbled into broken dead pieces at the moment it reached her nose. Then they were gone. The only thing remaining was smoke, thick and gray, with the sounds of screams and strange laughter.

My chest heaved, my heart raced, and moisture teased the strands at my hairline as my eyes sprang wide. The words vanished, like those beasts, evaporating the moment I'd awakened. Still, the song was haunting, as it always was.

***

The reflection attempted to convince me of who I was. It inhaled as I did, exhaling in turn. She was the image of a royal daughter. But I knew the truth. By now, my magic should be consistent and trustworthy, like all the royals who had come before. It was in me, as much a part of my being as the blood that coursed through me. I was a royal born, giving me the gifts of more than mundane magic.

Mundane magic was magic anyone could do through using the proper placement of tools like stones, salt, and candles. The other magic required a different connection with the light. I didn't feel special doing mundane magic. I wanted to do the magic that other royals had access to.

I'd done everything I was supposed to and more. I'd studied the books, the magic words, the use of the salt, crystals, and other tools that pulled on things natural to our realm. I knew what needed to be done to make my magic work. Yet, I'd been humbled by the knowledge that knowing and doing too often proved to be on very different spectrums of light. A light I desperately needed. The Dark Moon was fading into the morn, but I needed it to shine its light within me so that the magic from the stardust I carried would activate. Perhaps that was the problem. I'd asked, but it had yet to gift me with consistency.

I still wasn't certain whether I was a clar-gani who could see into others and situations, a clar-hadi who could connect with others' energies, a clar-waraka who could heal, or a clar-magana who could communicate with the light. Over the years I'd seen all four clar gifts come up for me. Still, nothing had come through like it should. The four clar gifts of the Dark Moon still lay shrouded in darkness.

Over and over, my magic fell into a different category than my family's and the other royals. I couldn't let it happen again this evening. It had been spotty, like a tree losing leaves as it approached the end of the giving season.

***

"Lafia Rinal Saleera Ketonga?"

Ajur Bellrin smiled the smile of queen who'd ruled and commanded others for a lifetime. One eyebrow raised and her chin rose ever so slightly.

I tried to smile back. The Demonstration of Magic was the defining coming of age moment for every Faduwatan royal. My sister, Kyari, had completed hers flawlessly. And now, having proven herself in more ways than I ever could, it had happened for her. And, they'd kept it from me. *How could they?* She was getting married, and they didn't think it worth me knowing. I'd had the most humiliating evening possible, and they'd added insult to every injury.

Nontu watched me, as everyone else did, as I struggled to control my expressions and not reveal the emotions rolling through me. Kyari stood beside her fiancé, Hakur, looking on as if she didn't want to understand what might have been troubling me. For once it had to be about me. Just once. Today. Now. This moment.

Every royal my age and older had gone through it successfully. It was my turn. I'd been preparing for years but my preparation had begun officially four years ago when I'd turned sixteen. The pressure rose in my chest, my heart pounding like the soft drums beckoning from the eds of the room.

Nontu calmly walked over. "Remember all you have practiced." She wrapped her arms around me, hugging me tightly and sharing her mighty energy with me before exiting the hall.

Nontu had come to us from the magical land of Zhiri to be our royal syte. She'd arrived shortly after I'd turned sixteen and gone through the initiation into magic training, as all royals. Since coming, Nontu had been there for me more than anyone.

"Are you ready, Lafia Ketonga, to begin your Demonstration of Magic?", Ajur Bellrin asked.

I could sense her impatience as my hesitation meant a delay to the fun of the annual Crossing of the Ties ceremony. As the host, it was something she took seriously.

With somber eyes my mother squeezed my hand gently, her eyes somber, and stepped behind the crowds until she was out of sight.

Our family ruled with the power of the clori stone and under the color red. I was a proud Narutian. Red and the clori stone were part of my power. I was cloaked in both the red and the stones, from my hair to the uncomfortable shoes. I should've felt courageous, being from Narut, but a weakness settled in my knees, threatening to cause my downfall.

I concentrated on my body and consciously lifted my chin. I considered the placement of each foot as I walked to the table with my supplies, including candles, a purple and blue hand-painted jar, two small boxes, a small pouch with stones, and my small finger-wand in a jeweled carved wooden box.

"This evening, Ajursun Lafia Rinal Saleera Ketonga will demonstrate the three levels of magic through three tests. In order to pass, she must successfully complete two of the tests. The first test is the *Ring of Concentrated Magic,* the basic level of magic, accessible to all people. Some of you may refer to this kind of magic as mundane magic. It's the magic of using items and tools to manipulate and control energy." Ajur Bellrin paused to see if I'd made progress towards the station set up for me.

My legs were made of the bollak tree trunks that grew throughout northern Faduwata, anchored in rocky ground as I made my way to the middle. A tight-lipped smile was the only assurance I could give her that I was indeed going to make it to the center of the room.

Bellrin, satisfied, continued, "The second test is to demonstrate the *Gift of the Clar.* Obviously, this is one that every royal should pass, as the gifts are within us by birthright. At least one of the four clar gifts should be demonstrated. Will she demonstrate clar-gani, clar-waraka, clar-hadi, or clar-magana? We'll have to wait and see."

The room spun slowly around me and I placed one hand on the table to steady myself, spreading my feet for balance. I'd made it and my nerves were much worse than I'd thought they'd be. The drums beat slowly and rhythmically in the background, making my heart feel off tempo.

Bellrin watched with concern before finishing the descriptive speech she or the other Clarhugabas gave before a royal tested. "And finally, the third test is the *Suspension of Natural Forces,* a demonstration of high magic. As you all are aware, it is the most difficult and very few are able to successfully achieve it as it requires the suspension of natural law. We add it in just in case someone is able to delight and surprise us!" Ajur Bellrin said, her eyebrows raising high. With an air of anticipation and intrigue, she added, "Will tonight be tonight? Let us find out. You may begin, Ajur Lafia Ketonga."

Ajur Bellrin raised one hand gracefully, calling for an end of the drums that helped mask the pounding in my chest. I fought to steady my hand as I focused on the neatly arranged ribbons on the stand and the crowd. I carefully slid the gold and silver colored wire-framed finger-wand onto my ring finger. The room fell silent, and everyone took a cautious step back, their eyes locked on me.

"For my first test," I squeaked and then loudly cleared my throat. The crowd's anticipation for the next royal to successfully join the ranks of those eligible to partner was palpable. "For my first test, I will demonstrate the *Ring of Concentrated Magic*."

I picked up the jar and slowly sprinkled salt in a circle around me. I then took out the five stones, one for each of the four regions and one for Faduwata. *Kyari was going to be a Sparakan and had kept it a secret from me.* I glanced at the newly engaged couple, watching me intensely.

Focus, Lafia. I turned back and put the stones in the center before getting up and bringing over four candles, two at a time, and placing them around the circle. I lit them and searched for Nontu, as I usually did at that point. But Nontu wasn't there, forbidden from being in the palace for the test due to the possibility of interference. I carefully stood and stepped back to allow the other royal sytes and the Clarhugabas of the other ajurdoms to inspect and make notes.

"Is your *Ring of Concentrated Magic* complete?" Bellrin asked. It was what they asked every royal child undergoing the test. Kyari smiled at me from where she stood beside Hakur. I glanced once more at my demonstration work. My mind was cloudy. I didn't want to forget something. I walked around the circle, my hands clasped behind me. The wire finger-wand pressed into my other hand.

"Ajursun Lafia. Is your *Ring of Concentrated Magic* complete?" Bellrin asked again.

I nodded slowly. *Ring, stones, and fire.* "Ya'i. I am complete."

"Very well. It is complete and will remain as you've set it for the remainder of your demonstration. You may proceed with your second demonstration of the *Gift of the Clar*."

"Thank you Ajur Bellrin." I turned toward the crowd. I'd completed the *Ring of Concentrated Magic* and only needed to pass my demonstration for *Gift of the Clar* and I could be finished with this pageantry. If I wanted, I could even choose not to attempt the final demonstration.

"For this demonstration, I need a single volunteer to join me in this circle."

There were no raised hands. This wasn't even the most difficult demonstration, but no one wanted their secrets revealed in such a public way. I'd only secured one volunteer and planned to save her for the last demonstration, but perhaps now would be a good time. I scanned the room for the person who had previously agreed to spontaneously volunteer a few months prior. I felt foolish. I'd been so caught up in the evening and assumed every royal and dignitary would be present. She wasn't. From the corner of my eye, Bletondu smirked.

"I'll provide evidence that perhaps you, and others you are close with, will know but is not confidential. Don't worry," I added jokingly, "your secrets are safe with me." My eyes scanned those looking on for any takers or anyone who might look interested. My stomach continued its awkward dance despite the smile on my face.

"Please don't make me come around one by one," I said with a nervous laugh which was received by an awkward silence.

I searched the dignitaries for a friendly face that hadn't averted their eyes. Even they refused to help. I turned to their children who seemed to have made themselves scarce. "Faru? Perhaps I can work with you on this demonstration?"

Faru's green hair bobbed slightly as he moved from behind his father, Sarkin Yandoka Felli. "Nothing I say will have anything to do with your father's role as Faduwatan Chief of Internal Security."

Faru sighed heavily and whispered a question to his father, who responded with a brief nod.

"Does that mean I have a volunteer?" I asked excitedly. This one was always tough for those doing demonstrations. No one in this group wanted secrets revealed but it had been especially tough for me. Not a single willing volunteer.

"Ya'i. Nothing on any governmental business." Faru's face was stern. He stepped forward and I invited him into the ring with me.

"Please close your eyes with me while I connect with you."

I took one of Faru's hands in both of mine and we closed our eyes. Despite being flustered, I needed to do this. The hall was silent enough that I heard Faru's breathing. My heart beat loudly in my ears. My hands warmed around his. This should be easy. Connecting with him right in front of me, his hand in mine. I breathed deeply to calm my mind.

My mind skipped from the image of Kyari and Hakur's engagement announcement to the juice spilling on Bletondu at the start of the evening. *Go away.* They were replaced by my father Rufan's words and what I'd heard outside. Then by smoke, beasts forming from smoke and the dying flower of my dreams. I forced them out and refocused my attention to the middle of my forehead, but it only showed irrelevant scenes I'd already witnessed. Nothing about Faru.

I opened my eyes enough to see through my lashes. They were getting restless. *Come on, Lafia. Do not fail.* My forehead throbbed as I forced a connection with Faru. I strained to see something. Anything. It had to be evidential. A dingy red sash, like the ones we wore, lay on the ground, and he appeared lifeless beside it, his hair was different, and I wasn't sure it was even him. Then it was all gone, eaten by thick gray smoke.

"I'm sorry." I opened my eyes fully. "It's been such an eventful evening with the excitement of my sister and Ajursun Hakur's engagement. I believe I'm a bit distracted. I need another moment." There were gracious nods throughout the room as I closed my eyes to try again. Inside I screamed, "Faru! Can you hear me? Where are you, dammit!?"

Nothing. Silence. That same smoke clouded everything. I let the smooth conical tip of the dunha stone mounted on my finger-wand graze his wrist to connect with his pulse. I hoped it would amplify the signal if there was one. Images and sounds from earlier in the evening flooded back into my head. I strove to block it all out and focus solely on Faru.

Still nothing. My throat clenched, and my palms went from warm to moist—not from the magic I was trying to use.

I dropped his hands. If I didn't pass this test, I still could get my status by miraculously passing the next one or requesting a special testing with the Clarhugabas and sytes within three moons, but it was risky.

If I failed now or later with the special testing, I'd have to wait until next Crossing of the Ties ceremony. I could also prove it by showing I could use the different levels of magic in real life. That was even riskier and less likely given my success up to now. It didn't matter.

Whether I failed today or later, it would ruin my reputation and bring shame upon my family and on Nontu. I thought about Kyari and how she told me to focus and relax and then my mind shifted to how she'd kept the biggest news of her life from me.

I didn't open my eyes or say anything as I turned my full energy to Faru. I took his hand in mine again and tried to feel the energy around him. If I could expand my energy field, it would be possible to connect to his and maybe get something useful. The energy around me grew along with the tingling sensation as I connected with him. *You can do it, Lafia. A little more.* "Show me," I whispered. Faru stood in front of me, and then he was gone. Nothing was there but the gray smoke. I let his hands fall and stumbled back out of the circle, nearly falling.

"Are you okay?" Faru asked. "What did you see?"

"N-Nothing. I didn't see anything. The power was overwhelming and knocked me off."

"I did feel you connect, even if briefly."

"Ni."

"Lafia. I know how much this means. Just share what you saw to pass the demonstration."

I shook my head. "Ni. I saw nothing evidential. Just smoke, fog. Nothing."

I couldn't make sense of anything I'd seen.

"Are you sure, Ajursun Lafia?" Faru asked firmly.

"I'm sure." I was unable to hide the tremble in my voice.

Before he could ask again, I stepped away from him and turned to face the audience. I'd tried listening, communicating, seeing, but there was nothing. Any of them would have been demonstrations of the clar, but I had no clar at all to use with any of them. There was only darkness.

"Please accept my apology. I must concede this demonstration of my *Gift of the Clar*. Thank you, Faru, for volunteering."

Ajur Bellrin stepped into the center, stopping near me. "Ajursun Lafia, would you like to attempt the final demonstration, *Suspension of Natural Forces*?"

My mind reeled from what I'd seen. To have any chance, I needed to focus. My Adon's comment from earlier replayed in my head, "Unless you have mastered connecting…" and I tried to push that out as well. I raised my eyes toward him, but my Adon looked away. Lifting my chin, I willed the tears to remain in my eyes.

I'd need another volunteer for this as well. It had been challenging enough getting one to demonstrate a message. If I succeeded, there might be redemption for me. If I failed, this night would be solidified as a complete and abject failure. "I will attempt the final demonstration."

"Very well. You may take a moment to prepare."

Bellrin along with the other Clarhugabas and sytes stepped back. I closed my eyes and took a breath before returning to the table. I picked up the small purple box and held it up before placing it back down with a forced smile.

"I need a volunteer for my *Command of Haskeal Magic Tools* demonstration." Everyone stared and several took another noticeable step back. My family couldn't volunteer. Now even a volunteer from Hakur's family would be suspicious.

"One volunteer is all I need for this basic demonstration of my *Command of Haskeal Magic Tools* using the deanimation dust." There was nothing. I smiled at Najurvod hopefully, but he averted his eyes toward my ring of salt. "Anyone? You don't disappear." I didn't want to beg but not a single person was coming forward. "You'll only be still a few seconds." If I heard the desperation in my voice, everyone else did too, which would mean any trust there might have been had been lost.

"We don't want you to resort to begging, Ajursun Lafia." The words dripped like slow tree sap from Bletondu's lips. "I'll volunteer for your little demonstration." She sashayed across the ballroom in a bright fuchsia gown with shimmying silver beads hanging from her knees to the floor. A matching feathered plume, rivaling the size of her arm, stuck out of her coily loose hair.

"Would *anyone* else like to volunteer?" I pleaded with my eyes.

Bletondu dramatically spun around to survey the room. "Looks like you're stuck with me," she said with a chuckle loud enough that everyone could hear. "Don't worry. I'm a willing volunteer." Smiles crossed the faces of several of the guests. She then turned her gaze to me. "It's so good to see you again, Lafia. I've hardly seen you since, well, since…." Bletondu lifted the skirt of her new dress slightly and raised her shoulder while smiling.

"I'm so sorry about the dress, Bletondu. But you look as lovely, beautiful in fact, as ever."

"Well, it'll have to do. Thankfully, I'm always prepared. I'm sure you understand. I like your dress as well. It looks familiar. Didn't Kyari don that very gown, minus the pants, just three celebrations back?"

"Ya'i. You have an excellent memory. I loved the gown, but I really liked the idea of pants," I smiled back.

"Hmmm. It's very brave of you."

"Brave?"

"Of course. I certainly could never be so bold, and on an evening as important as this one is for you."

I yelped and everyone again turned their attention to me. I'd been squeezing my folded hands so hard the finger-wand had nearly drawn blood. Bletondu walked in a circle around me, stopping on the other side of my circle.

"Thank you for volunteering for this demonstration. Can you please confirm that you have no prior biases that would cause you to assist me beyond your voluntary participation?"

"I can confirm this one hundred percent." Her eyes moved slowly to me, and for a moment, Bletondu's gaze locked in.

"Then we will begin." I picked up the box, held it gingerly in my hand and tried to remember the words under Bletondu's judgmental stare and hundreds of waiting eyes.

"I will demonstrate deanimation of a living being using the power of the tongue and haskeal deanimation dust."

Everyone except Bletondu took another step back. *Now you want to trust me?* Kyari had already stepped back once and now she probably wasn't even listening, her thoughts consumed by her engagement.

I unclasped the box and pulled the lid back before setting it down again.

"Please step into the ring with me."

Bletondu gave me a look that said, "Are you certain?" but moved inside the circle of salt anyway.

Once I began, I had to act quickly. My tongue suddenly felt heavy, and my mouth dry. I smacked my lips and tried to swallow, hoping to create moisture that would allow me to speak the words. Holding up my finger with the wand, I indicated I needed a moment and walked quickly to the beverage station, my steps echoing loudly in the quiet hall. I picked up a glass of water and swigged it, some missing my mouth and landing on my chin and dress. I dabbed both of them quickly and as discreetly as possible with a napkin and then hurried back, glass in hand.

"Are we ready?" Bletondu asked. "This is the longest demonstration I've seen since I began coming to this affair. By this time in the evening your sister was already done, and we were already back to dancing."

"Ready." I wanted to deanimate her condescending smile, but with this demonstration, I would deanimate all of her. *Much better*. With the haskeal deanimation dust and the words it should be a straightforward demonstration, but nothing had gone as it should yet. I pointed my finger-wand toward Bletondu, pinched the dust between my thumb and pointer finger on the other hand, and narrowed my eyes.

Bletondu's expression shifted subtly, and I wondered if she was concerned.

"Mai rai ni jiki gareni."

I relaxed the grip on the dust as I continued to point and blew it into Bletondu's face. Her breathing slowed, her restless fidgeting became barely noticeable and finally stopped. I'd done it. *Two demonstrations passed!* I smiled for the entire room, turning again for Nontu's approval, before remembering she wasn't there. It had only been a few seconds. The gasps around the room made me whip around to see Bletondu making stiff, jerky movements and then break into laughter, shaking her head back and forth.

Through her laughing, she said, "Something needed to entertain these people. It didn't work but I'm sure you'll get it next year." She leaned forward and whispered, "After all, to truly be eligible and be in a serious courtship, one must pass the demonstration. Well, at least if you aim to rule one day over an ajurdom or as Clarhugaba." She leaned back so she could look into my eyes. Bletondu's eyes didn't hold the smile her lips did. "But you know that, don't you?"

A wave of embarrassment rushed through me as I stared at her in disbelief, then at the wand on my finger, and finally at the ring and rocks and candles. *This couldn't be happening.* I tried to calm my voice enough to speak.

"I have not successfully demonstrated all of my tasks, and—" My voice stuck in my throat again as I looked for my Mada. She was still not within eyesight. "I accept the rules of eligibility and will reattempt through special testing with the Clarhugabas and sytes," I paused as I stared over the heads in front of me, "though real-life application or at the next Crossing of the Ties." It was what I was supposed to say if I failed more than two tasks. "Thank you for your time."

There was a light, polite applause as I curtsied.

Bletondu shook her head with pity. "I'm so disappointed for you, Lafia. That it didn't work out this year," Bletondu added for further insult.

My lips tightened as I bent to blow out the candles.

"By the way, you wouldn't have passed anyway. Your *Ring of Concentrated Magic* is not done properly. You don't need one for the haskeal dust magic to work, but I thought you should know just so you don't blame me for failing."

Words escaped me as she stood there smirking.

"Tell me, Lafia. Do you think Najurvod will ever find a partner?" she asked curiously as I examined my *Ring of Concentrated Magic*. I inspected what I'd done, the placement of every piece.

"Lafia?"

"What, Bletondu?"

"What do you think? Will he?"

"Will who do what?"

"Najurvod. A partner. Keep up."

"A business partner? Now isn't the time."

The annual ceremony was the prime opportunity to renew relationships and solidify important deals. Najurvod, as shrewd as he was, wouldn't have missed the chance, especially given his position. It had always been clear that as the crown Ajursun and only royal child of Emervy, he must ensure his title was put to the most beneficial use in every way possible.

"Don't be dense, Lafia. I'm not interested in his business dealings. Is he ever going to find himself a life partner, a wife, do you think? Surely, you've heard something. Your little sister must have shared some gossip. We would make quite a pair, wouldn't we?" she said with a toss of her head that left me tightlipped.

I visibly rolled my eyes. "Is that who you're interested in here?"

Turning slowly on my heels, I left the center of what was to be the dance floor once again. With my chin high and shoulders straight, I maintained the impression of dignity. In reality, it had been left behind with the salt in that ring. Despite my failure, I was not going to give any of them the satisfaction of any other reaction. They already had enough to talk about.

Bletondu strode quickly after me, as the cleaners came to the center where I'd been.

"Don't try to be smart, Lafia. It doesn't look good on you," Bletondu said with a smirk. "I'm only playing around. Don't be so serious. Now, is that dashing Emervian crown prince looking for a life partner or not? Kyari wouldn't say."

"I couldn't tell you either. Have you spoken to him this evening?"

"Earlier. But I wanted to get a dance in. He's quite the dancer. Tell me, is he seeing anyone? Seriously? That perhaps wouldn't be at the Crossing of the Ties?"

"If you want to talk to him, talk to him," I said firmly. "You have more years of experience in this than I do. Surely you or your friends can wrench an answer from him or someone else."

"Good idea. As a matter of fact, I believe I'll make all of my rounds. The evening is getting late."

Bletondu sashayed off in her over-the-top gown, leaving me to stand, as the last of the salt was swept away, and my stones and candles were put back in my case so I could gather them later. They carried it off the floor while I followed Bletondu briefly with my eyes. The evidence of my failure had been removed, but that didn't help. I'd done nothing right and had made a fool of myself, disgracing everyone I cared about.

2

ROYALS

There was nowhere to escape this time. In the open, waiting for our trains, he strode toward me, his confidence on his sleeve as proudly as the emblem across his chest.

"Are you alright?"

"I'm fine. I'm sure there are plenty of others you must see before all the trains come."

"You are correct but I'm speaking with you now. Listen, we're going to be family soon. We might as well try to get along."

I sighed deeply. "Ya'i. But our regions are quite far apart. Thankfully."

"Not that far with the stations. Look, Lafia, don't worry about anything yet. You're just now officially in play. Well, I mean…I'm sorry. You will be. At any rate, you should forget all of that for now. Well, forget almost everything. I'm sure you won't be forgotten. That spin on the dance floor and your demonstration will be seared into the memory of every Faduwatan here. Quite an *almost* coming out, don't you think?" he said, his fingers emphasizing almost.

"You may want to keep making your rounds, Jamil. I don't think I can handle any more of your titillating and inspiring conversation, and I wouldn't want to use all your remaining time. Besides," I paused and nodded briefly to Kyari and Hakur, "I couldn't handle any more news and surprises tonight."

His mouth opened in shock, "You didn't know?" Now it was his turn to whisper. He pulled me farther to the side so he could look straight into my eyes. He was tall and undoubtedly one of the best-looking *eligibles* in Faduwata. If I were to truly be honest, he was *the* best-looking.

My chest was heavy. "Am I the only one who didn't know?"

Jamil's mouth turned up on one side and his eyes softened, "I'm sure you weren't, but since I get all the news, I wouldn't know."

"Calling all Wallarins. Calling all Wallarins," the train conductor announced. The Wallarins separated from their small groups, where they chatted with each other and headed to the first few train pods.

"This union between my brother and your sister is good for Faduwata."

"Calling all Emervites. Calling all Emervites."

I glanced up hopefully when the conductor had begun speaking, only to be disappointed when it wasn't Narut.

"We'll talk soon. I'm assuming I'll see you at the engagement dinner."

"It is my duty to be there," I smiled tightly. It was the same smile I'd used for a great part of the evening.

"Calling all Narutians. Calling all Narutians."

I let out a sigh of relief.

"Well, that's me."

"Hand?"

Jamil held up his right hand and I reluctantly offered my left hand. "Until next time we meet, may the light of the Dark Moon be within you."

"And may it be within you. Wait. Where's your Faduwatan royal ring, Jamil?"

Jamil leaned over closely, "I may have lost it in Emervy, the last passing etawae moon." He shrugged and straightened. "I'm having another made. My mother believes it's just been misplaced somewhere in the palace. It's better if that's what she thinks."

"Do you at least have the Sparakan ring?" I asked quickly, holding up my left-hand finger to show the reddish jeweled ring on the finger next to my thumb. I rested my other hand on my hip.

"Ya'i," he said and held up his hand. "I had that one replaced immediately."

Unbelievable. I shook my head and headed toward the train before slowing my step and looking back.

"Next time, go a size up on your pants."

"Lafia. Leaving? I thought I heard them call for Narut." I winced at the sound from behind me. "Greetings again, Jamil," Bletondu said with a voice that almost sang. "What were you two whispering about over here? Hopefully not that terrible tumble from earlier? Did you see it, Jamil? It was just awful. Are you alright now, Lafia?"

"I'm fine. Thank you."

"It looked like the two of you were wrapping up and I wanted to make sure I said my goodbyes. Goodbye, Lafia." Bletondu reached for my chin and I pulled away. Still, her eyes managed to meet mine. "Watch your step as you go. You wouldn't want to take another spill."

"It was nice chatting with you, Jamil. Looks like you don't need to make rounds. They come to you," I nodded.

I carefully started walking towards the train, holding my skirt up so I wouldn't trip. I studied everything in my path. I was almost to the train.

My hands flailed in front of me as one foot stuck on an uneven stone that lined the path, and I fell forward, landing hard on my arms and side. My elbow and knee stung sharply.

Kyari hurried over to help me up. "Are you okay?" she asked, looking me over. I turned my elbow to see the blood running down my arm. Jamil rushed to my side and handed me his handkerchief.

"It's all I have."

I grabbed the handkerchief and held it on my elbow, pushing Kyari off me. "I'm fine. I can get up by myself."

"Does it hurt?" Kyari asked while searching the crowd. While I'd suspected Bletondu had something to do with my spill on the dance floor, I couldn't be sure. This time I knew it was Bletondu.

"I said I'm fine. You have other things to concern yourself with."

I limped toward the train, my hemline torn, my knees scuffed, and my palms scratched. I fought to muster the little pride I had left. I knew how to do a repel spell just as well as Kyari. And I didn't even need official words as the magic lay in the intention and the phrasing I used to get the effect I needed. I knew exactly what I wanted to repel.

This evening's young
But love is done
Repel Bletondu

From everyone
Til a week is done
And comes the sun
And if she tries
To steal his eyes
May she fail
May I prevail

***

Our platform, a round metal plate, had openings to enter and exit but was otherwise enclosed, with windows to see out of. Despite being a circle, seated on the thick cushioned seat next to Kyari and Naeemah, I was completely alone.

The train conductor rode smoothly, providing as safe and comfortable a trip as possible. He managed to keep our transporter in alignment with the magnetic lines that ran between the palace and the main transport station in Sparaka.

"Do you think we could rock this off the lines?" Naeemah asked, breaking me out of my thoughts.

"What?"

"Do you think if you and I start moving side to side, we can rock our little disc off the track?"

"Why on the whole realm of Maradobu would we ever consider that?" My face twisted at her idea.

"Well, Mada is completely preoccupied, as is Adon. We may as well do something."

I gave her a final sideways glance, refusing to engage in her immature prank that could cause serious injury not only to us but to everyone in the row of discs. I turned my head toward Kyari and then out past her.

The lines crisscrossed Faduwata, but trains only ran between the most populated and key areas and the main transport station. Otherwise, walking was an option, cycling, riding carsos, a large animal suitable for carrying one to two persons who knew how to manage it, or private transport operators, who often operated without a license, as long as they avoided the authorities.

I sighed audibly, unintentionally.

My Adon continued to stare out the window, avoiding any conversation. Perhaps he was deciding on what he would say about my disgraceful failure.

"Is everything alright with you, Lafia?" Selifaya asked with genuine concern. "Aside from, well…that is something we will resolve. It is done."

She was clearly speaking of my failure to pass the demonstration and Adon gave her a sideways glance, still choosing not to look at me. Mada had barely noticed my condition coming into our transport platform. She'd barely noticed me and had no idea about more than the earlier happenings of the evening.

"I'm tired. This evening has been long and—" I stopped speaking, questioning whether my concerns were important to them. "I'll be fine."

"I believe some rest is called for after this exciting evening," Selifaya smiled.

I nodded and returned my gaze to the lights ahead. We were entering the Sparaka Central Station, where we would arrive at the main transportation hub. Sparaka Central bustled, even beyond the main transport station. Other trains like ours, private transports, and Sparakans on foot and cycles came in and out of the station. Carsos weren't allowed in the actual station, but they waited along the road. I smiled, despite myself. They were as vibrant and colorful as their leaders.

They did everything with extra flair, from their hair to their clothes and makeup.

"Ohhh, I may have to come here when I'm of age," Naeemah gushed. She waited for a response, but I pretended not to hear. "They have the most beautiful and vivid colors in all the realm. Don't you think?" she asked and gently nudged me this time.

I shrugged in response.

"Right. I guess you can find this in Faduwata Central as well, but mostly because there are a lot of Sparakans there. I could live in Faduwata Central too."

Frustrated, I let out a slow breath and twisted my body slightly, bumping Kyari's leg, who barely noticed.

"And don't they wear their pins most creatively? Look, Lafia." Naeemah pointed toward a woman crossing the road in front of a late-night diner. "She has hers as a pin for that beautiful gold and green scarf. Is that gold and green? It's hard to tell in this light. Oh, and look at him. His is in an interesting place on his pants."

Unable to resist, I casually turned my head to see what she was talking about. He'd secured it in a rather noticeable place, front and center of his pants. I huffed to hide a laugh before resuming my position. Their pins were in creative places. Peering to the other side, the pins were stuck on belts, shirt sleeves, added to necklaces, and placed anywhere else they could think of.

"Don't be like that, Lafia. It's just going to be the two of us soon."

"We're getting close," Mada said to my sisters and me.

Conscientiously, I felt for my sash. It set me apart as one of the royals. I smoothed my gown and pants out and slipped my shoes back on. Selifaya checked each of us before having Kyari put on lipstick and Naeemah dab powder on her forehead. "Touch up your lips, Lafia. Here." She handed me a glittery gloss with rosy bits and gold dust.

I dabbed my lips and readied myself for the eyes that would be on all of us from when the door opened to when we were safely in the station and on the next transporter.

My train was also filled with the royals and dignitaries from the other stations, so perhaps it would mean less attention on me. A large crowd gathered at the entrance. Some held signs while others threw flowers and glitter. They were saying something I couldn't make out. After several seconds I realized they were chanting.

"What is this?" Rufan asked in frustration, to anyone who could hear him.

"It looks like a protest, Adon," Naeemah said with a tinge of excitement. "But look, some people are even giving us flowers."

"Protest for what?" he asked, looking to Naeemah this time.

"I don't know."

"Maybe they're upset we had a party," I said nonchalantly.

"We do it every year. For them. So we can have peace. They know this," Rufan argued irritably.

"Do they?" I asked.

"Not now. None of this now." Rufan glared at me and then the protesters.

"We all deserve water! We all deserve water!" could be heard clearly as we pulled into the station.

"Come. Quickly. All of you." A Sparakan guard opened the door and escorted us off the train.

Despite only having forty to fifty Sparakans protesting, they were loud. The guard ushered us quickly to the transporters, where an operator requested the coordinates and punched them into a machine. We all stepped onto the metal plate, held the dunha stones given to each of us by the operator as an energy booster, and stood still.

The operator said, "Thank you for riding the Faduwata Express," and pulled the lever.

***

"Has the news of our engagement already reached Sparaka, Adon?" Kyari asked once we'd arrived home in Narut.

"It's possible, perhaps, from the first transporters leaving. It's of no importance. The entire realm will know by morn anyway. You have more important things to concern yourself with. You are engaged to Ajursun Hakur and will soon sit beside him as Clarhugaba to all of Sparaka. You have a great deal for which you must prepare."

"Mada. I was under the impression that there wasn't to be a formal announcement yet."

"As was I, but good news travels quickly. As your father said, your concern is not about who knows."

"And what was that chanting about, Adon?" Kyari asked. "I heard them saying something about deserving water when we provide water equally to all regions of Faduwata."

"Don't worry about such things, Kyari. As your father has already said, you have more important things to concern yourself with."

"Mada. Should I not be prepared to understand what troubles the people if I'm to be a Clarhugaba?"

Selifaya smiled and nodded. "Ya'i, you should be. However, there is a time and a way for all things. The night is late. We can continue this tomorrow."

"Ya'i, Mada." Kyari pressed her lips together as she did when she was forcing herself to not speak.

"Mada. May I speak with you?" I asked.

"It's late and this day has been long. Let us speak tomorrow."

3

CLARHUGABA

Familiar footsteps in the hallway followed by rapping of knuckles on the door meant Kyari waited outside.

"Come in."

"Good, you're still awake."

"Ya'i. Can't sleep."

"Me either. So much excitement tonight."

"Mmmm."

"I'm engaged, Lafia. Can you believe it?"

"I can now."

"I know. It all happened so quickly. I'm sorry I didn't come earlier. I was with Nontu discussing what happens after the marriage. My duties."

"Of course. I'm sure you'll do very well, whatever it is you must do. You always do very well."

"Is everything okay with us, Lafia?"

"Of course. Why?"

"You've been quiet this evening on the ride to the transport station and then home."

"It was a long and terrible evening for some of us, Kyari."

"I'm sorry you didn't pass the demonstration, Lafia."

"Is there something I can help you with, Kyari?"

She shifted uncomfortably near the door.

"You're still up. Why are you up to so late?"

"Trying to go to sleep. That's all. You probably should get to sleep too. I'm sure you've got a lot to do tomorrow."

"I thought maybe I'd come and talk to my best friend," Kyari smiled and walked toward the bed.

I stretched my legs across the other side and moved my pillow closer to the middle. Kyari sat on the edge of the bed.

"It's late, Kyari."

"You don't have to be so formal. We're home."

"It's late, Kyari. I'm tired. I've had a long and disappointing day."

"Come on, let's lie in bed and talk until the moon is completely gone, drained by the dawn," Kyari said with a hint of girlish excitement.

"Not tonight. I said I'm tired. Not all of our nights were stellar, Kyari."

"Why do you do this?"

"Do what?"

She shook her head as if she didn't believe I was asking for clarification. As if it should've been obvious.

"This. You tamp it all down until you're frustrated and then throw words and act out without thought."

"I don't do that. If I have, it's not on purpose. Everyone gets frustrated and upset."

"But you throw your frustration and then leave it for others to deal with."

I stared blankly at Kyari. She'd already interrupted me and was it really so she could turn the blame on me?

"I'm sorry you feel that way."

"It's not so much that I feel that way. I'm not the only one."

My suspicions were right. They did talk about me.

"As I said, I'm sorry you feel this way. But tonight isn't only on me."

Kyari sighed heavily.

"I don't know what you must be going through right now but I'm not the enemy."

I pressed my lips together, rolled over onto my stomach and faced the other way.

"Ya'i. It is late. I'll see you at breakfast." Kyari waited for a response, and after an uncomfortable silence, she walked to the door. "Good night, Lafia."

The door opened, and Kyari walked out, leaving it slightly cracked. "Please pull the door shut, Kyari." This time it clicked closed and I sat back up in bed.

I wanted what Kyari was preparing to have, what my mother had as the Clarhugaba to Narut. To do that, I needed working magic and to partner with an eligible Faduwatan who would ascend to the role of Ajur. Najurvod was eligible, guaranteed to ascend, and therefore the only eligible I had any interest in.

By now, I should've known which of the gifts of the clar I had. Gani, seer; waraka, healer; hadi, connector; or magana, communicator. It was possible to have multiple gifts as Mada and the sytes, but I yearned for consistent proof that I had even one.

As a clar-magana, Mada was able to communicate with other dimensions of light. Clar-maganas were the most common in my family line. Kyari had the gift, and I suspected Naeemah had it as well.

Being a clar-magana was considered one of the more powerful gifts because if you could reach the light within a being or a place, and communicate with that inner light, you

36

could help it expand, grow, change, and heal. You could see what it saw from their perspective. Nontu had all of them. I wasn't sure what could have made her think I was a natural or special without a single, consistently apparent gift.

I'd followed Nontu's instructions, daily practice with her after breakfast and private practice before bed. Nontu had told me that my gifts were to be used to serve others and to help me create for myself. First within and then without. So far, I'd been unable to do either. I couldn't help myself and so I couldn't help anyone else.

"Focus," that's what Nontu would say. "What do you want? What's in your heart?"

That perhaps was part of my problem. It may not have been all my problems, but it didn't help once I'd gotten past the mundane magic. I thought about what I wanted at that moment. *Najurvod.*

I jumped at the soft knock on the door. "Who is it?"

"It's me."

"Come in."

The heavy metal door opened partly and Nontu peaked in. *What was she doing up here and so late?*

"Is everything alright, Basi Nontu?"

"Is it?" Nontu answered with her ears turning up, the tips coming forward ever so slightly.

I considered lying to her for a moment but thought better of it. She was a syte and would know whether it was truthful or not. Besides, I didn't want to lie, and she probably already knew. "I don't know, Nontu."

"What is unknown?"

"I don't know how to make my magic work."

"That is what you believe to be unknown to you? Is that what drew me here to you?"

I shrugged, not wanting to answer any other way and risk drawing her into a deeper conversation.

Nontu smiled. Her brown skin caught bits of the moonlight coming in. The golden amber freckles that began at the tip of her nose and continued just above the center of her brows into an arch over them were a match to the ones that dotted the tips of her pointed ears. Tonight, under the lavender full moon, they glowed amber.

While my ears were pointed as well, they were much smaller with a more subtle tip. On occasion I would choose to paint dots in gold or red on my face as many others in Maradobu did. However, my ears and dots didn't glow like hers. It was another reminder that she was different than me.

Nontu folded herself onto the large pillow on the floor.

"I know this evening was especially difficult, Lafia."

I shook my head to distract myself from what I knew was coming. I didn't want to get emotional.

"I can't. Not right now," I whispered.

"Tonight, you expected to pass your demonstration and enter the phase of eligibility. That did not happen."

"I know, Nontu. I failed. I know."

"Instead, your sister becomes engaged to the ascending Ajursun of Sparaka."

"I'm sorry, Nontu. Can I help you with something? It's late."

Nontu smiled and cast her eyes toward the window. "Tell me of your dreams, Lafia."

I studied the cover on my bed intently. She'd asked me the same question since she came to us on the first lavender moon following my sixteenth birthday.

"I haven't had any dreams lately."

"Ni? Not at all?"

"Ni. When I sleep, that's all I do. Sleep."

"I see," she replied softly. "Nothing at all." She put her hands together, finger to finger, the tips meeting each other. Her pointed nails matched her ears which were now pulled back.

I grimaced. "That's not true, Nontu. Everything is engulfed in smoke. I see a glimpse and then it's gone. There's still that little girl I've told you about. She's playing and singing something, but I don't know what it is. Then that's gone too. Even my dreams are useless. Nontu, I'll be okay, won't I?"

I'd finally told her about the smoke. After tonight's failure, what else could I lose?

"Always the same little girl?"

"Ya'i. I don't get much else."

"I imagine you will. You must determine what is keeping you from using your magic."

"Sometimes I think I'm blocked. Light talkers run in my family. All I see is darkness, smoke, gray." I paused as I watched her eyes. "It's possible that something else is wrong, Nontu."

"Do not overthink. That is a tendency you have. It can overpower the light trying to work through you."

"Don't think?"

"That is not what I said. There is a time for mental athleticism, and there is a time to let the mind rest while the light works."

"My mind doesn't rest, Nontu."

Nontu smiled and stood, rising as gracefully as she'd sat. She touched the center of my forehead. "All things will come to you when they are due. You cannot force magic. You allow it to flow through you."

"I know something is wrong, Nontu and I must figure it out quickly."

"What else do you know, dear child?"

I loved when Nontu called me *dear child*. "I must prepare for my Demonstration of Magic, Nontu. I must be ready to take my place as a Clarhugaba. Being a light leader, a Clarhugaba, is all I want. I know this."

"How do you know this, Lafia?"

"It's all I could think about when I tried using my magic and it didn't work. I thought about how I'd fail as a Clarhugaba. I'd fail my people. I didn't know until tonight how much filling this role means to me. How much it's always meant. I want to serve like Mada serves."

"It is good to first know our own hearts before seeking to know the hearts of others. Ya'i?"

"Ya'i."

"Is that what you want, to be a Clarhugaba and clar-magana like your mother?"

"Ya'i."

"Why?"

I wasn't sure why she asked me this when I'd already been clear.

"Why what?"

"Why do you want to be a Clarhugaba?"

"Nontu. I told you this earlier, I want to serve like Mada serves."

"Is it to be like your mother, or is it to serve?"

"That's the same thing."

"Is it?"

I sat quietly, observing Nontu's facial expression and demeanor. I wanted a sense of what she meant by what she was asking. Instead, I got nothing from the serene Nontu.

"Close your eyes, dear child. I want to show you something."

"I can't connect."

"You can. I can. We will."

I closed my eyes and Nontu moved to sit in front of me on my bed. She clasped my hands and her long, pointed nails tapped against my palms.

We began breathing in sync as we'd done for years. The energy began flowing from Nontu to me, making my palms warm and tingly. The tingling sensation crept through my wrist and up my arms to my shoulders. Then it passed through my neck, the back of my head and the top and over to the center of my forehead.

"Connect with me," Nontu said only slightly above a hush.

I tried but there was nothing. It was cloudy and gray.

"What do you see, Lafia?"

"Nothing. I think I'm blocked, Nontu."

"Connect *with* me," she encouraged.

"I—"

"Shhhh. Quiet that voice telling you that you cannot connect with the light and connect with me."

I took several more deep breaths and let my shoulders and back relax. That was supposed to help with the block, but nothing came through, even with Nontu sitting with me.

"What do you see and feel, Lafia?"

Nothing. Everything was clouded, but telling her I'd gotten nothing, again, wasn't an option. "I don't know. Nothing is clear." I dropped Nontu's hands.

"You were born with magic, as are all those with royal blood. As are my people."

"But you all have it, and it's stronger, and you can do so much more. Nothing I do works as it should with any consistency!"

"Did you dream last night?"

"The same thing as always, but it felt heavier. Closer."

Nontu nodded as if she understood.

"I think I needed to talk tonight, and I feel like I can talk to you."

"You can always come to me, Lafia."

"I know."

Nontu studied my face and smiled.

"You really should know that you are very special to me. More than you know. I see a young woman who has made a great deal of progress since we last spoke."

It was my turn to smile.

"You're right. I want to be a Clarhugaba. I know that now."

"Knowing is good."

"How can you always be so sure and confident, Nontu?"

"I see what I see. I know what I know. Only you can know what you see and know what you know." Nontu said calmly and without any space for argument.

"Do you miss your home, Nontu?"

"Of course. As you would miss yours if away for long periods."

"You only go home twice per year. Why?"

"If that. Do you want me to go more often?" she laughed lightly.

"Ni. I was curious why you don't go more. One day I want to see Zhiri."

"It is a place of wonder. A place of beauty and magic. I do miss it. Once one visits, it proves difficult to leave. I actually have not been back in quite a while."

"I thought you visited just after my birthday when you went on leave."

"I have many other things to do and places to visit when I take leave. I cannot always go home."

"Then you must miss it terribly."

"I consider what I must do, in this season, a priority. Sacrifices are sometimes necessary."

"You mean preparing Kyari?"

"My duties as a royal syte here and you and Naeemah are also a priority."

Nontu tried gazing into my eyes causing me to lean forward uncomfortably to get out of the light. She came closer and touched my hand. "I see. I see." Nontu let my hand go, grazed my forehead with one long finger and turned to leave.

"What? What do you see, Basi Nontu?"

"There is much, Lafia. You are aware of the things you know but not what you do not know. There is much unknown that you do not yet know is even unknown to you."

"How am I supposed to not overthink when you say a thing like that, Nontu?" I smiled.

She smiled back and touched my forehead gently once more.

"I would love to come to Zhiri with you the next time you go," I said with a breathiness I hadn't expected.

"Perhaps one day."

"I don't understand why I can't go with you now."

"I, for one, am not going now."

"When are you going? Perhaps you can help me convince Mada and Adon to let me come along."

She laughed out loud at the idea, "To Zhiri? Outside of Faduwata? Where they have no rule?"

"What's wrong with that?"

"Dear child, for your kind to enter Zhiri, you must be on official business or be a purposed guest. You have no official business and would be your purpose of being my guest?"

"So that I can learn magic from them. I must pass my test, Nontu. If they know my magic is broken, they might help. Especially since we're at the border between Faduwata and where our realm ends. Before we enter the other dimension. Isn't that why they send sytes to help keep an eye on things?"

"Where did you get that idea?"

"Despite what some might say, I'm very observant and perceptive. Remember, a lot happens up here." I tapped my head.

"You are quite right about it being late." Nontu pointed beside me on the bed. "Bring that bag of stones you have there with you in the morning, Lafia."

I checked the bed where she'd pointed. I'd been careful to tuck them near my thigh, out of sight.

"Good night, Lafia. Worry less."

4

TO KNOW

"Is the daily session going to be enough? Do we need to extend it or add one later in the day?" Selifaya asked gently once I'd taken my seat at breakfast.

"There are more pressing things than whether I've had or will get extra practice. There's a ceremony to plan. So much excitement there." I leaned back and picked apart a piece of fruit, putting tiny pieces in my mouth after studying them each intensely.

"Both the engagement party and the wedding ceremony dates will be set soon, correct, Mada?" Kyari beamed, her stress subsiding to make way for enthusiasm.

"I've already asked Nontu to look at the moon dates and read the other signs. She'll have options by this evening, and the messenger can deliver them to Ajur Orin and Clarhugaba Kima by the morrow, first light," Selifaya gushed, hardly able to take a bite for her excitement.

"It feels so real," Kyari said.

"Ya'i. It would be most auspicious to have this union when the Dark Moon is in its expecting or giving season and we have a beautiful full lavender moon again," Selifaya beamed.

"Oh, that would be magical, Mada. It would be good for our union and for Faduwata."

"We have to start planning our gowns, Kyari. What colors will Lafia and I wear? I know our colors are this red but maybe we can do something more fun?" Naeemah had come alive too, squirming in her seat, likely imagining the dress she'd wear.

They were giddy and I was relieved the attention was off of me and onto someone who wanted it. Kyari deserved to be happy. Even if she hadn't entrusted me with the secret.

My Mada turned her attention to my Adon. "Why so quiet, love?"

Rufan studied a random, uninteresting spot on the wall of the smaller dining hall.

"Why must we take all this time? Where there is love and promise, why wait?" he asked.

"It is our custom to wait. They are now allowed to court privately—within the set rules. You cannot rush that, my love. Remember? That's when we first truly fell in love," Mada smiled at him as if there was some inside secret we weren't to know.

"Ugh," Naeemah scoffed.

"I think we should consider a shorter courtship. Kyari is now getting to the edge of eligibility, and she has known Hakur since they were children," he said.

"Adon? Is everything alright?" Kyari asked. She glanced to Selifaya, me, and even Naeemah.

"Yes. I simply want what's best for you. We can aid Sparaka in arranging a splendid affair, unlike we've seen in many years. We don't have to make you two wait so long for that."

"Dear Rufan, my love. Let us continue this conversation after we hear about the dates from Nontu."

"When she returns this evening after consulting with Sparaka's syte, we'll pick the first one Nontu provides," my Adon smiled with satisfaction.

"The first one?" Kyari asked with a look of fear. "What if it's the next lavender moon? That would be impossible."

"Not impossible. We have two ajurdoms preparing for an important ceremony. Besides, the sooner we do this, the sooner we can welcome a new son into our family, bring joy to you, my dear Kyari, and strengthen Faduwata." Rufan held his juice up. For him, it was settled.

I was familiar with the look Mada gave Adon that said it was done and *not* done at the same time. He grew uncomfortable under her gaze and broke eye contact. Then Mada, satisfied her point had been made, turned her full attention to me.

"With that settled, speaking of Nontu reminds me. I haven't forgotten about you, Lafia. We want you to have whatever you need to be successful. We can reevaluate the schedule if you'd like, perhaps after today's practice." She took a small sip from her cup.

"Do you think I'm incapable of learning? Of practicing magic? Are you afraid I won't be good enough to be a Clarhugaba? Don't any of you believe in me? Ni. You believe in me about as much as you can see clearly that the smoke over the mountains isn't normal."

Mada looked at Adon with concern before meeting my eyes. I couldn't believe they acted as if they didn't see it.

"Where is this coming from, Lafia? Of course I believe in you. We believe in you. It's why we support you however possible."

"I don't need more practice. I just need another chance."

"I see you are upset, understandably. Last night, you clearly had difficulty with your demonstration. You'll have another chance, and between now and then we will take whatever measures are necessary. I thought this is what you wanted," Selifaya said.

Her tone meant she'd been insulted, but I wasn't taking it back, and I wasn't going to apologize for being right.

"What I want is for my magic to work. I wanted to be able to focus on my Demonstration of Magic without being distracted by surprises, secrets kept from me. Excuse my tone. I meant no disrespect by it." I pushed my seat back. "I must excuse myself from breakfast. Please tell Elna it was delicious. I need to rest a bit before the next session."

I tried to maintain my composure as I exited the room. Certainly no one would come looking for me, but rest was not on my agenda.

5

GIFTS AND THE GARDEN

The back gardens were quiet and peaceful, and the pluif tree blooms were now fully open. I headed toward the stepping stones that led to my favorite spot, the fountain. I meandered on and off the path, tapping the trees. The fountain and the garden were surrounded by flowers, plants, and trees with small houses for the haskeals, a small light fae that lived throughout Faduwata.

It was an elusive and rare occasion for anyone, save Nontu or the other Zhirians, to see them—except for the light they gave off at night or if you disturbed them, as I was, by tapping on the trees. They were as private as the ruwatane who lived in the waters bordering Zhiri.

They all had magic that worked. They didn't strain, constantly fail, and make fools of themselves.

Did any of them care anyway? After all, I was the middle child, and they had already secured our societal anchoring. Kyari was engaged to the eldest son of the Sparakan royal family. The fact I was broken wouldn't set our ajurdom back very much, especially with Naeemah already making such strong progress.

But it would mean I might be overlooked, becoming the unwed child and the princess who'd never be Clarhugaba.

Bletondu had already made her interests clear and nothing was stopping her from going after Najurvod now that Hakur was no longer available.

From my spot on a stone bench near the fountain, I watched the water rise and fall musically. The haskeals were likely watching me with curiosity, pity, or perhaps just laughter.

It's okay. I gazed upon the water drops and considered how they hit the pool and were once again indiscernible from any other drops of water. *It's okay to be ordinary. There are millions of people in Faduwata who are just as ordinary as me. I can be the ordinary Ajursun. That would make me special.*

I scoffed out loud. I didn't want to be ordinary, and I wasn't supposed to be. I was an Ajursun of the ajurdom of Narut, and one day, I was meant to be a Clarhugaba.

North of me, the skies were gray and overcast from near the top of the mountain until any visibility was gone. It had started a few moon cycles past and been steadily getting worse. With dusk came what appeared to be lightning and distant thunder.

"There you are, Lafia."

My mother approached wearing a flowing robe, in a hue of our royal color, that grazed the ground when she walked.

"Are you feeling well?"

I wasn't certain how to answer. I wasn't physically unwell unless broken magic was a symptom of an illness I wasn't aware of. I shook my head.

"Ni, Mada. I'm not feeling well."

Selifaya nodded and sat beside me on the cool hard stone, brushing off dirt and fallen leaves first.

"What troubles you, Lafia, my child?"

"I know you said you didn't tell me about Kyari's engagement because I wasn't supposed to know. But it bothers me that I wasn't trusted with this information. I feel like Naeemah knew."

"She didn't know either, Lafia. She simply was too excited about what it meant for her to care about that part. You two are very different. All three of you, in fact."

"That's not all, Mada."

"What else troubles you, love?"

I clasped my hands, one over the other, trying to still them. I avoided turning toward my mother as a tear rolled down my cheek. I feared that if I spoke or blinked, my entire face would be wet.

"Look at me, Lafia."

I closed my eyes. She moved closer and wrapped one arm around my shoulders, drawing me in. My hands relaxed as my breath caught in my throat before coming out in sobs. Tears flowed like the fountain we sat in front of.

Selifaya gently wrapped her other arm in front of me and held me silently. My tears wet her robe. When I finally managed to speak through the gasps, it was to say, "I'm broken, Mada. Broken."

"Where did this idea come from?" she asked softly while stroking my hair.

"I'm the only royal child I've ever known to fail their Demonstration of Magic."

"You have royal blood, which means it is in you. You'll make a wonderful Clarhugaba, especially when your magic opens to you. It is a great responsibility."

"I don't know what went wrong. Ni. Everything went wrong from the moment I arrived last night. Like someone put a curse on me."

"Last night was quite difficult, but a curse? Remember that our magic comes to us in different ways, Lafia."

"Yours comes straight to you."

My mother paused as she gazed into the fountain, deep in thought.

"Sometimes, when things appear broken, it's only that the pieces haven't found their proper fit yet."

"Why am I the only one who hasn't found their proper fit? Kyari is perfect and Naeemah is the life of the room. You and Adon know how to be, how to be…graceful and regal…then there's me. I am none of those things."

"I hear and feel how much what you are saying troubles you. I know it may be confusing because your experiences in this body are telling you this. But I will tell you something else. I'm your Mada, so you must listen," she smiled, one arm still around my shoulders.

I sighed deeply, not wanting to be talked out of what I already knew to be true.

"Mada. It is. Just as Faduwata is. *It is.* I am not like the other royals."

"Ni. You are not," Selifaya began. "You are not meant to be. Otherwise, you would be."

"That doesn't help me right now."

"Listen, Lafia. Each of us is here with unique gifts and purpose that is only unto us. You are young and your flower has yet to bloom. Like these beautiful pluif trees, there is no way to tell what will be inside until it opens. And as you've seen, some open as soon as the dawn breaks, and some are just now opening. Do you think the ones that just opened believe themselves to be any less beautiful or special? That they are less useful to the tree?"

"Ni. Why would they?"

"They each contribute to the tree and the tree's life. Just as you contribute to Faduwata, to Narut, and to the life we must maintain for ourselves and for our realm."

"That means one day, I'll be fixed right?"

"You are already right. You simply must look past what you feel and see in your flesh and know what is for you in the light of the Dark Moon."

I sat up and pondered her words.

I locked in on a haskeal house past the fountain. Maybe I'd catch a glimpse of the magical little creature. From their bright light, I knew they were small, only about the size of an adult man's hand. Their legs were long and slim, though I had seen some light shapes that appeared to have much shorter stout legs. Their wings covered their backs and up past their heads. I still wanted to know what they looked like myself. Not from just Nontu's description.

"Mada?"

"Ya'i?"

"Can I work with you? Like Kyari did."

Selifaya gazed upon the fountain before she took my hand in hers. "It is rare that a syte will accept the call to be of service to the royals of Faduwata. They can serve in their own home where they are also needed. She came not just to provide additional insights for Narut but especially for you all. My duties at this time are extensive."

"But we're learning this to be Clarhugabas, like you. I don't want to be an Ajur. Shouldn't we learn from you so we can understand the real duties of a Clarhugaba? Not just how to use the gifts, if I even have them. There's more, isn't there?"

"Our family is held in great esteem. We must all do what we must. Do you understand this? A Clarhugaba has many duties and responsibilities that extend beyond her home to everyone in her care."

"That means as a leader of the light, you don't get to really be our Mada and teach us to do the same?"

"I am always your Mada, and whenever I can, I will teach you what I know. You must understand that being Clarhugaba is difficult. An honor to serve in this way, but with it comes great responsibility and many challenges."

"It's what I want to do. More than anything."

"I know it's not easy to see others have such easy access, but once you step into your gifts, you can train specifically for this role, as Kyari has begun."

"Is that when I get to spend time with you?"

"We spend time."

"I mean you and me."

Mada was quiet for a moment and then wrapped my hand in hers. "I wish I had more time to be with you, all of you. The demands have grown, and while I cannot share or explain it to you, all of us light leaders have more to do to keep everyone safe and well."

"Why? What's changed?"

"You are in good hands and Nontu came here willing to fill a role that needed to be filled, to guide you in a way that timing would not allow me to do."

"I appreciate you bringing her here, and she has been wonderful over the past four years, but in two years, she'll be gone, like Fina is gone. Nontu will be back in Zhiri to serve there. I won't be ready in two years if I don't have my magic now."

"Don't fret about what might be, Lafia. You have now. You have this moment."

"Mada? I adored Fina when she was our syte. She taught me so much. Not just about how to use my magic but about so many other things. We were close."

"She was very special, wasn't she? She always spoke so highly of you. Said how special you are."

I leaned back to look at my mother. "She said that?"

Selifaya patted my leg and smiled. "She was right. Nontu is right. You are special, and one day you'll know it for yourself."

"How? I can't do anything right."

"There are things that take time, and it all falls perfectly into place when the time is right."

"I'm twenty, Mada. I made a fool of myself last night. Nothing went right. If there was any time for it to be right, it would've been now."

"You can't measure your progress based on some event like the Crossing of the Ties. It's arbitrary."

"Every other royal child has been measured at this event since the ajurdoms of Faduwata united. Why would I be different?"

"Perhaps, Lafia Ketonga, because you *are* different. Being different is alright. Becoming who you will be at your own pace is alright. I don't have the answer. As a future Clarhugaba, know that you will not always have the answers. But you must always seek first inside for the light of truth. Always begin within. That's where the seeds of every gift lie."

"What if the Dark Moon didn't give me any clar gifts, like the other royals? I should at least have the gift of clar-magana, like you. I thought the gift of communicating with the light was supposed to be in your line?"

Mada sighed deeply. "The Dark Moon gives everyone gifts."

"Everyone?"

"Without exception."

"Then why are royals the only ones with the four primary clar gifts?" I awaited her answer, knowing she couldn't have one.

"Do you believe the only gifts are the ones the royals possess?"

"They are the ones that matter to me, as a royal. I'm supposed to have at least one. I've been training and studying for since I started learning my letters and numbers."

Selifaya chuckled, although there was nothing funny in what I'd said.

"We have those certain clar gifts, and it happens that as royals, we possess those four clar gifts from the Dark Moon, in particular."

"So what about everyone else?"

"Do you see this garden?" Selifaya asked and moved her hand to indicate the whole garden.

"Of course."

"What do you think of it?"

"It's beautiful."

"A gardener from a village between here and Emervy designed this, and her team built it all when your father was a child."

"That's really nice."

"How does it make you feel to be in this garden?"

"Usually relaxed and peaceful."

"What a gift it is to have those feelings, isn't it?"

I guess this is what I get for having the Clarhugaba of Narut as my Mada.

"Ya'i."

"Now, I want you to go back inside and join your sisters and Nontu in your daily practice. There will come a time when you must know how to do the things you will one day do, even if today isn't the day you do them."

"Mada?"

"Ya'i?"

"Is it possible to test again before the next Crossing of the Ties ceremony? I can't wait that long."

"It's only next year. That gives you plenty of time to prepare for success."

"I know what I did wrong. I didn't do my Ring of Concentrated Magic right, which threw everything else off. I need to try again so I can be eligible."

"Is this about Najurvod?" Selifaya smiled.

"Ni. Actually. Maybe. Mada, I cannot end up with Hemole. I'd die. And Jamil is—he isn't an option. The only one for me if I want to be a Clarhugaba is Najurvod. And Bletondu—"

"Ahhh. I've noticed Bletondu isn't shy about showing how she feels with any of the eligibles."

"And she can do that because she is officially eligible and, honestly, she's older than me."

"There is a way to test again. It has to come before the Clarhugabas and sytes of the four ajurdoms. We meet again during the next lavender moon. I can add your request to our agenda."

"Thank you, Mada."

"But, if I do this, Lafia, there is no guarantee everyone will vote to allow you to retest. And, if you do retest, you must be ready. If you do not pass, there will not be another request, and you will have to wait until the next Crossing of the Ties ceremony."

"I understand. I'll be ready." There was no reason they shouldn't allow me to try again. It wouldn't harm anyone, and they were already gathering.

Selifaya sat quietly beside me—a few fine lines around her eyes—looking upon the fountain.

"I'm sorry, Mada."

"For what?"

"That I failed, and now I'm asking you to do this."

"It'll be alright. However, you're on limited time to prepare, so you may want to join your sisters in the dakruhi room for practice."

"I will."

"And one more thing, Lafia." Selifaya stood, her expression serious. "Kyari's wedding is the priority right now. You must understand that. You will be responsible for managing your practice time, but you must not cause any additional and unnecessary distractions."

I dropped my head back and caught another look at the skies over the mountain.

"I understand."

"From now until the wedding we'll have guests in and out, and everyone must play their part to make this ceremony and union a success."

There wouldn't be any help from my mother other than her asking to add my request to the agenda. Everything else would be up to me.

"Mada. I've been meaning to ask you something. I know you're busy, but I still need to ask. I don't think there is a right time, but I'm short on time."

"You can ask."

"Do you think Fina can come to visit? Or—" I began before letting the thought drop.

"They don't like to leave Zhiri often. You know this."

"But I thought she might want to see me too."

"What was your 'or'?"

I fidgeted with my clothes.

"Lafia?"

"I was thinking I could go to Zhiri to visit Fina?" I tried to see my mother out of the side of my eye.

I'd never been to Zhiri. I'd only heard of its wonder, people, and magic. Perhaps Zhiri would jumpstart my magic. Nothing else had worked.

"Go to Zhiri? To visit Fina?"

"Ya'i. For a little while. You'll hardly miss me."

"Fina is no longer in our employ. And Zhiri is so far away. And of all times, Lafia?"

"It's not that far with the stations. I could go for a short while. You don't need me here."

"They don't have a station there. Only a train that ends at the border. From there, you must travel by foot or carso."

"I can do that," I said assuredly.

"You've never traveled anywhere by foot, off the grounds of this palace or another palace."

"That doesn't mean I can't."

"You cannot go to Zhiri alone. You are a Faduwatan, an outsider to them. Besides, we do need you here. You must be properly sized and fitted. And you must rehearse. There are appearances to be made."

"I'll take Nontu. I can learn from them. Fina can teach me, and Nontu can continue to teach me."

"And what of your sister Naeemah? She'd be without a teacher."

"That isn't true."

"If Nontu is gone, she is without a syte here."

"Naeemah always has you," I sighed.

Selifaya stood and slowly walked from one side of the fountain to the other.

"Why do you wish to visit Zhiri, really?"

"I want to do what you and Kyari can do. I don't want what happened last night to ever happen again."

"I know you want to pass your Demonstration of Magic. That's what Nontu can help you with. You don't need to go all the way to Zhiri to see a former royal syte when you have one right here."

I didn't respond, choosing to study the two rings on my fingers.

"Going to Zhiri without working magic might only make matters worse. Do you truly believe going is the answer?"

"I don't know. I only know what I'm doing can't be the way for me."

"You need more time. More practice. More patience. That is all. I'm not permitting you to travel to Zhiri, with or without Nontu."

"I'm an adult, Mada. By Faduwatan law, I can go and come freely now that I am twenty years of age."

"What of your sister? Her wedding. I told you, Lafia, that you cannot allow this to be a distraction."

"Then after the engagement dinner. They can fit me before I go."

"You are also a royal child of the ajurdom of Narut. I am your Mada, and as your Mada and because of the special position you hold in Faduwatan society, I cannot allow you to travel across the realm just because you can't do magic!"

I sat back. I'd never heard my mother raise her voice. Selifaya took a deep breath and relaxed her shoulders as mine tensed.

"Lafia, there is much happening here. Your sister is engaged and set to become a Clarhugaba in the next year. I cannot allow this distracting behavior. You know what you must do, and you know where you belong. I expect you to support this family, support Narut, and support Faduwata. Now is the time to focus on this union and what must happen, not on your insecurities about something you need not worry about."

My heart beat from its fallen place in my chest; otherwise, I was frozen. There was so much I wanted to say. I studied my mother's stance, the crossed arms, the pacing in front of the fountain, and the avoidance of eye contact. *It doesn't matter. Ni. I don't matter.*

"If you cannot manage your responsibilities and duties to Faduwata first, I will not submit the request for you to retest."

"Mada! You can't."

"Lafia, this will all be past us soon. We need you to support where we are now. Do you understand?"

I nodded, my throat refusing to work.

"Do you understand, Lafia?"

I nodded again and gulped. "Ya'i, Mada."

"Is there something else?"

61

I contemplated whether to bring up yet another thing, but time with her alone was scarce.

"Have you noticed how overcast it's been to the north?"

An undeniable silence caused me to glance at my Mada who was now in deep thought as if she'd stopped breathing for a moment.

"Mada?"

"I'm sorry. I thought we were past this. You hadn't mentioned it in weeks. Why do you ask this now?"

"I've noticed it seems overcast that way every day. It's been like that for a few moons now. I didn't really want to bother anyone with it, but it's been bothering me."

"Is this what's had you distracted? Could it be why you struggled last night with your Demonstration of Magic?"

I was confused about whether she thought the smoke was the problem or me thinking about it had caused me trouble.

"I'm not sure. I didn't bring it up again because I didn't want you all to keep thinking I was going through something. But everyone thinks it anyway."

Selifaya nodded. "I see."

"Mada, I haven't done any recording, but it seems like it's gotten worse and it's starting to come over the mountain. I can't ignore it and keep it to myself. Is no one else bothered?"

Selifaya turned her head reluctantly in that direction. Her smile was strained as she stood and straightened her robe. "It does appear to be a bit overcast. The weather can be peculiar. But it's still such a lovely day. There is a lovely and gentle breeze, and over here, pink skies. Perfect."

"It is a beautiful day, but *that* hasn't changed, like normal skies." I pointed toward the foggy skies. "Usually, we have some foggy days and some clear days. It's just foggy over there every day. That doesn't seem normal, Mada."

"It isn't that peculiar. I can't say I've noticed it. Perhaps the stress of the past few months really has gotten to you. The pressure of performing and becoming an eligible. The demands of being an Ajursun can get to all of us."

"It's not stress. I can't be the only one who notices this."

"Lafia, even if what you say is the case, that it's been overcast, which I have not seen, even I, as Clarhugaba, cannot control the weather."

"You don't believe me, or do you really not see that? Or maybe it's not important enough?"

"I wish you wouldn't doubt that I'm on your side, Lafia."

"So is it that you haven't noticed it?

"I haven't noticed anything very unusual. You've been under a great deal of stress since you turned twenty. Perhaps you've felt the weight of the world. Felt as if you've been living under a cloud."

I shook my head in disbelief. "This isn't in my head."

"I don't know what it is then, Lafia. But you should try to clear your mind of those distractions and focus on serving the Faduwatan Alliance through support of this union and passing your Demonstration of Magic."

I tapped a small pebble under my shoe, then rolled it under my foot. I had to ask if it had something to do with the forbidden place. The place there was no life beyond.

"Is it possible it's the Tokahaya?"

Selifaya turned to me sharply. "Why would you wonder that, Lafia? The Tokahaya has not been an issue for Faduwata for a hundred years. Faduwata won the battle and there has been peace. We ensure this remains so."

"Does this...that strange smoke... have to do with the fourth rule of Faduwata?"

Selifaya stiffened and her lips set in a straight line.

I hesitated to push it any further, despite wanting to. There was already too much agitation in Mada's voice.

"I was just curious."

"Understandably. But you must return to your daily lessons and not worry about some foggy skies over a mountain where fog always lies. Especially fog and smoke that only you can see."

I glanced again at the top of the mountain. It was fog, but it was different and somehow familiar, even if no one else seemed to notice it.

6

DATES

Evening finally came and I questioned whether to join the family for supper. I'd managed to avoid them for the remainder of the day since successfully storming out, but Elna's meals were deliciously hard to resist.

If I went, there would either be questions about my behavior or even more tension. I put on a simple elegant dress that tied at the waist for dinner. As I made my way down the stairs, I stopped near the bottom to gather my nerves and planned how I might respond to what they would say.

"So glad you could join us," Adon smiled stiffly after a look from my Mada. "From what I gathered, it was in question."

"Of course I would join. I am a part of this family."

Rufan was the only one to have missed my mention of the smoke over the mountains. And now my Adon was actually speaking to me again, at least for the moment. I'd already gathered it was the consensus that I was going through something, since no one else could understand what my fuss over the fog and smoke was about.

They sat around the table, napkins already in their laps and glasses full. The first course was on the cart ready to be served.

"Have a seat, Lafia. They're ready to serve the first course," Mada gestured.

I sat at our custom hexagonal table, seated between Naeemah and Kyari. We waited politely while the first course of toasted bread with fruits was served around the table. Kyari's energy to my right made my skin tingle but in a different way than when I was attempting my magic. I decidedly avoided looking at any of them.

"Now that everyone is here," Selifaya clapped the tips of her fingers together excitedly, "we have several possible dates for the engagement celebration and the wedding ceremony."

Naeemah wriggled in her chair with excitement.

"Good. We'll set it as soon as possible," Rufan stated with authority before putting an entire piece of bread in his mouth.

"Rufan, love? Remember what we discussed?" Mada said sweetly.

"Ya'i. However, we must remain open to the most auspicious dates and not delay a moment longer than necessary."

Nontu came in holding a thick piece of paper and a calendar. She sat in the empty seat reserved for when she chose to share meals with the family. Nontu handed Selifaya the paper with a confident smile.

"What does it say, Mada?" Kyari asked eagerly.

They each leaned forward while I leaned back. Selifaya's finger traced the lines written on the paper.

"Mada?" Naeemah said "Will we have the engagement party before the next lavender moon?"

"Dinner not party," Rufan corrected. "Will we, Sel?" he asked, turning to Mada.

"A moment. Please. I'm looking," she answered without letting her eyes leave the paper, concern briefly crossing her face. "Nontu? Is this everything before the next Crossing of the Ties ceremony?

"It is everything when I have accounted for all that must be considered."

Rufan and Kyari met Selifaya's eyes with expectation, as she took a deep breath and placed the sheet face down in front of her.

"Please don't make us wait any longer or resort to guessing, Sel," Rufan said.

"What is it, Mada? What's wrong?" Kyari brow was marked with concern.

"Nothing. It's just that all of these are much sooner than I would've expected."

A broad smiled crossed our Adon's face. "Wonderful. When are the dates for the engagement dinner?"

Selifaya spoke as if she didn't believe her own words, "Before the lavender moon enters half etawae phase and while the dark moon still shines full and bright."

"Hand me the calendar, Nontu," Rufan commanded.

She slid it over to him and he quickly scanned the page, his thick finger landing on one spot. Even he was surprised. That's in a mere three nights from the morrow!"

"Three nights! That can't be right," Kyari stared across the table in shock. "Let me see that, Adon."

Kyari stared at it, looking at the overlapping range of dates between when the lavender moon was still full but heading towards passing half etawae phase. It was between then and the next seven days. The Dark Moon would still be bright and full as it headed into the next season of giving. That was in the next two to three days. She put the calendar down and her eyes skittered back and forth wildly.

"I won't have time to get a dress for the event and what about the menu. Mada! We simply can't do it then. When is the next date?" Kyari asked Nontu, her face fixed in defiance.

"It is possible to do this. We have access to the best dressmakers and planners." Rufan spoke with such assurance I almost believed him.

"Mada, please tell Adon that this is not possible," Kyari pleaded.

"What about the wedding, Nontu," Selifaya interjected calmly.

"The most auspicious dates occur within the three days of the next full lavender moon. The Dark Moon will not have yielded more than half of its bountiful gifts. Ideally, on the second day of the next full lavender moon," Nontu answered as she studied the paper.

"Surely, that isn't correct, Nontu," Selifaya said, taking the paper from Nontu and looking at Rufan.

"It is correct," Nontu said confidently "As I understand it, sooner is better than later."

I shook my head in disbelief. "Isn't anyone going to ask why it needs to happen so soon?"

They turned their heads towards me with curiosity. Then Kyari, Selifaya, and Naeemah gave their attention to Nontu and Rufan.

"Ya'i. Why does it have to be in three nights time? And a wedding by the next full lavender moon?!" asked Kyari.

Rufan fidgeted while Nontu shifted her weight.

"You have no place to question anything, Lafia. The information provided by Nontu shows that the most auspicious time for this engagement dinner is in three nights. The other is two nights," he scoffed. "We should honor the work she has done by providing these very vital dates."

"But that doesn't answer the question of why," I said more to Mada than him this time.

My father's face hardened as it had done the night of the Crossing of the Ties. I'd crossed the line again, but still, my question was valid. Mada avoided me and Nontu sought out Rufan's guidance through her eyes, neither offering any support.

"Are you not curious, Mada?" I asked, hoping for solidarity.

"Even if no one else is, I am now quite curious," Kyari stated.

"This is the information we have been given by our honorable and very knowledgeable royal syte," Rufan responded sharply. Nontu's brows raised at his colorful description of her, which was rare for Ajur Rufan.

"The information is not the same as the reason. We know it needs to be auspicious but surely there are auspicious dates in the normal range of six to nine moon cycles," I said and paused, waiting for a response from anyone.

"That's enough from you, Lafia," Rufan barked.

I raised my hands in surrender, looked at Kyari with a raised brow and sat back.

After several moments of silence, Kyari leaned forward. "Are we really expecting for everyone here in addition to the entire royal family of Sparaka to be prepared within three nights for the first engagement dinner in at least six years? I agree with Lafia. It's important to me to know why."

"Ya'i. Just like it's important to talk about the damn smoke," I said rising to my feet.

"Enough, Lafia. This is not your affair. This is about your sister Kyari and not you. And enough talk about this smoke!" Rufan boomed, causing me to sit back in my seat.

Silence descended on the table and the sharp crack of thunder broke it. For a moment I thought I got a glimpse of something else, but I couldn't be certain. It was as if no one else heard it or saw it as they continued to stare at me. What I did know for sure was that there was a reason. There most certainly was a reason.

"Fine. I'll let it go. I do have an announcement, if anyone cares to hear."

I received looks of warning from both my parents and Kyari.

"I plan to request a retest for my Demonstration of Magic," I said.

"That's great," Nontu said. "When?"

"You all gather again before the wedding. Mada will add the vote to the agenda for whether I can retest. If the vote passes, then it'll be that day."

"Why so soon?" Kyari asked.

"They will already be gathered together, so it doesn't inconvenience anyone."

"We just found out I'm getting married within the month and you don't think it will inconvenience anyone?"

"Lafia, it was reasonable to consider retesting next month, before. But with these dates and there being so much to do right before a wedding...It may be best to wait rather than have all your energy tied up on testing."

Kyari bobbed her head. "Exactly. Why can't it wait?"

"Maybe the same reason your wedding can't wait."

"Careful, Lafia," Selifaya glared.

"Mada, Adon? Please tell her this isn't proper. That she needs to wait. This is my turn."

"What brought this about so suddenly?" Rufan asked.

"I am testing again. At least I told you! All of you. I could've waited until I'd passed."

"You were testing. But given your behavior and the timing of the engagement and ceremony, it doesn't seem wise to request for you to test for demonstration. You'll need to wait."

"I can't wait. There's no time."

"You want to test so that you and everyone else can be distracted just to give you a second chance. What if you waste this and don't even pass? What then?" Kyari demanded.

"I will pass. I know what I did wrong."

"Everything. You did everything wrong, Lafia. From the beginning. Starting with not settling your nerves."

"Well next time, that won't be a problem."

"You plan on magically adjusting your temperament in the next month?" she asked curtly. "Mada, tell Lafia she can't do this."

"If she can show herself able to handle the demands, I will allow the request to be made. Everyone has their reasons. However, I thought I made it abundantly clear that this testing was not to be a distraction and that this wedding is the priority. Correct, Lafia?"

"I understand. I won't let it be a distraction. You'll hardly know I'm here, but I have to do this. I have to.

Kyari shook her head and got up. "I'm sorry. I've tried. Ever since the engagement last night, Lafia has been trying to get the attention off me."

"May the Dark Moon forbid its light to shine upon me and not just Kyari. Even for one night."

"Lafia Ketonga! Do not say such things. The Dark Moon shines its light upon and within all of us, equally."

"It's hard to tell. Seems I'm always stuck in some shadow," I cut my eyes at Kyari.

"Why, Lafia? Why do you have to do this now?"

"You're right. Now is never the right time for me. Later. Always later, Lafia. In time, Lafia. Not now, Lafia. You, Kyari. You are always now. You are always at the right time. I get it." I was on my feet, and my napkin was in my seat.

"Sit down, Lafia. I've already said you can retest but you may have me reconsider that decision."

"Lafia, you push things too far," Rufan scolded.

"My apologies. I don't mean to do that. But don't worry. I will not be in the way. If you don't mind, I'm going to excuse myself, so you all can get back to more important matters. I'm going to retire for the evening. Good night."

***

"Are you alright?" Nontu stood in my doorway.

I shrugged. Speaking was pointless.

"You do know how to make an exit," Nontu said heaving her shoulders.

"Am I being unreasonable?"

"I am sure it is completely reasonable to you. Each of us has our own reasons for everything, so naturally you are able to reason based on your reason."

"Nobody cares about me or what's happening."

"That is not true. Your family may be busy, even distracted, with all that is happening right now, but that does not mean they do not care."

"I heard Kyari this morning when I left the dakruhi. She thinks I'm—. I don't know what she thinks but she doesn't believe me. No one does."

"Come with me, Lafia. I want us to do something we do not get to do often when practicing with your sisters and when you are so focused on just those four gifts."

"What? If anything, I need to practice using those gifts. I need them."

"In time. Ya'i. You forget that while you, as a royal, are born with access to those four gifts, everyone can use magic. Just differently.

"What are you saying?"

"There are some things anyone can do, can practice, and do well without being born with the clar gifts. I have even heard of some who inexplicably access one or more of those clar gifts by practicing mundane magic which can at times require more on commitment."

You're saying I need to rely on practicing mundane magic because I don't have the clar gifts?"

"That is not what I am saying at all. I am saying while you wait on those gifts to reveal themselves, become stronger in your ability to use those gifts and practice magic well, by doing these other things."

I eyed her doubtfully. She didn't believe in me either.

"You study your book, right? Even though you may not be able to perform the magic in those spells, yet, you know them. When your magic works as if should, you will be able to use everything, together."

"Until then?"

"Come. I will show you that you have more to offer than you think."

I followed Nontu to the dakruhi.

"There is magic all around us, already. We can use that to amplify our own."

"You forget. I don't have magic to amplify."

"No more of that talk, Lafia. You use magic each time you speak."

My hands flew above my head in frustration.

"You've seen me. You've seen it. I'm not lying."

"You are not speaking your truth either. Now, unless you can do that, be silent and do the practice."

I mounted an argument and Nontu turned her gaze to me and then my mouth, pinching her thumb and forefinger together. My lips refused to part. "I told you, unless you can speak your truth, be silent."

This wasn't the first time I or my sisters had been hushed, but it was always frustrating.

"Fine," I said through closed lips, but it sounded more like, "hmmm."

Nontu raised a brow. "There is a great deal that you can do even if your magic gifts have yet to fall into place. Your sister never focused on these other very practical skills. She was never very interested. Now, you may speak but mind your words, Lafia."

"That's probably because the gifts through her royal blood will be enough to make her a great Clarhugaba." I didn't mean to let the tone of jealousy slip through.

"She has the same blood you do. We will do something you have control over." Nontu grabbed her bag of salts and bag of stones, a variety from around Faduwata, with special ones from Zhiri, given by the water people.

"What are we doing with these?"

"You cannot control everything. It is far too big. But perhaps you can manage something smaller."

I'd tried this before and my focus had wandered.

"Nontu, this isn't going to work."

Nontu shot a look of warning. "Is that what you know?"

"I'm going to be honest and say that it has been my personal experience that half the time, nothing happens."

"That means half the time something does."

The bags of salt and stones sat on the small table. I only wanted one thing specifically, to find out about Najurvod. I would try it again if this helped me achieve that goal.

"Do you remember what to do?"

I picked up the bag of salt and the one with stones and walked to the open area with a cleared floor. I set the stones down and reached into the salt bag, drawing some out and sprinkling it around me in a small circle. I repeated the steps to make a larger circle for Nontu and me to sit within.

"What's next?"

The energetic lines, powered by the four main stones of each ajurdom and the monedutse stone, ran throughout Maradobu. I searched for stones representing each area and laid them in front of me.

"Go on and continue."

The decision on what to name each station, many years before, brought a smile to my face. I placed the monedutse stone in the middle for Faduwata Central. Going from the top and around to the left, I laid the other stones, beginning with Narut's dunha stone, Wallarin's clori stone, Sparaka's eltris stone, and finally Emervy's jerhun stone.

Next were the clear stones, laid around with pointed ends facing the monedutse stone. Finally, I laid clear stones between the ones for each ajurdom. I glanced at Nontu again briefly. I'd forgotten something, just like I had the night of the Crossing of the Ties ceremony, but Nontu offered no hints.

Standing back from what I'd done so far, I repeated the rhyme I'd made up when I'd first learned this at sixteen.

Salt the circles
Set the stones
Bring the light
Make wishes known

I grabbed two candles and put them in the top quadrants I'd created, near the monedutse stone before getting two more for the lower quadrants. Then with a touch more confidence, I sat.

"I'm ready."

Nontu joined me in the larger circle.

"Good. That is the part you can fully control. The next part is the most important."

Make wishes known

The secret to this was simple but the execution wasn't easy. My hands rested on my knees, and I avoided Nontu's watchful eyes. What was my wish? *Najurvod? Clarhugaba? Both? Respect?* I opened one eye enough to see Nontu calmly looking back. *What is it I wish for?*

I picked up another jerhun stone from Emervy to represent Najurvod and focused on it in my hand while looking into the candlelight that glowed from the center of my circle. *Nothing.*

Staring harder and holding the stone tighter, I repeated his name in my head.

The stone pressed into my hand and the muscles in my fists hurt. I knew I was failing.

"I can't. None of this works, Nontu."

"Try again."

"I've been trying but even you can't fix this." I blew out each of the candles.

"Wait, Lafia. You underestimate yourself. So long as you do, everyone else will too. Know what you want. You have the rest you need to do what we set out to do this morning."

"You mean this mundane magic?" I scoffed. "Anyone can do a border of protection, but this is meant to help concentrate my magic. It's supposed to be more than mundane. Nothing happened, again did."

There was an annoying calmness in Nontu's unblinking eyes, and her long ears tipped back ever so slightly.

"You are upset."

"Damn right, I'm upset, Nontu. If something isn't working, don't you think it would be foolish to not adjust what I'm doing? I'm going to adjust."

"You have adjusted by choosing another way and asking to retest. As long as you can manage the demands on you, you will have another chance in a few weeks."

"But Bletondu and her magical eyes are only days away."

Nontu's expression changed as she realized what I'd meant.

"Please accept my apology, but I'm done here. There's something wrong, and nobody," I stopped to address Nontu directly, "nobody understands."

Nontu nodded and left the room, pulling the door closed.

7

ALWAYS SISTERS

Despite all protestations by Kyari, it was happening, starting with an engagement dinner in two nights and a wedding at the next full lavender moon. There was no time for anyone or anything else besides her and the hurried affairs to make this union final.

Selifaya had sent news out by special courier the prior evening, given the lack of time to plan. The engagement dinner was in two days.

Kyari came to my room early that morning, hoping to talk. This time I let her. For the first time in my memory, Kyari was not her usual composed self. She was on edge, pacing between the picture windows and the opposite wall.

"What's going on, Kyari?"

"This engagement dinner feels rushed, and I am sorry that I said those things and behaved as I did when you said you were retesting and trying to tell us about the smoke. I know it's important to you."

"I was out of line. You were right. I was upset. No one seems to know I exist half the time. But none of that matters now."

"It does. You do. I know that if they let you test, you can pass your Demonstration of Magic. Just remember to center yourself first and get your nerves under control."

"Me and my nerves," I smiled. "But your wedding is the priority. Faduwata first."

She nodded. "Adon is set on these dates and Nontu was most likely following all her signs and whatever instructions she was given to have it so soon. I just—," Kyari's voice caught in her throat, and I waited for her to clear it. Instead she shook her head and took a deep breath. "I want you to be my first lady of the bride."

After all that had happened, I wondered if she was being serious.

"I want you beside me when I say my vows, holding the necklace I will give to Hakur."

"Are you sure, Kyari?"

"I made a mistake, Lafia. I know our parents wanted this to be very private, but I should have told you. I should have trusted you like I have with everything else. This shouldn't have been different."

"You're my best friend. You have always been. I tell you everything, or at least I try to. You didn't come to me with something as big as your engagement."

Kyari nodded. "You really consider me your best friend?"

"And you are about to leave me, Kyari. Adon hardly knows I exist, Mada is kind enough, but we all know you are her favorite. And you're leaving me with never-stop-talking-Naeemah. I love her, I do, but you understand."

Kyari smiled as she ran her fingers down her leg and then clasped them, fingers interlaced, in front of her. Her only sign that she was anxious or nervous.

"You've always come to my rescue, Kyari, ever since we were little girls. What am I going to do without you?"

"I'm going to Sparaka. I'm not leaving the realm," she smiled before sighing and leaning against a wall. "I've thought about that too, honestly."

"It may be Sparaka but it's as far away as you can go and still be in Faduwata."

Kyari looked at a spot near the foot of my bed and nodded, her fingers dancing with one another during her silence.

"Do you love him? Hakur?"

Kyari's gaze shifted to the window and followed something flitting about outside. Then she took a deep breath to calm herself, as she'd do before walking into a crowded room where every one of her graces would be required. "I'm sure I will. He's a good man and will one day be Ajur and I will be Clarhugaba. He is funny and while he's certainly no match for Najurvod on the dance floor, he can hold his own. Besides, if you can look past all of that hubris, he can be quite charming."

I rolled my eyes. "So...that's a gracious ni."

Kyari smiled softly. "You are quite aware that the options are simply abysmal. I've waited as long as I could."

"I wish you could have what Mada and Adon have. I wish all of us could."

"We could have that kind of love if we're willing to do what others like Alari have done."

"Renounce ever having the throne or the option of being a Clarhugaba?" I asked incredulously.

"Or choose to love who you are with, using the power of will given us through the clori stone."

"It may be that same clori stone and the one who gains the most from the power of will it gives that ends up keeping me from being Clarhugaba."

"Things will work out, Lafia. For both of us. You didn't answer about being my first lady of the bride."

I sighed in contemplation. "I will be honored to serve as your first lady of the bride."

"Thank you, Lafia. I'll have my sisters by my side." Kyari was misty-eyed.

"What's wrong?"

"I'll be gone in a lavender moon cycle. All the way in Sparaka. Did you know they began updating the smaller palace for his future bride and him over a year ago? All in anticipation of Hakur's marriage. I've never known any place but this."

"You just made it sound like it wasn't a big deal. You're going to miss me too, aren't you?"

Kyari sat on the edge of my bed, her eyes still moist.

"I'm sure it'll be nice." I put an arm around her. "Sparaka is colorful and exciting. There'll be no shortage of activity and affairs to attend. You are going to be such a light there. They're going to love you. You were made for this role."

"I hope so. I've been preparing my entire life to fill a role like this, to be able to move and speak and make everyone feel welcomed and comfortable and of course to influence them to action," she added the last part with a tease. "But now it's real. Practice will be over."

"Nontu would say, if practice is over and the opportunity is presented, the student is ready," I recited in my best Nontu voice.

Kyari rolled her eyes. "It's interesting the things you choose to remember."

***

A few hours later we were exiting the train in Maradobu Central. Selifaya had dragged us, along with Nontu, to meet Kyari's future mother-in-law, Kima, and sister-in-law, Asabe. We were accompanied by half a dozen planners, two dressmakers, one tailor, and four guards. Back in Narut, Ajur Rufan would be fitted for his royal suit. In Sparaka the same was happening for Ajur Orin and Ajursun Hakur.

Naeemah bounced excitedly from shop to shop, regardless of whether it was for fabric, shoes, jewelry, or desserts. Her boundless energy even seemed to wear on Kyari.

I, on the other hand, couldn't focus on picking out materials and styles for our dinner attire and for the dresses we'd be wearing in less than one lavender moon cycle. The dressmakers' stress could be seen on their faces. Kyari went along, doing an excellent job of appearing interested and excited about what was to come. I suspected that despite feeling rushed for the engagement dinner and wedding, this was ultimately what she wanted.

As we entered another shop for fine fabrics, I paused, something crossing my mind.

"Lafia, you're blocking the door," Selifaya said. "Go on in. Hopefully there is something here in the right colors for you and Naeemah for the ceremony."

I scanned the shop, piled high with fabric on pallets, on rolls, hanging from the ceiling and stacked along the walls. I had no interest in looking and chose to find a corner where fabrics in the color scheme we required were lined up. What had they said? I struggled to remember the conversation between my Adon and Ajur Orin from the night of the Crossing of the Ties ceremony. It had dawned on me that the discussion hadn't solely been about the wedding but what it had been about I didn't know.

I glanced at Nontu from the corner I'd staked, surrounded by fabrics. She had been acting a bit unlike herself as well.

She must have felt my eyes on her and turned slowly before coming over. "You seem to have a great deal on your mind again this morning."

"Ya'i. But no one wants to talk about it."

"I do, but not now. I believe you. We can talk about it after the engagement dinner," she said with a tight smile.

"You believe me? About what?"

"That the smoke is indeed strange. There may be more to it, but I also believe with everything going on, it is best not to involve your parents or sisters."

Although I wish she wasn't, Nontu was right. Not only were they focused on Kyari, but they didn't believe me and there was something they weren't saying.

"I'll keep it to myself. Thank you, Nontu. I know I must put Faduwata first."

"Some things must be as they are." This time her smile was gentle and kind. "We do what we must for Faduwata and for Maradobu."

"Maradobu? Since when has that been part of it? I'm just trying to focus on the Alliance."

"Lafia, I'm not from Faduwata, remember? Zhiri is in Maradobu too. So are the oceans where the ruwatane live and the other dimension the haskeals use."

"My apologies. I wasn't thinking. But why?"

"Between now and your sister's wedding, just know it is for the best to keep some things to yourself. For everyone and you, if you want to retest," she said and touched my forehead as she often did.

"What are you two talking about? Find some good fabrics over here?" Selifaya asked.

"It seems Lafia has found some beautiful hues, especially for the union ceremony." Nontu patted a pile of fabric and then slowly walked away, leaving me with Mada.

"I see you have. Which ones were you looking at?"

I pretended to look through the pile, but my mind was elsewhere. I was an adult now, and nothing was working, including my attempts at courting and all because my magic was broken. I was the laughingstock of Faduwatan royal society, and my family thought I was stressed and going through 'something.'

"This one?" Selifaya's question pierced my thoughts. My hand had landed on a burgundy crushed velvet material. "I think it may be too warm for this fabric. Keep looking."

The truth was I hadn't even looked at the material. I absently rested my hand on the pile and then tapped one. "That undertone would do nothing for your skin. Here let me get in there and see," Selifaya said and stood next to me before frowning. "Wait. Let me get a dressmaker over here too. She can let us know if this will work."

I considered the way the smoke was the day before when I sat with Mada at the fountain. It had been thunderous, and something appeared in it the night before when we'd gotten the news about the dates for the engagement dinner and wedding. It hadn't made sense then, but it was brooding and angry. And, in some way, familiar Looking at it long enough and I would begin to shiver, a coldness that wasn't simply from being near the mountains. Still, I was curious and no one else seemed to notice.

There was some familiarity to my visions and dreams. I'd seen grayness and smoke. I'd heard and felt the pain. Whatever was up there, that was the only thing I ever saw—gray smoke. I'd tried to keep it to myself, with the exception of mentioning the smoke once to Mada, and in the dakruhi with my sisters. But the dreams, at least the part with the singing girl, I'd share with Nontu.

During practice, it had come through while connected with Nontu. I wondered if she'd seen it as well. Could she have? Nontu was more powerful than anyone in Faduwata, so it was very possible. Even then, it was my vision, so I had to see and know for myself. The smoke felt like a heavy weight resting on my neck and shoulders. It kept me from sleeping, from seeing, or connecting. It was keeping me from my magic.

What had Nontu said the night I'd failed my demonstration? Something about seeing and knowing. I tapped my forehead lightly. "Ya'i," I said whispered to myself. "But only you can know what you see."

Raising the subject had failed. No one would listen from the moment I brought it up. Save Nontu, and that was only from today. Unlike other times when I'd been ignored and invisible, this was different. This was important.

This isn't any kind of damn smoke. Not like this. This is the Tokahaya. I knew the rule very well, like everyone else. *There is no life beyond Tokahaya. It is the path to no return.*

But the smoke was usually more of a light gray mist above the mountains, not this. Not what I was seeing and what no one else was seeing. No one went to the Tokahaya, and I didn't know exactly where it was since it wasn't just on top of the mountain. That was how you got there. Something up there led you to the Tokahaya, but legend ensured we knew the danger.

I knew that smoke and my magic were connected. I didn't know how but I knew this much. It was the only thing I'd dreamed of since turning twenty. That and the singing, little girl. I would figure out that connection. Despite my mother's protestations, I was a grown woman, even if I hadn't passed the demonstration. That meant I had the right to come and go as I pleased.

I planted my fists on my hips. Clarhugaba. That was my destiny. It was my purpose. I needed my magic. To gain the respect of my family and the other royals and be recognized as eligible to sit beside an Ajur as the Clarhugaba, there was no option but to get it.

I needed my gifts to work if I intended to pass the Demonstration of Magic. While I'd sounded confident about knowing what I'd done wrong and being able to succeed at the next demonstration, Kyari had been correct.

I'd done everything wrong, starting with the *Ring of Concentrated Magic* and the gray fog blocking my *Gift of the Clar* demonstration. By then I was in no place to successfully attempt the final test, especially with the gazing eyes of Bletondu taunting me.

The upcoming demonstration would be different. I would have a temperament adjustment but more than that, I'd get my magic fixed and there was someone I knew could help.

8

THE ENGAGEMENT DINNER

Even as I lay in bed, awake, not wanting to move and begin the day, the energy of the palace vibrated around me. I felt it through the walls and windows. It was as if our entire home had come alive under the spell of the pending union.

I finally forced myself out of bed and took the small pouch from under my pillow to place in my pocket. Carrying the strength of the realm with me, made me feel more secure.

The morning had certainly come all too soon. After the recent events in Sparaka we were going back, gathered in the main home this time, but surrounded by many of the same people, including Bletondu. I found comfort in knowing that Emervy had also been invited and Najurvod wasn't keen to turn down an invitation such as this. The engagement dinner promised to be a lively and intimate affair of the four royal families.

Despite the day's events I wanted to practice. *I needed to practice.* Nontu wasn't in the dakruhi yet when I arrived, and I stared out the window as I waited for her.

"You seem anxious, Lafia." Nontu stood beside me, her hands behind her back.

"There'll be a lot of people there."

"Only the families. Nothing to worry about." Nontu's ears pulled forward ever so slightly.

"That's easy for you to say, Nontu. You are a venna, so graceful and at ease and your magic always works. I don't want this evening to end in ruin, again." She was rarely wrong. "You're right. There is a lot on my mind."

"Lafia. You are smart in many ways and when people get to know you, they can see that. They like you."

"While I appreciate that, how often can that ever happen? The moment I'm in a room of people I fade away." *Ideally, that will work in my favor this evening.*

"You will be fine. All will be fine. This is good for Narut and for Faduwata."

"It is good for Narut. Faduwata will be stronger," I said as if I believed it.

She stood in front of me as if searching for words. "We each do what we must, Lafia. We all have obligations and commitments and our decisions impact others. Do you understand this?"

"I have an obligation to Faduwata, my ajurdom, and myself. In that order. I understand."

"Now you must get ready."

"Next time we come together to practice, Bisa Nontu, my magic will not be broken."

Nontu smiled. "It is not broken, Lafia. I have told you that."

"Then, it will be right. Soon. You'll see." I stood and smiled. "I have a favor to ask."

"What is it?"

"Would you help make my case to the other sytes? They have to vote with the Clarhugabas. I only need four total to be allowed to test."

"I can help you with that. Or maybe you will simply demonstrate through real life between now and then," Nontu gently squeezed my hand.

"There isn't much chance for proving it outside the demonstration but thank you for always being in my corner. Sometimes I feel you are the only one who is."

Nontu now took both my hands, her eyes looking at our hands together. "You are very important to me, Lafia."

She watched me leave so I tried to walk normally from the dakruhi. There was much I needed to do before we went to Sparaka. Breakfast would be happening soon and then the engagement dinner that evening. I couldn't let anyone suspect I had something planned if I wanted it to work.

***

I stepped inside my room, checked the corridor behind me, and then hastened to close the door. I pressed against it gently, listened for the click and turned the lock. I took a deep breath.

I walked to my capacious closet and wondered what to take on the trip I had planned. Floor-length evening wear, mostly in various hues of reds and burgundies, hung in bags to my left, formal dinner attire and other dresses were in front of me. The dress for this evening's engagement dinner was slipped over a silver wire figure near the back of the closet with skylights and white tiled flooring. The sparkly cap-sleeved dress hugged my figure without fitting too tightly and the tassels hit high on my calves. My braids had already been taken down and my freshly twisted hair was pulled back and ready to be styled after breakfast. The idea to decorate it with a large feather had come from Bletondu, who would no doubt be there that evening. I wish I didn't care what she thought or what she said.

Black boots, pants, and a shirt would be practical for walking through the woods and keep me hidden. My family would likely question my attire, but they'd have to be satisfied with my response that it was comfortable travel attire. It was the truth.

Every one of my drawers had been combed before I stood with my ear pressed to Naeemah's door listening outside for movement. Satisfied I'd heard nothing, I rapped one knuckle against the door, calling her name softly.

"Naeemah? Are you in there?"

She didn't answer. I turned the knob, pushing the door open, confirming what I thought. The water ran in the washroom. In her closet, clothes were strewn across wire forms and laid across two small benches. Despite the disarray making it difficult to focus, I needed to find one thing Naeemah would have.

A bin on an upper shelf held assorted shaded glasses. What I needed couldn't be too dark and had to fit snugly around my eyes. After trying three pairs, a light green pair with bedazzled frames fit perfectly.

"What are you doing in my closet, Lafia?" Naeemah stood in a robe that grazed her ankles, her hair wrapped in fabric matching the color and texture.

"I needed some shades. I knocked, but you didn't answer."

"*You* are wearing shades tonight. That's going to be such a look. Are you sure? And isn't your dress burgundy? That color could work, red and green, but I'm not sure about the sparkly frame. What color is your feather? I could add some burgundy sparkles if you want. I have time before I get my hair done. You know what else you could do to match it? Have Helna paint your nails—"

"These will be perfect, Naeemah. Perfect. I'll have Helna paint my nails to match," I conceded. I walked past Naeemah who moved enough to let me through. "I'll let you get ready." I slipped back out of the door, grimacing as I closed it behind me.

"No problem. Let me see your nails when they're done. I like those pants too," Naeemah called through the door before muttering, "I might wear shades too."

Back in my room, I secured the door and slid the shades between the folded scarf. After a deep breath, I peered into the open bag in front of me.

This is crazy. What in the light of the Dark Moon are you doing, Lafia?

Getting my magic fixed.

"I'll show them I have what it takes to pass the Demonstration of Magic. They won't be able to ignore me after this," I whispered to myself, wearing the green shades in the floor-length mirror.

***

I considered the moss-colored polish on my nails and smiled. I'd had Helna keep my nails their regular length, unlike Naeemah, who'd gone for the dramatic again. It hadn't been my plan to wear the glasses to dinner, but if Naeemah was as well, I wouldn't be alone in the avant-garde fashion statement.

Before leaving, I needed one more thing. It was hidden somewhere in the palace. My mother called it Clarod, her light blade. Clarod was a wedding gift, and the Zhirian sytes had given it the insertion of the light of the Dark Moon to cut through the darkness.

She'd put it away and had only mentioned it once in recent months, saying it needed a reinfusion of light because the power had begun to fade after more than twenty-five years had passed. Clarod would be useful protection while traveling alone.

A knock on the door startled me. "Who is it?"

"It's me." Kyari's voice was edged with exhaustion.

"Come in."

Kyari opened the door, paused, and raised her eyebrows as she scanned my outfit. "Did Naeemah put you up to this?"

"I thought I'd be comfortable since we're changing there."

"You look like you're going to a different kind of social gathering than my engagement dinner. In any case, I want to give you something before we go."

"What is it?"

Kyari reached into the pocket of her wide-legged pants and pulled out a rich indigo pouch. "I found this in Faduwata Central the night of the Crossing of the Ties ceremony. At first, I thought it was just a regular rock, but it's a monedutse stone."

"You found a rock from the Dark Moon?" I was in awe as they usually required mining. "You truly are lucky."

"I did find a monedutse stone. It was bigger, but I gave it to our jeweler and asked him to cut it down into two and smooth them. He mounted them so we can wear them. I put it on a necklace for you."

I let the necklace fall into my hand. The black stone caught the light in the room, and the metallic bits sparkled.

"It's beautiful. I don't know what to say, Kyari."

"Soon, I won't be here to look after you, but remember, I'm always with you. No matter what, we're always together. The moneudtse stone is a great stone for protection too, so I still have your back." She smiled.

"Thank you so much. Help me put it on. I want to wear it."

"Tuck it into your shirt. If Naeemah sees it, she'll ask where hers is. I've got something else for her, but it'll take half of dinner just to get past her talking so I can tell her." We both laughed at the truthfulness of Kyari's statement.

"I have to finish getting ready. I'll see you downstairs."

She walked out, pulling the door closed. I fingered the smooth, round stone that hung between my breasts, the chain grazing my collarbones, slipped it under my top, grabbed my case and jacket, and headed downstairs to find Clarod.

***

The engagement dinner officially began in the early evening when there was still plenty of daylight. Our family had the entire southeast wing to prepare. Kyari took one room with an assistant already waiting. Naeemah and I shared a room, and Selifaya and Rufan shared a room where they were welcomed by a personal assistant with an entire pitcher of Golden Nectar plus a few added ingredients.

Naeemah had brought shades in a light blue, similar to the ones I wore and matching the fresh paint on her nails. Her pink dress was trimmed with jewels between the regular fabric and fringe that hung between the top and bottom of her knees and a deep v-back to complement the straps that highlighted her athletic shoulders.

"You look so pretty." Her hair was styled in a side bun with jeweled pins around the bun like a crown.

"You too, Lafia. And the glasses look perfect with that dress. I know Kyari is the highlight, but no one will be able to write us off tonight. Guarantee."

I hoped she was wrong. At some point, I needed to escape before it was too dark, to make my way to the train and into Sparaka Central Station. I tapped the monedutse pendant between my breasts and put my Narutian sash across my shoulder. I looked every bit the princess I was meant to be. A proper Ajursun, even if the truth was different. I put the clothes I'd worn into my traveling case and set it next to the bed, leaving Naeemah's clothes crumpled and strewn between the chair and bed.

"It has been such a long day, a long week, in fact," I sighed. "If I make it through half this evening, I'll be surprised."

"Well, at least there are beds back here if we need to crash," Naeemah giggled.

"I may have to leave early for a nap."

"You're so boring. Najurvod is going to be here," she winked.

"I don't care."

"That's not true. Hey! Let's call Helna in for our makeup. I've got some great ideas for you."

"Isn't that Helna's job?"

"Think of it as...inspiration. A color scheme for the day. We're always in these reds. We have to spice it up whenever we can," she smiled devilishly.

9

THE COLOR OF ENVY

Green hues covered my eyes and gold dots were added above my brows, merging into the bold gold eyeliner, further accentuating a deep copper-colored liner. My cheeks shimmered from the bronze. The gold dots were inspired by Nontu who was to arrive later.

Naeemah had been even bolder, choosing blue lipstick and a mauve eyeshadow with an ombre effect. She'd added three dots on either side of her eyes along with liner, both in sapphire. As usual, she pulled it off with complete style and ease.

In their elegant formal dinner dresses reaching their calves, Kyari and Selifaya could have been going to an entirely different event than Naeemah and I. Kyari wore a soft stole around her shoulders. Naeemah and I pinched our faces, wondering if she had chosen it for herself, or if had been Mada's choice.

"Are we all ready?" Selifaya took a moment to study each of us, from our hair to our makeup, jewelry, dresses, and shoes. She then did the same for Kyari. She adjusted a hairpin here, pulled a piece of fabric there, and then stepped back from one final look. "Remember posture and poise." She nodded with satisfaction and had Kyari step in front of her and Rufan. Naeemah and I walked together behind them.

I checked myself in every reflection, anxious that some part of my attire or hair would be out of place. "You look fine, Lafia." Naeemah grabbed my hand to keep me from using it to pull at my dress or check my hair again.

"You look beautiful, Naeemah. A true princess," I smiled and squeezed her hand back.

"Don't you all look lovely!" Kima, Hakur's Mada and Kyari's future in law, gushed.

I laughed at myself for even thinking our colorful makeup and glasses would stand out. If anything, they were understated.

"Let me welcome the House of Narut, family of Ajur Rufan and Clarhugaba Selifaya Ketonga, to our home to celebrate the pending union of Hakur Rityr of Sparaka and Kyari Ketonga of Narut."

Hakur stepped forward to take Kyari's hand. He kissed it with such tenderness that even I blushed. A part of him had gotten lost in her eyes before he said, "Welcome to my home. Welcome to Sparaka."

I rolled my eyes. He was absolutely smitten.

Standing around the enormous dining table, my stomach rolled. Across from me, Bletondu's eyes were trained on Najurvod. Arstut stood nearby, still scowling in my parent's direction.

"Thank you, Ajursun Hakur. It is my and my family's great pleasure to be guests here with you, the honorable Ajur Orin and the gracious Clarhugaba Kima Rityr. We are humbled that all of you have chosen to celebrate this special occasion with us."

Ajur Orin stood back proudly. "You all may take your seats. Cards have been set."

Orin's twin brother, Orfil's family, was present too. The brothers weren't identical, but they definitely looked alike. I'd been placed in the seat directly beside Jamil. His Adon Orin must still have hopes for the two of us. Clearly, he didn't know his son or me. I nodded at Jamil politely before we took our seats.

Bletondu sat next to Najurvod and Nontu sat by Sparaka's royal syte, Mareda. The royal sytes from Emervy and Wallarin sat together. Asabe and Naeemah had barely been seated, and they were already whispering. Yet, Bletondu was my focus. She was beautiful in her crushed velvet gold and magenta dress, smiling and batting her long lashes at Najurvod.

He wasn't as bothered by her attention as he'd made it out to be at the annual ceremony. I tried to catch his eye and give him a smile, but each time I was close to drawing it, Bletondu snatched his attention away. She was bold, even if she did have every right to secure a match for her ajurdom.

Ajur Orin cleared his throat and tapped his glass with his one long pinky finger. It was now decorated in lighter blue polish with dangling jewels. "Before we begin this most delectable meal made by the greatest hands in all of Sparaka and possibly all of the Maradobu realm, let us toast to the beautiful bride and handsome groom. They are a pair made to perfection by the light of the Dark Moon."

Arstut twisted his lips and gave a slanted eye to both Hakur and Rufan. Perhaps my suspicions were right, and he truly was upset that Kyari was not going to be with Najurvod.

"Everyone has their glasses?"

We picked up our glasses of golden nectar and held them in front of us, waiting for Ajur Orin to continue. "Hakur and Kyari. May your union be a symbol of hope and strength to all of the people of Sparaka, Narut, and to all Faduwata. May it shine a light upon our most inestimable realm, and may the commitment of our two ajurdoms, through this most precious of marriages in recent memory, stand the test of both the ages and the trials of leadership. May your graces and the ones who have to join us in celebrating this most illustrious event and—"

"My beloved is a fan of circumlocution when I'm most certain our guests understand full well that the first-born children of Sparaka and Narut will make a fine pair and represent Sparaka now, and whichever ajurdom they settle upon later," Kima politely summed up Orin's elocution.

"To Hakur and Kyari," Rufan said proudly.

"May the light of the Dark Moon always be within you," Selifaya finished as we all held their glasses high

"Ya'i!" was said in unison and we took a sip of our golden nectar.

Ajur Orin sat and the toasts continued, around the table, some short and some longer.

Arstut saved his for last, ending with a uniquely memorable toast in its brevity and content. "May you be all you need to be."

Selifaya sat up and leaned her head to the side, smiling but only with the side of her lips. "Would you care to explain what you mean by that? I don't think I caught the sentiment of that toast, Ajur Arstut."

Arstut was taken aback that my mother had questioned his intent. "Only that the duties are broad and can weigh heavily. I hope they have the power and support to carry those duties with grace and honor."

Selifaya smiled coyly. "Of course. They have the full support of their families and their community. Isn't that right, Arstut?"

He nodded curtly before settling on the glass he'd placed in front of him.

Dinner was eaten through bursts of laughter and talking, sometimes all involved in the same dialogue and sometimes in micro conversations. Arstut ate silently and painfully slowly. From how his eyes glazed with each bite, I knew he was mentally counting the number of times he chewed.

"What are you looking at?" Jamil had caught me.

"Nothing."

He watched Arstut for a moment before fixing his napkin on his lap. At the same time, Asabe and Naeemah unabashedly took cake, pie, and some chocolates and continued chattering about the wedding and their dresses.

"That color goes nicely with your skin," Jamil pointed to my nails.

I sneered. "That's an odd thing to say."

"What should I have said? The color is pretty on you, and it compliments you very well. Just as the color of those glasses do."

I readjusted my seat, cleared my throat, and narrowly saved the napkin before it slipped to the floor. "Thank you."

"You picked a very nice frame for your face shape."

"What are you doing, Jamil?"

"I'm giving you a compliment, Lafia."

"Really?" I challenged him.

"Usually, one might simply say thank you and continue the conversation."

"You are trying to rattle me or distract me."

"Ni. But do you feel rattled or distracted?" he smiled slyly.

"You know I cannot compete for the attention of an eligible royal tonight and so you tease me."

The formality of conversation had returned with the occasion. If it were a more personal encounter, my response would've been different. I had no time for his antics.

"From what I hear, that may very well change soon, and then lady sparkles over there will have some competition."

"Who? Her?" Even then she stared without rest at Najurvod. "I can't compete with those gazing eyes. She's probably seen every wish and desire he has and will certainly do what she can to make them come true."

"Don't count yourself out yet, Lafia. You'll be ready. Right?"

"I will be. I'm going to make sure of it."

"Then give yourself credit."

"For what? Even you know the difference between her and me."

"You may want to veer away from baseless assumptions."

"They aren't baseless. I'm basing them on what she can do and who she is. And the fact that his father," I nodded towards Arstut, "would clearly prefer anyone else for his son over me."

Jamil shrugged, "But in the end, it's not his father's choice. He's a grown man and he must choose his own path."

The assistants brought out three more special cakes to choose from, drawing Naeemah's attention. One came from Bellrin, who proudly brought a homemade cake to any occasion she attended.

Once the assistants left the table, I faced him, curious. "You're right. Absolutely. Just as you've chosen yours. To be a selfish and irresponsible prince."

"You know little of me, Lafia."

"I know more than enough."

"That's how this is, then? I'm trying to be kind and you cut me."

"You are trying to get a reaction and distract me."

"Maybe, but only from something that is clearly bothering you. Why worry about what's happening over there?"

"Because my life and future depend on it."

Jamil pushed his chair back and rose to his feet. "When's the music starting, Mada? I think it's time to get our guests on their feet and dancing."

His broad smile beamed for the entire table as his strong lean body stood beside me, close enough to touch. He was beyond frustrating with his politeness and conversation. He even noticed my hair was in twists and not braids.

Kima stood, "You all keep those mouths going in delightful conversation and enjoy those cakes, specially made for your delectation. I will have the band commence with the music!" She bounced out of the room, already dancing to a rhythm only she heard.

If it were anyone else besides Jamil, I might have engaged in the conversation he tried to draw me into. The music had begun playing in the other room.

Kima returned, this time moving to the music we all heard. "You all are welcome to accompany me, the dashing and delectable Ajur Orin, as well as our lovely future daughter Kyari and our dashing son Hakur to our gathering hall."

She had Orin on his feet and let Hakur and Kyari lead the way. The spacious room had been cleared to leave a sizeable dance floor. A knot formed in the center of my stomach at the familiar feeling. All I wanted was a place out of the way to go unnoticed.

Bletondu guarded Najurvod as if she couldn't allow a moment for anyone else to get close unless she were there too. There was so little space between them that her hips occasionally grazed his. She smiled at me from where she stood and waved with her fingers held chest high. Her wrists dripped with beads and jewels just as her neck did.

She was coming over, her arm wrapped securely around Najurvod's. Attempts to find a nearby escape failed and she was standing in front of me.

"Lafia. So good to see you. I'm sorry I didn't get to speak with you at dinner. Naj and I were having the most fascinating conversation. Weren't we, Naj?"

"Lafia. Good evening. It is a pleasure to see you again so soon." Naj took my hand and kissed the fingers as he'd done before.

"Naj? Weren't we having the most interesting conversation?" Bletondu asked again, with emphasis.

"Quite."

"Oh good, I see you two are already almost on the dance floor." Ajur Arstut had made his way over to us, stiff and pouty as always. "You should dance."

"We were just speaking to Lafia," Najurvod offered, his eyes still on me.

"Don't you look like a gift from the Dark Moon, Bletondu. Lovely and radiant as always." Arstut smiled before turning to me. "Lafia." His eyes barely crossed me as he nodded curtly, not hiding his displeasure.

"Ajur Arstut," I smiled and nodded politely.

"You probably aren't dancing this evening." Arstut's insult hung thick.

"I may."

The music picked up into a lively melody. Hakur led Kyari onto the dance floor, where they moved together, the only two on the dance floor before Orin and Kima joined. Naeemah nudged Rufan and Selifaya to dance.

"You two young ones should get out there and dance. You move so well together." With that, Arstut pushed Najurvod away from us and Bletondu went with him. "Not everyone is as gifted as you on the dance floor."

"Lafia. May I have this dance?" It was Jamil, standing behind Arstut.

Avoiding further assault by Arstut, I succumbed to Jamil's false charms.

"The music is good." Jamil smiled and extended his hand to me. Arstut frowned in a way I hadn't thought possible, given how tight his face always was.

"Ya'i. Thank you."

Jamil was commendable for being wise enough not to give me a repeat of the Crossing of the Ties ceremony. With him, I danced and moved with grace. However, I had no intention of giving him the commendation.

"Lafia Ketonga of Narut," he said, stepping back and lifting my hand just before placing a tender kiss on my knuckles, "I must excuse myself from the floor, but it has been a pleasure dancing with you this evening. Would you care to join me for refreshments?" He glistened beneath the beads of perspiration, as did I.

My heart pounded as Bletondu glared at me. I smiled back and curtsied, "Jamil Rityr of Sparaka, it has been my pleasure as well, and I would welcome refreshments." Dancing with him had been a pleasure. "Thank you."

He nodded once more and offered his arm to escort me off the dance floor. We walked to the refreshments where water and various nectars were available.

"You are a fair dancer, Lafia. Once you get into your rhythm."

"Thank you."

"So that half compliment is one you can accept. But not a full one?"

"I can admit there are a few things I must work on."

"Like letting Arstut slide in thinly veiled insults?"

"I was handling it fine."

"Or being mad at Bletondu for going after what you want?"

"What? You need to watch it."

He shrugged noncommittally. "I'm only saying you don't have to hide and pretend you aren't just as pretty as she is."

I wasn't sure how to respond. *Me as pretty as Bletondu?*

"That's only because she's all done up and trying."

"And? What's wrong with doing yourself up and trying?"

"For what? To please you or them?"

"Oh my, Lafia. You really miss the point. You like it. I know you do. I see how you admire your sisters, Ajur Bellrin, and even my Mada. You don't need to do it for anyone else. You think I look this good for others?" he smirked.

"Who said you look good?" I shot back.

"I do. And I look good because it feels good, and I like to feel good. Trust me, you look good then you start feeling good. Next thing you know, you'll walk through the room with all that confidence you admire in everyone else."

"I couldn't."

"Why?"

"Doesn't matter. No one notices me anyway."

"Forget them. This is about you."

"Look. It's not me. I wouldn't even know how."

"It's like anything else. If you can learn mundane magic, you can learn to see yourself and appreciate that and honor who you are by shining just as bright on the outside as well."

"What are you up to, Jamil?"

He shook his head. "You don't see it."

"I didn't pass my demonstration, so there's no evidence I can even do mundane magic, much less make myself look—"

"Look what? Confident? Assured? Like the light you are?"

"Stop it with all the compliments, Jamil."

"Does it make you uncomfortable?"

My cheeks and hands were warm. I fidgeted in the dress, smoothing it while simultaneously wiping fresh dampness from my palms.

"I'm a middle child too, Lafia. I know how it is. I was so used to not being seen I almost stopped seeing myself."

"That's hard to believe."

"Really? Why?"

"You don't come off as quiet or shy."

"I wasn't. I just had a way of going unnoticed."

I'd noticed him years ago before he'd grown into even more of a man.

"You come from a family with a flair for the extravagant."

"I come from a family that embraces their inner flare."

"You all can do it. People expect it."

"If you like nice clothes, don't let anyone, including yourself, feel like you can't or shouldn't have them. You've got no reason to deny yourself. My Mada always says, 'when we choose to amplify the light within, it can't help but spill forth in beauty.' I believe it."

"She's Clarhugaba. Of course she would say something like that. And of Sparaka, no less."

"You've got only two choices, really. Remain as is or go for it. Only a small and insecure person will insult another for trying and caring, after all."

"Point taken," I laughed. "Especially considering the opposite. Why would one desire to not try for themselves or to be careless with themselves?"

"I always knew you were the smartest of the sisters."

"Now you're pushing it, Jamil. At any rate, I'm far behind in the game of beauty, charm, and magic."

Bletondu crossed the dance floor with Najurvod firmly in her grasp under the approving eyes of both Bellrin and Arstut.

"Don't worry about them. Focus on you. I hear something important may be happening for you soon."

"You did? How?"

"When you've got as much experience as I do at being invisible, you hear a lot."

"I would spot you from anywhere!" I announced. "I mean, as tall as you are, you're not invisible."

"I decided I was done hiding. I'm a royal son of Sparaka. I am not hiding. Well, except when necessary or it serves my purpose," he grinned.

I needed to get away from him. *What kind of man says all this, trying to make me feel like I was something I couldn't be?*

"What was the look that just crossed your face?"

"I was thinking about my demonstration. I don't know if they'll let me do it."

"There are a few other things taking precedence now," he said, extending his hand toward the room.

"You certainly don't have to remind me. Everyone else has already made sure I know."

"Would you like a tour of the palace and grounds before dark?"

Bletondu spun toward our end of the dance floor, successfully handling the impressive move Najurvod had attempted with me.

"I'm both ineligible, and we'd be unaccompanied."

"You've met Denka, our assistant?"

I palmed my forehead. "Ya'i. Pleasant woman. And very helpful."

He laughed and walked away to find her. The song wound down as if on cue, and Bletondu bopped toward me as Najurvod fetched beverages.

"Isn't this a delightful affair? I'm so happy for Kyari. Seems she has exactly what she wanted. It's wonderful when that happens." Her eyes beamed as she glanced over at Jamil and back at me. "I see you're going after what you want too." Bletondu sounded sincerely pleased. As if by some grand design, we would all end up with the proper partner and happy.

I shook my head. "We're just talking since it seems you and Najurvod are inseparable."

Bletondu beamed. "Nonsense. I'm happy to switch dance partners. Wait. I guess it's more of an unofficial thing. For now, that is."

And there it was.

"My setback is only temporary. I'm not concerned."

"You're not? I don't know how you do it, Lafia. Even at your lowest, when anyone else would be in despair at the situation, you manage to keep a smile and hope."

"How was everything after the Crossing of the Ties ceremony, Bletondu?"

"Why? It was fine. My energy was a little off the next day. I figured I'd picked up some other people's negativity from the ceremony, which had changed my light spectrum. I recalibrated, cleared myself, and was fine," she sang. "Naj called on me just yesterday, so not just doing fine, but better than fine," Bletondu spoke with flittering hands and shoulders as if she couldn't contain her good fortune.

Even my spell had failed. I replayed it in my mind.

This evening's young
But love is done
Repel Bletondu
From everyone
Til a week is done
And comes the sun
And if she tries
To steal his eyes
May she fail
May I prevail

Her resistance was stronger than the intention and magic I'd used. I watched Najurvod and Bletondu and wondered if Bletondu had used her gazing eyes on him to enchant hi. He was behaving as if she'd put a spell on him.

I nodded while placing my hands behind me to conceal my fidgeting. "Glad things are going so well for you."

"You too. Are you working on changing the heart of the one royal committed only to Faduwata and Sparaka more than his life as a bachelor? Good luck. Even I couldn't put a crack in his love armor." Bletondu smirked as she followed him with her eyes.

"What do you mean by even you?"

Jamil's words about letting Arstut make snide remarks and doing nothing about it must have stuck somewhere.

"Only that I'm more experienced in matters of the heart."

"But you're still single, aren't you?"

"Only because I do not like to rush these things. These partnerships are critical and affect the balance of Faduwata, our ajurdoms, and even Maradobu as a whole. I don't take this lightly."

"I know this."

"Do you?" Her eyes glanced at me and then at Jamil as he sauntered over.

I never relished the sight of him more.

"Jamil! Lafia was just saying how she wanted to dance with Najurvod. Would you care to dance with me?" Bletondu leaned forward, her eyes saying more than my words could ever manage.

"When we return from our stroll, I will take you up on that offer, and Lafia can have that dance with Najurvod as well."

From the look on Bletondu's face, his response wasn't what she'd expected. She lifted her shoulders and turned sharply to rejoin Najurvod who was now in the company of one of my cousins and a dignitary's daughter. Bletondu swept in and cleared them out as she pulled him to another table to sit.

She was relentless.

10

JAMIL AND I

"It is a pleasure to see you again, your royal highness. Have you been enjoying the party?"

"Denka. It's nice to see you too. You all have done a wonderful job."

Her eyes sparkled, pleased by the compliment. Then she raised an eyebrow. "You'd like a tour of the palace, I hear?"

"Ya'i. Jamil has offered."

"Well, I'll follow the two of you."

I paused, hoping to catch Najurvod's eye. It was pointless to go through this gesture if he didn't even know. He needed to see that someone else was interested in me as well.

Supporting the glass of golden nectar with two fingers, I raised it, checking for any eye contact. *Nothing.*

"Can we start the tour that way?"

Our paths would pass by Najurvod and Bletondu, and he would have to notice me with the most handsome man in the room.

"Most certainly."

Jamil placed his hands respectfully in front of him as he walked. I did the same, ensuring a gap of several inches between us.

As we passed Najurvod, I nodded politely to him and then to Bletondu. I wanted him to consider the possibilities.

Selifaya perked up at seeing me walking next to Jamil and heading away from the great room. She began to follow until she noticed Denka was already on duty. Even then, her eyes bore into me.

Out of the room, I was now uncomfortable. He was a gracious and kind host, but I could hardly look at him.

"Did you know that after Narut, Sparaka was the next ajurdom founded? Before the alliance?"

"I did. We had to learn that in Faduwatan history. They wanted to ensure the northern and southern ends were secured. Five hundred years later we are still securing those ends."

"Indeed."

"They've redone this palace three times. By the time Hakur is ready to pass it on to the next Ajur, it'll be time to do it again."

"Why so often?"

"It keeps the energy fresh."

"I believe ours has only been redone twice if that. You know my family. They aren't ones to waste."

"I do know this," he teased with one side of his lip turning up.

"Maybe Hakur and Kyari will choose to come to Narut instead of Sparaka."

"Why? Your sister desires to be Clarhugaba, not Ajur. And my brother probably isn't well suited to being a Clarhugaba. Not sure what he would do without a title."

"He could have a title, even if he weren't Ajur or Clarhugaba. There are many other people needed to run an ajurdom."

"As much as he loves to be seen? Ni. Sparaka gives them both what they desire."

"What about you? Why do you desire to be single?"

One eyebrow raised in surprise. "I don't believe that is any of your business, Lafia."

"I'm curious. There are so few of us royals already, and you've taken yourself out of the circle."

"We all make choices. Some for ourselves, some for others."

"Why do you want to be married?"

"I wish to serve as Clarhugaba. I do not wish to serve as an Ajur. The thought of that role makes me ill to my stomach."

Jamil laughed.

"There you go again, laughing when I've said nothing funny."

"Ajur Bellrin serves in both roles. I'm sure she can give you all the tips. Bletondu will most certainly not give up her chance to be Ajur. I can hardly imagine how she'd go over as Clarhugaba."

We both giggled at the thought of her serving in that capacity. "Maybe she'd grow into it. If I can learn, so can she."

"Ya'i. Difference is, you actually want to learn."

I nodded. "I want to be Clarhugaba. There are limited paths to it." I paused at an arched doorway. "This room is beautiful. What do you use it for?"

"Mada likes to entertain the other Clarhugabas or sometimes visiting officials here. I try not to step in. She can tell if anyone does."

I stepped back from the door. "It's so bright and airy and warm. Very inviting."

"She'd be happy to know you said that. Over here, on the other side, is my Adon's private study. Nearly the same purpose, but the energy is different."

"I love it. He's such a collector!" I desperately wanted to go in.

"You can step inside."

"Some of these carvings look as old as the realm. Has he always been a collector of artifacts and random old things?"

"You can say that. He's taught me some about collecting. It's an art."

"Maybe you can show me sometime."

"There's more to see of the palace."

He walked in silence for a bit and then stopped to point out a wall. "I always have to show this wall when I give someone a tour."

"What's special about it?"

"Touch it."

I placed my hand against it and then pulled away from the strange vibration that ran through in my fingertips. "What was that?"

"That wall is one of the original walls from when the first palace was built over four hundred years ago. Those who laid the foundation never saw it completed. They built the whole palace to align with the paths we now use for transport. They didn't know what it was then, only that they felt the power of it."

"That is amazing. And when they redo the palace, this wall always remains." I placed my hand back on the wall to feel the subtle vibration.

He put his hand against the cool surface as well and then asked, "Ready to see more?"

"Lead the way."

"You've already seen the grand ballroom. Enough of it. After all, you did take a spin around the floor and saw it even from outdoors."

"Don't tease or you'll be as bad as Ajur Arstut."

"My apologies."

"And what is this room?" I asked as we came to a closed door.

"That's the studio."

"Studio? What kind?"

"Mostly painting but some sketches as well."

"Can I see?"

"Ni. You cannot." He kept walking and I stayed in front of the door.

"Why not?"

"Because we have other things to see."

"Is it your studio?"

"Come, Lafia."

I placed my hand against it. "It's your studio, isn't it?"

"It is, but we aren't going in. It's private."

"Because I might mess up the energy?"

"Come on. Let me show you one of my other favorite spots."

He refused to indulge my curiosity. I tapped the door lightly and followed him down another corridor, touching the smooth walls as we went. The ocean air wafted in from down the hall.

He pushed open a set of glass doors that led to a solunarium with tinted glass that provided shade during the day and allowed a full view of the night sky and our beautiful moons. In the distance was the ocean that connected us with Zhiri.

"The view is breathtaking. I see why you love this place."

Plants nestled in each corner, hanging or in beautifully painted boxes, as bright as the Rityr family personality.

"Would you like to go outside?"

I would have loved to; the days were getting longer, but my time was running short with the day peeling away. The shadows of night would be here soon, and I still had other plans.

"Perhaps we can walk out and back around to the other side? I'm sure my parents are beginning to look for me."

I also wondered if Najurvod had begun looking around for me or thinking about me being with Jamil. I wanted him to wonder, but I needed to get back to have at least one dance with him before I continued on with my trip.

"We can do that."

He let me walk ahead of him and my hand grazed his. It felt like the same currents that ran through the original wall of their palace. I pulled my hand closer to my body.

Denka pulled the door to the solunarium closed after we exited. I walked with enough distance between us to ensure I didn't accidentally bump into him, and our shoulders didn't meet. I wanted to allow the fabric of my dress to meet his shirt, for him to feel the magnetism that was between us without even having our skin touch, but he was as resolute in his desires as I was. Time could not be wasted.

"You've seen this end of the palace and private residence since this is where you are staying."

Everything was vibrant. Even the hedges were manicured into intricate shapes, some as the magical creatures that lived just south. A cerulean blue veranda jutted out past the room I shared with Naeemah, and colorful vines spilled over its sides.

"Your home is lovely."

"Thank you"

"Will you stay here, or do you plan to venture out to live somewhere else in Sparaka?"

"Time will tell."

"You truly are without a care in the world, aren't you? It must be nice to live so freely with no responsibility or the need to be accountable."

Jamil stopped in front of the doors that led back inside. He took in the sun in the sky and the Dark Moon beginning to make its appearance. The Dark Moon was always there, its long cycle moving us through our seasons, giving itself to us, sharing its light. The lavender moon had begun to wane as it deepened in color, advancing to the etawae phase when it was but a sliver in the sky. It still hung nearly at its peak fullness but with a richer color than the night of the Crossing of the Ties. Jamil's shoulders sagged, yet he didn't respond.

"What? Nothing to say to that?"

I'd managed to shake him.

"We should return to the party. I wouldn't want any rumors getting started or to have Ajur Rufan searching for me."

He reached to pull open the door, and I stopped him.

"You should know something, Jamil. You could have more than this lonely life you've chosen for yourself."

"And you, you could be an Ajur, Lafia. But that's not what you want, is it?"

He yanked the door open with a force that made him stumble backward.

"Denka? Lafia? After you."

Denka narrowed her eyes at Jamil as she entered and waited for us to pass before continuing to trail us. This time we didn't walk with each other as he took quick long strides toward the grand hall, and I struggled to keep up.

"I'm sorry if I upset you back there. I just thought you should know."

"You've made yourself more than clear." He stopped and turned to me, his tone returning to formal. "A moment, Denka, please."

Denka took a few steps back and pretended to check the dust on a doorway as though she couldn't hear.

"You want what you want. I will respect that. I ask that you return the courtesy. Do not doubt that I am and always will be a royal son of Faduwata and Sparaka. I know very well where my duty lies. You have one thing you need to do right now. Pass your demonstration or else that one you are pining after won't matter. He'll be someone else's."

Denka cleared her throat loudly.

"Hakur," she said from further away than normal.

"I'm looking for Jamil. I thought I saw him walking out, and you were with him."

"I'm right here."

Hakur paused, noticing my arms crossed in frustration.

"They are about to play our song. I need you."

Jamil smiled. "One moment." He faced me again. "I hope the tour was pleasurable and do enjoy the remainder of your evening. You can follow Denka back if you need more time."

He trotted to the dance floor to join Hakur in a dance the two brothers had mastered over the years. I walked ahead of Denka to where the music played and bodies bounced in time.

Everyone gathered around Hakur and Jamil until they were gone, behind a sea of bobbing heads. All eyes were on them. He would have a great time dancing, drinking, laughing, and dancing some more. With the awe and attention of the crowd, he wouldn't give me another thought.

Najurvod stood shoulder to shoulder with Bletondu, their eyes on the entertaining duo as well. If I waited to dance with him, I'd miss my chance to leave; dancing with him wouldn't matter if that happened. Without working magic, nothing else would be of importance.

Food enough for a gathering three times that size filled one of the tables. I grabbed several pieces of the assorted fruits and breads as a snack for later, then nibbled on various cheeses. The next song was in full swing when I slipped out of the room for the washroom.

From there, I snuck to the southeast wing bedroom, where I shimmied out of the cocktail dinner dress and into my traveling clothes. At the bottom of the case was the zipped lining. I opened it to reveal the bronzed handle of Clarod.

With the gentleness I'd seen my mother use, I removed Clarod from the thick sheath, turned it over in my hand, and mumbled, "This is it, Lafia," before placing it in the rolled-up bag I'd stuffed inside the case.

The scarf was the perfect protective wrap for the glasses as I put them, along with the napkins filled with fruit and bread, inside the bag and cinched it closed. Now, I simply needed to figure my way out of the palace unnoticed. Through the window was the veranda I'd spotted earlier. It wrapped around the east side of the palace.

I opened the bedroom door and checked both ways before scampering to the room used by my father. It was farthest down the hall, with a large window overlooking the veranda. Carefully, I unlatched it and slowly lifted. Once through, I would only need to avoid the guards at the corners of the palace.

I slid through the cracked window and dropped to the tiled surface, sure to dampen the sound of my boots. From my crouched position, I listened for anyone coming before skirting along the palace walls at an excruciatingly slow to avoid disturbing the guards perched farther out or the haskeals. Too much noise would cause the haskeal homes to light up, drawing unwanted attention.

The path to the next train station was clear. Based on the map I'd saved from Faduwata Central Station days before, the walk could be done quickly, as long as I wasn't caught.

Something moved behind me. I hesitated to listen. When the sound didn't continue, I gingerly moved along the bushes and under the trees, acutely aware of the haskeals houses on their branches. I spun in the direction of another sound but there was nothing to see through the darkness. *Focus, Lafia.* It wasn't the time to let my nerves get the best of me. I was determined not to be caught by a guard and delivered to Rufan and Selifaya.

Above my head, haskeal homes lit up as I lifted the latch and pushed the gate at the far side of the palace. Finally, on the other side, I took a breath and scuttled through the trees. If I arrived too late, all of this would be for naught.

II

FINA

It was difficult to know how long I'd been moving along the tree line, disturbing the haskeals, before I finally felt the hard road beneath my boots. Despite my attempts to blend in, I was certain the locals could tell I wasn't from Sparaka. That was not a problem as long as no one recognized me. I pulled the scarf out and put the glasses on before wrapping it around my head, letting it rest low on my forehead.

Ahead were the lights of the train stations, which would take me to Sparaka Central Station. Shrouded in dark clothing, I picked up my pace, glad that I wouldn't have to worry about the haskeals much as I left the wooded area.

My legs sought to carry me faster and my bag bounded against my back as I neared the station. The sights and sounds of Sparaka Central Station surrounded me. I loved Sparaka, even with my misfit status. Standing at the edge of the path, I was keenly aware that not only was I not wearing my Narutian pin, but my royal sash was tucked inside the bottom of the bag. To avoid being questioned I needed one of them.

The pin we used when we didn't want to draw unnecessary attention was tucked into the side of the bag. I dug it out and placed it on my chest as usual before abruptly removing it, instead placing it on my shirt sleeve. The station bustled with people of all types coming in and out. Once in the transport area to Sparaka Central Station, I found a place in the regular line.

***

I passed towering walls with murals depicting Sparaka's formation as I made my way to the main area, searching for a station map. In a corner that felt as if it had been forgotten was a series of framed maps for each major station. Studying the Sparakan map long enough to commit to memory without drawing attention, I departed in the direction it had shown. Several corridors led to me a doorway to the bustling and beautiful city of Sparaka Central, overflowing with visual delights, a cacophony of sound, and people with a soothing vitality. The last of the sun's glow had faded long before but that would only serve to help me.

I patted my pocket for the pouch of stones. It served as a reminder of what had to be done and of Nontu. When I returned, it would be proudly, magically, and worthy of becoming eligible. Between my fingers, I anxiously rubbed the small purple stone Fina had given me.

"Looking for a ride somewhere this evening?" A tall thin woman with skin the color of the coastal beaches leaned against the wall casually.

"Ya'i."

"Where can I take you?"

"Zhiri," I answered with confidence that wasn't mine.

"Zhiri? You have business there?"

"I do."

"Because you do know they don't let outsiders in easily."

"I'm aware. Thank you. Can you provide transport?"

She looked at me askance and pulled the small stick she'd been chewing out of her mouth. "I can take you, but if they say you can't stay, I have to charge you for the ride back." She placed it back between her lips, waiting for my confirmation.

"That's fine. I can pay you."

"You don't even know how much it is yet."

"What is your fee?"

"Sixty-two."

"Sixty-two? For one person?"

"Do you have a problem with that?"

Between paper and coins, the fee wasn't an issue. However, if this was common, what I'd brought might not last as long as I'd expected. I reached into my bag, angling my back for privacy. The fifty cullon bills had pictures of first-born royals. The twenty cullons had pictures of the second-born royals from across Faduwata. I pulled out one of the fifty cullon bills.

She waited impatiently, tapping one foot against the ground, and twisting the stick between her lips, letting the wood grind against her teeth. I shoved the bill back, found one with Hakur and then flipped through the few bills I carried for a twenty or ten cullon bill. The tens had the third-born children, and if there were none, it carried the station emblem as did the lower bills. I pulled out a twenty with my face on it and grunted.

"Is there a problem?"

"Ni." There had to be a ten-cullon bill. I sighed in relief at Asabe's face and then found two single cullon bills with emblems of the Sparakan and Emervian ajurdoms.

Once more, I thumbed through the bills to make sure neither my face nor my sisters' faces appeared on any.

"Here you go. Sixty-two cullons."

"Good. And you've got enough to return?"

"Ya'i. If necessary."

She waved her hand and walked away, assuming I'd follow. We rounded the corner of the main transport station and walked across the street. Several other private transport operators stood in the street and on the sidewalk. Their conversation promptly ended, replaced by curious stares, when they spotted me following the lanky woman.

"Don't pay them any mind," she said, swinging one long multi-colored braid over her shoulder as she pointed to her platform. "Come on and get on in."

"Where are you two headed, Juxi?" someone called cheerfully from behind.

"Don't worry about it. I'll be back tonight."

"Be careful. It's getting late," the woman said while watching me.

"I will. I always am," Juxi said before turning back to me. "I have seat belts. You may want to put one on. It's a long ride to Zhiri. Hope you're ready to be disappointed."

"I will be fine. I'm going to see a friend," I told her, unsure why I felt compelled to explain. Perhaps because, until that point, I had told no one else of my plans and in moments I was heading into the darkness with a stranger to a place where I might be rejected.

"Hope they're a good friend."

"They are. One of my best."

***

We wove along the main streets of Sparaka until the area became sparse. Densely packed buildings gave way to free-standing businesses and homes and finally to farmlands and sprawling spaces.

"So you're from Narut? You don't look like you spend much time here—Sparaka, I mean," Juxi said once we were surrounded by open air. Her teeth still clenched the stick as if she feared losing it.

"Narut, ya'i. Only coming through Sparaka for this visit."

"Where in Narut you from?"

Her tone made it difficult to tell if she was looking for information or being polite.

"I'm from the north."

"Narut Central or one of the outposts?"

"You ever been that way?"

"Of course. I make sure I get around."

I nodded. A vast emptiness lay between where we were and Zhiri. The salty ocean air reminded me of where I'd just left. And of Jamil and what I'd said to him about being selfish under the rosy sky. I rested my head against the hard bar behind me and studied the stars that began to dot the darkness. The trees stretched their branches, trying to touch the Dark Moon and sand danced beneath the transport.

"You didn't say which part." Juxi's lips turned up on one side.

"Just looking for a ride."

"You're not on the run, are you? I can't lose my operator's license for transporting someone evading the law." She was now scrutinizing me, starting with the way several twists hung beneath the scarf and the pin that held it in place. Her lips pressed against her twig, and she swung back around.

"Ni. I'm not a criminal. I have some personal matters I'm trying to take care of, and my friend in Zhiri can help me."

"So running from something else." Juxi nodded as if she was right about what she'd assumed I was doing.

"I'm not running from anything. I'm visiting a friend."

"And it seems like you're doing it so that no one knows."

"I would rather not talk."

"Fine with me. We're close. Once we cross that bridge, you'll be there." Juxi paused and then she slowed the ride. "Are you going to be alright?"

"I'll be fine."

The bridge loomed in front of us, high above the waters that separated the magical island from the mainland. As we approached Zhiri's borders, I stood in the transport to peer through and over the edge of the bridge. My breath caught in my chest at the shimmering light beneath the surface as they swam.

"You ever seen one up close?" Juxi asked with a gentle smile.

"A ruwatane?"

"Ya'i."

"This is my first time."

"It's hard to get close. On this side of their island, they stay by the shore. Never seen one come all the way up. Maybe you'll get lucky while you're here."

"That would be amazing to see," I agreed.

"A little warning for you. You're the outsider here. Be respectful and humble."

"Why wouldn't I be?"

"You'd be surprised how people of your status behave when they come to a place like this. Even as special as Zhiri is. Some act like they are owed something. They owe you nothing. This is their land and their home."

"My status?"

"I can tell you're someone. Dignitary's daughter? Tradesperson? You're young, so probably one of their children."

"Oh. Ni."

"You don't have to tell me. Just know they don't take kindly to posturing from outsiders."

"I would never."

Juxi shrugged and slowed the transporter as we approached a golden metal gate with crisscrossed bars that reached at least fifteen feet into the air and spanned the bridge's width. Two women with spears, clad in gold and silver armor that covered their chests and arms, stood on either side of the gate, watching our approach.

The knot that frequently visited had returned, settling in my stomach. As we reached the stopping point, metal flashed near their waistlines. I thought of Clarod, safe in my bag and uselessly out of reach.

"Will you wait until I'm through?" I asked nervously.

"I'll wait a few minutes, but I need to get back. Elumu's waiting on me. If I'm too long, she'll worry. If she worries, she's calling for help."

I pressed my lips together, uncertain about coming to see Fina unannounced after four years.

I put the bag over both shoulders and stepped off the platform. The women guarding the gate took a menacing step forward. Two appeared to be vennas, like Nontu. The other two were small giants who made me feel like a child from where I stood.

Behind them was a tall stone wall with heavy doors. The wall continued until it blended into the horizon in both directions. Occasionally the glint of metal reflected from the top. Someone, or something, moved along its surface.

A woman with hair cut short on the sides came to the gate, her gaze never wavering from mine as I approached.

"How can we help you at this *late* hour?" she asked.

I checked back to make sure Juxi hadn't left.

"I'm here to see a friend. Her name is Fina."

"How do you know Fina?"

"I knew her in Narut when she worked there."

The guard walked over to the others and whispered something. She returned to the gate and peered into my eyes through the bars. "What business would you have had that you would know Fina?"

"She was a family friend."

"She was a syte. How do you know her?"

The woman held the spear several inches between from the ground. Its deadly point aimed at my foot

"She worked with a family I know. We were friends. She'll confirm."

The mohawked vennan woman whispered again with the other guards before coming back. "Wait. I'll find out if Fina will vouch for you and allow you to enter or if we'll detain you for coming to our borders without the proper authority."

"How much longer?" Juxi called out.

"They're checking with my friend." I hid the concern from the threat of arrest.

"This extra waiting time will cost you if you have to go back."

With a slow roll of my eyes, I looked over the side of the bridge and into the water. The ruwatane did stay close to the shore. The few that could be seen stayed beneath the surface, casting a luminescent glow.

I'd waited for what seemed to be nearly an hour before there was a loud click and one of the gates slowly opened inward. "A little longer. I want to be sure."

"It's your money."

"I had to come and see for myself who this young woman was that claimed to be my friend." It was a voice I hadn't heard in years. Still melodic yet full.

"Fina! It's you. I mean, it's me."

"Who you are is clear to me. What is not clear is the reason you are standing on this bridge at this hour, alone, no less." Fina's eyebrows raised as they had when she would chastise me.

"I had to see you. I must speak with you, Fina. I need your help."

Fina took a deep breath and stared at me with piercing eyes. "I will vouch for her, a daughter of Narut. I will take her under my watch."

"How long, Fina?" the mohawked guard queried.

"We will start with one night. It is too late for her to journey back to Narut."

"Very well, you'll need to file a report and register your visitor first thing on the morrow. Otherwise, we'll send someone to your home. You understand the rules."

"Thank you." Fina nodded to the guards. "Follow me so we can at least sign you in for tomorrow and then I want to know what you are doing here."

"Wait. I have to pay my operator for staying."

Fina's eyes followed the bridge to the transport and Juxi standing beside it, two fingers twisting the wood in her mouth. I walked back over to her.

"How much for waiting?"

"Twenty cullons."

"Twenty?"

"What did you expect?"

I shook my head and found a twenty that didn't have my face.

"You sure do care a lot about what bills you use."

Ignoring her comment, I handed her a single bill for twenty cullons. *Jamil.* "Thank you for the ride and for waiting. I hope you get back safely."

Fina's arms were folded across her chest. Once I was back through the gate, the guards immediately closed it with a loud clang. Fina marched quickly, forcing me to trot to catch up.

"What are you doing, Lafia? Coming all the way here?"

"You were the only one I could think of that could help me."

She stopped and swung around, one fist planted on her waist. Then she started again. "You are not like everyone else. You can't just turn up in Zhiri. Not like this."

"But I needed to see you."

"That changes nothing, Lafia." Fina yanked me in until my nose was an inch from hers. She put her hand on my chin and pulled my head towards her, so her lips were to my ears. "You are a royal child. There are rules, customs, procedures that must be followed. You've broken every one of those coming here and have put me in the middle."

The back of her head bobbed as she strode ahead, her ears up and ever so slightly back, a clear sign of her displeasure.

"Where are we going?"

"This first checkpoint. We must sign you in so they know I've vouched for you. Then, we're going to my home. But, at first light, we'll make this official."

"Does that mean notifying Narut?" I asked, trying to hide my concern.

"That is customary when we have visitors such as you." Fina stopped near a pair of carsos standing next to the great wall that hid the rest of Zhiri from view. "Hop up," she ordered, pointing to a brown and white speckled carso.

I stepped back, taken by surprise at its sides. It should've had soft fuzzy fur.

"It has wings," I said with awe.

"And his own spear."

"What?" I backed up to see what she meant and spotted the pointed bone spiraling from his head. It glistened under the moonlight. "How is this possible?"

"Our carsos have wings and horns. I hope you aren't afraid of heights," she said with the slightest hint of a smile.

The truth was that I was quite afraid of heights, especially if untethered and left to rely on holding on to what amounted to a piece of cloth and the strength of my legs. I stepped up and Fina sat behind me. She grabbed the reins while I leaned forward, resting my head on the carso and holding on tightly while trying not to hurt him.

"Let's go home, Saren," Fina said sweetly. The carso backed up to face an open area before going into a light gallop and flapping its wings. Slowly it lifted. I peeked out of one eye to see us rising higher into the sky and heading over the foreboding wall.

On the other side was an entirely different world. It was quiet yet busier than I'd expected. Zhirians of different types moved below on paths of both land and water. Streams wove their way through what must have been the commerce district.

"Do we come here tomorrow to register me?" I asked hopefully. I wanted to see it in full light.

"Ni. Our security and our assembly offices are nearer the other coast. You'll see the city on the way out after that, though."

She said it with finality, as if my visit would be quick. What I needed her help with couldn't be accomplished in such a short period.

***

Art in the most vibrant hues did its best to capture the magnificence and beauty of the world Fina was privileged to live in. It hung from every wall in every room. Some abstract representations and others with fine detail only possible with a magical replication, protruding from the canvas with dimension. Like Fina. Full of vibrancy and dimension. Yet now her colorful exterior, a big bright pink skirt beneath a sparkly top, and sparkly soft-soled lace-up low shoes contradicted her demure reception. Her reserved attitude no doubt brought on by me.

"I was holding a gathering for the light when I received notice of an unexpected guest." Her tone was part irritation and curiosity. "Naturally, we had to discontinue for the evening, but some treats are left. Considering how you just walked inside, you may want my tea instead."

Fina handed me a cup with dark ocean-colored liquid in it. "You probably need to drink something, and this will settle your

stomach after that ride. It can bother those who aren't used to
it."

"Thank you, Fina."

I sat in a comfortable velvet armchair that reminded me of
the sea when the sands were settled. It was spacious enough to
fold my legs in.

Fina leaned against a small hearth with a water feature
rather than a fire. It babbled as she studied me. She was, as I
remembered, except for the color and style of her hair. She'd
always made a point to dress for special occasions and to
change her hair. She said that since energy often came through
the top, she didn't want her crown to be stale. A pair of black
heels and long black boots were set by the door. That evening
I'd unknowingly interrupted her gathering. She'd no doubt been
wearing one of them before she and Saren had come for me.

On the counter were a few covered dishes and several cups
were left on the kitchen table. There were other remnants of the
evening's events prior to my arrival. A small bag of salt rested
on the table and several stones were scattered about, left by
guests as Fina hustled them out.

A rosy gold pendulum lay near a small box on top of a silky
cloth. I remembered it, or something like it, from her time with
us. She'd use it to prepare for our time together or ask the light
for guidance. The candles were blown out but remained at each
seat.

"I'm sorry for interrupting your magic meeting, Fina." I
brushed the velvety arm of the chair, smoothing the fibers in
one direction before glancing at Fina. She still wore her finger-
wand.

Noticing me looking, she slid it off and held it in her hand
before scanning the table.

"I don't think I'll need that for the rest of tonight."

She picked up a purple box and lifted the lid, gently placing the wand inside before letting it snap shut.

"What brings you to Zhiri, Lafia?"

I took a long sip of the blue liquid. It had a tinge of bitterness and she'd given me more than I ever wanted to drink.

"If the tea is too bitter, add some joju syrup. It'll sweeten it up. If I recall, you never liked bitter foods and drinks."

I shook my head and took a sip, passing on the joju syrup, despite wanting it. I wanted her to see I'd grown up and took this visit seriously.

"You."

"Me? Ni, Lafia. I did not. For what purpose are you here?"

I struggled with how to tell her or whether she'd think I was foolish as well.

"Go on, speak."

"Fina. I need you to help me get my magic working. When we worked together, I felt it coming in as it should have. I know that was before I was supposed to learn, but I felt it. Then you left right when my real training was to begin."

"And you started working with another syte. My time with your ajurdom had come to an end. That is the way of the royal sytes. One season ends to welcome the next. We return to our home to serve."

"But my magic didn't come in like it was supposed to. I'm twenty now, Fina. Twenty, and it's broken." I searched her eyes. "I think I'm broken."

Fina sat on a small chair that rocked under her weight. She crossed her ankles and placed her hands on the armrests. Finally, she leaned back and asked, "What is it you think I can do for you, Lafia?"

"Help me fix it. If you can't help me, I'm not going to pass my Demonstration of Magic."

"You're only twenty, Lafia. There is next year. You'll have time and motivation to prepare."

"Not for me. I need to be a Clarhugaba and so I must pass before the next full lavender moon."

"That's in a matter of days. Why is there such a rush?"

"There are other factors at play, and I may miss my chance if I don't pass my Demonstration of Magic and become eligible.

"Other factors? What other factors would require passing within days?"

"That's not important. What's important is that I fix my magic. And it means I won't be here that long."

"The reasons why are always important." Fina looked at me curiously before continuing. "If something is wrong with your magic, truly, you're taking a great risk coming here with such little time."

"What other choice do I have? You all have magic to spare."

"What do you mean? You have a royal syte in your service. That is one of her purposes."

"I want to train with you. For a little while. Perhaps being in this magical place will jumpstart my gifts. It'll be an immersive experience and my magic will have to turn on."

Fina smiled and shook her head. "Your magic isn't broken." She leaned forward and stared into my eyes as Nontu often did. Her smile dimmed as if she saw something she didn't quite understand.

"Then what is it?" I asked, hoping she might have a better answer than anyone had given me.

"I do believe you're experiencing something unusual with your magic."

"Then you will help me?"

Fina shook her head slowly back and forth, pursing her lips and fidgeting with her hands. "Sometimes, a person's magic can get blocked for one reason or another. Ultimately, others can only do so much and the only one who can get their magic to work is the one whose magic isn't working."

"So you believe I'm blocked?" My eyes narrowed slightly.

"I believe you believe you're blocked."

"That's not the same thing."

"Lafia, what do you think has you blocked?"

"Please don't laugh when I tell you this. I know what you're going to think."

"You haven't changed that much, have you? Seems you know things about everyone else before yourself."

"Will you at least consider that maybe I'm not being dramatic?"

"I'll listen to you, Lafia. Haven't I always done that?"

I took a deep breath and another sip of the bitter drink, which left my opinion of it unchanged. I rubbed the stone she'd given me between my fingers.

"I think it has something to do with the Tokahaya." I tensed, waiting for her response. Unlike Nontu, she could be blunt and honest at the same time, and her goal wasn't necessarily to spare my feelings.

"The Tokahaya?" Her eyes narrowed as she peered through the large window and into the darkness. "You believe the Tokahaya has decided that of all the people in the realm of Maradobu, it would block your magic? Why?"

"When you say it like that, Fina, it seems unreasonable."

"I'm asking if you know why that would be."

"Only those born of royalty have the four gifts of the clar. I'm supposed to have at least one of these four gifts of light and what if they don't want me to have them?"

"Why you? Why did they not block Kyari's? Or your mother's? Or the other royal-born members of Faduwata?"

"I don't have that answer."

"Is it possible you're overthinking this?"

"If it hadn't been four years of practice and study only to end in the complete failure of my demonstration, I'd say yes."

Her expression changed and she leaned forward. "No royal has completely failed their demonstration in all my years."

I wasn't sure if that meant she believed me or that she was in disbelief I would be the one in her lifetime, which was longer than Faduwata had been united, to have completely failed.

Her eyes flitted back and forth as she tapped her fingers.

"This doesn't feel like a coincidence."

"Coincidence?"

"The timing of it. It's unfortunate as well, obviously."

"Is there any way you or the other sytes here can help?"

"We aren't to interfere or involve ourselves in your affairs outside official duties. I'm no longer a royal syte and have no official dealings with Faduwata."

"But you did, and you know me."

"Why haven't you asked Nontu? She has as much experience as I have and came highly recommended. Granted, there weren't many volunteers, but still."

I wondered if she wished she could be with us instead of Nontu. Regardless of how Fina felt, there wasn't a good answer that didn't make me seem inappreciative.

"She has helped me, but I thought you and I had a special connection and that being in Zhiri would help. Nontu is in Narut, not here."

"True. We haven't seen her in quite some time. Look. I can't help you with what you've described, especially not without approval. But you can speak to someone in the assembly if they grant you an audience in the morning."

"If?"

"You are an uninvited and unscheduled visitor. We have rules for our safety in Zhiri."

"But you can get me in?"

"We will see." Fina paused and bit her lower lip. "If you are blocked, and not because you're blocking yourself, they may be able to tell you. At least then, you'll know."

"Can't you ask that pendulum you put away?"

"You don't understand. I can't.

"Why not? I just saw the pendulum and I know you know how to use it."

"I don't have the authority. I serve here in Zhiri as a syte. To serve a royal family member doing work of a syte or for something like this when that person has an official syte assigned? It's out of the question. I could get in trouble. Lose my position."

"What if it were an emergency?"

"This isn't an emergency. The Faduwata realm is not in imminent danger, nor are you, your family, or anyone else."

"What if danger was coming?"

"In what way?"

Nothing I could say would be a good argument, but she was asking, and I had to try.

"At home, the skies over the mountains are changing. It's like the smoke is coming. Something angry is coming."

"What do others think about this?"

"Nothing. It's like they don't even notice it."

You've mentioned this to Nontu as well?"

"I have. She believes me."

"And what did she advise?"

I thought about it a moment. "That I keep it to myself for the time being. Kyari just became engaged, and her wedding will be before the next lavender moon."

"Congratulations to her. Who has she chosen?"

"Hakur of Sparaka."

Fina nodded and smiled. "So is your sister's wedding the pressing factor or is it something else?"

"Her wedding is pressing to everyone, but it's not my pressing factor."

"And Nontu only said to keep it to yourself."

"And that we'd talk about it later. But I came here. I had to see you, Fina."

"You still have that." Her eyes went to my hands and fingers as they played with the stone she'd given me.

"I always keep it on me."

"Good. It's been infused by the light. It won't hurt to have it done again. Leave it with me tonight and I'll take care of it."

"Will it help my magic?"

Fina chuckled softly. "When I gave this to you at your sixteenth ceremony, I knew there was something special about you. I didn't know exactly what it was, but there is something special about you, Lafia. I've always felt it. I'm going to reinfuse it."

"Thank you, Fina. Wait. Why can you reinfuse this stone but not check me?"

"The stone was a gift from me, that's different."

I placed the stone in her palm and she held it up to the light.

"I'll also add in a little something extra, seeing that you've got some particular concerns. Tomorrow we'll go to the city. You can get registered and then it's a short walk to the assembly.

"Thank you so much, Fina."

"I am bound by the rules of Zhiri, and the Zhirian High Assembly sets those rules and how they are enforced. But, being who you are they may at least offer you an audience. There are limits to what I can do for you, but know that if I could, I'd take care of it."

"Fina. You said you were blocked from seeing what was special about me."

"Ya'i."

"Is that normal? Couldn't that mean something? That something is blocking me?"

"I was blocked from seeing but that doesn't mean you are blocked."

"Whatever blocked you could be what's blocking me."

"I don't want to guess about this. Just be patient. The morn isn't far."

It wasn't the answer I'd wanted, but if the assembly could confirm my suspicions, I would know what was happening was real. I'd know my mind was all right and it was, in fact, my magic that was an issue.

"I take it this little trip wasn't approved by either Ajur Rufan or Clarhugaba Selifaya?" Fina asked, raising one of her brows. "As I suspected. We'll have to deal with that as well."

"Does that mean telling them and sending me home?"

"Let's save tonight for tonight and tomorrow for tomorrow," she sighed. "Since you'll be here for the night, we may as well catch up. You've grown into a young woman since I last gazed upon that face of yours."

I smiled at my former syte and friend. "You haven't changed a bit."

She stood and took my hands, helping me to my feet. "You've seen this part. Let me show you around the rest of my home."

12

ZHIRI

With the daylight filtering through the sheer curtains, it was there. A distinct energy poured in and surrounded me. This was why I'd come here. Magic was in the air. Everywhere. I needed it.

I twisted onto my back, and it dawned on me that I hadn't had the dream which had been a constant for months. Something else, almost equally disturbing, had taken over my subconscious. I tried to shake off the residual memories of Jamil. Somehow, he'd snuck into my sleep state. Beneath my skin was flushed and warm. While it was becoming harder to remember the longer I was awake, he'd been charming, handsome, and kind, just as he was in real life.

We'd danced as we'd done the prior evening. But in my dream, he'd held me closer, my arm grazing his, and our fingers locked. His breath was soft and warm on my cheek as he moved with me across a dance floor that belonged to us alone. He'd whispered something, his lips brushing against my ear, and I smiled. What he said, I no longer recalled. The moment was fleeting, gone like the shadows of the night.

None of it mattered. He wasn't on my list of eligible Faduwatans, which greatly annoyed me.

I'd barely sat up when there was a gentle tap on the door.

"Come in."

Fina pushed in the door, already fully dressed in a blue top with a large pin that reminded me of a pluif tree bloom. The shade of blue, like the color her hair had been when I'd seen her last. She wore gray pants with a sash around the waist and two small pouches tied to it.

"The morn is upon us, Lafia. How does it find you?"

"The morn shines upon us, Fina, and the night, the Dark Moon's gift brings us renewal."

"It's time to prepare for the day and get you registered," she smiled. "Don't worry. It'll be fine."

"Is it necessary to notify Narut? After all, I am an adult. I can travel."

"You can travel. But you are first a royal. It's improper to travel all the way to Zhiri, which has closed borders, without a clear purpose or official business."

"Can't my purpose be to visit a friend? You?"

"I did not summon you before you arrived. You did not seek an invitation or even inform me of your visit. We'll have to file the registration. Hopefully, you'll have a chance to speak with our Assembly Leader about what you're experiencing. Then they will likely send you on your way."

"That's it? I came all the way to Zhiri as a royal daughter and they're going to make me leave?" I was in disbelief. "They can't treat me like a commoner."

"It's precisely because you aren't a commoner that you'll get this much consideration and an audience."

"I'm sorry. I know I did this all wrong. I'm desperate, Fina." I remembered Juxi's comments about being humble.

"Do you think they should allow you to stay?"

"Ya'i. Once they know who I am."

"Your leaving is also due, in part, to who you are."

I sighed in frustration. "I'll get ready."

"Very well. Shower's through there." Fina pointed to a door that appeared to lead outside. "I'll see you out here. We can have a light morning meal before Saren takes us to get you registered." Her ears waggled and she closed the door.

I fingered the clothes I'd put on the evening before. They were cleaned and folded on a small chair near the bed. The black outfit lived in my closet, picked out by Naeemah. Despite being rarely worn the color had a faded appearance. There was never a proper time for an outfit such as that, or at least that was what my mother would say.

The stone shower was indeed outdoors. Fresh air rushed into the room as I opened the door to step onto the shower floor tiles. The trees and a tinted fibrous netting surrounded the opening, creating shade and privacy but the sky filtered through. The water cascaded from several small clear tubes built into the stone wall.

A small bench designed seamlessly into the shower was a perfect place to sit and collect my thoughts. They were likely going to send me away empty-handed. All I wanted was to pass my demonstration and win Najurvod's heart before Bletondu could charm him even more than she already had. The Tokahaya wasn't new, but if it really did have something to do with my broken magic, the magic and fae people of Zhiri were my answer.

Once dressed, I emerged from the airy room I'd slept in and into the open living space. Fina sat at a small table by a window with a view of a magnificent small garden. Haskeal homes dotted the landscape, plentiful, varied, and in colors more vibrant than back home. I gasped as one flew out and waved to Fina before taking off. They were real.

"I take it that was your first sighting?" Fina smirked at my expression.

Before I had a chance to answer, there were more. Coming and going from their tiny homes in trees, bushes and even some on the ground.

"They're everywhere!" I was in awe.

"You think this is something? Wait until we get out of this little enclave. Not everyone gets to witness Zhiri. You made a bold move last night, Lafia. If nothing else, you'll get to see us up close."

I smiled. It was already magical. I ate bread stuffed with berries and nuts, and an herb tea Fina had prepared. Her fingers still bore the green residue.

"You'll have to forgive me for last night, Lafia. You took me by surprise. I'm not accustomed to guests of any kind from outside of Zhiri. Even here, I keep mostly to myself when I'm not doing my work as a syte."

"I'm sorry. I couldn't risk telling anyone what I was doing. Or they might have stopped me."

"That would've been the appropriate thing for them to do," she said matter-of-factly. "Alas, you are here and it's unlikely this will happen again for quite a long time, if ever. You may as well see what you can." She smiled as we left through the door covered in moss. The top held a garden. The haskeals who spotted me quickly dodged and vanished.

"Are they afraid of me?" I asked Fina. "They hide themselves in Faduwata too."

"Just like you came in disguise to protect yourself and your identity, when we're outside of the safety of our homeland and not among our kind, some of us do the same."

I nodded, wishing they might trust me enough to get a better look, but I wasn't one of them.

We mounted Saren who walked out of the enclave. There were several other homes like Fina's, shorter homes she said the smaller people lived in, and then haskeal homes. As we approached a stream with a wooden bridge, a tail descended into the water, vanishing before I could get a clear glimpse.

"Do the ruwatane show themselves?"

"Not to you, if they can help it. You might get lucky though, once we're closer to the other side of the island. They're more plentiful as we get nearer open water. Inland we have the freshwater ruwatane. Because of how rare they are, they are quite keen to protect themselves from any outsiders. Even other Zhirians."

We galloped the rest of the way out of Fina's enclave and then Saren did what he'd done the night before and flapped his wings, creating space between us and the ground. This time I held on but kept my head free to look upon an entirely different world. The buildings were made of stones created by the sand on their island, matching the color of the ground below unless they'd been painted. Open windows allowed the breeze to flow through. Airy curtains in light pastel colors added to the mystique.

Another carso passed us in the air and both carsos made a sound as if greeting each other. In every direction, creatures, including fae, began their day. Below us, haskeals flew about, around and in between those walking. A set of two small giants like the ones I'd seen guarding the bridge were walking a child who was as tall as me toward a building that must've been a school. Children and adults of different types and sizes were also entering or approaching the building.

I was embarrassed by my surprise that they did this too. Then I realized that my embarrassment was likely driven by the fact that I'd never gone to a school, having been privately tutored, like all royal children.

Fina, Saren, and I continued past the school and other enclaves and flew over streams that wound alongside the cobbled streets. I spotted ruwatane swimming in the waters. They were making their way wherever they needed to go as well.

"You're going to catch a haskeal in your mouth if you aren't careful," Fina joked.

Closing my lips did nothing to curb my awe. Despite feeling ill to my stomach, I didn't want the ride to end, especially considering where we were going.

Saren slowed his flapping and landed with a trot, finding a space along a wall with other carsos. He made a similar greeting sound as we got off of him.

"Thank you, Saren." Fina smoothed his beautiful fur and feathers. "I think Lafia enjoyed it." Fina paused for a second and then giggled. "Ya'i. I did too."

"You can speak to carsos?"

"Saren is like a carso, but here we call then bintas. And yes, I can, but so can anyone here. It's not a big deal."

She made it sound as if it were even below mundane magic.

"How?"

"We just can. Not with words, of course. But they have thoughts and feelings like you and me. We communicate that way. We're heading in there."

Fina pointed to an ornate building across the street. Detailed stone carvings of winding flowers and geometric shapes covered the edges and top border. Along the top were small statues representing the various Zhirians. It was easy to understand why Nontu said it was hard to leave and why they were so particular about outsiders.

"Everything is magnificent here, Fina."

She nodded as her eyes scanned around us. "Indeed."

I followed Fina across the street, my bag on both shoulders, feeling like an obvious outsider, despite being essentially ignored, except by the haskeals who vanished whenever they came near me and then reappeared a few steps away.

"What do we do once we're inside? Can I plead my case to stay?"

"We'll see the registrar and complete your official paperwork. They will send notice to Narut. Then we can go to the assembly office and request a meeting with the Assembly Leader who goes by Otema Pular or Leader Pular."

"Is that the ruler, like an Ajur?"

"Unlike in Faduwata, our leaders are elected, and then the Assembly Leader is chosen by the other assembly members," she said as if to make a point.

"How long will it take for Narut to receive the notice?"

"It should only be a day once they get everything processed. Bureaucracy. Hopefully, you won't have to wait long."

"I'm glad for that much time but why so long? Don't you have magic for that?"

"We don't use magic for every task. Some things take time for proper decisions through due diligence and cannot be rushed. Besides, there is value in doing things beyond magic and while we do have magic not all of Maradobu does."

"It's better for me. Does the Assembly Leader typically meet with uninvited guests?"

"Not usually, but the uninvited guest is not often a princess. You've got that going for you," Fina shrugged.

We stood in a short line waiting to register behind a group that included a couple and several other individuals wearing Sparakan pins. They all presented previously approved requests to enter. The process seemed quick and simple for each of them. They requested to go to the special ceremonial section for a wedding. They received a daylight pass before being escorted out of the room by the wedding official, a vennan in long cream robes.

My hands quivered as I waited beside Fina. One day was hardly enough to accomplish what I needed. If the Assembly Leader, Pular, couldn't help me, I'd need as much time as possible.

"Where are you entering from?" Behind a large desk was a male vennan with a sharp nose, wiry spectacles, and gray hair. He had an air about him that suggested neither an interest in small talk nor wasted time.

"Narut," I answered hesitantly.

The registrar shuffled a few papers and then pulled out a form with a red top border. "Fill out the top here." He then turned to Fina. "Are you her responsible party?"

While saying, "Ya'i," Fina smiled and shook her head in the negative.

"Fill out the bottom and return it to me when you've completed it. You can go over there." He pointed to a tall table and handed me the paper and a writing utensil.

Fina followed and I set the sheet down to complete what I could before handing it over to her. Fina took the liberty to write *one day* in the intended duration space I'd intentionally left blank.

The registering agent finished with another person from Emervy who'd been prepared and approved already before calling me to the desk and taking the form.

"This will take a while. I'll release you into the custody of your responsible party until your forms are processed. But you can't go outside of a one-mile radius. Your wrist, please."

I held my wrist out, and he clamped a small bracelet onto it.

"That'll beep if you get close to the perimeter. It'll alert security if you cross it. You'll have five seconds to reenter the perimeter or risk being arrested. Understand?"

Fina gave me a look of warning, likely in response to my shock at possibly being arrested. "Understood," I said solemnly.

"I'm going to test it now," he said and pressed a button, making a spot on it blink green. He pressed a different button, and the blinking was gone. "It works. If you've been approved to stay, the flashing light will be green and stay that way. If it turns red, you must return here immediately. Keep that on until you check out and return it."

I nodded, realizing that my *visit* to a friend was approaching criminal status.

"Come on," Fina said. "Let's go to the assembly office and see if we can get you an audience."

I touched the black metal around my wrist, searching for the spot where the green blinking light had been. Fina led me outside where we walked down a long cobblestone street with a raised sidewalk over a waterway. While the Zhiri were polite enough not to point, many couldn't help but stare, giving me an excuse to return their curious looks. I was fascinated.

"Do we have to go in immediately, Fina? Maybe I can find Kyari a gift for her wedding. Or Mada a new beaded bracelet. You all have the best stones."

Fina looked at the building ahead to our left. It was painted purple with double sets of rust orange doors. Block symbols were placed above it.

"Is that it?"

Fina nodded. "I thought you wanted to know what was blocking you? Now you want to go shopping?"

"I do want to know."

"There's no reason to be afraid. We should go."

"I'm not afraid."

"Then what's this about?"

I averted my eyes from her gaze. I might be rejected, again, just by a different group of people. Maybe they couldn't tell me anything to help, and I'd get sent home with no more than I came with.

"Fine. Let's go."

Fina tapped her finger on a spot next to the door and the large doors opened slowly. I walked in first to find Zhirians of all types crossing the grand lobby.

The back wall was spotted with circular windows and small balconies that went to the top. People gathered by the small pillars on each level. One group after another vanished only to appear on one of the other balconies before walking to either side.

The outside wall of a large winding staircase was painted with the ocean and Zhiri in the background. Walking towards the back wall we passed the staircase. Each landing had a small sitting area where people gathered.

I followed Fina to one of the spots people transported from. Our official buildings didn't use the technology that leveraged the magnetic lines within the same building. I wondered how they managed to make it go vertically, and then thought of the wall Jamil had shown me in Sparaka.

Standing shoulder to shoulder Fina tapped her ring on a small pillar beside us, which lit up. She then pressed a symbol which then filled the screen taking us to the top floor after a momentary void. She turned left from the wall and our footsteps were hollow in the open space. Unlike back home, this felt comfortable. The furniture was soft, the windows had billowy curtains, and entire walls were covered in tapestries or murals, like the stairs had been.

Fina stopped in front of a door with more symbols I couldn't read but underneath in letters known in Faduwata it read 'Office of the Zhiri High Assembly'.

"Lafia, only speak when you need to, be mindful of where you are, and anything they do for you is a favor."

"Ya'i. I get it."

Fina pushed the door open and held it for me. Inside, a haskeal flew into a back room carrying several papers. A painting to the left appeared to be a vennan woman but she didn't wear the same ear decorations as the other vennan women I'd seen.

A vennan woman who appeared my age but was likely several years older than my mother stood at a desk, sorting papers. Both of her ears were decorated in the traditional female vennan style.

"The morn shines upon us and brings us renewal," Fina said with a lilt.

"Oh, Fina. It's been a while! The morn shines upon us and brings us renewal indeed! How are you, my friend?" She eased around the desk and hugged Fina tightly. A hug I'd wished I'd received instead of the chastisement.

"El! I am well. And you?"

"Work. It's been busy here. All of these requests. Everyone wants something and no one wants the same thing. The most difficult is the ruwatane requests. I'm just not sure how we safely get water access inside the schools. But we're looking at it for the upper schools," El paused, appearing slightly overwhelmed. "Anyway, all in a day's work. They have to review all of these to see what gets assigned to committees before the giving season comes." She pointed to a stack of wooden crates, each filled with paper.

"You've certainly got your hands full, don't you?"

"Always, but work is good for the light within. How can I help you?"

"I'm here because an old friend unexpectedly came to town." Fina nodded at me. "She wants to see if Leader Pular might be available to meet with her today."

"Today?" El said as if we'd asked for a water route through her office. "Pular's got meetings back-to-back today."

"It's a special guest," Fina said, leaning closer. "I think Leader Pular will want to see her."

"Well, who is she?" El twisted to face me directly. "Who are you?"

"My name is Lafia Ketonga."

"Ketonga? Ketonga as in Narut Ketonga? As in one of the ajursuns of Narut?"

My hands clenched. She'd made such a big deal of it. "Ya'i. I am an Ajursun. I would like an audience with Leader Pular."

"And a princess of Narut came all the way here, alone, without a prior arrangement?" El asked skeptically.

Fina sighed. "Is it possible to make it happen? It doesn't have to be a long meeting."

"I'll see what I can do. Only because of who *you* are," she said to Fina. "You two can have a seat while I check with them."

El put down the papers she'd been working through and walked the way the haskeal had gone when we'd first entered.

The haskeal returned and paused upon noticing us sitting there. In a high-pitched voice, she said, "Have you been helped?"

"We have. Thank you," Fina answered politely.

Satisfied, the haskeal zipped to the desk El had been working at and picked up another stack of papers before whisking off again.

Moments later, El marched back in with a large grin. "Their assistant said you all can go in when the current guests leave. They're wrapping up."

"Is Leader Pular a group?"

El was confused for a moment before saying, "Ohhh. Ni. Leader Pular is one person. Leader Pular uses they and them."

"Oh, of course," I said as if I was fully aware of what that meant, and my insular life hadn't made this possibly the first time I'd heard of this. I made a mental note to call her—I meant them—by their preference and hoped I didn't mess up. I needed to make a good impression but the added stress to not mess that up like I did everything else was already making my anxiety rise.

El must have noticed the pained look on my face because she added, "If in doubt, just call them by their name."

I nodded gratefully.

Voices were getting closer to us. They must've been Leader Pular's guests. I rose and smoothed my clothes as I was accustomed to when in formal meetings and gatherings. As the group passed us, they each noticed me, extending the briefest nod before continuing out the door.

El walked us back to Leader Pular's assistant. "This is Lafia Ketonga and her former royal syte, responsible party, and host while in Zhiri, Fina of Darong. They are here for Leader Pular."

The haskeal working in the back was giant compared to the other haskeals I'd seen. She was the size of a very petite small Zhirian person. Fina nudged me to stop staring at her and her iridescent wings. She was the most spectacular large haskeal, and until that moment, a haskeal type I hadn't even known existed.

The assistant knocked on the door.

"Come in."

She opened the door, and inside was a handsome vennan sitting at a round glass table. They extended their hand in an invitation to sit.

"Lafia Ketonga, is it?"

"Ya'i, Leader Pular?"

"I am. To what do I owe this unexpected visit from Narut?"

"It isn't a visit from Narut. I'm not on official business. I came here for help with a personal issue, and Fina thought you may be of some assistance."

"Oh. Did she? I don't have much time," Pular glanced at the bracelet on my wrist, "I see you're still being processed. Tell me, what is the nature of your personal issue?"

"I need help getting my magic to work and I believe if I stay here in Zhiri for a while immersed in the magic here, my magic will begin to work as it should."

Pular scoffed. "Why doesn't your magic work? You are, after all, a royal."

Fina nodded slightly. Out the window beside us was a world of magic and I needed to be a part of it if I wanted to take my magic back to my own world. "I believe I'm being blocked. I hope that whoever or whatever is blocking me down here can't reach me here."

"Nontu is your royal syte now, correct?"

"Ya'i. I don't know of where, but she's a vennan like you and Fina. She wasn't able to help me, so I thought Zhiri could. Magic is everywhere here."

"She suggested you come here?"

"Ni. I thought of Fina and decided to come on my own."

They were obviously skeptical. "I'm sorry you journeyed here to be told that we cannot help you with your magic issue."

"Wait," I said reluctantly. "I believe it's being blocked by the Tokahaya."

They gave the same look Fina had the night before. "The Tokahaya," Pular said, almost to themself. "Why do you believe this?"

"It can't be a coincidence that in Narut, my magic is never consistent. It never works properly. I completely failed my Demonstration of Magic to enter my phase of eligibility. *Completely.*"

Pular's eyebrows raised in surprise. "This is unusual. But it may have nothing to do with the Tokahaya." Their ears moved back and forth in thought. "Have you considered what that means? If you are correct, that is."

"That there must be some magic to undo the hold?"

Leader Pular leaned back, rubbing their chin. "Make sure that door is closed, Fina."

Fina stepped back and shut the door firmly.

"We have heard of a person's magic being, what we call, siphoned."

"Siphoned?"

"Something takes part of it for themselves. We believe the Tokahaya has the ability to siphon magic." Pular tapped their long fingers against the desk.

"Why would it siphon magic?"

"To help power its realm. We don't have proof. Entering the Tokahaya is dangerous and there's no guarantee you'll come out, at least not as you went in."

"How do they take it?"

"We can't be certain? We believe someone on this side has to help or be willing."

"Am I able to discuss my case with the Zhirian High Assembly?"

"You mean the full assembly? On such short notice?" Pular looked at me as if I'd asked something shocking.

"I was hoping that, given the situation, you might all be willing to see me."

"There is no situation here that warrants our full assembly."

"But I need your help."

Leader Pular stood and smoothed their clothing before placing their hands behind them and looking at me studiously. "That is not an emergency for us. If there is siphoning by the Tokahaya, there are two things that can happen."

"You've got magic that can stop it?"

"We have a way to test it. If your magic is under attack, you can wait until the attack ends on its own..." a concerned look crossed their face.

"Or?"

"Nothing. The best thing to do is wait for whatever magic used to wear off."

"What if it doesn't?"

A knock on the door made us all turn.

"Who is it?"

"Wulana."

"Come in," Leader Pular said and stood to greet her.

She was a lovely full-figured woman with wavy hair that hung like a mane down her back. "Wulana, I'm glad you're here."

"El said you had a special guest."

"What do you know of siphoned magic?"

Wulana's wide brows nearly met, and her lips pressed together firmly. She twisted her mane into a messy bun and, in what sounded like a soft growl, asked, "Who wants to know?"

"Our guest here, of Narut, is asking."

"Why?" Wulana stepped closer to me, her colorful hair like a halo.

"I think mine may be siphoned."

"Who gave you that idea?"

"My magic doesn't work as it should."

"Most people of Faduwata don't have the special gifts. Why would you expect to be different?"

"I'm Lafia Ketonga. I'm supposed to have magic."

"Ketonga?! I didn't know we were expecting royal guests in Zhiri today. Why was I not informed?"

"We weren't," Fina said crisply. "She came for help."

"What do you know of siphoned magic?" Pular asked Wulana again.

"We don't know much. It's not typically a concern here. Usually, it's only an issue if someone makes a deal with the Tokahaya. Siphoning not just magic but the light from others to power themselves. The Tokahaya needs energy and that's one way it keeps its power."

"It takes other people's power too?"

"Siphons some of the energy. It can also take people and hold them there, using their energy, usually through fear. It's one of the strongest energies. I don't understand why this would be a problem for you."

"I don't either. Only that I failed my Demonstration of Magic."

Wulana's brows raised high, pinching at the center. "For a royal child, that is *odd*."

"This is why I need your help."

"You've come all this way in the hopes that our people could help you when we already help you by providing one of our strongest magical citizens, our sytes?" Wulana said sternly.

"But she wasn't able to help."

"You can wait to see if it resolves," Pular suggested.

"Have you seen that happen? That the Tokahaya stops siphoning magic?" Fina asked curiously.

"When we had those former residents, they were siphoning and then once we banned them, it ended," Pular said.

"I don't think that's the same."

"It may be the same principle," Wulana said.

"Can you help me make the magic I have stronger then?" I asked. "Maybe then I won't need what's been taken and I can still pass my demonstration."

"Is that possible, Wulana?" Fina asked.

"For a non-Zhirian?" Pular scoffed.

"It's against our laws to act in such ways. Our magic is honored and revered and must be handled as such. We must guard it," Wulana grumbled. "On the outside, we have found trouble and our people mistreated and abused. Our magic is best put to use protecting our people and ensuring our life continues."

"What I'm hearing is that because I'm not Zhirian, you can't help me, even if it took nothing from you."

"To give you something of ours, by nature, requires something of us. Nothing is free," Pular said.

"Magic is everywhere, in excess."

"So you believe we should give it to you. In exchange for what?" Pular came around the table and stood near the window.

"What do you mean?"

"As I said, nothing is free, daughter of Narut. And you are unable to make bargains."

"I'm powerless?"

"Ni. You still have power within you. Your light is there, even if not all of it." Wulana circled as if measuring me.

"You could wait and see, Lafia. You don't have to do this," Fina added.

"If you refuse to help me, I won't have a choice."

"A choice about what?" Fina asked with concern.

"I *am* getting my magic."

"How?" Wulana asked.

"I'll go and get it."

Pular joined Wulana, standing in front of me. Their eyes searched deeply for something I knew wasn't there.

Finally, Pular spoke. "Look, Lafia. You are still a child. Young, naive. You must return home and allow those in charge to handle this. The Tokahaya is nothing for you, without your magic, to deal with. Even those with magic have failed in their dealings. Why do you want to mess with the peace you've had, and, by extension, we've had all these years?"

"I don't want to mess with the peace. I just want my magic so I can be who I'm supposed to be."

"And what's that? A queen and a Clarhugaba?" Fina asked gently.

She made me sound small and selfish. But it was what I wanted. "In fact, being Clarhugaba is what I want. It will be good for Faduwata."

"And the rest of us? How does Zhiri benefit if you disrupt the peace we've had all these years?" Pular challenged.

"I won't. That's why I need you."

"Can you at least check to see what's going on?" Fina asked.

"If it's the Tokahaya, there is nothing I or any of us in this room can do. That's the truth. If you're blocking yourself, there's nothing we can do. If it's someone else or something else, maybe."

"Good. Can we please check? If it's something besides the Tokahaya, maybe you can break whatever bound my magic."

"Fina. I'll be speaking with you after this."

"Ya'i, Leader Pular." Fina shook her head. I had indeed gotten her in trouble.

"Come here, Lafia Ketonga of Narut. Stand here in front of me."

Immediately I felt their energy and power. My entire body tingled as they penetrated my thoughts using their eyes. They walked around me with closed eyes and their hands raised toward me, discerning the energy around and within me. They took a large step back, clapped their hands three times, brushed them off and blew in the air.

"What did you see?" I asked.

"It is not just you blocking your energy. It is not someone else or something else in our dimension."

"So, what does that mean?"

They shook their head as if not wanting to speak this aloud. "There is no certainty I can give you that it is the Tokahaya. I can only tell you what it isn't."

"I understand. Even knowing that helps narrow things for me."

"It also means there is nothing we can do against it, even if we wanted."

"You could give me some of your magic to boost what I have."

"We can't give you our magic. That isn't what we do."

I paused for a moment, remembering what I'd brought.

"I have a request. Not to give me your magic." I raised my hand to acknowledge I'd heard them already. "I carry a blade that belongs to my mother, the Clarhugaba. It was given an infusion of light by sytes. That is something you do. But she said the power of the infusion fades after twenty-five years. Whatever power it has, isn't full. Can you give it another infusion to restore its full power?"

"You don't ask for much, do you, Lafia Ketonga?"

"I need this. Will it work throughout all of the realm? Other dimensions that may be beyond our realm?"

"We can restore its power with an infusion of light. However, you are asking about the Tokahaya. There are no guarantees with the Tokahaya." This time it was Wulana who answered. "Are we sure about this, Leader Pular? Her questions lead me to believe she may be willing to put herself in danger, and thus us, in danger."

Pular paced about the room with Wulana watching their every step. "What will you do once you leave us, Lafia Ketonga?"

"I will pass my Demonstration of Magic."

Pular's eyes narrowed. "How?"

"I will get my magic back as planned."

"You must return home, to Narut."

"There are many things I must do. If returning home to Narut is one of them, so be it." I had no desire to return there without my magic and risk failing my demonstration again, losing Najurvod to Bletondu, and being a source of disgrace to the Ketonga family and all of Narut.

I waited while the Zhirians exchanged looks, understanding, and finally came to an agreement.

"If we do this for you, you must promise to do something in return. Nothing is free."

"What is it? If you can help me get my magic," I paused, unable to imagine there was anything I had or could do that the Zhirian High Assembly needed, "I'll do whatever you want."

"The Zhirian people have maintained what we have, ensured peace with the mainland of Faduwata and the Tokahaya and we intend to continue doing so."

"Of course. How can I help?"

"Lafia Ketonga, you carry something within you. Something we have not seen since the peace."

I turned to Fina, concerned. *Was this what was special about me?*

"You must promise to choose the light and to use Clarod to cut through the darkness."

"Of course."

"At every turn," Pular said firmly.

"Lafia, understand you may have temptation. So they are asking you to make the promise to always choose the light." Fina grabbed my hand.

"What are you not telling me?"

Pular ignored my question, turning to Fina instead. "Get El and have her bring the file. She'll know which one."

Fina dropped my hand and quickly hustled out the door.

"What's going on? You've already told me you can't do anything besides infuse Clarod with light. Why is that such a big deal?"

"What do you know of this blade you carry?"

"It's my mother's and it's been a while since it's been infused with light. Mada hasn't used it or even taken it out since I was a little girl. Why?"

"That's all? You don't know why we gifted your mother with this blade and gave it the infusion of light?"

"We never talked about it," I answered sheepishly. There were many things I hadn't been told.

"Does your mother know that you have taken her blade as part of your excursion?" Wulana chimed in.

"I did not tell her before I left. I plan to return it safely. With your help, it'll also have more power."

There was more silence as Wulana and Pular considered my answer.

"You must return home and take the blade to Clarhugaba Selifaya. You are not prepared to wield its power."

"It's a blade. I lift it and cut."

"Ni. She is not ready. We infuse this and she may misuse its power," Wulana argued.

Fina pushed the door open with El behind her, holding a small device.

"I have the file, Leader Pular."

I didn't understand. She held some gadget that looked like a clear cubed crystal and nothing more. Pular reached into the drawer and took out a black metal box with silver coils wrapped around it. It was no larger than their fist. I'd never seen anything like it. He took the cube from El and placed into a slot on the top. I heard something click and then in front of him was a picture of me as a child. It was taken shortly after Fina had come to us.

"What is this? Why do you have an old picture of me on this thing?" I waved my hand over the black box and my hand cut through the picture. It was a different kind of magic, like their use of the vertical transports in the building.

Pular ignored me as he put a lens over one eye and nodded his head, making the image move up and symbols appear below.

"What is this? What's it say?" I demanded.

"Just as I thought," Pular nodded, making the screen move again. They took the lens off and put it away.

"You cannot wield Clarod. Not without functioning magic. Not with what is inside you."

"What's inside me that is so bad I can't use a simple blade!"

"It's not a simple blade. This blade has been made and infused to cut through the darkness. You, Lafia Ketonga, carry both the seed of light and of darkness."

"Everyone has good and bad in them. It's being alive."

"Ni. We have only seen this once before. You must leave and return home. Do not return here without your magic and a commitment to the light."

"You're sending me away because of something you think I might have in me and because my magic doesn't work? That's why I'm here. That's the only reason I'm here and you are rejecting me too!"

Pular stood firmly, hands pressed together. "We are helping you. You must come into your power and strength the right way. Fight back in your mind against whatever you believe is holding you."

"If I could do that I would."

"You said yourself, something is siphoning my magic."

"Ni. I said, sometimes that can happen, and you said something is blocking me. It must be the Tokahaya. You're afraid I'm going to go there?"

"Your people teach, wisely, that there is no life beyond the Tokahaya. Even this blade may be no match. What if it consumes you?"

"That's what worries you?"

"That I might be consumed?" It worried me too. I couldn't admit to them my plans, but I didn't need to. Going home with Clarod was an option. Returning it to my Mada and waiting for whatever spell had been placed on me to wear off was an option.

"I will go home and Clarod will be returned to my mother."

"Do you promise?"

The first signs of moisture escaped from my palms. Though I planned to get home with Clarod when I was done, it wasn't in my plans now.

"I promise."

"She's lying," Wulana said.

"I will personally escort her to Narut to ensure she returns," Fina said irritably.

"Are you satisfied? Can I please get the infusion?"

"You still want it? Just to take it home to your mother?" Pular asked suspiciously.

"I do. And I want you to tell me what else you saw. What else you know."

Wulana shook her head at Pular. "Some things are better left unspoken. We do not risk giving it breath and word and bringing it into existence."

"You think just telling me will make a spell of it? That it'll give the power of the tongue?"

"Spoken from the lips of any of us in this room? Ya'i."

I collapsed into one of the chairs at the table in Pular's office.

"That's it? I came all this way to infuse my Mada's blade?"

"You got more than that. You know it's not just you, but you need to wait."

"As powerful as you are, you can't break it? Pause it? Or something?"

"So that you can pass your Demonstration of Magic?"

"Ya'i."

Wulana leaned towards Pular. They were doing it again. Nodding and shaking their heads in silence.

"Tell her," Pular said.

"We can't do that, only you can. You have everything you need already, Lafia. When you believe, you will know it to be so."

There was no other argument I could think of. Pular and Wulana were wrong about me. I turned to Fina for help.

"Listen to them, Lafia. They are wise."

"You have chosen the solitary life of a syte in Zhiri. I mean to be a leader as Clarhugaba and serve my ajurdom and all of Faduwata. I cannot do that by waiting around."

"The blade still needs to be infused if it is to be of any good magical use to Selifaya," Fina said.

"Then we do that and be done."

"I'll accept the infusion," I conceded, holding back tears. "And I thank you for the time you've taken to look into my situation."

"Very well. Let us commence then," Pular picked up Clarod and turned it over in their hands. "I need multiple sytes to do this infusion."

"If we do this for you," Wulana said, her face scrunched, "you will need to return home. We cannot have you here when you've come without the permission of your ajurdom. We don't wish to be entangled in any disputes."

"Then it is settled. Let us give this blade a clar infusion to renew its light," Leader Pular held Clarod up in the air.

***

Red blinking lights reminded me of my status in Zhiri. They were sending me away, as suspected. However, Clarod was freshly infused by sytes, including the very powerful Assembly Leader Pular.

"You must go home, Lafia." Fina grasped my hand. "I don't want anything to happen to you and you shouldn't be out here alone."

"I've done alright so far, haven't I?"

168

"You got here. And now you need to get home. You don't need to try and find whatever's got your magic. I'll take you back to Narut personally.

"I need to pick up something in Sparaka first."

"And then Narut?"

"Thank you, Fina. For everything. I know you can't help me with what I need, but you let me see your beautiful home. I know why it's so special now."

The Zhirians went about their business outside of the building and within. To them, this was normal, all common. To me, every bit of this place was magic and wonder. If I'd been allowed, I would have stayed. But my magic hadn't been impacted, despite being surrounded by it.

"We will go to Narut after Sparaka, Lafia?"

"Take me to Sparaka since I have to leave here. When I'm done, we'll go home.

We walked back to the registrar's desk, and he pulled out my paperwork. He scribbled notes on it and gave me a ticket. "Exit through that door there."

Signs attached to the door and hanging overhead read No Reentry in the Zhirian language and in words I could read. It would lead us to an official transport station that took us back to where Fina had met me the night before.

"What about Saren?"

"He'll meet us there," Fina said with certainty.

"I'll take that." The registrar pressed a button on a machine and tapped the band on my wrist. It opened and he slid it off. "I hope you enjoyed the time you had here," he said politely before moving on to the next guest.

Walking out of the sculpted building, soon I'd be thrust back into the ordinary world after experiencing something fantastical. I would take in every sensation of Zhiri and brand it into my memory.

"Returning to the entry point?" a male haskeal asked in a pitchy tone in line with his size.

I nodded reluctantly.

"That way." He pointed to a giant waiting near transport platforms designed much more intricately than ours. A uniformed attendant scanned my ticket before walking us over.

Instead of bars and seats, the floor had cushions spaced out for sitting and straps that crisscrossed the body. The other option was to stand between cushions unless there were several small giants as there were boarding with us.

I squeezed in between Fina and a giant child. The top of my head only reached his chin which he bumped several times while fidgeting with the straps crossing his torso. The flexible straps against our backs bent with our movements. I held tight, certain it had to be easier than riding Saren.

"Everyone ready?"

There was a chorus of mumbled agreements before a bell rang. I stumbled as the power surged beneath us. It wasn't true that they didn't have transport stations. They chose not to connect to the Faduwatan system.

When we arrived at the border city, most of those riding got off and walked in various directions. The transport operator pointed to me. "This way. I'll escort you to the exit."

My hands clung to the straps on the transport and the bag I'd carried sat at my feet.

"Lafia? It's time to go," Fina urged gently.

I didn't move.

"You must exit the transport. Please have your guest step out," the giant said to Fina impatiently.

"Lafia, come on. It's time. Saren is already waiting on the other side of the wall."

I frowned as I stepped from the platform and grabbed my bag. I lingered, soaking in the border city and all its people. The fae, small people, vennas, giants, and even the occasional hint of a ruwatane in the stream that ran alongside the street.

"The door to exit is there. Once you're through the gate, the bridge that leads to Faduwata will be right there," the giant smiled and nodded. He tapped his large foot waiting for Fina and me to move toward the door, and then he followed behind, casting his shadow over us.

At the door, he paused. "Enjoy your day." He said it so casually as if he hadn't all but told me to leave paradise.

Outside the foreboding wall that hid their world, Saren trotted over. His tail was limp and ears down. I know he felt the same way I did.

"We don't get much company. We don't even get out much, especially not up this way. You're going to miss her, aren't you, Saren?"

I smiled, hoping to make him feel better. "We get one more trip. I'm going back to Sparaka."

"You mean through Sparaka on your way home," Fina corrected. "Your parents will be searching for you if you aren't sent home today. We will not be entangled and will be honest about your unsanctioned visit and your stop in Sparaka."

I winced at the idea of Adon and Mada and how they'd already alerted Sarkin Rusya who'd undoubtedly be waiting for me in Narut. Even still, I had something I had to do. They would understand it was worth it when I made it home.

"Please leave out the stop in Sparaka. A woman my age needs to have one secret or two. What I'm getting in Sparaka is personal."

"Do I need to be concerned with that trip too?"

"Listen, Fina. As soon as I'm done with my business, it's to the palace. Just please leave Sparaka out of it."

Fina stared into my eyes, and I fiddled with the purple stone between my fingers. "Don't do that. It's impolite."

"Now it's impolite? Convenient, I'd say. Hop on and let's get you back before your parents send the head of security to get you."

I imagined Sarkin Rusya coming after me. Or worse, the Chief Internal Security Officer for all of Faduwata, Sarkin Felli, coming with a small army to bring me home while threatening Zhiri with their mere presence. It wasn't inconceivable, given his position. However, from what I'd seen in the short time there, the Zhirians were quite capable of taking care of themselves. It was no wonder they didn't need us.

My head rested on Saren's neck as I wrapped one arm around him and held onto the grab strap. This time he didn't take off in flight. As we walked toward the gate that kept us out of their home, he changed. "Saren! Your wings! What happened to them?" And then the beautiful horn vanished, leaving him indistinguishable from a carso.

"He's hidden them. Imagine him flying into Sparaka for all the world to see."

"He's alright? They'll come back?"

"Once he's safe back here, they will. Some Zhirians must do more to obscure our identities or protect themselves as they've been mistreated and harmed at the hands of those on the main land. It's the same reason the haskeals who live in Faduwata portal hop and often spend time in other dimensions."

"Why bother living there when they could be here in Zhiri?"

A guard slowly opened the gate to let us through.

"We need to ensure what you all do won't negatively impact us. We are only across a bridge and what you do in Faduwata, what we do in Zhiri, impacts everyone in the Maradobu realm. They are there to help and to heal. They do often visit, though."

"I can't blame them," I smirked, wishing to remain in Zhiri, even as a stowaway.

When we finally arrived after several stops, it was nearly dusk in Sparaka, and stores and shops were beginning to close. I ran my hands over Saren's head and leaned into him again, not wanting to dismount the majestic creature.

"Where are we heading?" Fina asked, glancing at the few stores with lights still on.

"I need to find something."

"I'll come with you."

"You don't trust me to go shopping alone?"

"You ran off all the way to Zhiri, Lafia."

"You may want to do some shopping too since you're here."

Fina cocked her head to one side and folded her arms. "You're not leaving my sight, Lafia Ketonga."

Dusk was already upon us. I'd have to manage having her there with me a while longer.

13

MAGIC AND MYSTERY

Jamil once told me of a special shop in Sparaka during one of his tales of his escapades. I scanned from where I stood near the transport station.

"I knew you'd be back."

I swung around, and Juxi stood against the outside wall.

"I saw my friend and she's visiting Sparaka with me."

"Got what you needed?"

"Ni."

"I told you; they don't take much to outsiders," Juxi shrugged with a sideways glance at Fina who ignored her.

I inhaled and clenched my jaw at the fact that she'd been right.

"Can I give you a ride somewhere else?"

"We're fine. Thank you."

"Alright. Suit yourself. You know where to find me unless I'm already on a trip or home," she smiled.

My hand motioned in what was meant to be a wave but appeared as if I'd injured myself. I did know where to find her and would be certain not to come back that way when it was time to leave Sparaka.

Her eyes bore into the back of my head as I scampered toward the shops, making Fina trot after me.

"Slow down."

"It's already late so I don't have much time."

Several shops had already shuttered for the evening. I glanced back at Fina and saw Juxi had found someone else to hold her attention. On one side of the street sat a brightly painted shop with blues, yellows, greens, and reds, the colors of the ajurdoms. The sign was cut to resemble a polished monedutse stone with the words *Stones and Scents* engraved in a white wash. Through the window were containers filled with both local and Zhirian stones. Shelves in pale Faduwatan hues held assorted candles, finger-wands, books, and other magical tools. Spacious aisles were filled with more of the same, plus tapestries, beaded jewelry, incense, and other items.

"What are you looking for?"

"I'll know it."

On any other day, I would've gone in. But I was searching for a different shop and the lights were being turned off even as I peered through the glass. A man waved through the window and continued his meticulous neatening of the shelves.

"Looks like you're too late for this place anyway."

I ignored Fina. She was a distraction. Jamil had described the other shop as time-tested, eclectic, and bordering on cluttered.

A reflection from across the street caught my attention. I left the colorful storefront for the shop with no overhead sign to say what was sold there. On the window in gold and black letters read *Faduwatan House of Magic and Mystery*.

"Where are you going now? We need to go soon. I don't want Saren out here alone that long."

"He can trot back and then fly home. We both know that."

"That's not fair to him. Or me."

"You don't' have to stay, Fina. I am grown. I can do this and get home."

"You're right. You can. But that doesn't mean you will."

Through the windows were stones of every color imaginable, candles, bottles of sand, earth, and salt. There were scarves, glasses, bowls, and an assortment of magical, mysterious things that were simply random. Some were well-used, while others appeared brand new.

My mother and Nontu had also mentioned it, but Jamil had made it seem like a place I had to go. I never imagined walking inside before I'd passed the test and was on my way to becoming a Clarhugaba. It was where the sytes and Clarhugabas went from all over Faduwata. Others ventured through those doors as well for the practical tools they held and some out of curiosity. What I could see through the windows had me intrigued.

"This is it," I whispered.

Being this close, my heart quickened, and the palms of my hands tingled with anticipation. Nontu had mentioned using an item several times in her magic, and I hoped to find one for myself. There was another rare item I sought as well. A book rumored to exist with only a few copies remaining in all of Faduwata.

I took a deep breath before opening the heavy wooden door with large brass handles. A musty scent was thinly veiled by candles and incense. An irritating chime rang out and then there were heavy footsteps from somewhere in the back. Despite having no magic title and failing my demonstration, being inside felt magical. More importantly, I'd been told that very special and magical items occasionally wound up there.

"Well, come in, to the Faduwatan House of Magic and Mystery, with a little miscellaneous thrown in," the high-pitched voice said, sing-song laughing the last part about miscellaneous things.

"Thank you." No one was in view and then a head of beautiful gravity-defying curls in a mauve purple, bobbed around a shelf stacked high with books, knick-knacks, figurines, and other odd treasures.

Her striking locks were the same color as the outside of my parents' ceremonial robes back in Narut. The satiny inside was made from the same red fabric as our sashes. I thought of home, my mother's certain angst, and my father's certain anger.

"Can I help you find something or offer you a glimpse into your destiny?" The woman reached up to take my hand and turned it palm-side up. "I may see something she doesn't," the woman enticed.

I looked down at her head. A flower stuck out the top middle. I gently pulled away. "I'm looking for a swinging heart pendulum. Do you have any?"

"A pendulum?" Fina shook her head in disbelief. "All this time for a pendulum? We have those in Zhiri."

"You wouldn't let me shop in Zhiri, remember?"

The pendulum would help me find my heart's desire. My magic. They were made in Zhiri, infused with light by the sytes, and exported to Faduwata. I'd been told by Jamil and Nontu in the past that they could be found in that shop.

Her head had been going from one side to the other, studying me, one hand on her chin. She was likely wondering why I'd refuse a glimpse of my destiny. After standing there awkwardly, her eyes a full foot below the top of her hair, she smiled and pointed behind me.

"Follow me. I've got a very nice selection."

"I'll wait here for you," Fina said, sitting in a seat with a view to the door.

The woman watched her sit and then waved at me. "Come. People buy them and then they sell them back because they don't get what they thought they wanted. They think it's broken." She chuckled before noticing the look of doubt on my face. She cleared her throat and added, "This business has been in my family since Faduwata began. We've seen many happy customers who get exactly what their heart desires. I'm sure that will be true for you."

I twisted my lips. The swinging heart would give me a chance if I was going up into the gray smoke to find my magic.

"All of these right here will work the same. You just pick the one that calls to you the most. And today only, you buy one and I'll throw in a quick look at your destiny."

"Thank you for the offer."

"Well, I'll let you be with them so one can choose you. I'm Meyrnul. Let me know if you need any help or want to see some of the lovely loose stones I've gotten from the ruwatane people. The nice ones, which I have, they won't sell or trade to just anyone." Meyrnul glanced out the window and across the street to the other shop.

"Thank you, Meyrnul. The swinging heart is fine for now."

A glimpse of my destiny wasn't necessary when I knew I was destined to be a Clarhugaba and those swinging hearts would help. The pendulums hung on the stand. Not one of them called to me. "Hello," I whispered, but nothing came back. It was supposed to be magic so there was no harm in trying.

My fingertips gently grazed the first one. It was a lavender stone heart. Although pretty with darker lines that ran through it, there was no response to me. My eyes moved to one that was royal blue. I swayed my fingers in front of it, and the pendulum moved toward me. Startled, I snatched my hand back quickly. Meyrnul raised her brow and nodded for me to try again.

I reached my fingers toward the blue heart once more and it slowly swung toward me, this time undeniably. I'd never seen one work before. "Does this mean it's calling to me?"

"Ya'i. It's not usually so clear. That is unmistakable. You must have strong magic," Meyrnul beamed, her head leaning as she began studying me as Juxi had

"I must've been lucky, or this is a very powerful stone."

"They certainly don't respond like this to everyone, even when they do call someone. Shall I wrap it up for you?"

"Ya'i. Thank you." I stepped back and fingered the loose stones in a bowl near me.

"You should pick one for the pocket," Meyrnul said and lilted away.

I patted my pocket. My stones were there, secure. Following behind Meyrnul, I ran the words in my head, searching for the right way to ask the question that had drawn me through those doors. I looked back towards where Fina sat. She looked relaxed, confident I wouldn't sneak past her.

Even asking could get me in trouble, and everything I'd left my family to do would be over, leaving me with nothing but a pendulum that would be useless if my plans failed. We were halfway to the register when the door chimed behind us.

"One moment. Feel free to keep looking. There are wondrous things here. I'll take this to the register for you." Meyrnul left, her purple hair heading toward the door to greet the new shopper. "Well, come in. Please let me know if there's anything I can help you find or if I can give you a glimpse of your destiny."

I went to find the register and Meyrnul. The question required discretion and now there was someone in the shop to avoid. I rounded a tall book case and nearly collided with someone's back. "Excuse me. My apologies."

The person spun around.

"Nontu? What are you?" I stopped, unsure how to ask what Nontu was doing there without facing the same question.

"I checked the other shop across the street first. They were closed."

"What?"

"I admit my trip here was much easier than yours, not having to sneak out of a palace and walk along a wooded path and go all the way to Zhiri and convince them I was going straight home and then wind up here."

"You followed me here?"

"I most certainly did not. I did not go to Zhiri but received word through the haskeals that you had. And then your mother received notice. She nor your father are pleased."

"How'd you find me?"

"This afternoon, I told Fina I'd help take care of this business without drawing too much attention, walked out the front door and took the train straight from the palace here." Nontu craned her neck to get a view around the shop in search of Meyrnul. Satisfied she was out of earshot, she pulled me to a corner. "You've been behaving most strangely of late and sneaking off in the middle of your sister's engagement dinner was not something I could ignore."

"I'm fine. And I'm an adult. Plus, as you know, Fina is here."

"And you are coming back with me. You must put this other business out of your head."

"Ni. I'm not. I can't."

"Lafia, it's time for you to go home with Nontu," Fina said coming from behind Nontu.

"I can't believe you told her?"

"I am a responsible adult, and this is not a discussion, Lafia," Fina declared.

"Your parents are already concerned. It is either I who brings you back or the Narutian Chief of Security." Nontu's hands were on her hips now, in frustration.

"As I said. I'm an adult."

I looked back and forth between Fina and Nontu, feeling cornered.

"Lafia Rinal Saleera Ketonga. This is not a debate. If they learn you are out shopping when you are supposed to be making your way back to Narut, they will be even more furious than they already are. You cannot behave this way. Think of how your parents must have worried until they knew you were with Fina? How do you think your sister feels, you leaving her engagement dinner for social calls and shopping?"

"This isn't about any of them."

"It is not just about you either, Lafia. You have been behaving as if it is."

"You don't understand, Nontu. No one does."

"Do not be so certain."

Nontu faced Fina and I could feel her frustration even as she spoke calmly to my former syte.

"Fina. Thank you for letting me know and making sure I got here. I know you have duties back in Zhiri. I will take it from here."

"Thank you, Nontu. Take good care of this one. She is truly special and needs to get home. She seems bent on doing anything but that, so be careful."

"I can handle it. It was good to see you again after all this time."

"And you," Fina said, grabbing Nontu's hand. "Lafia, it's time to get home. Come out and say goodbye.

I followed Fina reluctantly out the door listening to the chime again.

I'll miss you, I thought and stroked his face. He lowered his head, letting me get nearer and I felt him say it back.

"Thank you for trying, Fina. And for listening."

"You really are one of a kind, Lafia. I'm glad to have seen you, even if it may not have seemed like it. You had me worried. I'm still concerned about what you plan to do. Whatever it is, you don't have to do it all alone."

"Even if no one believes me or—" I inhaled the less than Zhirian-fresh air "—if no one believes in me?"

"Even then. Sometimes believing in ourselves will bring others to our side. You did that with me and even with Leader Pular. Neither of us knows, but you believe. Keep that."

I shuddered inside at the gap between Zhiri and where I had to go but smiled and nodded. "I may not believe in myself, but I believe that the Tokahaya is connected to my malfunctioning magic."

"It may be. I hope you get the answers you seek, so you can get your magic and become the Clarhugaba you desire to be." Fina hugged me tightly, as she'd hugged El earlier that day, leaving me with a warm and safe feeling. I held her even as she released her arms.

"I hope to see you again." The tears wanted to fall despite my efforts to keep them under control.

Fina mounted Saren as I hugged him. She waved from where she sat and walked him around to face the direction of Zhiri.

Her world was safe and enviable. Yet it had given me little more than a light-infused blade and the knowledge something was indeed wrong. Returning home wasn't an option for me but moving forward meant I needed some direction. I would find that back through the doors I stood in front of, even if I had to deal with Nontu now. There was no time to waste.

Nontu waited at the door, on the inside. Likely to ensure I didn't escape again. When I came back through, she stopped me.

"You think I don't understand, Lafia. But there is much you don't know."

"You don't understand. I tried to talk to you, to Mada, to all of you. None of you get it. I'm not going back to the palace. Not yet."

"What are you doing?" She waited for an answer before adding, "Running away?" Her eyes squinted and she secured the bun and headband over her forehead and ears. Finally, she took off her large, shaded glasses and peered into my eyes. "Try me."

"There is something I must do, Nontu. I know what I saw, and I know what I know. My magic isn't just broken. It's stolen. Siphoned, actually." My voice rose enough that Meyrnul looked in our direction. I leaned toward Nontu to whisper, "I'm getting it back."

Nontu stared in disbelief, speechless for long enough that Meyrnul decided to return to check on us.

"Was there something else I could help you find?" Meyrnul stopped. "Nontu? Is that you?"

"Meyrnul. My apologies for not making myself known. I was being discreet."

"No need for that in here. It's been a long time. Why haven't you been in? Have you been going straight back to Zhiri? Or shopping in Narut? My shop is so much closer to your home."

Nontu laughed. "I go to Zhiri occasionally, but I have been busy with my royal duties. I am only here because I thought I saw a friend come in. And I was correct."

"You know this young lady?" Meyrnul's smile spread across her entire face.

"Indeed, she does," I interrupted the reunion to continue my business. "Please accept my apologies but I am looking for something else."

"Oh, what might I help you find? Any friend of Nontu's is a friend of mine."

Nontu's head tilted as I stayed focused on Meyrnul. "Ya'i. I'm looking for something very rare and special."

"I *specialize* in the very rare and special. This is the most special magic and mystery shop in all of Faduwata." Meyrnul's voice rose as she shimmied. "What kind of rare and special thing are you looking for, dear?"

"I'm looking for a book. A very old book."

Meyrnul squinched a single eye at me as if measuring my seriousness. Then she cast that same eye on Nontu who mirrored it.

"A very old book about Faduwata and her history from the beginning," I added.

She wound her head to face Nontu again, this time the eyebrow raised in a high arc. "Is she with you asking this?"

We both waited for Nontu's answer. Her eyes met mine with uncertainty.

"Are you with me, Nontu?"

"I will not let you do anything foolish, Lafia."

"Nontu. Are you with me?"

Meyrnul clasped her hands, her thumbs going round in circles. After an uncomfortably long silence, Meyrnul huffed, "I can take you this way to my special collections, but this area is reserved for serious patrons. Do you understand? I can let you see this first collection only."

Nontu still hadn't answered, and I needed to know before going any further. "Are you with me, Nontu?" I couldn't have her decide to use the authority my parents had granted her to drag me back to Narut or call Sarkin Rusya from home to return me to the palace. Or worse, have Sarkin Felli sent after me.

Nontu nodded once. "I have always been with you, Lafia."

"Then come with me to see the special collections." I took her slender hand.

Nontu shook her head and then smiled at Meyrnul. "Lead the way."

"You won't be disappointed. This collection contains anything and everything written about Faduwata's history and formation. Not that there is much on the formation, but it'll be here. That and more, even about Maradobu. As you know," she said to Nontu, "this realm goes beyond Faduwata, though some forget that."

We followed Meyrnul's quick steps to a wall tucked into the rear corner of the shop. She carefully pushed unlabeled buttons on a rounded pad embedded into the wall, pressing her ear close to small blocks. Something moved inside and then she tapped it with her closed fist before sliding it into a cavity in the wall. It opened into a small dusty study, absent any windows or doors.

"What is this?" I asked.

"Everything I've found about Maradobu and Faduwata's history. If the book you're looking for exists, it'll be in this room."

I walked in, with Nontu stopping at the wall's opening, ensuring it wouldn't close accidentally or on purpose.

"I seek a book I heard about that tells of," I looked around the dim space to ensure there was no one lurking behind books or in the shadows of the corners. Satisfied we were secure, I whispered, "the Tokahaya."

Nontu whipped around sharply and Meyrnul's eyebrows raised nearly to her hairline. "It's been years since someone has come in asking about that. Oh, Nontu! What a friend you have!" she trilled. "One moment." Meyrnul scurried back through the wall she'd opened and vanished.

The light chime sounded, and we heard the click of the door locking. Her quick shuffling steps brought her back, breathing heavier than before. "Here, this in there if you're worried." She handed Nontu what looked like a small walking stick to put between the opened wall. Nontu, with minimal embarrassment, accepted the stick and placed it in the gap.

"Come with me. This other room doesn't have many books, and you must be a syte, light leader, or one of the magical beings to come in unless, of course, you're with one," she said, beaming at Nontu. She turned to me to say, "Lucky you to know two vennan people and a syte! So few people ask about this. This is everything my family has found so far. I don't have to tell you that it's frowned upon to speak of," she slowed her stride and turned to whisper, "the Tokahaya, so I keep it here."

Meyrnul repeated the wall-opening process at the back of the dim study after sliding a bookshelf out of the way. This room was the size of a small closet with a table and one chair. It smelled as I'd expect an old wooden chest would when opened after years of being forgotten.

"Thank you, Meyrnul. You've been collecting this? I mean, your family?"

"Ya'i. We are the keepers."

On a single bookshelf, three books were arranged neatly. Two were bound in soft material with string. They could have been bound when the various ajurdoms and cities that would become Faduwata began more than five hundred years prior. The third was thinner, like a personal journal. The material was the same as my blade Clarod's sheath. It was the color of the soil after blood had been spilled and mixed into it.

"That one." My voice came out breathy but with a sense of certainty.

"Are you sure?" she said and picked it up from the shelf. "One of the other two has a great deal of information about the formation of Maradobu and the gray smoke, well, the Tokahaya. And this small leaflet is one of the earliest copies of the *Sacred Truths of the Dark Moon*."

"That can't be correct. The Truths we learn are much shorter. That must be more than the Sacred Truths."

"Perhaps there is more here than you learned."

"The Sacred Truths of the Dark Moon are inerrant, sacred, and without question." I looked at Meyrnul. *Had she not learned of this? Especially as she had a copy, which she shouldn't have had.*

"It may be the closest to the original writings. Never mind about that. The book you're holding is an unreferenced personal account, and who knows how much is true."

"I feel it. I'm sure."

"You wanted some history, I thought. We don't even know how old this little journal is. The paper is old, but my brother only found it a few years ago. It had been buried in the hills on the north side of Emervy."

"This is the one." Even the feel of the book in my fingers told me I was right as I picked it up and sat in the single seat. From the very first page, I knew. Inside, in beautiful scrawling letters, someone had taken notes. I thumbed through the pages, and it mentioned getting into the Tokahaya realm and strange smoke that shifted and transformed. I flipped toward the end. At the top of a page, *Leaving the Realm* was scrawled more hastily than the other writing.

"Nontu, this is it. This is what I need. How much is it?"

"I'm sorry, but these books aren't for sale. They don't leave this room."

"What? This is a store, but you won't sell these?"

"Ni. You're welcome to copy them." Meyrnul pointed to paper and ink on a shelf in the room we'd come through. "I'll bind it once you're done. You only pay for the paper and the ink. The binding is free," she smiled.

"You want us to hand copy this entire book?" My frustration was beyond being hidden as I glanced back and forth between Meyrnul and Nontu.

"It's not very long. I suggest one of you work on the right side of the page and the other on the left side. You'll be done before I officially close shop. Unfortunately, due to the hour, I won't be able to give you those glimpses of destiny this evening. But the special still stands if you make a purchase and come back tomorrow."

"Why do you want this book, Lafia?" Nontu rubbed her temple, shifting her weight uncomfortably.

"I need it. If I'm going into the Tokahaya, I need to know what I'm up against and how to get back."

"If what?" the two women asked in unison.

"You heard me. I'm going and I am coming back. This book will help me get there and get back. Someone did it before and lived to write about it."

"This book is a hundred-something-years-old. It came into our care after the battle. No one has done it since. We aren't sure someone did it then. It could be made up. Besides, it was before the peace." Meyrnul scrunched her face and silently pleaded for Nontu's aid.

"If it's been done once, it can be done again."

"Lafia. Whoever wrote this journal had to have functioning magic to get in and out," Nontu said gently.

Her expression was clear. She would've taken me away immediately if it had been up to her. But I would not go willingly, and I knew she didn't want a scene.

"You said you were with me, Nontu. Are you still with me?" My eyes begged for her support, despite the authority I tried to carry in my voice.

"Lafia, this is not something you need to do. Your magic is—"

"My magic has been stolen by the Tokahaya. I'm getting it back. I want you with me, but even if you aren't, I *am* going. My life depends on it. The life I want requires I have my magic, Nontu!"

"That is one life. One version of what your life could be."

"It's the only life that matters. You wouldn't understand, Nontu."

She fell silent. One foot rocked back and stayed, creating more distance between us. A sadness crossed her face and settled in her eyes. "You should not presume to know what I understand, Lafia."

"This is what I must do. Tell me you've never had to do something no one else understood. I have to do this, Nontu. I have to."

"I cannot condone a quest that will lead to your demise."

"You aren't with me," I snapped, trying to overpower the heat washing over my chest. "Will you at least help me copy the book?"

Nontu pensively flipped through the journal. She closed her eyes and lowered her head. "I am with you. I will help you, and when this is done, it will be done." When Nontu's eyes opened, a tear escaped.

Meyrnul watched us, her mouth agape and her eyes moving back and forth as if she were watching an unfortunate accident occur in slow motion.

"We'll take the paper and the ink. Thank you. And I'll also take the blue swinging heart pendulum." I held the small journal in my hands, afraid it might disappear if I put it down.

"Swinging heart pendulum?" Nontu asked. "Oh, Meyrnul. We will also need one extra sheet to send a courier letter."

"For what reason?" I narrowed my eyes.

"Unless you want the Narutian royal guards and Sarkin Rusya herself descending on Sparaka this evening, I need to send notice back to your parents. It will buy us tonight. I cannot promise you any more than that."

"That'll have to be sufficient then."

***

When we emerged from the shadowed room, we found Meyrnul in a chair with a pillow. Most of the lights were off. I held the copied journal in my hands to be bound.

"All done?" Meyrnul said, rousing from her nap.

"Ya'i." I handed her the papers and she waddled to the register to bind them and ring up my purchases.

Before I could follow, Nontu grabbed my shoulder. "It is far too late to do anything with that information tonight, Lafia."

"I'm afraid if we don't go tonight, you'll try to convince me to go home. I'm not going home. Not before I do this."

"You are being unreasonable. It would be best to have one or a dozen guards accompany us and have a caravan with food, supplies, and weapons. The Tokahaya is not something to play with or go into without preparation."

"The woman who went in and came out did it without an army."

"That was over a hundred years ago. Things have changed since the battle, Lafia."

"It's a realm. Whatever magic rules it has, I'm sure it still has."

"Leadership can change. A lot may have changed."

"Nontu. Listen to me. I know people only see the not-so-graceful, shy woman who gets lost between Kyari and Naeemah. It's easy to forget that there is a life I want as well. I want to have love, respect and be of service to my beloved home, wherever that is in Faduwata. Most importantly, to be of service as Clarhugaba of an ajurdom. I can't do any of those things if I don't do this. If I don't do this, nothing else will ever matter."

"We're all set. I can take your payment over here," Meyrnul called out.

"Without all of that, you still matter, Lafia. I wish you would be sensible and stop this. We can practice together. As much as you want so you pass your demonstration," Nontu reasoned.

"Coming," I called back before I responded to Nontu. "You weren't there for my demonstration. I failed every single test. The mundane, the haskeal deanimation dust, and the demonstration of what is supposed to be my gift."

"I know. That is why I will work with you."

"Are you coming this evening?" Meyrnul asked impatiently.

"Yes, just looking for something." I dug around my bag for more cullon bills. "Nontu, the Tokahaya can siphon magic. Did you know that? It can use it to give itself more power in its realm. And it even takes people and holds them to access their light to give itself power."

Nontu stared off into a corner, her gaze unfocused. She then returned her pained eyes to me. "I have heard of such things. Why do you think I do not wish for you to go? Do you want to be one of those people held in the Tokahaya?"

"What if by going, I can help free them too?"

"You are not listening, Lafia! You could put more than yourself in danger. You could risk everything! Why? Because of your impatience?"

A wave of heaviness crashed through my chest. "I'm not being selfish. What I do, I do for Faduwata. I do for Narut."

"Tell yourself that, but if you fail, what you do will be on Faduwata and Narut."

My hands quivered at the thought of bringing harm to all that I loved. Meyrnul came over, her large brows now furrowed with concern.

"Is everything alright, Nontu?"

"Ya'i. I'll pay for the book and pendulum. How much is it?" I answered before Nontu could.

"I, well. I don't recall. Come to the register."

This time Meyrnul didn't walk ahead and waited for us to move first.

"Help me, Nontu. You followed me because you care about me. I know you do. You wouldn't have stayed and helped if you didn't."

She was pained or possibly afraid.

"I'm going to be okay," I assured her.

"She's a big girl, Nontu. I'm sure she'll make the right decision."

Nontu ignored Meyrnul's comment. Standing in front of the counter, she touched my forehead and ran her fingers along my cheek. "I do care about you, Lafia. This is why you must understand that you cannot beat the Tokahaya. It will either consume you or take everything you care about. That is what it does."

"You don't believe in me either?"

I stared at the book sitting there and the small box with my pendulum inside. Meyrnul leaned on the counter, her hands resting as she listened curiously, no longer impatient.

Nontu grabbed my arm and pulled me away from the counter, speaking in a low whisper. "It is not that I do not believe in you. There is a reason no one goes into the Tokahaya, and one of Faduwata's rules is that there is no life beyond the

Tokahaya. It is the path to no return. I do not want to lose you, Lafia."

"You won't. I'll come back stronger and with my magic. And when I do, they—everyone—in my family and all the royals will have to respect me."

"There must be some other way that does not put you at risk like this."

"This is the only way, Nontu."

She moved her head from side to side as if arguing with herself. Nontu placed her hand against the long pointed tips of her ears and walked farther away, pacing between me and a stack of crates. Meyrnul's head was on the counter, either from restlessness or she'd gone back to sleep.

"If we do this—"

"Ya'i! Thank you, Nontu!"

"Listen, Lafia. If we do this, we do it together. We are both risking our lives and you have to understand there are no guarantees."

"I trust you, Nontu." I picked up the book and held it tightly to my chest. "We're ready, Meyrnul."

Meyrnul startled. "Oh. Oh. Oh. What were we doing? Ya'i. I wasn't sure you two would ever work out whatever that was. Now, that book and," she muttered and closed the small pendulum box, "this swinging heart pendulum. Will that be all?"

"I'll take this hat." Nontu grabbed a knitted cap from a stand beside the register. "And this." She picked up a scarf as well after glancing at me. "I see you already have one. Wise."

I pulled out bills and coins from those I'd already separated and handed them to Meyrnul, grateful that I didn't have to go alone, even if I'd been prepared to.

"Alright. Let me get your change."

"You can keep it. We've taken far too much of your time. Thank you."

"Thank you! And thanks for visiting the Faduwatan House of Magic and Mystery."

Meyrnul unlocked the door, and it chimed once more as we walked out onto the much quieter street. The sound of the lock clicking behind us was way past due. A few late-night establishments for food and drink were still open, but most of the regular shops were darkened.

"Tonight, we create a plan and rest, Lafia. Let us find a place to sleep."

"I'm not going back to the palace, Nontu."

"I know. You have been clear. We will find a place here in town. I am hopeful one of these lovely establishments has a room to let."

The idea of staying inside one of the buildings down here made me a bit nauseous. "Is there another section of town we can stay in?"

"I did not think this would be to your standard, as it should not be. We can go to the finance and business district. Unfortunately, the two of us would be much more recognizable there."

Groaning, I checked up and down the street once more. "The place up there with the sign above it. It says—" I craned my neck, "Does that say, ROO OR LET?"

"That is exactly what we are looking for. Come on, dear child. Let us get in before the night gets wild."

I put the straps of my bag around both shoulders, and together we marched toward the ROO OR LET sign, attempting to ignore those in the street. The door opened on an

establishment under a sign that read SPARE NONE FOOD &
ALE, and two men shoved a third man out.

I tried to dodge him, screaming, "Watch out!" as I lost my
balance, stumbling toward the road and the oncoming train.

14

ROO OR LET

Nontu whipped around and reached for me with surprising reflexes as I hung briefly over the street, staring into the oncoming lights while a horn blared. She yanked me back to safety on the sidewalk.

My heart fought to stay inside my chest but that wasn't going to stop me from yelling, "You fool! You almost killed me!" I fixed my clothes. "You need to be—" my words dried on the tip of my tongue as I recognized the face even under the large glasses and hat. "Jamil?"

He stumbled around to look at us. "Lafia? And Nontu?! What are you doing here?"

"We could ask you the same thing!" I glowered.

"You could. But I asked first!"

"We said get out of here. Your money's no good!" One of the men who'd shoved him onto the sidewalk yelled out the door. "Get from in front of here."

"I better start walking," Jamil said, keeping his head down.

We scampered quickly to catch up to him.

"Why am I not surprised? What was that about, Jamil?" I asked after we'd gotten past the building.

"That was nothing. I was trying to settle something up."

"I take it that the settling did not go in the way you would have hoped then," Nontu reprimanded.

He shrugged, put his hands in his pockets and said, "It's okay. Next moon, they'll have forgotten all about it. What are you two doing out here? Last I heard, they couldn't find you. You abandoned your own sister at her engagement."

"You wouldn't understand. I had important matters to attend to."

"More important than the engagement dinner?" he challenged without stopping.

"For me, it was. Besides, I wanted to do some shopping. I wanted to check out Sparaka for myself now that I'm twenty and this was one way."

"You? Wanted to check out Sparaka? That's not like you."

"It's very much like me if you'd ever stayed put long enough to get to know me."

"Not now, Lafia."

"We're even spending the night here in town. Isn't that right, Nontu?" I said proudly.

Nontu simply did a curt nod before directing a question at Jamil. "Do your parents know you're out here this evening, unaccompanied?"

"If they don't already, it won't matter, as I'll be back before they notice or start to worry." His grin made me look away. "So, where are you staying? I've got a friend who I stay with in town."

"We'll be fine. In fact, we're staying right here." I pointed up to the ROO OR LET sign.

Jamil let out a loud "Ha!" from his stomach as if I'd said something terribly funny. "That's funny. Ni. Where are you two staying tonight? Really."

Nontu's expression had no hint of a smile. "We are here for the evening."

"Ni. I can't let you two stay here. Not in my town. Come. Let's hop on the next train. I promise it'll be great, and your personal health won't be at risk." He raised his shoulders and lifted his hands. The building did look seedy. Wherever Jamil might take us couldn't have been worse than this.

"Who is this friend?" I asked.

"I've known him since I was knee high. His mother, well, the woman who raised him most of his life, trades with the Sparakan government. He's good."

"Does that mean he'll recognize us?" Nontu questioned.

"I'm sure he's never met either of you in person."

"We can stay at the inn here, Jamil. We'll be fine." I stopped walking, not wanting to risk being recognized by someone associated with the government.

"There? I've been in there. Once. That's not a place for one of the premier daughters of Narut to lay her head. Or for a royal syte." Jamil flashed a smile at Nontu.

The crooked sign swung tenuously on rusty chains. Cobwebs had claimed every corner of the windows, and some had even stretched across the windows. Something scurried from the doorway and along the sidewalk before disappearing into a crevice too dark to see. I stumbled back, nearly colliding with Jamil.

"Easy there. If that's too much for you, wait until you're inside."

"Nontu? Maybe we can go with him to his friend's place. It's just one night. At least he knows the town and his way around."

"Ya'i. Come, Nontu. Lafia's already on board. Let's hop on this next train. It's already coming."

Nontu spoke in a firm low voice, "The two of you are royals and I am a royal syte. We cannot be seen gallivanting about Sparaka without so much as a sash or a guard and," she said with added emphasis, "at this time of evening."

"You aren't gallivanting. Ni. You're having a tour, and one of the royal sons of Sparaka is personally giving it to you." He put his hand across his chest and leaned forward in a mock bow.

"My point exactly. The three of us!" Nontu pulled her hat low on her forehead, to ensure her ears remained covered.

The train slowed to let riders off, and Jamil stretched out his arm, inviting us to step up. "Come."

"I'm trusting you, Jamil." I took his arm and boarded the train.

"Surprising after the engagement dinner. One might think from the way you behaved I was one of those loathsome creatures from old lore."

The shaded glasses covered his eyes. There was no response I could give to that without opening a door I refused to step through. Rather, I needed to focus on what lay ahead. I secured the scarf around my head, making sure my hair and forehead were hidden, changing my face shape. We were going to the home of someone who dealt with the government and arriving with Jamil. I fixed the green-shaded glasses over my eyes. There wasn't much more I could do.

Jamil secured his hat and glasses. He flashed his perfect teeth, made brighter by his deep sepia tones. It was difficult to tell if he was about to search for trouble or was simply willing to let it find him.

15

SPARAKA

One leap and Jamil was off the train, reaching back to help Nontu before offering me his hand. I grabbed the handrail instead and jumped off the lowest step. Nontu was still obviously displeased.

"See, that wasn't so bad and isn't this part of town nicer than where you were planning on staying?"

"You mean the same part of town where you ran into us? Quite literally," I said smartly.

Nontu studied the buildings and their shadows as if expecting someone or something to emerge at any moment.

"Trust me. You're in good hands." Jamil touched Nontu's shoulder.

"You were just thrown out of the establishment back there," Nontu reminded him.

"Minor misunderstanding that will be cleared up by the next full moon. I told you that. This way. My friend lives a couple doors down."

Nontu continued checking each shadow and doorway until we arrived at the front of a stone building with vines creeping along the front. Music came from somewhere close.

"Are you sure about this, Jamil? It looks," I came closer checking the area around the building out as Nontu had been, "unsafe."

"It's not a palace if that's what you were expecting."

A plain metal door on the side of the building was secured by a handle and a lock requiring a key.

"That's the side door, Lafia," he laughed. "Give me more credit than that."

"How was I to know?"

"I've been here more times than I can count. And I'm alright. And it's definitely better than your ROO OR RAT," he chuckled.

"It said ROO OR LET, not rat," I retorted.

"Come on up the stairs to the main entrance." Jamil ignored my defense, focused now on getting into building.

Nontu and I followed him, and he rang a huge overhead bell.

"Was that really necessary?" Nontu asked, covering her sensitive ears.

"Sorry, but it's loud in there, and I wanted to be sure he could hear it." Jamil smiled and then pounded three times on the door.

The door swung open, and a man filled the doorway, blocking most of the light that would've come from inside. He rubbed one hand down the beard that ended at his chest. "Jamil! My friend! Finally here," he laughed before looking around him. "And...company?"

"Well, you never know what to expect with me, do you?" he joked. "These are my friends. They need to stay with me tonight. They were actually prepared to stay in the ROO OR RAT."

"It was ROO OR LET!" I said again in defense.

The man feigned shock and offense, then laughed from the belly, his head leaning forward, spilling long twists. Then he stood, showing a broad and inviting smile. "ROO OR RAT! No friend of Jamil's stays there. Disease. Rats. Who to call to clean up?"

"I have no idea but I'm sure I can find someone with connections," Jamil chortled to groans from Nontu and me.

"Come. Friend of Jamil's, friend of mine. Olug."

"Thank you, Olug, for letting us stay in your home this evening," Nontu said, still inspecting the grounds and the house.

"Thank you," I added. "It's a lovely place."

"You never say that, Jamil."

"You're already making his head bigger, and that's not an easy thing to do," Jamil chided me.

"Try sometime." Olug put his elbow around Jamil's neck. His large forearms and towering size made Jamil look below average, which he was not.

"Can we get all the way in and close the door, please?" Nontu asked.

"Sorry. Ya'i. Come in. Get comfortable," Olug said, moving inside and out of the way.

With the door closed, the music was even louder.

"Is there a party? Here?" Nontu asked, clearly annoyed by the music that vibrated through the room.

"Ya'i. Surprise guests too."

We turned to each other at the same time and then to Jamil.

"May we have a moment with you, Jamil?" My smile stretched tightly across my teeth. He could be infuriating.

"What is it?"

"Over here." I walked to the door with my back to Olug who was already at the foot of the steps. Nontu glared at him, in full sight of Olug.

"A friend is one thing, but we can't be seen here at a party."

"You're with me and in disguise."

"No, you lug! We can't," I argued.

"Olug."

"Ugh! We are going back to ROO OR LET." I grabbed the handle of the door.

Nontu and Jamil protested simultaneously in their own ways. Nontu blurted out, "Let us not get ahead of ourselves."

Jamil threw his hands up. "Don't be foolish. It's too late. No one will ever expect a princess to be here," he whispered. "I do this, and no one suspects I'm me."

I huffed at Nontu. "If we'd left earlier, we could've stopped at one of the small villages along the way, and it would've been better than this."

"We would hardly be less recognizable there. We would stand out more, especially done up the way you are. You look like you belong in Sparaka."

"Olug, can you give us a minute?"

"Party must happen, Jamil," he said, holding his glance.

"I understand. I'll be up soon." Jamil sighed and returned to me. "She's right. You do. And it doesn't look bad on you," Jamil gulped.

"Thank you, I suppose."

"You should do whatever you were going to do, Jamil. We will be fine once we know where we can rest our heads for the night."

"Either of you ever been to a party that wasn't hosted by a royal family?" Jamil asked, ignoring Nontu.

He said royal with a hint of disdain and Nontu narrowed her eyes at him.

"I most certainly have," Nontu said. "But I do not intend to indulge in what is happening upstairs." Her crossed arms and widened stance meant she had no intention of leaving the house either.

"You really think we're going to sleep through all that noise?" I asked Nontu.

"We need to try. Otherwise, tomorrow will be difficult."

"Or you could live for one night." Jamil's eyes beckoned me.

Nontu lightly tapped one foot as she waited for me to come with her.

"I'm twenty, Nontu."

"What does that have to do with anything? It is you who has plans for tomorrow that you have said are most important."

"And tomorrow will come, whether we sleep all the way there or not. We should have fun, Nontu. Who knows what tomorrow will bring," I pleaded with my eyes.

"How often will she get this chance, Nontu. Surely, you were young once. It might have been what would seem like a lifetime ago, but you were." Jamil attempted to use his charm on Nontu who turned to face the stairs that led to the music.

"You hardly look like yourself, Lafia. Keep the wrap on, and those glasses, and you'll be good. And you, Nontu, just keep your ears covered and the forehead markings too. Syte ears aren't very common outside of Zhiri and a dead giveaway you're probably a royal syte, so…," he said with a shrug of his shoulders.

Nontu checked that her hat was still secure over the tips of her ears and across her brow.

"We're really going up there?" The panic in my voice was obvious.

"What's the plan?" Olug called from the middle of the steps.

"Is there somewhere quieter where we can rest for the night?" Nontu asked Olug hopefully.

"Study's around there." His shoulders heaved in a shrug. "Missing the party now. Here? Up?"

"We will take the study." Nontu wrapped her arm around mine.

"Is that what you want?" Jamil asked me. My cheeks warmed as they all stared, waiting for my answer.

"I suppose that's fine. If there's space for both of us to rest comfortably."

"Study's small. Don't mind being close, study's fine," Olug said hurriedly. "Large rooms upstairs. Proper."

"This will be fine," Nontu said firmly, holding me closer.

I felt the vibration of the music against the door. The smell of incense wafted toward me, making me heady. Jamil leaned against the wall waiting for a decision as well. I'd never been somewhere like this.

"Nontu. We need to be rested, and that's not going to happen if we are squeezed together in a small study on—" I frowned and turned to Olug, "What's in there to sleep on?"

"Sofa. Two chairs."

"Ya'i. It won't be comfortable squeezed together on a sofa."

"It is also difficult to rest when you do not sleep." Nontu tried to catch my eyes with hers, but I chose to study the intricate handrails where Olug stood. I didn't want her to connect with me.

"I'll be fine up here, Nontu. Don't worry."

"That is my job."

"I'm an adult. A young adult, but an adult. I'm with Jamil, a premier son of Sparaka, a royal son and his childhood friend. He may not be the most responsible person in Faduwata, but I know," I glared in Jamil's direction, "he wouldn't let anything happen. Right?"

"She's in good hands and I will be on my best behavior to make sure she gets settled in to rest for the night. If that's her wish."

"Good." Olug came off the step and pointed a thick finger past Nontu. "This way."

She followed him out of the large foyer, her eyes remaining on me until they couldn't any longer. I stood arm's length from Jamil in awkward silence. I desperately wanted to see what was at the top of the stairs and was willing to risk Jamil's company to be there.

"Ready for fun?" Olug asked as he lumbered back into the room.

"Let's go!" Jamil grabbed my hand before looking at me and letting it go. "Come on."

The music boomed louder with every step until we were in a large room with a partial glass ceiling. The stars and the lavender moon were high above. People stood in clusters, casting uninterested glances at me, before returning to their dancing, talking, drinking, and playing games. A game of two fingers was being played at one table amidst groans and cheers.

"I see you looking at them playing over there. Do you want to try it?"

"Ni. I've never played two fingers with anyone except my sisters and Nontu."

"Come on. I'm sure you'd be great. I can be your partner."

"You? Is this how you lost your rings?"

"Keep your voice down, La— They know me here as J, but what should I call you? And I wouldn't wear them here."

I thought for a moment. It was only for a night. "How about you call me Larsa."

"Larsa?" he said as if it made no sense.

"Well, you can thank yourself for the La part since you already started with that. You have something better?"

Jamil sized me up from top to bottom before shaking his head. "Larsa it is. Now, do you want to play two fingers with me?"

"I told you. I've never done it like this before and certainly not for money."

"And you've probably never done it like me before."

"What do you mean?"

Jamil led me away from where the game was being played and turned his back to the players.

"You play with one person holding up the finger on each hand you choose, right? The other two of you have to guess the fingers."

"Ya'i. And then if you're playing with someone like you," he winked, "when the other player locks in, I change which fingers I have up, and you connect your energy to mine and change your fingers to match my new fingers. You win."

"What! That's chea—"

"La...rsa! Watch it. Do you want us thrown out of my friend's party?" he warned.

With a look of disdain, I had him lean over so I could whisper in his ear, "That's cheating, J."

"What did you come up here for?"

"I wanted to see. I've never been to a party like this."

"Of course you haven't. Everyone cheats. We just don't announce it," he whispered in my ear.

"That's ridiculous," I whispered back.

"It's expected. It's a sign that you've got good magic," he winked.

Confusion became panic. "I'm not playing a game where you are expected to cheat."

"It's not cheating if you're using your gifts or someone else's."

"Is that why you want me to play?" I challenged, avoiding a woman passing behind us.

"Can't hurt having you on my team."

"You were at the same ceremony I was a few days ago, weren't you?"

"Ahhh. That was nothing. Bletondu got you flustered, and you fell for it. Nobody is out for you here. You can relax."

"Nobody is *out* for me, just to *use* me."

"Loosen up and have some fun."

That smile made me want to stay if only because he'd asked. Ni. I wanted to stay because I could, and I might never get the chance again.

"I'll watch. That's all."

He studied me for a moment before conceding. "Good idea. You should watch it being played first."

"I'm only watching, Ja…J," I caught myself.

He either ignored me or put my comment aside because he continued unaffected. "You probably play with one sister and the other sister is the setter, deciding on the two fingers. Am I right?"

"Ya'i"

"Same thing here but we use cards."

I shook my head. It didn't sound like a good idea. "Maybe we can dance instead." I pointed to the dance floor and saw a couple at the edge, their sensual moves causing me to blush as if I'd intruded on a private moment. "Or we can enjoy the view of the skies."

"Let's play one round. If we lose, we can do something else."

"One round? And the cards are on the table?"

"Absolutely. It'll be fun. Something I'm guessing you could use more of."

"I have fun."

"Then let's do it. Only twenty-five possible options. Should be easy for you."

My lips turned down as his strong hand reached for mine and took it before pulling me toward the table.

He thinks I have gifts. I stopped walking.

"What's wrong?"

"I thought I made it clear I don't want to play."

"Don't get cold feet now. We can win."

"They were already cold. You wanted to ignore it, but I'm not playing. Besides, have you won before?"

"Of course."

"More than you've lost?" I folded my arms.

"I haven't kept track."

"That's unlikely."

"Look, La-rsa. One round. That's all. What can it hurt?"

"Do you have something you want to lose tonight? Because from what I'm hearing, this isn't your game."

"I admit, sometimes it's not. But I feel lucky tonight. I ran into you, didn't I?"

"And knocking me over and nearly taking Nontu down with me, that was you being lucky? I might be dead if it weren't for Nontu's quick reactions," I snapped.

"You're scared," he said, changing his expression.

"How often do you win?"

"Like I said, I don't keep count."

"You'll need to do it on your own. I'm only crashing for the night. Not risking my crown jewels on a game I use for practice," I hissed.

Jamil let out an exaggerated sigh. "Now you're being dramatic. You aren't risking anything. I am. What good is practice if you don't use it for real."

I glared at him before pivoting to watch a different part of the room.

"Have it your way. Come with me or not. I'm playing a hand." He blended into the crowd and stood by the table for the next challenge.

He paid me no mind as I watched from the side. I tucked my hands under my arms, to hide my fingers and rings. There was cheering from one end of the table, and someone said, "Who's next?" Jamil's hand shot up in the air.

Something pulled me closer in to see. The setter shuffled the deck and placed it on the table before carefully sliding the card on the top toward him, face down.

"Card is set. Timer being set. And go."

Jamil stared at the card under the timer and the bills in front of the setter. I caught his eye, and for a moment, he seemed pleased before resuming his focus. The winner from the prior round sat across from him. The divider hid most of her face. Jamil clenched and unclenched his fist repeatedly.

"Time is almost up. Lock in your fingers in three, two, one. Time!" The last few grains of sand fell to the bottom.

"Locked!" the two callers yelled from either side of the competitors.

Jamil regarded me briefly before his attention returned to his fingers. This was a stupid game for someone with or without gifts of the clar to play, especially if you risked playing with someone with gifts. Jamil wasn't a seer, yet he'd chosen to play. For any of them it was a guessing game or one of luck. Or, as my mother had said when I was much younger, there may be some with royal blood in their veins who'd become unknown when they'd landed on the mainland shores or during the war. This was risky. The setter pulled the divider back to reveal both sets of hands and flipped the card over. "Left Three, Right One. Do we have a winner?"

The callers both answered, "Ni!"

"Would you like to play a second round? Remember, you can only play three rounds. If by the third round, either champion or challenger fails to secure a win, the party or parties having failed to secure a win will lose everything wagered in those rounds. If either party secures a win, they take all winnings. The house takes the tie."

The woman nodded without shifting her eyes from Jamil. "Stay."

Jamil smirked at me and then checked the bills on the table. "Stay."

"Add your bets," the setter instructed.

Jamil reached into his pocket and pulled out two more bills. It seemed foolish that he was bothering with this game at all. He didn't need the money. *Did he enjoy this?* This time, with more confidence, he winked.

"Ugh," I groaned and walked away. He could play his little games, but I wouldn't indulge him.

"Are you here alone?" I turned and found myself staring into the chest of a man even larger than Olug. I wondered if he had even been speaking to me. I crept farther away, unsure how to answer him. Except for the past two days, I couldn't remember any time I'd been anywhere outside of the palace walls alone.

Over the crowd's noise, Jamil moaned and I eased closer to see what had happened. *Figures. He lost.* I waited until he saw me in the crowd and then shook my head hoping he'd know exactly how I felt. Then I realized it wasn't that he'd lost, only that he hadn't won.

The setter addressed both parties. "Do you want to play the final round?"

"Stay," the woman said, her eyes narrowing beneath her hat.

"Stay," echoed Jamil with a look of determination that I could only interpret as willful stubbornness or stupidity.

The woman across from him wore her hat pulled down tightly over her head and fit snugly to her brows. Her hair exploded from underneath, resting on her shoulders. Her eyes lifted, and found mine just before I stepped back. It was the same feeling I had when Nontu stared into me. Ni. It was like when Bletondu did. Perhaps she was a royal. Ni.

She's a vennan! They all have magic. There was no way Jamil would beat her. I tried to get Jamil's attention as he reached into his pouch again. He stood and patted his pockets before a realization crossed his face. He sat back down.

"I challenge you for a higher wager. This ring." He held up his finger. "What do you have?"

213

The vennan tilted her head quizzically and then reached inside her bag. "Is it real?" she asked Jamil. "Absolutely," he handed it to the setter, who took out an instrument, briefly examined it, and nodded his agreement.

The syte felt around inside her bag until she paused and pulled out a small gold box. It was no more than half a finger high and wide. She set it on the table gently. I wager this.

Jamil scoffed, "What is that?"

"Haskeal deanimation dust." She picked up the small box enticingly.

I leaned forward. It was a rare thing, but not for a Zhirian.

Jamil narrowed his eyes, "Where'd you get it?"

"I won it."

"Where'd you get that?" She pointed to his ring.

"I won it."

"Fair. Do we have a wager?" she asked, her pointed nail tapping the side of the tiny box.

"Wait." The word came out before I even realized I'd spoken.

Everyone turned to look at me and my mouth went dry. I coughed and tried to swallow as I walked around the huge man from earlier and to Jamil's side.

"I need to speak with you. Now," I said through my parched lips.

He glared at me as if to suggest I was being audacious for interrupting his game and speaking in that tone.

"Now," I said more emphatically.

"One moment, please. I'll be back," he said and picked up his Sparakan ring.

I leaned in to whisper and said, "Don't do this. She's a vennan."

Jamil stiffened before turning his gaze toward the woman who sat across from him. In the dim light of the room, her hat pulled down low, he couldn't see any clues.

"How do you know?"

"I don't know exactly how I know. I just do. The hat, for one thing. She's so confident and I'm pretty sure she's baiting you. You're not getting that haskeal dust."

He crossed his arms and nodded to his spot at the table. "I've already accepted the wager and she's already offered a suitable wager. If I back out now, my name is as good as the dirt in Emervy."

"They have some of the best dirt, J," I replied, drawing out the 'a' sound.

"Well, of course. It'd still be the best of dirt, but my name wouldn't be the best among men."

"J. You're missing the point. She's a syte. She's going to win."

"Maybe not."

"You can't beat her unless there are some other gifts you've got you've been keeping secret? Can you do this as a connector? That's what you are, right?"

"I can connect with a person, not a darn card. And I don't know what she's doing, but it's like she's scrambling everything up inside, so she's not locked until the last second. I barely caught it last round."

"And with all that, you want to play still?"

"I'm committed. But there's also you. You can help."

"Don't do that. Don't drag me into your mess. I told you I wasn't playing, and I don't think you should either. You'll lose that ring again and have nothing to signify your status should you need it."

"And that matters why?" he asked curiously.

"It matters because...because...it just matters, J. Just in case." I glared at him. He was infuriatingly stubborn.

"If it matters so much, help me."

"I will not help you." I crossed my arms.

"Are you coming back to play? This evening?" the setter asked.

"Another moment," Jamil said and returned his attention to me. "Help me."

"Ni. I can't."

"Is it that you will not help me as you said before, or that you cannot help me as you say now? There's a difference."

My head bobbed back and forth, trying to decide the best answer to his pointed question. He couldn't know how serious my issues with magic were.

"I will not."

"Then you'll have to be satisfied to watch me lose."

"Suit yourself. I'm finding Olug and turning in. This is foolish and I want you to know that is exactly what I think."

"You see the difference between you and me." He was close enough to feel his breath on my ear, "Princess Lafia. You are afraid of losing. I'm not."

"Good night. Enjoy your loss," I scowled.

Jamil walked back and took his seat. "I'm in." He glanced once more at me and set the ring on the table.

I wanted to leave and find Olug as I said I would, but my feet took me to the other side of the table, opposite the setter. I stood a row back from the action and watched him shuffle.

Haskeal deanimation dust. It was rare, powerful, and finicky, as I'd demonstrated. Bletondu hadn't paused a second or been in any state of deanimation. That night tried to replay, but I took the memory and imagined squashing it under one thick boot. I would have loved to have another shot at blowing a pinch of dust in her face leaving her with a most unattractive expression, like the moment before a sneeze, locked on her face for everyone to see.

The shuffling ended and the setter took the card off the deck and placed it face down on the table. He picked up the timer.

"Card is set. Timer being set. And go."

My eyes darted between the syte and Jamil. He was focusing on the drawn card and then staring at his hands. My hands began to tingle and then my fingers as I kept them wedged beneath my arms. I squeezed them into balls and relaxed them again, but the tingling didn't stop. Instead, it intensified.

It was different than when we played at home. Not all my fingers tingled. Only a couple. Only two. My right thumb and my left ring finger where my Faduwatan ring lived. I wondered if he had gotten it too. If he'd picked the same two fingers held out on my hand.

"Time is almost up," the setter announced. He checked Jamil and the syte. "Lock in your fingers in three, two, one. Time!"

"Locked!" The two callers, on either side of the competitors, called.

Jamil sat stone-faced. A part of me hoped he hadn't lost, despite wishing he might learn the lesson he'd missed at the other establishment. However, I also didn't want him thrown out of his friend's home.

The setter pulled the divider back to reveal the syte's hands and Jamil's hands before turning the card over. "Left Four, Right One. Do we have a winner?"

My hands had somehow been right. I'd been lucky enough to get it right! It was a fluke but perhaps Jamil had gotten the same good fortune.

The syte's caller said, "Ni!" while Jamil's caller shouted, "Ya'i!"

My jaw fell. *How'd he do it? How'd he beat a syte?* He jumped up victoriously while the syte stood and kicked her chair with her heel, causing it to careen back. She eyed the small golden box of haskeal deanimation dust. One fist slammed into the table, causing it, the timer, cards, and anything else on the table to jump. Before I could see where she went, she vanished into the crowd.

Jamil gathered his winnings and put everything into his pouch before leaving the table. There'd be no gloating now or saying anything at all. Instead, I ducked away. It was a good time to find Olug. Walking toward the bar, I felt a light touch on my shoulder. I whipped around to find a smug Jamil behind me. His smile spanned his entire face.

"You look pleased with yourself." I continued walking.

"I am. Thank you."

"That wasn't meant to be a compliment."

"I am sure it wasn't. But I need to thank you anyway for your help."

"I didn't help you. You managed to win on your own. As I said, you must be very pleased with yourself."

He followed me to the bar, but I didn't see Olug where I'd spotted him earlier. "Listen, La-rsa." His voice was suddenly much softer. "Despite all your feigned protests, thank you."

"What under the light of the Dark Moon are you talking about, J?"

It was his turn to be confused. "I'm talking about what you did back there."

"I watched you play. That's all. You're welcome for the moral support. But it's not a big deal."

"Moral support? I suppose, if that's what you want to call giving me the right fingers," he said with a shrug.

The befuddled expression now belonged to me. "Surely, you're mistaken. I could never."

"But you did."

16

ONE NIGHT

My eyes bore into his uncomfortably, seeking understanding. I couldn't help but wonder if this was a ploy to have me forgive his foolishness or if he was flirting.

It was impossible to tell which, but I refused to be toyed with either way. "It's late and I have an early morning. Please take me to my quarters for the evening."

"Where do you have to be that you can't enjoy this one night?"

"I have very important business to attend to."

"In Sparaka? If that's the case, I should accompany you."

"Ni!" I spat with instant regret. "I mean, it's not necessary. I already have Nontu." My hands pressed together. Whatever he was trying to do to me with his easy smile, sparkling eyes, and whatever spellbinding scent he was wearing had to be ignored. "Now, where will I be sleeping?"

"As you wish. I'll show you." Jamil turned sharply, marched through the crowded area, and back towards the stairs. He went down to the middle landing and opened a door to the side, revealing a large suite. "This is where I'd normally have my quarters, but tonight, it's all yours." He gestured for me to enter.

"And you? Where will you sleep?"

"Not very likely I will before this little space is open again. It's very comfortably appointed and sound-proofed. He entertains here rather frequently and energetically."

He'd shifted to the more formal tone, the one he used when he chose to distance himself.

"I have a question for you, and I want you to be serious. No games, Jamil."

"I'm a little offended, but alright. What is your question?" He leaned against the door jam, arms folded into one another.

"How did you beat that syte?"

His eyes pinched together as if trying to figure something out. "Is this a trick question? A test or something?"

"Ni. I told you to be serious and no games. How'd you win?"

"I already told you. You helped me."

"For the love of Faduwata, Jamil! Can you not find a way to be serious even when I ask you point blank?"

There was no way I'd helped him, not knowingly. And if I had, why should he benefit from my magic when I couldn't?

Jamil checked up the stairs to see if my exclamation had drawn eyes. Then he stepped all the way inside the door, his stare intense. My neck flushed warmly as I held myself steady, waiting for a sensible explanation.

"I don't know what you want me to say. In fact, I don't know what you want, period. I answered your question. You are the reason I won."

"Fine. If you want to stick with that. You could've said your magic works. That somehow you tuned in with time to spare to that vennan. But...I don't know what you're up to," I fumed.

His eyelids flapped repeatedly, and his mouth opened and shut several times as he shook his head and then tapped the open door.

"None of that happened. I don't know what else you want me to say."

"Good night, Jamil. I'll be gone by the time you wake but please give Olug my thanks for our accommodations this evening. And thank you for inviting us to join you here." I stood stiffly, avoiding his mocking gaze.

Jamil's face twisted and contorted in a range of conflicting expressions. I waited to see if something other than more lies would come through his soft full lips. Instead, he straightened his posture as I had done mine, nodded politely, and took a long breath in through his nose. "Good night, Lafia. I hope your business goes well. I'll see you at the wedding."

The wedding. "I have one more question before you go, Jamil. This time, please be honest and answer me truthfully."

"I'll do my best." His voice was laced with frustration.

"You always seem to know what's really going on. Do you know why this wedding is happening so quickly?"

Jamil poked his head through the open door, listening to the music booming from above. "Do you want the right answer, or what I know of the real answer?"

"Are they not the same?"

"I can give you whichever is most acceptable to you."

"I want what you know about the real answer, obviously."

"May I close this door?" One hand rested on the partially open door, preparing to seal us from the party above.

"With me in here alone with you? Certainly not."

"Then you'll need to come closer because I am not speaking this loudly, and you will not say you heard any of this from me, understood?"

"What is the big deal? It's a wedding. Oh my! Is Kyari with child?"

"Quiet, La-rsa!" he hissed. "Do not make such assumptions. And so loudly. That's precisely how rumors begin."

"If it's not that, what else can it be?" I allowed myself to come close enough to Jamil that we could whisper.

"You've heard of the Tokahaya? Beyond its reference in the four rules?"

My eyes widened. He'd called it by name.

"If saying that much is going to unsettle you, I'll stop now," he warned.

"Ni. Ni. Don't stop. Ya'i. I've heard of it. I know something about it...now."

"Do you know how it, well, became?"

"I've learned a version of how it came to be."

I didn't want to admit more ignorance. I only knew of the battle and that there was now a very delicate peace. From the Zhirians, I'd learned that the Tokahaya siphoned power and magic from our world, but how it had come about was still a mystery.

"Then you know it requires sacrifices." He focused on a spot on the floor between us and the bedroom.

My eyes followed his eyes before returning to him. His handsome face now carried shadows.

"What do you mean?"

"It's a legend but legends are based on some truth, aren't they? People go missing, vanishing practically or quite literally into thin air."

"I have only heard a few made-up stories of that." However, it made sense if they were being held as power sources in the Tokahaya.

"And I can't prove anything, but I've heard it's the Tokahaya that took Ajur Arstut's wife."

"That's ridiculous. She passed in childbirth."

"There was no body—hers or the baby. I heard there was a ceremony for their passing, but that's it."

"Jamil, please be serious. A royal sacrifice? Faduwata defeated the Tokahaya a hundred years ago. At least it will be in a few weeks. Everyone knows that."

"Did we? Really?"

"Of course we did. We have peace. The ajurdoms wouldn't allow what you're saying without another war."

I cocked my head to one side, curious about how much he knew. I didn't want to let on about what I'd learned but a royal sacrifice wasn't discussed in the journal we'd hurriedly copied. Only how a Zhirian woman had gotten in and out.

"A sacrifice would be one way to keep the peace," he shrugged.

"So what if there is some kind of royal sacrifice, which I admit I am highly skeptical of? What does that have to do with Hakur and Kyari having to marry so quickly?"

"If it does demand a sacrifice, it's time again. At least from what I've been told." Jamil stopped to peer through the cracked door.

"And? What does that have to do with what you're doing?"

"The consecration of their union by the next full lavender moon gives Faduwata a level of security we need in case—" he stopped to check outside the door again.

"In case what?"

"In case things don't work out according to plan."

I searched his face. "Wait. I get it. This is you mocking my insular existence again, isn't it? Oh naive, Lafia, sheltered by palace life and her royal upbringing, always surrounded by the high life. Very funny."

His expression didn't change. For the first time, I felt a seriousness in him.

"That's why I'm here, Lafia. I needed that haskeal deanimation dust. Thanks to you, I have it. I don't have the same magic you, your sisters, and mother have, but I'm a connector. I get the energy of people and I still use what you all call mundane magic. I just can't see, not like you."

"That's why you're here?" I studied his shoes and pants and continued slowly up his frame until I looked at his face. "What are you planning to do, Jamil?"

"I did most of what I came to do. Tonight will be a success."

"So you're going back home tomorrow?"

"You asked why the marriage was happening so quickly. What I'm doing isn't your business."

"Wait. You didn't finish telling me why." I came closer, my voice quiet.

"Right. I didn't. From what I've gathered, this sacrifice requires a royal, untouched woman eligible for marriage. This wedding can protect your sister."

"But what of Bletondu? She's just as much at risk."

"I mentioned it demands an untouched woman."

"So failing my demonstration means I'm safe."

"From what I have gathered, ya'i."

Still, something didn't feel right. It didn't make sense. "Arstut's wife wasn't untouched."

"But she was with child. I don't know why she was chosen last time but I would guess that's why. Why, this time, an untouched woman? I don't know, just that your sister and my brother need to get married before the next full lavender moon passes."

I nodded in understanding about Bletondu while still processing the sacrifice and Arstut's wife. Even what it meant for me.

"I don't know how much of that is right but it's what I've heard. Every ajurdom has had to make sacrifices. It is Narut's turn. If we help, your ajurdom helps all of us secure a future without this sacrifice and a few other things we need here in Sparaka. But as you know, rumors grow, and one never knows."

He stepped toward me, causing me to take a step farther into the room, my head still reeling from what he said while thinking about a few evenings past.

"At the Crossing of the Ties ceremony, my father spoke to someone outside." I waved off the curious look he gave me. "I spent a lot of time outside that night. Whoever he spoke with said something about him only having until the next full lavender moon for something and then the following full lavender moon for something else."

"The next full lavender moon and then the one following? Hmmm."

"Hmmm, what?"

"Look. You've got important business to take care of. I've answered your question and—"

"There you are, Lafia." Nontu stood in the doorway, large earmuffs over her hat.

"What's wrong, Nontu? Why are you up?"

Her eyes were filled with displeasure as she stood between us, "I felt something was off. I was not expecting this."

"Nothing is going on, Nontu. Trust me." A hint of disgust crossed my face. "Jamil was telling me about," I glanced at Jamil, "the Tokahaya."

At the mention of Tokahaya, Nontu closed the door behind her. "What did you say? What do you know?" she demanded.

"I'm not sure?" Jamil hesitated, looking between Nontu and me.

"You can tell her. You can trust Nontu," I reassured him.

"I only know what I heard. Don't know how true it is."

"What do you know?"

"I've heard that the Tokahaya is preparing for the next sacrifice. It's part of why my brother and Lafia's sister are getting married so quickly."

Nontu's eyes locked on his. She didn't blink or waver as he agitatedly shifted from one foot to the other. "That's what I know."

"That is not all you know." Nontu stepped even closer to him until he could feel her breath.

"She's going to make you answer, so you might as well tell her what you know."

"I'm trying to find answers. Father has charged me with getting information and trying to stop it. It's why I'm here. It's why I'm always—" he stopped. "Never mind. That's all I know."

Jamil's eyes narrowed and he stepped back from us. "You two, in Sparaka. Why are *you* here?"

"I told you I have important business." I faced the window.

"You can stick with that line if you'd like, but you should understand, Sparaka isn't like Narut. Ni. They see you out in the day and someone is bound to recognize you. And sorry to say, the Narutians aren't very popular right now, what with the water situation."

"Water situation? I did hear someone chanting after the Crossing of the Ties ceremony about everyone deserving water."

"Ya'i. Everyone deserves it, even if Ajur Rufan doesn't believe it."

"Watch yourself, Jamil. Don't speak of my father with disrespect."

"I said nothing disrespectful. The water comes here much more slowly, and many times it's not even ready to consume. We're in a drought, our water is undrinkable, and nothing has been done."

"You're surrounded by the oceans. You aren't in a drought."

"You know we can't drink that. Our system is set up so that Narut manages the water as we provide safe fishing that protects the ruwatane and the waters. We handle commerce with the Zhirians. Narut isn't upholding its end."

"How dare you? I didn't hear you complaining at the engagement dinner as we drank and danced without care."

"We all play our parts. You may want to take your drinking water from the pot over there. At least you can boil it. It's okay to bathe in, but the tub only fills so high to conserve. Between the low rains down this way and Narut holding back water, this is what you've got."

"Your lips speak loosely. Some words should be held," Nontu said with a glare that Jamil ignored, choosing not to meet her eyes.

I pursed my lips, "Are these more lies? Taking an easy shot at Narut and my father?"

"While rain may come there, we're dry down here. You can test it yourself. Everyone knows Narut runs the fresh water in Faduwata."

"I don't need to test anything. I'll be fine. We're leaving bright and early to make the most use of daylight."

"I can't say the same for myself. I still require two things before I leave the city. At any rate, the night is not getting any longer, and the time you have for rest only gets shorter," he smiled tensely.

I cast my eyes toward the window, feeling silly and childish.

"What are you doing here, Jamil?" Nontu asked and took his hand. He removed it from her grasp immediately.

"As I said, I seek answers."

"And? What do you intend to do with those answers?"

"I must also acquire two more items. One of them I can get without aid, but only for a little while longer. Therefore, Bisa Nontu and Ajursun Lafia, I must let you both retire as you desire, and I must return to my duties."

"Not so quick." Nontu stood in front of the door. "What do you intend to do with those answers and those items?"

Jamil's expression changed. Like an animal when cornered. Then he closed his eyes briefly, straightened his clothing, and stood straighter, lifting his chin as he did. "I do not have to answer that question. I am on official business at the request of Ajur Orin. I do not answer to you. Either of you. Now, please stand back from the door."

Nontu stood back reluctantly and let Jamil open the door.

"I'm going to the Tokahaya," I hastily divulged.

He stopped, one foot still in front of the other. "You're what?"

"I'm going to the Tokahaya to get my magic. It's been taken."

"That's outrageous. Both the idea of going there and that your magic was taken."

"Is it? You said yourself they want a sacrifice. I spoke to the leader of the Zhirian assembly and was told they, indeed, siphon magic and power. I need my magic if I'm ever to be of any use to Faduwata or Maradobu."

"You spoke to Leader Pular? You didn't mention that," Nontu asked quizzically.

"I did. They confirmed something is taking it. It can only be the Tokahaya."

"You have no idea what you're going into. It'll take you alive. Besides, you've got magic. It's in you. It's in all of us." Jamil stood back to study me. Concern and confusion crossed his face.

"Ni. Mine is broken," I said before looking at Nontu. "I know you said not to say it, but right now, he needs to know it's true."

"But you used it earlier to help me win."

"I don't know if I did, or you tapped into that vennan. Maybe it was a fluke, or you got lucky. Even if I did help, I can't use it consistently. It's like it's trapped somewhere behind a wall, and that wall has a few cracks that let a tiny fraction through every once in a while. But I can't be a Clarhugaba like that. I need my full magic."

"I will ask you again, Ajursun Jamil. It is your choice if and how you answer," Nontu urged gently. "What do you plan to do with the answers and with these last two items you seek to secure?"

His lean fingers ran across his forehead, and he tapped the open door with his other hand before pushing it shut. His arms dropped to his side and his lips trembled slightly before they opened. "I'm going to the Tokahaya."

I remained in shock at his confession, while Nontu's was quickly replaced with concern. "You are not serious, Jamil. You…why? What is happening here?"

"I'm not going alone. I'll be fine."

"You're going to the Tokahaya? You? And you called me going outrageous? Will your magic even help you there? Do you have someone like Nontu to help if it doesn't?"

"I'm getting what I need. I'll use the items along with the magic I have. My connecting with others has gotten me this far. Not everyone has to be a light communicator. It helps but I'll be fine. Besides, I have Olug."

I shrugged and twisted my lips. "Is he magical? Is he special or something?"

"You can say that."

"We shall journey together," Nontu said matter-of-factly. "You will need to hurry and gather whatever these last two items are and be prepared to depart by early morn."

Jamil opened the door. "You can't tell me what—" he stopped mid-sentence as Nontu gave him a look I thought only mothers had.

"Between the four of us, we will be able to help each other get what we each need."

"What is it you have to get before leaving?" I huffed and then said, "Maybe there's something I can do to help."

"Well, if you're offering."

"Offering what?" Olug cast a shadow from behind Jamil.

"To help," I smiled.

Olug frowned and beckoned Jamil with one large hand. "Been looking all over, Jamil. Not much time. Crowds thin. Chance going." He turned to Nontu and me and said, "Rest now."

"We need to go," Jamil nodded.

"I can help somehow," I said more forcefully.

"Do you even know what you're offering to help with?" Jamil asked.

"Not yet, but you can tell me. Just be warned that even though there are some things I'm not good at, what I am good at isn't always reliable."

"Lafia, even if it's not perfect, it's better than nothing. Help us win this next game. Olug needs something before he'll come along. You can play it with him while I secure the map," Jamil said with an air of command.

"Ni. Inconsistent magic," Olug said, put off by Jamil's suggestion of my help.

"You told him that, didn't you?" I sucked my teeth and considered whether my helping was risky.

"I try to be honest. And inconsistent or not, you are the one who offered to help."

"Isn't there something else I can do?"

"Do you know how to play Runkles?"

My face twisted as if trying to translate another language.

"I didn't think so. It's a simple card game but it is high stakes. Kind of like two fingers."

"Then I can probably learn it."

"Rather than just help Olug? All he needs is for you to identify which person has the item so he can get it from them. It hardly takes magic if you can pay attention."

"How's he going to get it?"

"He knows the house. He can handle it. I told you he's special."

"I do not like the sound of that," Nontu chimed in. "Listen, I will help you with Runkles. My magic is consistent. Lafia, you may not consistently see what you are trying to see when you connect with the light, but you can connect, and that is all you need, correct Olug?"

"Even less. Watch, act."

The muscles in my chest tightened. The Crossing of the Ties ceremony and the unsuccessful attempt to connect with Faru flashed in my mind. "What if I don't get anything?"

"You will, Lafia. Know that you will," Nontu reassured me.

"And if not, keep eyes open," Olug instructed

"Divide and conquer. The four of us." Jamil winked at me and Nontu. "Be prepared to move quickly. This door has a lock for a reason so meet back here. Olug will shut down the party for the night."

"I am ready, but I have only seen Runkles played once, so you will need to refresh me." Nontu fixed her hat again to sit low on her head like the other vennan had earlier that evening.

"I guess we are doing this." I followed Olug, Jamil, and Nontu out of the suite and closed the door.

17

WYRDEN

"Must find Wyrden," Olug said before entering the party room.

"Who's Wyrden?" I asked.

"Not who, what. Sword from mother. Stolen. Deep market. Here tonight."

"A regular sword?"

"Ni. Special, but not to ords. Beautiful handle artisanship. Intricate. This long." He showed me the space of his forearm. "Blade retracts."

"It sounds beautiful. But why not just get another sword and look for this one later?"

"Won't go without Wyrden. Ords cannot fathom power of sword. With me, Wyrden is more."

"Is that what you call people without the clar gifts of magic and who use mundane magic only? Ords?"

"Jamil is right. Insulated. Limited. Come. Time wasting."

"We'll find it, Olug." I tried to sound confident, despite the palpations that had already begun.

I slid my finger-wand out of my pouch and slipped it onto my pointer finger. Following behind Olug, we slowly weaved through people at tables playing games, dancing, drinking, and talking.

I held my hand out, trying to pick up on the sword. I picked up a lot, but nothing specific. There were more items in that room than I would've imagined.

"Olug, I think everyone here has something secret on them," I whispered. "I can't tune in like this."

"How then?"

"I need one at a time."

"Won't happen. Best chance? Shufflescape. Back corner."

I tried to follow his eyes but had no idea what Shufflescape was to even know if I were looking at it.

"Follow. Stay close. Pay attention."

"Olug, the greatest host in Sparaka!" a man with a beard as colorful as the pluif trees and a bald head called out as Olug approached a circle of people standing around identical long cylinders on a spinning board. "You come to play or observe?"

"Jeno! Friend, no more losses tonight." he laughed.

"And who is the lovely lady?" Jeno winked at Olug. "You finally have a friend?"

"Friend of friend. New to Shufflescape."

"Well. Maybe next time. What's your name?" Jeno asked.

"Larsa."

"Come on in closer, Larsa. You can stand by me."

"Excellent hands to learn quickly. Enjoy," Olug said, patting me on the shoulder.

He was leaving me, and I could barely conceal the terror on my face.

"Hosting. Check in on guests."

"Oh, don't be scared. Watch. We're about to start the round. Every person playing has to put an object inside the cylinder in the hopes of winning something better. Thing is, not every cylinder has an object, so you may end up with nothing."

"What happens if nothing lands in front of you?"

"You see if you can find something you want in one guess. If you guess yours, you can take it off the table. Everyone gets the chance to do this. Anything left, others get one chance to find."

"That seems unfair. Who gets to start?"

"Before we play, everyone rolls for placement and lines up in that order. You don't have to play if you don't like the odds of your placement."

"And if you still wind up with an empty container after your guess, you go home empty?"

"You get a container, and if it's not what you want, you can try to trade or buy it. Time to get this thing going," he smirked. "Players set?" He held a long lever connected to the round table.

Everyone took a step back and placed their hands down in front of them or behind them. Their full attention was on the table, intensely focusing on their cylinders or the cylinders holding something they wanted. That didn't matter. I'd already spotted it. It was on the opposite side of me, under a cylinder, in front of a small man wearing thick wire-framed glasses and a shock of bright orange hair and eyebrows.

The top of his head came only to the top of the cylinders, meaning he could not see the entire table spinning. He quickly pulled a stool up and stood on top, giving him a view of all the cylinders. I couldn't help but smile at his ingenuity. Still, I needed to watch that cylinder. At least three other people's eyes were on the same prize.

Jeno pulled the lever down, causing the table to spin quickly. I wasn't expecting the speed, and within a few spins, I'd lost track of the cylinder I'd been tasked to find. I tried to figure out which was my target by following the eyes of the other three who'd been watching the sword. Two were looking at the same cylinder, their eyes somehow able to keep up, at least for the moment.

Olug should've been there so I could point the right person out to him, and he could figure out how he'd get the sword without resorting to this game that wasn't much more than chance.

It was too risky to glimpse away to look for him. The table began slowing its rotations, and it didn't appear any of the three players who'd been following it at the beginning were more certain of its placement than I was.

"Player one, make your pick," Jeno called out.

A young woman with amber-colored hair walked around the table between two tall men. She reached between them and confidently lifted the top of a cylinder to reveal nothing beneath. She scrutinized the one beside it and her eyes narrowed as she exhaled slowly. She stomped one foot before carefully placing the cylinder on the table. She carefully slid through the crowd, defeat plastered on her face.

"Replace the lid in the proper spot, please," Jeno told one of the tall men, who moved the empty container. "Player two, may you have better luck."

A man overdressed for the party in leafy green suspenders and a matching top hat walked directly to one of the three containers in front of where the woman had made her failed selection. He studied each of them, placing his hand above one and then shifting his hand one over. He held his hand there, seemingly in thought, before lifting the cylinder. He pulled the sword out of the container, turned it over once, and then placed it securely in a satchel he wore across his body. Without a word, he strode from the table.

"Wait? Trade?" someone called out to him with no response.

Jeno called for the next player to choose, but my eyes followed the man who'd gotten the sword. I slowly backed away from the playing area to follow him and find Olug. The top hat made its way straight for the stairs. *Where are you, Olug?*

I followed the well-dressed man until he stood at the top of the stairs, securing the satchel. Olug's large frame should've been easy to spot, but I saw him nowhere. Nontu and Jamil were heavily involved in the game of Runkles and the sword was about to leave with the top hat.

The staircase would lead him out of Olug's. The suite was on the right and there was another door to the left. *That must be the other exit.* Even if I followed him, getting the sword was a different matter.

There'd been no real-world use for the years of combat training at the palace. I considered the front leg sweep. That might take him down long enough to pull the bag over his shoulder and run. *Run where?* I didn't know a thing about Sparaka, especially not this part. I rubbed one of the crystal rings on my hands. I knew how to throw a punch, but I'd only been taught to do it for self-defense. *A knockout punch to rob someone? Seriously, Lafia?*

He'd started his descent. *No Olug. Anywhere.* I lingered near a crowd at the top of the steps, keeping watch of his path. He could escape through the side exit door or venture down to the main entrance. He pushed against the side exit and slipped out. I threw my head back in disbelief before bolting down the stairs and out the front door.

A streetlight cast an eerie glow as he scuttled across the road toward a carriage. If he entered the carriage and the carso trotted off, the sword would be lost, possibly forever. I checked over my shoulder to see if Olug had managed to catch up yet, but I remained alone. The man with the top hat could not leave with Wyrden.

Despite being the only one able to stop him, my legs defied me, refusing to move. Olug needed Wyrden as I'd needed Clarod, as I needed my magic. I willed my legs to charge. It was the only way I'd get enough momentum behind me to land a punch hard enough to knock him down and keep him down so I could get to the sword. *Olug wouldn't go without Wyrden. Jamil wouldn't go without Olug.*

He turned at the sound of me dashing toward him, but any chance he had vanished with my fear. He tried to raise his arm to block, but my arm was already pulled back with my opposite leg planted. I connected with the side of his temple as my other foot came down firmly to the ground. He stumbled backward, flailing, and then crashed onto the street, landing on the satchel. The carso whinnied and stomped one hoof.

I lifted the fallen man enough to drag the bag from beneath him and grabbed the sword.

"Hey, you! What are you doing?" a woman's voice cried out.

I looked up but saw no one.

"Thief!" she yelled.

I lowered my body into the shadow of the carriage, contemplating my options. The streets were otherwise quiet. The woman leaned out of a window a couple stories up, watching. I had to move quickly. I sprinted across the street and into the shadows of the building walls.

"I'm alerting enforcement!" the woman yelled. Going through the front door of Olug's would compromise the entire place and possibly his operation. The bells rang. The woman hadn't lied. Moments later, the flashing began.

The side and front doors of Olug's slammed open, and people poured out grumbling. Her sounding the alarm wasn't what I'd wanted, but now there were others on the street in addition to a suspendered man regaining consciousness. I ran around the building, concealed by those filling the street. I needed an alley or another entrance.

Every royal had to undergo safety and physical training to protect themselves, ajurdoms, and Faduwata. By the light of the Dark Moon, I hoped it would help now.

A window glowed with a soft blue light on the back side of the building. I recognized the light from the one that glowed on the stairway, reflecting into the room I was to sleep in at Olug's. I jumped and pulled the fire ladder down. The whir of the enforcement vehicles coming on the main street was getting closer. Once up the ladder, I tried to open the first of the three windows. The second refused to budge as well. I pulled on the third one and a light turned on.

A sigh of relief escaped when Nontu's face looked back at me through the glass. She unlatched the window and flipped it open, relief on her face as well. Behind me, lights were rounding the back side of the building. I tumbled to the floor inside the room and ducked below the window frame.

"Turn off the lights, Jamil," Nontu whispered and quietly closed and latched the window.

I carefully drew the curtains as lights began scanning each of the windows.

"What happened? We looked around, and you were gone," Nontu asked in a tone between worry and frustration.

"Friend gone." Olug burst through the door out of breath. "Friend went outside. Enforcers there. Bad for Faduwatan friends."

"I'm here, Olug. I followed the man who got Wyrden and got it back for you. I got Wyrden," I panted.

I pulled it out of the sleeve. The fragments of moonlight and searchlights that came in caught the handle and shimmered against the cool metal. Olug fell to his knees, shaking the floor. His eyes were moist when I handed him Wyrden.

"Thank you, friend. Wyrden back. Hug?"

"Ya'i."

Olug reached over and engulfed me in a hug as we sat on the floor, waiting for the enforcers to pass.

"We can't stay here until day. We need to leave soon," Jamil interrupted.

"There are too many enforcers out now," I argued.

"Safe here tonight. Known for royals," Olug said with some assurance.

"You know?" I asked with surprise.

"Olug knows. Friend safe."

"Good. When the enforcers have stopped searching the area, and things have settled, we'll depart," I smiled.

"We won the map." Nontu flashed her teeth.

"So that means we're ready to go," I added.

"We'd have to go through Narut to get to the Tokahaya. If I were your parents, I'd have guards at the station, looking for you to bring you home." Jamil rubbed his chin as he paced in the dimly lit room.

"He's right. We can't go to Narut." I anxiously reached for Nontu's arm.

"The shortest route is through Narut. Narut, the outposts, and up the mountain," she sighed.

"Ni. We'll go through Emervy. The smoke can be seen from Emervy and Emervy's borders touch the lower mountain. All we have to do is go up. They won't be looking for me there."

"She has a valid point. However, Emervy is not pleasant this time of year. We have not prepared for the cold." Nontu pulled on her shirt to make a point.

"I brought a jacket," I said more smugly than I'd intended. "I mean, I already planned ahead, just in case Zhiri didn't work out."

"Olug prepared for all." Olug patted his bag, which appeared twice the size of everyone else's.

"A jacket may not be enough, Lafia. Unless Olug's packed coats for both of you, Emervy isn't going to work." Jamil's jaw was set and his feet planted. "We can go to Narut and get out before anyone has a chance to see us."

"Lafia right. Guards at Narut." Olug paced in circles tapping his thigh as if that would yield an answer he otherwise wouldn't find.

"Ya'i. There will be. They'll be looking for a syte and a princess," Jamil said. "There's gotta be a solution."

Nontu was in what she would have called her traveling clothes. Lightweight pants and ankle-high boots were usual for a trip to Sparaka that time of year. In another month, it would be too warm for boots.

"Hello. Nontu and I look like that. That's why Emervy is our answer. You two can stop tapping your thighs and struggling so hard to come up with an answer."

"Together, you do look like a syte and a princess," Jamil said slowly as if a thought was forming as the words passed through his lips.

"Then we split up," I said.

"I do not like the idea of leaving you, Lafia."

"Splitting never good. Common knowledge," Olug argued.

"I was thinking of better disguises," Jamil nodded.

"Considering no one is looking for you, Jamil, I think splitting up breaks the connection between us." I sniped. "What do you think, Nontu? Do you know if they are there?"

"Your parents or those looking for you could be. Neither Emervy nor Narut are good options, but if we must, Narut is more direct."

"Going through Narut as we are, will end this before it begins. Perhaps better disguises like you said, Jamil, and splitting up will give us the best chance," I suggested.

"I'm not leaving you in the hands of Jamil or a stranger. No offense, but you do not have a reputation for being responsible."

"Nontu, I went to Zhiri by myself and got back here. I can catch a train. You need to trust me."

Nontu's eyes darted back and forth as she went through what must have been a series of dire scenarios. "Jamil Rityr of Sparaka, I know you. I know where to find you, and I know your syte, and if you do not ensure that Lafia arrives safely to whatever destination we will meet, I'll come looking for you. Do you understand me?"

"I understand." Jamil fidgeted nervously but still met her gaze.

"Then it's settled," I said. "We'll go to Narut. What in that body-size bag of yours might be used as a disguise, Olug?"

"First, we get to Sparaka Station," Jamil cut in. "That alone may be difficult enough. Speaking of difficult, how did you get the sword, Lafia?"

"Ya'i. How?" Olug echoed.

"I guess I'm not completely useless. I paid attention. I followed the winner. I used some of the things I practiced in real life." I directed the last part toward Jamil with a smirk.

Olug nodded as if that made complete sense.

"So you used your charm to disarm him?" Jamil asked with a raised brow.

"I knocked him out if you must know."

Jamil took a step back and quickly schooled his face.

"The only thing we need now is sustenance and a few other supplies for the journey," Jamil said.

"Got it." Olug slipped out of the room. Before the lights had even left the rear alley, he returned, carrying three more packs.

"Don't look surprised. He had two ready to go for us. The other two he keeps for emergencies. You never know when you'll need to get out of town quickly."

Olug nodded and smiled. "Like now."

"I see," I said, although I didn't. "The morn will be upon us soon, and we don't need to be around here when it is. No more delays. We must go."

"There's a way out. We've used it before. We just have to be careful," Jamil said. "Grab a bag and follow us. You lead, Olug."

Olug opened the door and went down the second half of the stairs to where we'd come in. He turned toward the study and then continued past it. He pulled out a light wand and lit the inside of the corridor.

"Come." Olug ducked to enter before resuming his regular height. We moved from finished and painted walls to unfinished walls. The dank air held the smell of decaying vermin, causing Nontu and me to gag several times. Olug pushed on another door which screeched against the stones beneath as it struggled to open.

"We're entering some of the original tunnels that held the first transit system that used the grid. Now the trains run about eight feet over. They go all through Faduwata," Jamil boasted.

"That means we could walk all the way to Narut from here," I said hopefully.

"If you want to arrive in the replenishing season," Jamil teased. "Besides, there are things in these tunnels. We don't want to spend more time than necessary down here."

"Things?" It was the first time Nontu had spoken in a long time.

"Ya'i. Generally, the type that slithers, creeps, or crawls," Jamil stated. "And other things."

I closed the gap between myself and Jamil as Nontu gripped my arm.

"How much longer down here?" Her voice trembled as her grip tightened.

"Soon." Olug's voice carried differently now.

"We're close. When we get out of this tunnel, we'll need to blend in and follow Olug straight through," Jamil instructed.

"Where are we going?" The moment I asked the question, music carried to us through the tunnel.

"Another party? Seriously?" I asked incredulously.

"Listen. The music isn't party music." Jamil slowed his pace and I pressed against his back, listening with him and Nontu.

He was right. It wasn't any party music I'd ever heard.

"You may want to grab the coat from your bags."

"We're in Sparaka. Why do we need a coat?" I asked.

"It's one of the cooling grounds. They were built once the transport system moved up."

I pulled the coat out and gagged. "This smells horrid. Worse than the tunnels. I'm not putting it on."

"It is quite wretched." Nontu held her nose away from the foul outerwear while keeping it at arm's length.

"Perfect. Put them on before we enter. When we get in, don't speak. Don't do anything to draw attention."

"Can we breathe?" I asked sarcastically.

"Good question. Only through your nose."

"Was that in jest?" Nontu queried.

"Ni. Nose breathing gives cooler air than through the mouth. Put on those horrid wretched coats so we can get in and out as soon as possible." Jamil slipped his on and buttoned it all the way to the collar.

I practiced taking shallow breaths as I pulled the long coat over each arm.

"How am I supposed to breathe through my nose without the risk of vomiting?"

"If you think that's going to happen, hold it down."

Jamil stopped in front of us and looked more serious than I'd ever seen him. He pulled the hood over his head and held the haskeal deanimation dust in his hand.

"What's that for?" I asked.

"In case we need it."

"For what?" I grabbed his arm and closed the small gap between us. The smell made me nauseous.

"It can be dangerous in these undergrounds. One other thing. Don't get bitten." Jamil twisted away and lined up behind Olug again.

Olug pulled the door open and let out a blast of frigid air. The stench flew up my nose, forcing me to stifle a sneeze while gagging. I wanted to say something but one look inside and I changed my mind. I felt for a hood and put it up too. The coat's rancid scent was preferable to the odors coming from the room.

18

UNDERGROUND

Jamil was on Olug's heels, and I stayed close to Jamil with Nontu close to me. Between us, we'd left no space.

Grayish brown people with large empty eye sockets, some with one and most having two, sat around tables talking and drinking. They were dressed for the warm southern climate we'd just been in, not northern Narut, as the temperature would have warranted.

I'd never seen anything like them in real life. Slim limbs and round bellies. Their hands and feet too large for their small frames. One of them threw a mug to the ground in boisterous laughter, shattering it around them. No one was bothered by the act. Their conversation was in words I couldn't understand.

They were fascinating and nothing like the pictures in the books that had tried to make them look…better or at least more like Faduwatans. If they had hair, it was scraggly and hardly distinguishable from their skin. Where eyes should have been were either one large useless eye hole in the middle of their foreheads or two placed as ours were. Their noses were the size of their overly large thumbs. With flaring nostrils like that, I wondered how long they'd been down in the tunnels to be immune to the odor.

We walked gingerly one after another until we stopped abruptly. I plowed into Jamil and Nontu into me, causing a different sound than had been in the room. We stopped where we stood, nearly on top of each other, Olug's hand held high in the multiversal symbol to wait.

"Echrugen au?" Someone turned in our direction. "Echrugen au?" they repeated, standing up and coming toward us. We'd drawn their attention, and now all heads had turned, their noses high in the air.

Olug checked back. We weren't even halfway through.

I mouthed, "What do we do?"

Before he could answer, someone banged a mug on the table, then another, and another until they were all banging and clanging.

"I said, who goes there?" the same voice growled.

No one spoke. Jamil shook his head and nodded to the left. Some of them had knives out and their pointy teeth bared. I gulped hard and a head turned my way.

"What strangers are in our midst?" the angry voice asked.

Olug turned to Jamil and shrugged his shoulders. Jamil twisted his lips in frustration but answered anyway.

"Apologies for me and my comrades seeking safe passage. We mistakenly found ourselves here."

The little vial of haskeal dust was now open.

"Do I look like a fool? You've worn clothes to hide your upper-ground smell. We have intruders!"

"Ni! We're not. We're just passing through."

"We don't let upper grounders just pass through, do we?"

"Ne weide oull! Ne weide oull!" they chanted.

"See, they don't like you upper grounders."

"Please let us pass and we'll be without trouble."

"Hehe! They want to pass without trouble. So do we? You know what you weide oulls do when one of us comes up?" he asked angrily. "Do you?"

"Ya'i," Jamil answered meekly.

"Why shouldn't we do the same to you?"

My body trembled uncontrollably. Olug was mouthing something as his head slowly turned round the room. He was counting. *Why?* Then it dawned on me. He was thinking about starting a brawl in this cold pit. No one would ever find us, and we were woefully outnumbered.

Olug rolled up his sleeves, revealing Wyrden strapped to his forearm, and Jamil situated his pack so it wouldn't get in the way. Nontu caught my eye, clearly skeptical, and we both shook our heads. Olug was about to pick up the under grounder speaking and do something that wouldn't end well.

"Wait," I stammered.

"A girl? There's a girl in here?" their leader raged.

"Please," I started. Suddenly the mugs were clanging on the tables and the room filled with shouting. I tried to continue, "Perhaps we can make a trade," I yelled.

"We don't trade with girls!" Spittle hit my hand from the creature ranting nearby. The clamoring continued.

"What if it's something you want?"

"We don't trade with girls!" It now became a chant, almost rhythmic, as the mugs thumped, and feet hit the floor. Their voices rang in a chorus against me.

"Would you consider it if it were me?" Jamil asked loudly. He shrugged in resigned embarrassment.

"Perhaps if it is of value." The chorus quieted and only a few thuds of mugs against the scrap metal and wood tables could be heard.

"A trade and you can return unharmed."

"But we mean to receive passage through. We must get to the other side," Jamil said with as much humility as he could muster.

"Ha!" The leader's laugh was condescending. "Ne for you weide oulls. And definitely not for a su'heim. You bring her here! This is our territory. We don't walk free up there, and you don't down here."

"What will it take to pass through?"

"What do you have?"

Jamil scanned each of us. "These coats, some old clothes, and—"

"Silence!" The leader sniffed the air above him. "Are you traveling with a Zhirian?"

Nontu shook her head furiously.

"Why?" Jamil asked, stalling. "I'm sorry. We must've gotten lost. We just left a party in Sparaka and must've gotten turned around."

"Liar!" he pointed in the direction of Jamil's voice before inhaling deeply with his large nose bobbing towards Nontu. "I know that smell." He stood on one of the tables and walked toward us, sniffing as he came. "You bring one of them in here? To us, the oulls?!" he growled furiously and leapt from the table onto Olug, his teeth chomping in the air.

They were everywhere.

Olug whipped his sword out from his forearm strap and exposed the blade. "Stay back. No harm!" He didn't want to hurt them. "Pass through only."

"Too late, weide oulls!" the leader yelled.

I fumbled inside my bag for Clarod. I'd never used it, but any weapon was better than nothing. I kicked one off my boot and grabbed another, climbing up my back.

"Sorry." I flung him against an under grounder, ready to jump on Nontu who hung back.

"Get close and hurry," Jamil yelled. He had the dust between his fingers.

I turned to Nontu. "Come closer! Quick"

Nontu was spinning some magic behind me but there were too many. She walked quicker while her hands continued to move furiously along with her mouth. The ones who were behind us were moving but in slow motion. The ones beside and in front were jumping, clawing, and trying to bite. Thankfully, the tallest of them barely reached my chest and they were light. Easy enough to toss out of the way.

Nontu worked on the ones on the side as I fought them off with Jamil and Olug. We moved forward at the same time that Olug kept pressing through.

"Come on!" I yelled back to Nontu.

Despite our progress, they were still coming, even if they were slow. Jamil held up his pinched fingers to the under grounders at our side and blew, *"Mai rai ni jiki—"*

Jamil shrieked and cursed one of them who'd latched onto his arm. The sharp teeth had broken through, even with the thick coat. The small box fell to the ground, scattering dust all over.

"Mai rai ni jiki gareni!"

They went from slow to still. I paused in disbelief before grabbing the head of the under grounder that had locked onto Jamil. Its grip was like a vice. Pulling was useless, and we had only a few seconds left from the magic dust before they'd be back in motion.

"Get it off!" Jamil screamed.

They started moving again, slowly as before. Nontu continued slowing them, but the under grounder wouldn't loosen its hold on Jamil's forearm, and more were coming. They were crawling up Jamil's legs, my legs, and Nontu's.

That didn't matter. It had already bitten Jamil.

I tapped the blade in my hand and pointed it at the under grounder's head. "Get off or die!"

He didn't budge and Jamil yelped. "It just went deeper. Get this piece of vermin off me!" He was trying to fling others off with his good hand while shaking the creature who'd taken residence on his opposite arm.

I slid Clarod between his mouth and tried to pry him off. It clamped down. *Fine. Have it your way.*

Back and forth, I moved Clarod until it squealed and finally let go, holding its mouth and falling to the ground. I kicked him out of the way, trying to take down more than one at a time. Nontu had managed to get them all in slow motion, but we were still too outnumbered, and I had no idea how much farther we had to go. Clarod was now ready for action as we moved faster through the gray sea of angry under grounders.

I swung at them as they launched from the tables or tried to climb up our legs. Slicing into some, dodging others, and sending some flying into the tables. We stepped over the fallen under grounders as we advanced through their lair.

There was something ahead.

"Close!" Olug bellowed, still barreling through and clearing a path. His large fists flung them left and right out of the way.

The only time they didn't move at the reduced speed resulting from Nontu, was when we were throwing or kicking them.

"You'll be sorry, weide oulls, just you—" the voice soared as the under grounder hit the wall and Olug pushed open a door.

It was dark on the other side too, but at least it wasn't in the cold room.

"What in the haya was that?!" I huffed once safely on the other side of the heavy door.

"Usually, no one is in there. Or at the most, just a handful."

"So this is a regular thing for you, but this one time, they were having a club gathering?"

"You put us in danger," Nontu's solemn yet shaky voice cut through the darkness.

"That wasn't my intention. We were only trying to help, to get us on our way faster," Jamil winced.

"And you got yourself hurt! How are you supposed to go to the Tokahaya now?" Nontu demanded.

"I'll be fine. We'll get out of these tunnels, and I'll get it cleaned up and bandaged. Olug certainly has that in those bags."

"Good plan." Olug moved forward at a faster clip.

"What happens if you get bitten by one of those things?" I asked.

"It depends on how bad the bite is and how long it takes to treat. Infection. Maybe worse," Nontu answered firmly.

"What do you mean by worse?" I asked.

"Worse," Nontu said as if it was an answer in itself.

"You've come across those things before?" Jamil held his arm and tried not to wince with each step.

"Ya'i. That is why they are no longer permitted in Zhiri," Nontu said. "They are dangerous and therefore dangerous to our desired way of life."

"They were in Zhiri?" I couldn't hide my surprise.

"They were. They are called epers. They burrowed there too, which is why they look as they do, brownish gray."

"So what's the worst that can happen from getting bitten by one of them?" I asked again.

"The worst thing," Nontu paused as if remembering something, "is that you are transformed into one of them."

"What!" Jamil yelled.

"Why haven't we heard of that? Have you seen this before, Nontu?" I panicked.

"Ya'i."

"When we came across them, they were small and annoying, but we always got past them. I didn't know they were like that. I promise. I'm sorry," Jamil sighed, holding his arm.

"There were stories about things like this, not like that, exactly, but I thought they were made up." I looked at the tear in Jamil's coat. The evil thing had ripped all the way through."

"Hidden. Hide danger," Olug grunted. His shoulders sagged as he studied Jamil's face and arm.

"There's an antidote or a healer that can help, right?" I asked.

"There may be. In Sparaka Station. There's a magic shop there," Jamil said.

"Nontu, you've been around almost as long as Faduwata. Have you seen someone get better?"

"I have."

"There's hope. We have to get to that shop immediately, Olug," I yelled from behind Jamil.

Olug said nothing as he shined his light ahead. In my worry, I could almost ignore the damp air, odors, and the sensation that critters were lurking above and beside us, watching. I wondered what other slithery and crawling things waited in those tunnels.

Olug pushed through another door that led us into an unfinished corridor. The air was different. We'd slowly been walking at an incline, and I felt the shift. Soon the unfinished corridor led to another door and a basement. We walked past crates and bins of fruits and glass jars.

"Coats off," Olug ordered, finally taking a moment to stop.

In the dimly lit basement, I took off the coat and helped Jamil out of his. The bite had broken his skin, and four deep punctures bled down his arm.

"This is bad, isn't it?" Jamil asked Nontu.

"It is, but perhaps if we catch it in time, no real harm will come."

"We have to hurry to Meyrnul's shop." I shoved the coats into the oversized packs.

"As long as she has a salve, I can enchant it to stop the poison from their teeth."

"Is that why they were kicked out of Zhiri?"

"It is part of the reason. They are not good. They are not born."

"How can they not be born?" I asked.

"They were made and deposited in Zhiri when Zhiri was new. They do not procreate as we do. If they want to have more of their population, they must make more, and you cannot return from it. You can understand how that would be a threat."

"I can't wind up as one of them. Faster." Jamil pushed ahead of Olug, out of the basement and up a flight of stairs that ended in a small produce shop. Olug scurried ahead of him.

"Olug? What are you doing here?" an old man asked.

"Heading to town."

"You do know there are better ways to travel, right?"

Olug nodded but kept walking through and out of the door.

***

Getting to the Sparaka Station had been surprisingly simple compared to what I was certain lay ahead. A few dodges between buildings, lowered eyes, and a consistently quick pace had us at Sparaka Station in no time.

The poison from the eper's teeth was beginning to bother Jamil. Thankfully he was strong in body and will and refused to acquiesce to the pain. He allowed himself an occasional moan but nothing more.

The bandages may have been helping, but only to keep blood from seeping through his clothing.

"You'll be fine. We're almost there." It was all I could say, and I hoped I was right.

"I know." He sounded more confident than I felt.

"This way." Nontu had spotted the familiar area of the street and picked up her pace. "I hope she is open this time of the morning."

"If not, we'll wake her up. Even if it means throwing rocks at her upper window."

No one argued with my solution as we pressed our faces into the window that read Faduwatan House of Magic and Mystery. Inside was dark and there was no movement. Nontu and I knocked on the door together, peering in through the glass. Nothing happened.

I knocked again—harder—while Nontu stepped back to look at the upper window. She shook her head toward us, "No lights."

"Find some small rocks. I don't want to break her window," I instructed Olug and Nontu. I checked Jamil. He was okay so far. "Stay with us, Jamil."

Olug handed me three rocks that might be mistaken for small in his hands but would've certainly broken the window with one hit. I dropped them and searched the street for others as Nontu held her hand out, offering a few. Together we tossed pebbles at Meyrnul's window.

"I hope she's here," I said.

"They can be hard to rouse. The kanamu people work hard and sleep hard." Nontu twisted her lips and pressed two fingers to her temple.

"What do we do? We can't yell up and draw attention to ourselves."

"Speaking of which, we may want to do something about our disguises while inside." Nontu glanced between Jamil and me. "The three of us, together, as we are, will certainly draw attention."

"And not just in Narut," Jamil added.

"You mean if we get inside," I sighed.

"We'll get inside." Jamil forced himself to stand straighter.

"How. The door is locked and Meyrnul is asleep or not here. Either way, she's not opening the door." I tossed another pebble at the upper window.

"Back up," Jamil said shakily.

We stepped back as Jamil took out a tool with a pointed metal tip. His hand trembled as he aimed into the keyhole. He struggled to hold it steady, clenching the tool tighter as he pushed it in and fidgeted with the lock, lifting up and wiggling it from one side to the other. I had no idea if it would work but it was taking too long.

"Someone is going to see us breaking in." I stood to block his view from one side. Nontu and Olug covered the other angles.

"Ni." Jamil pulled the tool out and pushed open the door at the same time. "Hurry."

We rushed inside and quickly shut it behind us, sending the bell chimes off repeatedly. Footsteps approached from the back.

"Who's there? We're closed and I'm about to call enforcement!" The voice was hidden but it was clearly Meyrnul's.

"It is us, Meyrnul. Nontu and some…friends."

"Nontu?" Meyrnul came around a shelf of books. "What in the light of the Dark Moon has brought you here this time of morning?"

"We need your help, Meyrnul. He's been bitten. By an eper."

Meyrnul's eyes opened as wide as small saucers and her mouth dropped in shock. "How long ago? How long ago was he bitten?" she asked quickly.

"Not long but he already shows signs. He is getting weak, and his eyes are coming in and out of focus. Can you help him?" pleaded Nontu.

"Who's this?" Meyrnul pointed suspiciously at Olug. "Why is he here?"

"He is no harm. He is with us," Nontu smiled.

"Take a seat and keep that mouth of yours shut," she ordered rudely.

We all raised our brows in confusion at Olug and then her.

"Hold on." Meyrnul's little legs flew across the store to the apothecary section.

"Do you know her?" I asked Olug who simply shook his head and shrugged. "People assume. Don't know Olug."

I walked closer to where Meyrnul stood by the wall filled with vials. "Can I help you find it?"

She was reading the labels of different glass bottles lined up on the shelves. "Got it!" She grabbed it along with a small wooden stick and rushed back with me right behind her.

"Is that the salve, Nontu told us about? What's in it?"

I reached for the salve from Meyrnul, curious, but Meyrnul held it tightly. Her words came out quickly as she rushed towards Jamil and Nontu.

"We must hurry. It's a concoction of pressed and strained leaves from the pluif trees, ground bark from the bollak trees, oils and, of course, a secret ingredient imported from Zhiri." Meyrnul winked at Nontu knowingly.

"Nontu, do you know how to use this for an eper bite?" Meyrnul asked as she opened the bottle and set it down.

"Ya'i. I have done it before."

They'd already rolled his sleeve up his arm and were unwrapping the bandage. It oozed a greenish-gray puss.

"It is worse than I thought," Nontu said, looking unsure.

"But you can heal him, right?" My words were both a plea and a command.

"Put the salve on his wound, cover the entire thing. It needs to be thick enough that neither the puss nor any blood can get through."

I took the open bottle and stick from Meyrnul and slathered it on, trying to ignore my impulse to gag and forcing my failure back down while silently asking the light of the Dark Moon to help. Once it was covered, Nontu put a clean bandage on top of it and then her hands on top of that. She closed her eyes and told Meyrnul and me to stretch out our hands and touch his arm or hand somewhere. I placed my hand on his bicep and his muscles tensed in discomfort.

"You can defeat this, Jamil," I whispered.

Nontu murmured something I couldn't understand and occasionally whispered directly into Jamil's ear. She went back and forth for several minutes, speaking the words of healing and speaking to the light inside him. First, his bicep muscles relaxed, and then the tension in his back released.

"He will need some time to rest before he can begin moving again. It is best for him to return to the palace," Nontu said.

Meyrnul took the bottle and walked back to her apothecary section.

"We don't have time and I will not return home," Jamil argued despite his eyes still going in and out of focus.

"If you move now, before the salve and magic have time to work, you may set yourself back. You risk yourself if you do not go home," Nontu warned gravely.

"If we don't keep going, we will all be set back," he argued stubbornly.

"How about this? We do what we discussed and figure out better disguises. That'll give you more time for the salve and magic to settle in," I suggested.

No one argued, to my relief.

19

THE PRICE OF LIFE

The moons had long since faded into a deep rose-colored sky. Only the silver, nearly round, outline of the Dark Moon remained. I nodded thoughtfully. Disguises were what we needed but my mind was elsewhere. I studied his eyes, felt the moist warmth of his forehead, and wiped the sweat from his brow. What good were disguises if he was gone and replaced by an eper?

Nontu pulled me a few steps away and we stood shoulder to shoulder.

"What is on your mind, Lafia?"

"Everything. What if he doesn't get better? What if this whole thing is a mistake? I could fail again and forever be the disgraced daughter of Ajur Rufan and Clarhugaba Selifaya. Then no one will ever want me as Clarhugaba."

"That is a lot, Lafia. Do you believe in your heart that this is a mistake?"

Did I believe it was a mistake?

"If I don't have my magic, I won't be able to help with anything else."

I glanced at Olug, who seemed unbothered as he swallowed his second sandwich while Jamil napped.

"You are correct, dear child. You could fail at getting your magic. This entire trip could be for naught. But that does not mean you have failed or that it is a mistake."

"Maybe this is a sign. That we aren't supposed to go to the Tokahaya. Look what just happened with those under grounders. Jamil's life is now in danger because of what? Some rumors he heard? This stupid idea I have about my magic being stolen? What if I'm wrong and I put all of us in danger by going to the Tokahaya?"

"You have many questions. Doubts. Do not forget that he was going anyway. This is not because of your plans."

"Still, maybe it's a sign."

Even with the book we'd copied, there would be a great deal to figure out. Given we didn't know when it had been written, it could be completely useless, or it might save our lives and help. The scariest part was that we didn't know how thorough it was and what might be missing. Before that day, I thought I knew about under grounders, only to find out I didn't have the right information or even the most important information.

"What else might be different than we think we know?"

"What do you mean?"

"I didn't know about the undergrounders. I thought they were just fantasy. It makes me wonder."

"There is a great deal unknown and there are risks. Do you wish to stop and return home? It is not too late."

Here I was surrounded by magical things, as I had been in Zhiri. I wanted it for myself. I hesitated with my answer. Truthfully, what we had was how *one* person had managed to escape. Maybe she'd done it seventy years ago. Maybe it was only five years ago. They'd taken nothing with them when they left, but they saw the leader of the Tokahaya. The one who'd written the book left no indication of who they'd been, why they'd been there, or what they'd done after, but it was what we had to go on. That and the map Jamil and Nontu secured.

"Jamil is injured. We don't know what his fate will be," I finally said, shifting focus.

"We do not know what any of our fates will be. Do we? Not until we make it."

"What if we fail to get my magic? What if I fail? What if you get hurt? This part was my idea and it's on me if something happens to you."

"I have been many places and seen many things in my years, Lafia. I do believe I can take care of myself." Nontu nodded quaintly, understating the importance of her words.

"At the same time, it's not only my magic anymore, Nontu. What if I don't go with them? What if they can't get there?" I nodded to Jamil and Olug. Jamil had fallen asleep in the chair Meyrnul had used the night before for a nap. "What if Kyari's life is at risk? They had their own reason for coming, true, but that reason also affects my family and me."

"What are you saying, Lafia?"

I took a deep breath and stomped my foot hard against the wooden floor, jogging Jamil awake. But a moment later, his breathing had returned to a slow and deep rhythm.

"If we stop now, Jamil can go home and get better, right? We can try again when I'm more prepared. I don't know what I was thinking. Me? Go up there? I couldn't even get my magic right at a ball filled with regular people and Clarhugabas. What am I going to do against the Tokahaya?"

Nontu gulped.

"Even now, you know what I'm saying is right."

"It is not certain about Jamil, whether now or later. We need to see how the wound is healing when he wakes."

"I'm going no matter what." Jamil's raspy voice came from across the room, surprising everyone.

"Going too, with reasons." A look crossed Olug's face that I hadn't seen the night before.

"Jamil? How do you feel?" I rushed to his side.

"Only if you are well enough, Jamil," Nontu corrected him.

"I will be. I can walk. My arm is still killing me, but a sling may help."

"Let me take a look at that." Meyrnul brought over more wrapping. She pulled back the damp wrap that had been over it and twisted her lips. "Hmmm."

"What does that mean?" I asked.

Nontu studied the wounds and sighed. Meyrnul surveyed Nontu's face for a long while.

"Why are you looking at her like that?" I finally asked.

"There is a stronger magic, but...." Nontu's tone yielded little hope.

"But what?" I asked, standing eye level with her.

"There is a high cost for it."

"How much? We have plenty to pay," I said, feeling better.

"The magic that can heal him cannot be paid for with money or jewels."

"Then what?"

"Can we please have a moment, Meyrnul?" Nontu asked somberly.

"It's my shop, but sure. There's always something to neaten up or put away. The work never ends. I'll be here if you need me." Meyrnul's hair bounced until it disappeared behind some shelves.

"I think it may be better to see what happens. He may heal on his own." Nontu's answer was, in fact, no answer.

"I'm going to the Tokahaya, whether you all are with me or not," Jamil said weakly.

"Please, Nontu. What is the cost? I'm sure whatever it is, we can get it, between all of us."

Nontu collapsed into an uncomfortable chair near the cozy seat Jamil rested in. She shook her head back and forth, opening her mouth and then closing it again repeatedly.

"Tell me what it is, Nontu. That is a direct command."

Nontu stared at her hands and then at Jamil and the wound on his arm.

"You do not have authority to command me, Lafia. Do not be mistaken."

I continued to glare before averting my eyes. She was right. It was a favor of her service through Zhiri that she was with me.

"Please, Nontu. Tell me."

Nontu shook her head before softening her eyes. "I am sorry that my magic is not strong enough. If we had been a few minutes sooner, maybe, but it has been too long."

"Nontu! The cost!" I yelled, catching myself before adding, "please."

They all stared in shock and then Jamil turned to Nontu, the question in his eyes as well.

"If you want to keep him as is and not have him turn into an eper," she paused to swallow, "it will cost a light of life. One light of life."

"A light of life? What's the good of restoring him if he loses his light?" I asked angrily.

"And," she continued slowly, "the fee is payable only within the Tokahaya, where he can be restored."

Jamil sat up, concerned but still confused.

"He will not lose his life or his light, but another light of life must be exchanged so that he may keep his."

"That can't be right. There has to be another way." I paced the way my mother did when she was nervous and in thought.

"I told you, they are not good. They were not created with good and those who created them are not good either."

"What's that have to do with the cure?"

"Everything? Nothing? I do not make the rules. I only know the price is very high."

"So you've seen this before when you were in Zhiri?"

"I have. Many of us have, which is another reason they were banished and relegated to the underground."

"Look, we do whatever it takes to heal you now and then we'll deal with the exchange issue later." I grabbed Jamil's hand.

I couldn't lose him, not like this. If I were going to the Tokahaya anyway, I would help save him. I shook the next thought out of my head. *He is off-limits.* He'd always been off limits, even if my heart might have wished to consider him as an option.

"We get there and leave, and then we find an answer to the problem of trading a light of life later." I nodded at Jamil before turning sharply to Nontu. "Or does the Tokahaya want one immediately?"

"Later. Usually, later," Nontu answered, her voice flat.

"We can't turn back, Nontu. Jamil might lose the life he has. Getting my magic means I can help." It would also mean I would matter. "But it would be unfair to ask you to do this. You have duties to all of Narut."

"I have already told you, I am with you, Lafia."

"Could this truly be a mistake that the light of the Dark Moon saw fit to bring us all together at this moment?" I asked with the innocence and hopefulness of a child. "Before two nights ago, I'd never been alone outside of the grounds of a palace. Actually alone, with no guards or anyone accompanying me. I admit I don't know much about the world, only what I've read about or heard from Jamil," I whispered. "I've seen some of it, and honestly, it has taken me aback. I knocked a man out cold last night for that!" I pointed at Olug's sword, strapped to his forearm arm.

"Impressive," Olug smiled.

"And I admit that while I don't care very much for you, Jamil, please take no offense."

"Some offense taken." He took the damp cloth from his forehead and held it.

"But I believe you are here with good intentions, and I'm not going to stand by and let one of the handful of royal children turn into an eper. You are useless to Faduwata that way. I'm getting my magic back. If someone is trying to set up some sacrifice of my sister, I will help stop it." I glanced around to ensure Meyrnul was still out of earshot.

Nontu nodded at me, and I wondered if there was something she knew and hadn't told me. She seemed calm, but that was her general demeanor and not a good indicator of whether she was as scared as I was.

Meyrnul wandered back over and stood beside me. "Would you like to get that glimpse of destiny now?"

"We need your help with something else. Is there somewhere the two of us might change?"

Meyrnul put on a pair of glasses and scanned Nontu and me from our hair to our shoes. "You look fine. Do you not like the scarf and hat you purchased?" A shadow crossed Meyrnul's face as if she were insulted.

"They are perfect. We…we want to try something else, and our friends here have a couple things for us."

Meyrnul folded her arms and studied Nontu, Jamil, me, and finally, Olug. She turned her nose up at Olug. "This isn't a changing room, and I don't like any funny business."

My eyes widened at the realization of what Meyrnul must have thought. "Oh! Ni! Ni! Never. I need to not look so much like myself and Nontu as well."

"Why? Did you do something? I mean, besides getting your friend bit by an eper. One would think that was enough excitement."

No one said anything.

"I'm not being serious, of course," she said with a nervous laugh. "Wait. I recognize you," she said, suddenly stepping back and studying the four of us together.

"You've got the royal son of Sparaka with you, Nontu? And then, who is this, really?" she asked, pointing to me. "And again, who is this?" she raised her finger at Olug. "I can't afford to get in trouble."

"You won't. Please let us change quickly and we'll be on our way. You can forget we were ever here."

"That's hardly possible," she scoffed. "You've already put me in the middle of something I had no desire to be in the middle of."

"We won't be but a minute. You can even give me that glimpse of destiny if you want."

At the offer, her eyes lit up. "I'd love to give it to him, a royal son."

With a dramatic roll of my eyes, I said, "Fine, you can give him a glimpse of destiny."

"I don't want a glimpse of destiny. I want to get out of here."

"Well! I won't give you one and most certainly not him," she snorted at Olug. "I'll do yours. There's a room in the back. Come with me." Meyrnul walked off immediately, expecting us to follow.

Olug shook his head, acting as if he hadn't been bothered by the repeated slights. I grabbed his bag, and Nontu and I followed Meyrnul. We ducked through the door and into the back room behind her. "Don't mind the mess. Inventory."

"Thank you, Meyrnul. I promise you that the next time I need salt and sand, I will come to you," Nontu said graciously.

"You better," she said with the smallest hint of a smile. "I'll wait out here so I can finally give you that glimpse of destiny when you're changed."

Meyrnul skirted through the velvet curtain, leaving Nontu and me alone.

"How are you so calm about all this?" I asked Nontu, suddenly feeling it odd and suspicious.

"What do you mean?"

"How are you calm when we're about to do what we're about to do," I asked in hushed aggravation.

"I don't believe it would be helpful to you or anyone else for me to behave excitedly."

"Are you afraid too?"

Nontu's eyes softened at me. "I am not afraid. Do not go into this with fear. I do have concerns."

"Then why do you hardly say anything?"

"Until my concern has a stronger counterpoint, or I have something to offer that can remove that concern, I'd rather not give anyone else those concerns to hold."

"Why is Meyrnul acting like that toward Olug? She doesn't even know him."

"It is not my place to answer that or make assumptions. For as good a person as she is, she retains some old beliefs. Most of us have some of one kind or another. She will get through them, and in fact, she has gotten better."

"This is better?"

"Yes, believe it or not. You have got your own too."

I tilted my head at Nontu. I'd hardly seen enough to have beliefs like the ones Meyrnul must've had. "What do you mean?"

"Based on your life as a royal, you see the world in a way most common people never would. You have not seen things most common people have. That can limit you."

"I know my life has been insular but that is changing as we speak."

"It is. And next time you cross these streets, you will see it with different eyes."

"Point made."

Nontu smiled as she held up different items from the bag, avoiding the tightly wrapped bag holding the undergrounder coats. Despite the wrapping, some of the odor slipped through. "We are going to need to ask Meyrnul for something to cover the smell."

"I don't know if this is going to work, Basi Nontu. I don't. I think what I'm most afraid of is, well, I'm afraid of failing again, but I'm afraid that something may happen to you."

"I understand. I appreciate the concern. I love you too, Lafia. Danger and even the Tokahaya will not keep me from doing what I can to help you get there. And as I told you, you cannot enter any of this with fear. The Tokahaya feeds on fear."

"Why? Why do you care so much? More than...." I pulled another item from Olug's bag.

"We all have our reasons. It is hard to explain but you are important in this world, and you are important to me."

"You're the only one I'm important to," I muttered under my breath. "Thanks, Nontu," I said loud enough to be heard. "This might work for you."

"What is it?" Nontu turned the cloth around in her hands.

"I believe it's a shirt?" I shrugged.

"That I do not see," she smiled and put it over her shirt. It was loose and baggy. Definitely not the fashion of a syte, even in her traveling clothes. "This must be Olug's."

"Ahhh. Here. I'll put this jacket on. It's lightweight enough, but it's long. Actually," I smiled approvingly, "I like it, even if you and I both could fit in it."

"You will need a belt or something else or it may draw even more attention. Hand me those pants. If I am going to undo myself, I might as well do it."

Nontu slipped on Olug's pants. Even with the drawstring completely pulled, they were large and ballooned around the legs. I laughed at the sight.

"Ya'i. This is not a good look. What else is in there?"

I felt around inside the bag, looking confused for a moment.

"This?" I held up what might have been a skirt, but it had pants underneath and a belt with a built-in sheath.

"That was in there?" It was Nontu's turn to be confused. She appeared to search her mind for an explanation.

"Why? I know it's unusual, but it looks like something you could wear. And with pants, it's functional."

"It is functional." Nontu held the item up with her fingertips. "But I cannot wear it. Neither can you. It has a hole where your bottom would be. Put it back where you found it. I'll have to find something else for the bottoms. These pants are a giveaway. Everyone in Narut knows I wear these kinds of pants anytime I'm off the palace grounds."

"There's—"

"You two alright or did the guards come get you through a back door?" Jamil called.

"We need pants for Nontu."

Nontu and I came through the curtain and Jamil let out a whoop of laughter that almost woke Olug from his nap in Meyrnul's chair.

"I see you're on your feet now. That's a great sign." I nodded and smirked.

"I'm sorry. It's just—"

"Just what? It's a disguise. Don't be fatuous." I tossed him the oversized bag before immediately regretting it as he stumbled under the unexpected weight. "Sorry." I stopped, studying Jamil, looking between him and Nontu. He was tall and slender. "This might work."

"What?" Nontu asked curiously.

"Switch pants. No one is going to look twice at his pants on you and vice versa. It'll be enough to draw away attention."

"In Narut? It may not be enough." Nontu said, "But if I am not traveling with Jamil, it brings separation to us as a Narutian royal Ajursun and syte and breaks that visual connection."

"Whoa. You want *me* to travel with him? I thought you were against that?" I asked, not hiding my repulsion.

"What do you have against me, Lafia?"

"If you want to go through Narut, this is the only way I see possible," Nontu said with certainty.

I rolled my eyes, ignoring Jamil's question. "Then I suppose you two should swap pants and we can go."

"Not so fast," Meyrnul stood between where the velvet curtains separated, having appeared out of nowhere with a look of anticipation. "I still owe you a quick glimpse of destiny. Are you ready?"

"We really don't have time."

"Sure you do. It won't take long."

My eyes pleaded to Nontu for help. I didn't want to be rude to Nontu's associate but more importantly, I didn't want her to see who I truly was and or worse, the fact that I was a failure. Instead, Nontu smiled and said, "She has the time while we finish up. Besides, it will give Jamil a few more minutes to steady himself for what lies ahead. He needs to be careful if a bag can almost knock him over." Then she turned to me. "Know that it is a quick glimpse. It is not going to answer everything."

"I don't want it to answer anything," I grumbled as Meyrnul beckoned.

"Come this way, young lady." Meyrnul bounced ahead toward a table set near the back of the shop. "I believe this glimpse may give you enlightenment for whatever you seek."

20

GLIMPSE OF DESTINY

The small table was decorated with a cloth bearing the shop's logo and name. She moved the assorted stones to one side and lit the candle before closing her eyes. "Close yours too, young lady," she ordered. Meyrnul muttered something and said, "Thank you to the light of the Dark Moon."

I opened my eyes and Meyrnul picked up my hands and gently touched them from the wrist to my fingertips. She peered into my eyes curiously before putting one hand down. "Is this your dominant hand?"

"Ya'i. Why?"

"This hand shows what you are doing with the potential you came into this world with."

I pulled my hand away.

"It's okay, young lady. You're young. What nineteen or twenty?"

"Twenty."

"You have much time to bring out the potential." Meyrnul smiled and gently picked both hands up.

I sighed and tried to relax my palms.

"You come from a line of power, but you feel disconnected," she said, touching both hands and looking back and forth. "You are more than you think you are, and when you understand who you are, you will connect to your power and be able to do great things."

"Oh. That's pretty good," I smiled.

"Do you want to hear the rest? Even if it may be difficult?"

"I don't know. I hadn't even really wanted to hear the first part."

"Then, that is all. A glimpse of destiny."

"Wait. What's the other part about?" I asked curiously.

"It may be difficult. From what I see in your hands, you may not wish to know."

"What do you mean I won't want to know what you see?"

"What if I said you'll be faced with a darkness?"

"At some point, everyone is faced with some darkness in their lives," I brushed off her question.

"True. You want to know, then?"

Meyrnul's hands were warm on mine. I had a vision filled with dark smoke and silver eyes before screaming cut through. It felt too familiar. I yanked my hand back.

"What was that? What did you do?"

"I didn't do anything."

"What was that?" I demanded.

"What was what?"

"The smoke. The screams?" I asked again. "How'd you do that?"

"I didn't see smoke or screams. I only know there will be a choice you must make, and it will be difficult."

"You didn't see that?"

"Ni. I read hands. I don't have the clar gifts to share what I see in my mind with you accept through speaking to you like I am right now. I only saw a darkness around you."

I pushed my seat back and stood on unsteady legs.

"It's a glimpse, young lady. Better to know, ya'i?"

"Perhaps ignorance would be bliss."

"Are you alright, Lafia?" Nontu had come up from behind, wearing Jamil's dark gray pants. He was farther back in Nontu's loose burgundy pants. It somehow worked for both of them.

"This was a bad idea." I pointed at the table and everything on it.

"What she's upset about isn't something I told her. It's something she saw on her own," Meyrnul chimed in. "I think her glimpse was pretty good overall."

"Pretty good?" I scoffed.

"Your words, young lady."

"That was before you ruined it with your darkness."

"Oh, that isn't my darkness." Meyrnul shook her head emphatically and looked at Nontu with concern.

"What did she tell you?" Nontu asked. "If you don't mind me asking."

I remembered it exactly, at least the first part. What she'd say had been pretty good. Promising. But I wasn't sharing any of it.

"I'll tell you later. It's time to go if you two are set."

"We are. Why don't you meet them at the front?" Nontu paused and lingered at the table with Meyrnul.

I glanced back a few times to see them talking in a whisper and Meyrnul touching her hand and pointing at her fingers. I studied my hands, palm side. *She could be wrong about a darkness around me. I could even be wrong about the smoke and screams. Every seer gets it wrong now and again. No one is perfect, and this was just one of her off days. Afterall, I'd had several off moon cycles,* I reasoned.

"You look scattered," Jamil said.

"Nice pants."

"Alright. Seriously, Lafia. What have I done to make you dislike me so much?"

"What makes you think I dislike you?"

"Everything. We're about to go to the only forbidden area spoken of in all of the Maradobu realm, and then beyond the realm, and I need to know we're doing this together and you aren't going to sacrifice me to the Tokahaya."

I smiled at him teasingly, as if I hadn't considered that an option before, but now the idea was possible.

"I wouldn't do that, considering you are one of the reasons we're going there. We could've gone home, tried this again later, but you know, you might turn into an eper and then it would be too late. But there is also the fact that you don't wish to marry or continue your line anyways, so if anyone were the ideal sacrifice, you would be. If the Tokahaya takes men. Maybe it does."

He glared at me.

"My apologies. That was terrible of me to say. You . . . just . . . never mind. I'm sorry."

"Yeah. And we're supposed to travel to Narut together," Jamil sneered.

"Everyone ready to go?" Nontu asked before noticing Olug. "Everyone ready to go?" she asked loud enough to rouse him.

"Ready." He tried to lift himself out of the chair, clearly made for someone half his size. It stuck to his hips, and he shimmied out of it, yawning and stretching.

Meyrnul glared at him and immediately checked the condition, making sure it had held under his weight.

"Did I miss something?" Nontu asked Jamil and me.

"Not at all. We're ready," I answered before Jamil could.

"Can you manage that pack, Jamil?" Nontu asked.

He'd taken offense even though he'd barely been able to stand not long before. "Of course, I can. I have two arms and a strong back."

"Good. Olug and I will go ahead of you, and if we are caught, we will create a delay so you can get through and back out."

Jamil stood awkwardly beside me, avoiding looking at me and me at him.

"Is there something I should know before we leave?" Nontu's eyes searched out mine while I found a colorful set of scarves to finger.

"Ni. We'll wait a few minutes before we leave. Make sure there are a few groups between us. We'll be fine, Nontu." I still didn't look up.

Olug grabbed the large bag and slung it over his back. He pushed the door open for Nontu and nodded toward Jamil and me, "To Narut, friends. Go easy."

Jamil nodded. "We'll be fine. We'll see you in Narut or Kanir."

"Do you think they're actively looking for us?" I asked Nontu and Jamil.

"Your parents are likely panicking and preparing to send out a search and rescue unit operated by Sarkin Yandoka Felli himself," Jamil answered.

The sound of his name alone scared me, even if he would be coming to help.

"I sent a message back, but by this time, they expect our return." Nontu had done her duty, but unfortunately, it only assured that my family would have people looking for me.

"Then we better hurry and get out of Sparaka." I put the bag over my shoulders.

"We'll want to be through Faduwata Central before commerce begins for the day as well. Once they haven't found you here, they'll move to the other regions, starting with Faduwata Central Station."

"Why is it just me? You're missing too, Jamil."

"I'm always missing. They expect it."

"Put your scarf back on and take off those rings," Jamil said.

"My rings? I told you before I never go anywhere without them," I protested. "I'll do what I did last night."

"It is for the best, Lafia," Nontu said. "If you do not wish to stand out, you must remove all clear signs of who you are."

"Use these." Olug came back in, letting the door close and chimes ring. He handed Nontu a Sparakan pin and then pressed one into my hand.

"How'd you get extra pins?" I asked surprised.

"Of all the things you wonder about how he's gotten, these should be the least of concern. Did you not experience the party last night?" Jamil asked mockingly.

"You are starting to feel better, aren't you?" I turned my rings around like I'd done the night before, so the jewels were palm side. "I'm not taking them off." I grabbed the pin and stuck it on my scarf, securing the closure. "Let's go."

***

Back on the streets, it was still early, but we'd lost valuable time. There were very few people to notice us, but the ones outside had a clear and disturbing purpose. The signs and their bearers, proclaiming an issue with water distribution and cleanliness, were already forming small groups.

"Why are they out here? No one is paying them any mind."

"I suppose it gets people to ask questions, usually those who come here and haven't seen it before. Mostly it makes them feel better. You noticed them."

"Has anyone filed a petition to query about the water situation?" My curiosity came out sounding more like judgment.

"Of course. Our government has. This union between Sparaka and Narut had better mean we stop getting the dregs of water after it's passed through Emervy with all their mining." This time he had been offended by my comment.

"But Emervy has touted their commitment to the environment and conservation."

"They've touted many things. Come. They are ready for us."

"You make it sound like everyone is against Sparaka. You do know that's not true?"

He shrugged and winced. "We'll see. Everyone comes here for fun and entertainment, leaving without a second thought about the people who live here. As long as they're entertained, the price Sparakans pay doesn't matter."

I stole a glimpse at him and then his arm and thought better than to say the thing on my mind. *What did he know about the price Sparakans paid? He was a royal.*

The conductor was waiting for us, ready with the polished crystals and to enter the coordinates. "Are you okay to leave Sparaka?"

"I'm going." He stepped forward to the conductor. "Besides, Olug and Nontu will be waiting for us."

"Please enter your payment," the conductor requested.

I took a couple of one cullon bills out of Jamil's satchel. They each bore the Sparakan emblem. I slid them into the machine, and we stepped onto the platform.

"Station?"

"Faduwata Central," I said.

"One for each of you," the conductor said, handing each of us a monedutse crystal for transport. He entered the coordinates and I took Jamil's hand out of habit, even if it wasn't necessary.

"Have a safe journey," the conductor said, but his voice faded into the void.

21

NARUT

There was no longer time to spare. From Faduwata Station, we needed to be quick, although Jamil remained steady. Nontu's magic had slowed the poison's effect, as it had slowed the epers earlier.

The salve helped too, but between the medicine and the magic, it still wasn't enough. If his condition worsened before we reached the Tokahaya, we could lose him. I could.

Despite my concern, I was still upset at him for who and what he was. Jamil had put on a cap and dark glasses, but I wondered how much that would lessen the attention he'd draw. He was the kind of man that drew looks. The kind of man I'd never have. Who'd never have me.

None of that mattered anyway, and those thoughts claiming space in my head now weren't going to help anything. I would not allow myself to want a man who didn't want to be Ajur, didn't want to marry, and didn't want to secure the future of Faduwata as I did. Beyond all of that, he'd never want me anyway.

"We'll catch up with them in Narut and immediately get on a train to the outpost of Kanir." My tone was matter-of-fact as I did my best to keep any emotion out.

"Fine."

"Fine."

Arms folded across my chest, I put distance between us, as I'd done back at his palace. We kept our heads down and walked quickly to where the connections for Narut were.

"You may want to pretend we're together, so they don't think you are, say, a royal daughter being held hostage," he whispered.

I huffed irritably.

"The way you're moving is going to draw more attention, especially since the alerts have already gone out."

Silently, I moved closer to him and took his good hand in mine. His fingers were lean and gripped mine back. I wanted to pull away, but the guards were looking at everyone going by.

"Act normal. Not normal for you, but for a normal person," Jamil said.

I wanted to elbow him in the side for his jab, but not only would that possibly make him worse, it would likely make him yelp or do something else to draw more interest. I squeezed his hand and kept walking.

The sign for Narut was mere feet away.

"You two. Stop." A guard's footsteps approached quickly from behind.

We kept walking at the same pace, pretending he wasn't talking to us. My coat bumped against my knees and my fingers squeezed around Jamil's.

"You with the long coat," the guard said.

I stopped. *This was it. It was over.* I turned my head partly toward him.

He walked toward us, holding something in his hand. My body tensed, squeezing Jamil's hand even more.

He stood just behind us, his arm outstretched. "I think you dropped this back there." He handed me a folded paper. It was the map.

"Ya'i. Thank you. Very much," I said.

"Is everything alright?"

"Ya'i. Trying to catch our train is all."

The guard looked at the sign in front of us and nodded. "A safe journey to you."

"Thank you." I turned and we walked under the sign for Narut.

"You almost lost the map, Jamil," I said through clenched teeth that pretended to be a smile.

"I know. I guess I didn't have it deep enough in these pants you all decided I should wear."

"I'll hold onto it then," I continued to smile. "We're almost there." I walked toward the transport entry I always used. No one was in it. Jamil pulled me back.

"Where are you going?"

"Narut." It was as if he'd asked whether haskeals could fly.

"We don't use that entry. Not today" He pulled me to the much longer line for Narut, filled with those beginning the day.

Aghast, I stared in front of us at the winding line. That alone could mean his demise into an eper.

"The more time in this line, the more chance someone will see us and the less time for you," I whispered.

"It'll be alright. It moves fast." Jamil kept his head down, but I saw the discomfort in his stance.

I exited the line and walked up to the attendant at the information desk.

"I'm traveling with someone who's been injured. We need expedited travel to Narut to attend to his wounds before they become too severe. What line is best?"

"What kind of injury?"

"A bite. We believe it may have been venomous. He's been treated with a salve but needs professional attention."

"This way," the attendant said, motioning for us to follow.

I waved to Jamil to come with us. He shook his head, not wanting to follow, but I nodded and waited for him to join me. He ambled over reluctantly as the attendant continued toward another unmarked door, nearly racing ahead on a replacement leg.

"La-rsa, what are you doing?"

"Getting us there faster. You can't wait."

"This is a bad idea. We should've stayed in line."

"Trust me."

"Right this way," the attendant said and waved us through the door.

Jamil kept glancing behind us, and even with the shades on his eyes, I could tell he was checking all around us.

We walked down a well-lit corridor with administrative offices. Ahead was a sign that hung from the upper wall. It read Medic. He glared at me and all I could do was grimace. I'd thought we would cut the line but instead, the attendant had taken us directly for help.

"I think there's some mistake. The assistance we need is in Narut," I said politely.

"We can help you here, as this is urgent," the attendant said in a most professional tone.

"But our family expects us in Narut with medical staff that knows what to do about his particular issue."

"We can give you treatment here and call ahead to inform your family. They can meet you at the next station."

"Ni!" I instantly knew my objection was too aggressive, drawing the eyes of the attendant and others in the hallway. "I mean, we have it taken care of. If we can have expedited transport to Narut, that would be the most helpful thing."

"Not without an assessment by the medic," the attendant said, whose eyes revealed no emotion.

I was hopeful Jamil might hint at what we should do now that my plan hadn't worked.

"The medic can take a look at it," he agreed with resignation.

"Straight inside. Sign in here and complete the waiver." The attendant directed us to a machine on the side. "You'll need proof of identity to be seen. Once you've registered, take a seat, and the medic will see you when she's ready."

The attendant walked out, leaving us alone in the waiting room to stare at each other.

"Look what you've done, Lafia. How are we getting out of this?"

"We walk out, back down the hall, and get on the transport we always get on. Not the one everyone else does. We don't have time to wait."

"We don't have a choice. You don't get it, do you?"

"I get it. If we don't get back soon enough, you won't be you. I think you're the one who doesn't get it," I said with a raised voice.

"We can't, Lafia. You walk into that transport, and this is over. I walk in there. This is over. Understand? They'll have me back at the palace, where I will likely die! And you will be

287

taken straight to Narut and probably not permitted to leave until the next Crossing of the Ties ceremony," he whispered gruffly.

"I'm not stupid, Jamil. I'm trying to save your life. There aren't enough of us as it is, and we can't risk losing you!"

My words momentarily stunned him. "Wait. Who is we?"

"Don't be foolish, Jamil. Faduwata. Sparaka. We need you. Now we have to get there quickly, and that line will take us all morning, and by the time we're in Narut, it'll be fully active, and those guards will be everywhere. Do you have a better plan?"

He walked around the clinic until he stopped in front of the desk.

"Ni! We aren't stealing medic outfits, Jamil!"

"Shhhh. We're borrowing. We'll leave them in Narut, and they can get them back. We can get on the transport, no question in these."

"This is crazy, but you have an idea that might work this time."

"This time?"

"I didn't misspeak. Come on. We have to hurry." The closed door currently read *With Patient,* but it could open at any moment. I tried another door. "Locked," I mouthed to Jamil.

"Try the sliding window."

I pulled against it, and it slid open easily. I set the large bag down and climbed through and behind the counter. Long green jackets and caps hung on the hooks.

"Here." I tossed them to Jamil before spotting a stack of bandages and wound dressings. I grabbed a handful of each and put them on the counter before scurrying back through.

"Just throw it on over your clothes," I said.

My coat couldn't be concealed beneath the medic jacket. I yanked it off and shoved it into the bag. I was buttoning the green medic jacket when I noticed Jamil struggling.

I pulled the green jacket over his wounded arm and then helped him ease it over the other arm. He exchanged the hat he'd worn there for the green medic cap. I unwrapped my hair and pulled the twists into a low bun before putting my cap on as low as possible.

"Lose the shades too," Jamil said.

I slipped them into the pocket of my green medic jacket before buttoning Jamil's jacket.

"It'll have to work. Let's go."

I cracked the door from the waiting room back to the corridor and peeked up and down the long white administrative hall. There was a ding, and the sign changed to *Medic Available*. We slipped through the opening and closed it gently before striding toward the exit. I tried to keep my breathing measured. I couldn't risk panicking, even though the heat was already rushing to my chest and neck, my heart beating faster.

We hustled back through the doors to the transport area, heads down as we made our way toward the sign that said Narut Special Transport.

Please let this work.

Footsteps quickly approached from behind and I glanced at Jamil out of the side of my eye. He heard them too. They were boots. Guard boots.

"We need to run. Get through that door. Can you?" I asked.

Jamil nodded and we sprinted toward the special transport area for Narut. The boots ran too.

"We're in pursuit. We believe we have her."

"Keep running," I called to Jamil as I stopped to close the door. I knocked over a check-in station, thrust it against the entry, and wedged it in. They were running full speed toward us. I backed away from the slit of glass in the door. They could see us too. There had to be six or seven of them, all large and intimidating.

"Narut, please. It's an emergency." I rushed up behind Jamil, my body between the conductor and the glass window, hoping to block the view.

The conductor looked between Jamil and me and shook his head. "I'm sorry, the special transport is out of service at this time. It should be operational momentarily. Or you can take the regular transport." He checked behind me, causing me to crane my neck to see.

"If there was a time to act, it's now," Jamil leaned in to say.

In sync with each other, I grabbed the crystals, and with his good side, Jamil rushed the conductor and pushed the button for Narut as he'd seen many times. The conductor stumbled to get back to the controls as the boots were about to enter the room.

"Stop! You are ordered to stop," they yelled through the closed door.

Jamil held his arm in obvious pain as he backed away from the glass. Before a thought could form, my foot jammed into the conductor's shoulder, taking him to the ground. I leaned over him and pushed the big *Go* button.

"We have to get out of here!" I yelled.

"We will."

I froze for a moment as they got closer. They were almost through. The conductor grabbed our feet. The buzzing of the transporter and the sound of a tranquilizer bullet whirring past made us lean back. There was more firing, but it faded into the distance. I was grateful for the faster transport available directly between the stations, versus what I'd ridden to Zhiri. Still, if they had noticed we were here, all the other stations were likely on alert as well, especially Narut.

"We're going to have to be ready as soon as this arrives in Narut." I clung to the bars, the speed pulling my lips back from my teeth. Had I known we'd be moving that fast I would've sat and strapped in. The thought left as quickly as if came. There hadn't been time for that.

He said nothing, only nodded as he held on. He must've hit the button for the top speed. Despite going straight forward it was still dizzying with the lights that lined the tunnel flashing as we passed, different colors to signal our speed, distance, and eventually our approach.

Trouble would be waiting on the other end of the tunnel. The red blinking light meant we were approaching the station. Shadows moved ahead of us. My heart pounded against the green jacket, and I squeezed Jamil's hand. Any moment and we'd be surrounded. I dropped to the floor, pulling him down with me. I was dizzy from the speed causing the room to spin in a kaleidoscope of colors. As they turned into fixed images I turned to Jamil, who groaned in pain.

I was right. We were surrounded and the guards began shooting their tranquilizers as soon as it showed our arrival. They weren't expecting us to be flat. We slid off the plate, holding our bags in front of us.

"Ajursun Lafia, please stop. For your safety."

My eyes darted about the room. They'd likely hit us if I ran, and it would be over. Only three of them fit inside the special transport room but we were still outmatched. Jamil opened his eyes wide with a little nod, expecting me to do something.

I'd only tried it in real life once, hours ago. My finger-wand wasn't in immediate reach. I only had the crystal I'd transported with, and my magic was always inconsistent. My heart raced, even as he squeezed my hand back.

"Do it," he said through an almost closed mouth.

I swallowed hard, trying to create moisture in the desert that had become my mouth. The words scattered, scrambling in my head and tripping on my tongue. The guards stepped slowly toward us.

Everything was garbled. After several attempts, I got out the words for the deanimation spell, but without deanimation dust, I didn't know what to expect.

"Mai rai ni jiki gareni."

It worked like it had in the cooling room with the epers. They didn't stop, but they slowed. I ran back to the platform as one of the guards slowly pressed the trigger on the tranquilizer gun. The darts moved at regular speed. I pushed Jamil out of the way, and he knocked over one of the guards. It wouldn't last long. I shouldered another guard onto the platform and tripped one, causing him to fall next to the control station.

In slow words, the last standing guard tried to appeal, "Aaaajuuurrrrrsssuuuunnn Laaaaaffffffiiiiaaaaahhhh, stoooooop fooooor yooooouuuuurrrrr saaaaaafetyyyyy."

Jamil swung his good arm and landed his fist across the guard's cheek. The "safety" drawled out even longer as he crashed to the floor.

"Let's go," he said.

We stepped over the guard on the floor. They were reacting faster, which meant we had to as well.

We crashed through the door, searching for something to jam it. The snaps gave way as I ripped off the green jacket and tied it to the handles of that door and of another near it.

"Come on!" I tossed the green hat and helped Jamil out of his jacket. "How do we catch up with Nontu and Olug now?" I gasped.

"There's no station like this In Kanir. We could've gone straight to Kanir's small station, but with them waiting for us, that's out of the question. We get out of here and I know someone who can help."

"Of course you do."

At the main station door, guards were posted everywhere.

"We can't go that way. Look for an unlocked door. There must be emergency exits." Jamil moved back and yanked at a door.

The handle I tried was also locked. We'd pulled all but one, and the guards were now clamoring at the door of the transport room.

"Can you do it again?" Jamil asked.

"Do what?"

"Slow them."

"Maybe. I don't know." What Jamil was suggesting was improbable. Two of us against several trained guards.

"If we can somehow get back in there, we can go take the transport straight to Kanir. We lure them out and go quickly."

"That's not going to work. We're stuck, Jamil."

"Ni. You just did it."

"It was a fluke. We can't rely on my magic. Not now!"

"You did it with those epers."

"Another fluke."

"Do you have a better idea?" His head turned to the side impatiently.

"Give me a second."

"That's all we have," he warned.

"Be ready. I'm going to untie this jacket. They're going to shoot as soon as the door opens. Use our jackets to trip them up and we get inside. We'll only have a few seconds." My voice shook but we couldn't wait any longer.

Jamil unwrapped the jacket from the other door, leaving it tied slightly before loosening it from the door with the guards banging against it. It was already bouncing open.

"Get ready," he yelled.

The door burst open.

"Mai rai ni jiki gareni!"

I directed all my energy to the three guards and the conductor falling through the door.

This time my words hit them like a jolt, their bodies moved as if they'd been hit by a wave of water, and then they were again in slow motion.

Was this another fluke?

Jamil jumped over them and pulled me with him.

He tapped the control panel to find Kanir. "It's off. They turned it off!" He scrambled to find a switch to start the machine again.

"Crap. They're getting up. Slow, but still. Can you turn it on?"

"Get out of here," Jamil said, avoiding their hands as much as I was.

294

We stepped back over the guards and conductor trying to detangle themselves from the pile they were in.

"Try that door on the right," I shouted. "It's the only one left."

He turned the knob and pulled. "Come on, Lafia. There are more coming."

Behind me, they'd already burst through the door to the special transport area. I recognized someone following behind them. My mother.

"Lafia?" Selifaya called out, moving through the guards. "Lafia? Wait."

"Shall we tranquilize her?" the lead guard asked.

I kept moving away, glancing back at them as we made our way toward a door.

"Wait! Lafia," Selifaya called again, concern etched across her face. I'd never seen her like that.

"Shall we tranquilize her, Clarhugaba Selifaya?" the lead guard repeated.

"Ni." My Mada began pushing her way past the guards in front of her. The look on her face told me we didn't have much time. She lifted one hand in front of her, aimed at me and began to say something I couldn't heart, her eyes focused. She knew magic I had yet to learn, and hers would work.

"I'm sorry," I mouthed before pulling the door and locking it from the other side. The darts pinged as they hit the metal.

"How do we get out of here?" I called out to Jamil.

"Underground tunnels run all through Faduwata. We just have to find them."

"Ni. We can't do that again. Those things could outright kill you—kill *us* this time."

"They don't stay under stations. The creatures under stations are harmless. Annoying and disgusting, but harmless."

I glanced at him skeptically, but the other way was my mother and her band of soldiers.

"Try the handles." Jamil was already pulling on the doors. "There should be one that's an emergency exit or takes us to the lower controls, basement, and then the tunnels."

"This one's open." I'd hoped it would open to daylight, but it opened to what I knew would be the basement as the stale air hit.

"That lock isn't going to hold them since they have the keys," Jamil called back. "We need to go fast." He bounded down the stairs despite the agony I knew he was in.

"Wait! Jamil. I'm stuck!"

He ran back up, trying to see how I'd gotten stuck through the dim light.

"The back of my bag is stuck in the door, and I can't get it open. I can't pull myself away."

"Hold on."

I nudged over to the side as he stood chest to chest with me, trying to wiggle the handle. It was wedged. "Come on," I cried.

"It's stuck. Watch out." He stepped back and rammed his shoulder into the door, knocking it open. He pulled the bag through and yanked the door back. The guards had just opened the other door and I was certain the lead guard had seen us. "They're coming." He was winded and his voice raspy.

"Was my mother with them?"

"I didn't see her, but she may have been behind them."

"We can't let her catch up with us. She will stop us. She almost did."

"She did?"

"Ya'i. Before we got through that door. She was about to use her magic, so she'll try again."

"You can block it, right?"

"She's Clarhugaba, Jamil. I can't even pass my test. I can't block her magic. It's strong."

"You'll have to. Put something up around us. Do something."

I'd never considered having to block my own Mada, but he was right. Would a protection spell work if my Mada was trying to protect me from something?

"What are you doing?" Jamil asked irritably.

"Thinking. If this will even work."

"Just try it. We don't have time."

The magic I knew to block the energy of someone else seemed insufficient and I'd never used it successfully, or needed to. Jamil stared at me waiting.

"Fine." I put the finger-wand on and held Jamil's hand. "Here it goes." I drew a circle in the air with my finger-wand.

"Toshe makamashi marasoda haske."

"We're going to have to find a place to stop, Jamil. So you can rest, and I can check your wounds."

"Not now, Lafia. I know a place if I need to stop."

We bounded down the stairs. At the bottom were two doors. Jamil peeked through one and I through the other.

"That's the control room." I pulled the door shut.

"Then it's through here."

I pulled the door behind us, closing it firmly. Exposed rocks, cool beneath my fingertips, surrounded us. Noises came from every direction as we ran. I stepped on something slimy, stumbling into Jamil, and something hanging from the ceiling grazed my hair. The lights on the sides of the tunnel were too dim to allow us to see the details.

"Do you think we'll catch up with Olug and Nontu?" I asked as we paused to decide which of the three underground corridors to go through.

I pulled out the swinging heart pendulum and watched as it began to swing, but not in any helpful direction. It didn't point to any tunnel.

"Which way is it saying to go?" Jamil asked hurriedly.

In my head, I heard *middle*. "Middle."

"You're sure? How do you know?"

"Ya'i. I'm sure." I wasn't sure how I knew as the pendulum hadn't shown me the answer.

He nodded once before taking the middle corridor. We'd been running for a while when he became slower.

"Are you alright?"

"I need to catch my breath. I think we're far enough we can walk for a bit." He'd overtaxed himself and his voice was as weak as it was when we'd arrived at Meyrnul's shop.

"Let's sit down then. So you can rest."

"Ni. We can't stop. They're waiting for us in Kanir, and we must get to the Tokahaya."

"They're waiting if they didn't get caught trying to get through Narut already. Or maybe even once they'd gotten to Kanir."

"Still, we can't stop. I won't."

His steely eyes bore into mine. There wasn't any certainty that they'd made it, especially since they'd gone through the station transports. They were only located in the four ajurdoms and Faduwata Central.

"We don't know if they did. And you need your strength, Jamil."

"Trust me, they didn't. If we got away and they were ahead of us, then they certainly did."

He was likely right. Nontu's magic was better than mine and Olug was strong. "Is there a way to get a message to Kanir? I don't think we should meet them there, not with everyone searching. My mother was out there, Jamil. I just ran away from my mother."

"Your mother," he said thoughtfully. "Kanir is still the best route for us. We're headed in the right direction, and once we're in town, we find Olug and Nontu. Then we rest."

"You're struggling, Jamil."

He held his wounded arm with his other hand. The sling we'd made had long since been lost.

"Stop, Jamil. This ugly green jacket has served every other purpose. It may as well serve another. Let me see your arm."

He faced me and I took his bag and put it on the cool ground. I twisted the jacket and mounted his arm inside before tying it around his neck. "How's that?"

He took a deep breath. "Better."

I got the distinct feeling it wasn't much better, but he didn't want me to worry any more than I already was.

"Let's keep moving. Then you'll find that *someone* who can get us to Kanir?"

"Ya'i. He runs a transport stand. We should wind up near the road to Kanir once we're out of here."

"We must be close. The air feels a little drier." We'd steadily been going up.

"It looks like a service entrance ahead. We'll need to climb a ladder." Jamil glanced at his sling. "At least I've got one good arm."

22

TO KANIR

The light shined through the metal bars, making them difficult to see through. I slid the shades back on, letting them give me anonymity and relief from the blinding light. Jamil pulled his hat down and put shades on as well.

"You were right, Lafia," Jamil smiled. "The middle corridor."

I smiled back. It wasn't often that was said of me.

"Maybe you're my lucky charm." The words were out to my immediate embarrassment.

The corners of his perfect lips turned down, frowning. "We need to find our ride."

"Agreed."

"Wait." He stopped and grabbed my bag to slow me.

"What is it? Do we need to stop again?"

"Ni. I need to tell you something."

He paused and I wondered what else there could be.

"Let's not use names. Any names here. It's safer that way."

"That makes sense. Just don't try to ignore me," I laughed and started to walk again before he touched my arm.

"There's something else."

"What? I don't think we need more surprises."

"I'm sorry. I should've told you before, but I was distracted."

I looked at Jamil's wrapped arm and nodded anxiously.

"I'm not going just because of the coming sacrifice. There's a stone that allows the Tokahaya to wield power over us. I destroy it, and there are no more sacrifices. So understand, no matter what, I have to get there."

"A stone? There are a million stones, Jamil."

"No names," he chided before looking around and pulling me back against the wall that held the gate we'd just come through.

"What kind of stone then?"

"It's more than a stone. It's a special crystal in the ruler's possession. I get it from him, and your sister is safe. You're safe, even Bletondu and all of Faduwata. It'll end this."

"That's why you're doing this?"

"Ya'i. I have to or none of us will ever really be safe."

"Why are you just telling me this?"

"It's my special charge. And only one other person knows."

"Olug?"

"Ni. My father."

"That's who was speaking to my father in the garden! The second time."

"I must do it by the second full lavender moon, Lafia. It has to be done. I have to get to the Tokahaya."

The lavender moon had been bright and full just days before at the Crossing of the Ties ceremony. Our lavender moon, our larger moon, worked in sync with the smaller, yet sacred moon of power, the Dark Moon. When those two moons passed, so would the current giving season. The second full lavender moon from now would have to be enough.

"We will get there. We will save Faduwata."

He nodded weakly but as if something had been lifted from his shoulders. His movements were a little lighter as we found the gate for the metal fencing and ambled into the open marketplace. Jamil pushed past vendors selling everything from food and fruit to clothing and potions. Twenty years and I'd never seen this part of the Narut ajurdom before.

"We don't have time," Jamil reminded me, stealing my attention from the wonder surrounding us. Above, near the mountain's edge, the sky had changed in just the time I'd been gone. The smoke hung lower, casting over the ridge.

"Look, Jamil." I stopped him to point at what I was seeing.

He paused and shook his head, confused.

"It's getting worse."

"I thought you said we had until the next full lavender moon. We still have the moon cycle we're in and that's more than three weeks, plus the next one and that's the full twenty-nine days."

"That's what whoever was speaking to my father said. Who I thought must've been your father. Wouldn't you know?"

"My father didn't mention anything about the second full lavender moon from now, only the next lavender moon when they wanted a royal sacrifice. Still, we should have plenty of time."

"Perhaps it's just a threat?"

"I don't know. The Tokahaya has never been known for its trustworthiness."

"You know a lot about something that we've been taught to avoid."

"And yet, here we are. Together. This way. His tent is over here."

A dingy rust-colored tent with a mossy substance growing on the outside was ahead. We maneuvered around several small transport platforms to get inside, where we found him. He was slumped over in a chair. Beside him was a tall glass with a brown liquid and the ash remains of the substance locals called the good root, according to Jamil.

"Tamki! Tamki! Wake up. We need a ride," Jamil called out, throwing his good hand up in the air.

"He's in quite a state," I whispered.

"Good as the two of you. Just well fueled." Tamki sat up shakily before his eyes focused. "Who's this. Looks familiar."

"Don't worry about her. We need a ride."

"Where ya gotta go, Tulu?" Tamki continued to twist his head at me forcing me to fix the scarf around my head and the shades while looking at Jamil with confusion. *Tulu? Did he have a different identify for every region?*

"Kanir. Did you see a couple other folks heading that way this morning?"

"Ya'i. I did one trip already. Cheap. Didn't want to pay extra for the big one. That's a lot of weight to lift."

"It doesn't cost you any more to move someone because of weight, Tamki."

"He took up space I could have used to squeeze another rider on. Instead, that other one rode with someone else."

Tamki turned to me and nodded at Jamil. "You know Tulu is the spitting image of that Ajursun down in Sparaka. Gets paid to fill in for him sometimes," he paused with a twist of his lips before pursing his lips at Jamil. "So I know ya can pay."

"We need a ride, Tamki," Jamil said irritably.

"How much?" I asked

"Two of ya? Five cullons."

"Five?" Jamil and I both asked in disbelief.

"You pay extra for the big one, or ask someone else. I know that spoiled prince down there pays ya good to stand around and do nothing. Ya may as well pay me fair to do something." Tamki leaned his head back again and closed his eyes.

Jamil huffed loud enough to cause Tamki to open them again.

"After that big one and that other one with the big hat come through, I figure you got folks looking for ya. What ya do, run off with the no-good prince's girl?" Tamki laughed before whispering, "Ya gonna have the whole royal guard coming for ya rear parts and for her. Longer ya wait, the more it costs. And ya won't get as far." He squinted one eye a bit.

"You don't know what you're talking about and would do good to mind your business, Tamki."

"So formal. I see you've been practicing your pompousness. I'm the one ya need. Five cullons or find another transporter willing to take ya up there."

"You know I can't. I dug inside my bag and turned to Jamil. "I only have three."

"Check mine. Side pocket."

I flung the flap on the side of the bag open and scrounged around for any bills or cullons. I pulled out a bill with Naeemah's face. I felt for the other bills and pulled them out. I needed either five bills with station emblems or one with the image of a different third born, of which there were few. My sister and Jamil's sister included. Feeling around a bit more, I pulled out a faded red bill with Asabe's smiling visage.

"Here," I said to Tamki.

"Come on then," he said, getting up and walking out of the tent to his transport. He hopped up and beckoned us to follow.

Tamki sat, forcing me into the space opposite Jamil. He then reached an arm over me to close the door before blowing a horn to move people off the path he took. The transport platform grumbled irritably and then whistled to a start. After lurching and tossing us back and forth, it slowly lifted, wobbling as it did.

"Hold on, it can get a little bumpy, especially at the higher altitude. Oh and put these on. Don't want anyone to know I was carrying the two of ya." He handed us big woven floppy hats to put over what we already had on. "Leave them here when you get out. They're not gifts, ya'i?"

"Just go, please." Jamil slapped the hat on.

I clumsily struggled to push it over the mass that was already on my head.

I gripped the bar in the middle and pressed against the padded seat back, crisscrossed with stitches and patches and stitches. Tamki pulled the front of the hat down, using two hands and stepped back.

Satisfied we were covered, he pushed a button and the transport platform shot forward, lurched once, and then continued in a mostly straight line from his tent. He'd positioned himself well to be routed along the magnetic lines crossing Maradobu.

Unlike the conductors between the palace and the station, Tamki's platform wasn't always straight and spun this way or that at random moments, jerked, sped up and slowed down depending on who or what was on the unofficial electromagnetic lines he used. The bar in the middle felt like my salvation as I clung to it out of fear I might fly through the caged platform and onto what had now become a mix of dirt and rocks as we continued up the side of the ridge to Kanir. And this, after flying with Saren.

With a sigh of relief, I spotted the buildings and people in the distance. Jamil seemed to be enjoying the ride or my discomfort, or perhaps both. I glared at him, and he smiled back. I bit the inside of my cheek to keep from smiling, but one crept out anyway.

"Here you are. I do accept tips," Tamki said.

I ignored his comment and slowly got out, holding my unsettled stomach. Fina's blue drink would've also been helpful for Tamki's rides.

Jamil got out and nodded to Tamki, "Thanks for the ride."

"Hats, please, or keep for another five cullons."

I took the hat off and tried to keep myself still.

"Or ya can trade something else."

"Here you go." I handed him his floppy hat. "We've got it. You may want to go easy on your fueling."

Tamki shrugged and spun around. "Heading to Narut? Anyone heading to Narut? Save one cullon on your ride."

We shook our heads but kept walking anyway. I reached in my pocket for the swinging heart pendulum.

"We need to find Olug and Nontu quickly," Jamil said noticing me hold it up. He paused briefly as he scanned the landscape of shops.

It began swinging again as it had done in the tunnel. I huffed as I stared at Jamil who was looking again for any signs of Olug or Nontu. It kept swinging towards him even when I'd been clear about my magic being a priority and him being off limits. I pulled the finger-wand out the side pouch of my bag before shoving the pendulum inside.

"We also need to check your wound. It's time to clean it and apply a little more salve."

"How about we do both? Find them and get me reset like we agreed."

"Fair." I scanned the small town curiously and then turned back to Jamil. "I have no idea where they'd be."

"You ever been to Kanir?" Jamil asked softly.

I didn't want to answer.

"Do you know this area of Narut?"

"I've been to the home of Kanir's leader, but that's it."

His mouth opened briefly before closing again. He nodded understandingly. "Knowing Olug, he would've wanted to get inside someplace to eat. Let's check anywhere selling food."

We started up the main street where Tamki had dropped us. Small shops lined both sides. They were quaint and not nearly as busy as Sparaka Central had been.

"Finally!"

It was Olug, coming out of a door just ahead of us. Nontu then appeared but was nearly blocked by Olug as she stood in the open door before making her way out.

"You made it!" I cried and hugged Nontu like we hadn't seen each other in years.

"I am so glad to see you." Her eyes were filled with concern. "We just picked up some fresh bandages from here and Olug was beginning to worry."

"We're here now. Finally. But we do need to check Jamil. Where can we go?"

"Good light there. Good food too." Olug walked ahead toward an establishment with bars on the windows.

"Are you sure?" I asked skeptically.

"We're in the nice part of Kanir. This is fine." Jamil's reassurance did nothing to ease my tension but at least we weren't splitting up again.

Inside, Olug found a secluded table in the back and ordered a pitcher of hap, a fermented juice from a mix of fruits. Likely what Tamki had been enjoying. Once it arrived and the table attendant left, I helped Jamil out of his sling. His arm was swollen, and the bandage was damp even on the outside.

"I'm so glad you're here, Nontu. You have to do more healing so he can make it." I gripped Jamil's hand.

Nontu locked on where our hands joined, a frown crossing her lips before she looked at both of us curiously. "Remove the bandage. Slowly."

I unwrapped the fabric and saw the skin underneath. I shuddered, afraid to keep going. "Something's wrong. His skin."

Nontu sat beside me to inspect for herself. "You are right. It may be too late. All I can do is slow it." She stood and wrung her hands.

"What's wrong, Nontu? If you can slow it, we can make it."

"You should know that his body might reject the poison."

"That would mean it repels it?" I asked hopefully.

"Ni," she replied.

"Then what does it mean?" Jamil asked, keeping his eyes lowered.

"If your body rejects it or this continues to spread before we get the magic, it will be too late. Rejection means it will kill him. If it spreads all the way through, he will be one of them."

"We can beat it. We'll get there before either of those things happen. Let's clean this up, you do your healing, and we go," I urged. I didn't want to mention the Tokahaya here, but that's where the only one who could heal him was.

"I do not want you to be disappointed or to blame yourself, Lafia, if he does not make it."

"What? Blame myself? He's making it." I finished removing the bandage and poured the hap on the wound before rinsing it with water. Then I picked up a clean spoon and smoothed the salve across it and rebandaged his arm. "Your turn," I said to Nontu and stepped back.

This was the first time Nontu had been this doubtful. She sat and put her hands over the fresh dressing. I placed my hands on Jamil's. I didn't want to feel this way, at least not with him. But when he was around, I felt ways I didn't want to. It would've been okay with Najurvod. Najurvod had been my remedy to his unavailability. Now, my hands closed around Jamil's ringless fingers. On my hand, the gold band that was normally inside was the only part showing from the outside. It was a reminder of the importance of my duty.

I whispered into his ear, "I promise you, Jamil, we will get the cure and do what we came to do. I'm going to make sure we get there."

"That's the first time you've been so sure of anything," he smiled weakly.

Although I nodded in agreement, he was wrong. Since I'd seen him at the Crossing of the Ties ceremony when I was sixteen, I'd been sure I loved him and just as sure that I wouldn't let myself ever fall to that emotion because I could never have him. I was no longer as certain about the second part. I couldn't lose him. I would rather have him as a friend if that was my only option than have him dead or changed due to this eper poison.

"I am sure. You need to rest a bit and let that healing do a little work. I don't believe we've been through the worst."

I pulled out the bound paper Nontu and I had copied and turned to where I remembered the discussion about entering the Tokahaya. For several moments I read silently.

"Nontu? Something's wrong with what we copied."

"What do you mean?" she asked nonchalantly.

"We each copied a page, but we copied the same page and then there are some that look like we skipped them entirely. We are missing every opposite page and then some!"

Nontu took the book and began flipping through, reading a few lines on each page. "It appears you are correct."

"This was supposed to help us. It's not even half there!"

"Eat." Olug returned with a plate piled with breads, cheeses, and meats and another small plate with fruits.

"Ya'i," Nontu said, removing her hands. "Once we begin, we must move quickly and make sure to have all of our strength."

"Nontu? Did you hear me? We don't even have half of the information. There was something in here about a necklace as well. It's not here." I flipped a few more pages. "Look! It says an important crystal is held within a necklace, but that's it. There's nothing else." I stopped speaking, feeling a sense of panic. "Nontu! Did you hear me? This book is useless!"

"I did. It was an error. One we cannot go back and correct," she said with an air of aloofness. "And, what of this necklace anyway? Do you believe it is where your magic is?"

"It's not just about the necklace. Never mind about that. It's the fact we don't have what we need!" I groused.

"You didn't look before now?" Jamil asked.

"As you've seen, there wasn't necessarily a great deal of free time for reading."

"How'd you manage to copy an entire journal and not realize you were writing the same thing?"

"Judging us isn't going to help now. This is what we have," I said defensively. "From what is here, entering and exiting is no easy task. And there's nothing about that piece of jewelry with the crystal except that there is one. At least I have my swinging heart pendulum, though I can't say it's been of much use thus far guiding us to my magic. Suppose to lead me to my heart's desire, but Meyrnul was probably right. It doesn't work."

"What do you mean? I've seen you use it several times," Jamil asked with concern.

"Ya'i, but that doesn't mean it helped. So far, it hasn't directed me toward my magic. Besides, you don't need Nontu or me to help you find your way. You were already going."

"We will help you find your magic, Lafia. I know that's what you need. I think it's what we all need."

"Must go. Enforcers coming," Olug said under his breath.

"He hasn't had enough time!" I worried.

"No choice." Olug helped Jamil to his feet. "Go now."

Reluctantly, I reached inside my pocket to get the swinging heart pendulum, ready for it to mock me once more. Again I asked it for help, this time to show me the best way out. It was supposed to guide me to what my heart wanted. It pointed to him again as it had done each time before. I stuffed it back in my pocket and threw the bag over my shoulder, ignoring the raised eyebrow Nontu gave.

23

ONWARD

Nontu motioned with her head for us to follow her into the kitchen. The cooks said nothing as she held her hand chest high, her fingers extended, except the smallest one bent halfway down. *Zhirian magic.*

We weaved through a hallway and out a rear door, where we found Tamki leaning against the side of the building, sheltering from the downpour.

"What are you doing here?" I asked him.

"This is a regular route and I saw the enforcers coming into town. I thought my prior fares might be future fares. Ya know?"

I rolled my eyes. "I'm not getting on that thing with him."

"Suit yourself but they were already coming up that hill and ya don't look like ya got many options. The rain might slow them, but it won't stop them." He pretended to look around as if looking out for them. "And I'll give you one cullon off for the sick look-a-like. Seems he's getting worse, fast."

"No choice," Olug said, supporting Jamil.

"Ya might wanna listen to the big one."

"Dear child, you may wish to accept the gift before you. Do you desire to reach your destination?" Nontu asked.

"Ya'i. But I'd like to reach it alive, which is a great uncertainty with him. And we've just eaten. I'm sure my meal will be all over his ride."

"I have bags, don't worry. But they're not free."

Nontu stood beside me. "I am with you all the way there. We can take another way, but we risk capture and may lose time."

"What's it gonna be?" Tamki tapped the top of his transport platform impatiently.

"Anything happens to us, to him, the people he works for won't have mercy. How many look-a-likes can there be. Tulu needs help and that's what you're going to provide.," I told him, our eyes squared.

"Whoa! She has some spark. Must really like ya, Tulu," he laughed.

I ignored his comment as we loaded on and got settled.

"I can take ya up to Ronk, the next village, but that's far as the lines go."

"How much will that be?" I asked.

"Fifteen cullons."

"Fifteen!? We don't have fifteen."

"And that's a cullon off. It would've been sixteen, but I don't charge ya full for the ill friend."

"We still don't have it," I said indignantly.

"Then what do ya have?" he asked, studying our hands, necks, and ears.

"We can pay you when we return," I tried to negotiate.

"Tamki, don't do that."

"You can have this ring," Jamil offered. "Olug, can you get it from the side of my bag?"

"Again?" Olug's voice was gruff and tinged with irritation.

"It's just a ring, but it's worth much more than fifteen cullons."

Olug pulled the ring out, and Jamil took it. "If you get this, we don't pay for transport again between now and," he paused to think, "and the next full lavender moon." Jamil held the ring between two of his fingers.

Tamki leaned in, squinting one eye and tapping the jewel with his fingernail. "Ya stealing from the Ajursun this way too? Took his girl, jewelry? What else?" Tamki asked curiously before shaking his head. "I can't take this."

"I didn't steal it. It was given to me, and I didn't steal his girlfriend. We came to get some help. Do you want the damn ring or not Tamki?"

"It's real?"

"Of course. We have to go. What's it going to be?"

"Ugh. Fine. Deal. Give it here." Tamki grabbed the ring and turned on the power. He tossed us each headwear. "Ya know what to do. Oh, and if ya need a bag, they're on the side. If ya use one, I charge a cullon. That's not for the ride; it's for the bag."

The platform wobbled and sagged under our weight, the lean favoring Olug, before balancing out, lifting higher, and taking off. Through the rectangular openings, I saw the enforcers entering Kanir in heavy boots and armored tops. We'd just missed them. Lowering myself in the seat, a silent sigh escaped my lips. Nontu touched the hat on her head nervously as she noticed the scene outside the transport behind us. I was grateful for the cover given by both the rain and Tamki's ridiculous hats.

"Nontu. Back there, you did something I hadn't seen you do before. It was like you made us invisible."

"Not invisible. I do not have that power. I made us of no interest."

"Why didn't you do that with the epers?"

"I tried that first, but they originate through Zhiri. Some of my Zhirian magic cannot be used on those from Zhiri."

"I thought they were created and put in Zhiri," I said thoughtfully.

"Their origin in this realm and in this dimension is through Zhiri," she said matter-of-factly. "I do not have that power over them, though I wish I did."

"So do I," I said sadly.

"Zhirian, hmmm?" Tamki smiled. "I see it now. Vennan? Even with the ears covered. I once knew a vennan woman. She was something special. She didn't like Faduwata, though, and visiting her in Zhiri was a chore. Told her if she ever came back to Faduwata, even all the way down in Sparaka or Wallarin, tell me. I'd be there fast as these lines could take me."

"Why's it have to be so hard to visit Zhiri anyway, Nontu?"

"It is for security, you know that. If Zhiri allows people of Faduwata to come and go freely, it puts itself at risk."

"But we welcome you." I gripped the rails tightly and tried to ignore the growing nausea as I considered Nontu's home and what they thought of us.

"Ya'i. Before the war, things were different, but we have had to become more secure. I see we are close to Ronk."

"Straight ahead." Tamki's mood had turned more somber. "Be careful. If ya plan on heading up that mountain, ya wanna hurry before dark. It's wet, slippery, and can be dangerous without the light. I hear people go up and don't come back and I don't want the royal security coming for me." He made eye contact with each of us, his face firm and serious.

316

"But we still have a deal, till the next full lavender moon."

"Ya'i. Let's hope ya need it."

Tamki came to a jarring stop, throwing us back and forward, depending on our seating position around the platform.

We took turns glaring at him from where we sat, plastered against the bars behind us or leaning into the bars in front of us.

"You've arrived. I do accept tips, and please leave the hats. They're not gifts," he nodded.

We climbed out of the caged platform, and I tried to steady myself. Tamki held out one of the hats we'd worn as if expecting us to put something in it.

"Come on, we need to hurry," I said to Olug and Nontu, ignoring his bold gesture.

I walked ahead and pulled out the pendulum. We needed to go up the mountain to get my magic, but the pendulum still refused to point to anything other than him. Jamil clung to Olug, distress lining his face with every step. I shoved the malfunctioning pendulum into my pocket and readjusted the bag on my back. Nontu easily caught up with me.

"It is not broken. It appears to work quite well." She took me by the arm and stretched her stride to create more space between us and Olug and Jamil.

"Not now, Nontu. Everything has gone wrong."

"I understand," she said before a lengthy pause. "Lafia, I need to tell you something."

"You don't need to tell me you 'need to tell me something.' Just tell me, like you always do."

She nodded thoughtfully while following the path we would take. "From the look of his wound," Nontu whispered in a low voice, "he only has until the morning."

My feet melded with the mud beneath me, refusing to move forward as my breath caught somewhere between my chest and throat. *Breathe, Lafia. Breathe.* I let it out and inhaled sharply, trying not to let my alarm escape through my expression. The morning was only hours away as night was nearly upon us.

I closed the soft jacket I wore. Despite the stench, I put the coat Olug had packed over it. I wrapped my scarf over my hair and pulled the hood up, ensuring my ears were covered. There are moments failed by words. Instinctively, I reached for the smooth stone in my pocket. I pulled it out and let it rest in my tightly closed palm. My other hand patted the small pouch of crystals in my other pocket.

Jamil leaned heavily on a long, thick wooden stick while Olug carried both their bags. Nontu may have slowed the poison, but it continued to spread. The brownish-gray skin on his hand had begun to snake around the side of his neck.

I walked back to them, leaving Nontu alone.

"We're getting close. At least it doesn't look like it's raining up higher. Seems we might catch a break after Kanir," Jamil said.

"Ya'i, but the clouds are still thick, and I see flashes up there. Lightning," I said. "Do you all see that? Or is it still only me?"

"I see clouds. Maybe it's lightning?" Jamil answered. Nontu remained silent and Olug's expression suggested he was more worried about Jamil than a storm.

"Whatever the weather, up there somewhere is what we need. You need to bundle up, Jamil, or you may get sick. I mean—"

"I know what you mean, Lafia. Maybe you can help me with pull this hat over my ears." He'd gotten it down on one side so that it sat lopsided on his head. I pulled it down on the other side. He reached toward me and pulled mine back over my ears. "You need to stay warm too. It's only going to get colder with the altitude and thinner air."

Jamil and I slowed until we were out of earshot of Olug and definitely Nontu.

"Do you remember anything else about the crystal?" I whispered.

"I will take care of it, Lafia."

"In your condition?"

"I'll be better soon."

"Just tell me how you plan to get it?"

"Legend says it's on a chain in a secure location. Find it, get it, destroy it."

"That's it?" I asked in shock.

"Wyrden will help destroy it."

I looked back. "I thought you said only your father and I knew?"

"He's got good ears. Better than you might expect."

"Alright. I guess it's not a secret."

"Not from him or you. The map will help us get to the gate to enter. The only other thing is finding it once inside."

"You don't have a plan. And now you aren't well. Jamil, if you don't get it, this sacrifice doesn't end."

"I know. Thankfully you two are here to help. And if you get that magic of yours back, you probably won't even need me."

"Why would you say that? We're all in this together." Maybe he wasn't himself, but he was still inside and trying to get a reaction.

"We should fill our canteens before the rain slows further. You can't get dehydrated. None of us can, not up there. Right, Nontu?" I called ahead to her. "If we're not hydrated, our magic isn't going to work. And I need all the help I can get."

She paused and came back toward us. "You were always such a good student. You are correct, it will not work well, and you will tire quickly. However, if we stop, we lose valuable time."

"It won't take long. The river flows over there but it won't be settled right now. We should find a table that's good and high right now, not more than a hundred feet up to our right. Let me see that map, Olug."

Olug fished it out of his pocket and handed it to me.

"See over there? Looks a bit more than a hundred feet, but we can do it. Besides, we need extra water to clean the wound."

I ignored Nontu's eyes telling me not to get too hopeful he would survive this and still be who he was.

"Good luck. Water running down this side is what comes to Emervy and Sparaka."

"But from here, it's fresh," I argued. "Emervy hasn't polluted it yet."

"More water is good," Olug agreed.

"Then we need to go up that way." It was noticeably dark, and the gray clouds rolled angrily, despite it not looking like it was raining.

***

Water babbled nearby, faintly, obscured by the winds picking up around us. The heavy air that filled the gusts dampened my hopes that it was merely a storm.

"This way." I walked into a small clearing. "It has to be near here."

Olug stood over a small area of rocks and weeds.

"Did you find it?" I ran over to see what had caught his interest.

"Not sure."

I knelt beside what was supposed to be water. "What is this?" I waited for Olug to respond, but he said nothing and only shook his head. "Olug, why does it look like this? Like it has layers of dust and dirt. From here, those rocks should've filtered most of it out." I moved the water with a small twig. "This is fine. Like ash." I grabbed a leaf and lifted some from where it had pooled. "We can't drink this. Even if we used our filters. We can't drink this!"

"I told you the water was bad," Jamil said weakly.

"But we're at the source." I spoke the words almost to myself. I searched for another pool that should have contained fresh rainwater. "Same over here."

"And here," Nontu called, kneeling several yards away.

"Help me move some of the rocks. Maybe it's cleaner farther down," I asked Olug.

Olug grabbed a large rock and heaved it to the side effortlessly. I used a smaller stone to lift a few others, hoping the water might be drinkable beneath.

"My father needs to know it's not Emervy contaminating the water." When Nontu and I made it back I would let him know what I'd found so he could make sure it was fixed.

"Perhaps your father already knows," Nontu said, looking askance.

"And he hasn't done anything? I doubt it." I asked confused.

"Some solutions require time."

"Everyone needs water to live," I argued, surprised at my own words.

"Be assured, this is something he and the staff are working on," Nontu said.

"In their slow time," Jamil said under his breath.

"While that may be true, at this moment, we still don't have a source of fresh water," I sighed.

"Keep going." Olug turned around and began walking again as if that were the entire discussion.

I had no argument or alternative, and no other options were offered by Nontu or Jamil.

"We don't have a choice," Jamil said with determination, even as the grayish color began spreading around the front of his neck.

Nontu held back, climbing slowly and deliberately. She was muttering what I assumed were spells to keep Jamil as strong as possible or help us in some way. Perhaps they were to give us strength. A small smile crossed my lips at the thought of Nontu. Since coming to us, she'd always been with me and had refused to abandon me.

We'd climbed long enough that the sun was no longer visible, though its light still crept across the sky. Olug stopped and dropped the two bags he carried. "Masks and goggles," he ordered.

"What?" I asked, confused.

"There are masks and goggles in there for us. They'll help with the fog or the smoke or whatever this is. I've heard it can be hard to see." Jamil knelt with a grunt after explaining. He reached into the bag Olug had for him until he found a pair of large goggles with an attached mask and filter. "Yours aren't connected. Olug is prepared but didn't know you'd be joining us."

"I guess that makes sense, that it's not smoke. It just looks smoky. It's thick fog." The gray fog danced and drifted ahead of us. Even from where we'd stopped, I felt it.

"Goggles help," Olug said, fixing a pair on his face.

I felt inside the expansive bag until I found the mask and goggles. I pulled them out and fit them on my face. Then I helped Nontu tighten hers and finally asked Jamil if he needed help getting them on, glaring at Olug, who had his mask and goggles on, both bags on his back, and was waiting for us to finish.

"I can do it myself." Jamil once again tried to put the contraption over his head, failing.

"Let me help you. We don't have time."

"If I can't even do this, what good am I going to be?" He dropped the goggles beside him and he moaned in pain again.

"If you don't let me help you do this, we'll all have to crawl through that mist and we'll run out of time. For you. For everything."

"You don't have to remind me. I know what's happening." He handed me the mask and goggles set.

After securing them on his head, I held my hand out to help him up. "Come on."

"I can get up."

"Why the stubbornness now?"

"I'm not. I'm a man, Lafia. I can stand on my own."

"What's that supposed to mean?"

"I have one purpose. One."

Jamil struggled to his knees and then, avoiding my help, finally got to both feet, his long walking stick, the only aid he'd accept.

"Ready?" he asked.

"Now that we all have our goggles on, we are." A pinch of salt in my tone went past Olug as he studied the fog we would soon enter.

Olug had been right. As we moved into the smoky mist, it became dense and thick.

"I bet whatever's contaminating the water has something to do with this." I nearly lost sight of my friends in the grayish mist and stretched my hand out in front of me into the fog that enveloped it.

"Where are you all?" Jamil asked.

"Here." I followed his voice until I could see him two feet away.

"Where?" His voice was close.

I grabbed the loose strap on the back of his bag.

"I'm here."

"Olug?" he called out.

"Here."

"Where's here?" Jamil asked.

"Put your arm out?"

A moment later, Jamil uttered, "I've got you."

"Nontu?"

"Behind Lafia. I have hold of her bag."

"Stay close," Olug grunted loudly.

We couldn't have gotten any closer to one another without tripping over each other's boots or being compacted between the bags we carried. It was like back in the tunnels.

"What did you say?" I asked, not sure who'd said it.

"Stay close," Olug repeated.

"Ni. Not you. Was that you, Nontu? Did you say something?"

"Ni."

"I thought I heard someone say my name."

"It wasn't me either," Jamil said.

"Let's just keep walking." I heard again. This time I knew Jamil had called my name and then said something I couldn't understand.

"Gate ahead."

"Gate? It's fog," I said unbelievingly.

"Games? Now?" Olug called back.

"Ni. I just didn't expect a gate."

"What did you call me?" he stopped.

"No one called you anything, Olug," Jamil said. "Let's go."

"Heard you," Olug heaved. "Not a wifferin!" Olug yelled back at me.

"What are you talking about, Olug? Where'd that come from? Wait. What'd you say? A spoiled prince? No use?" Jamil turned and his face came close through the fog. "You think I'm spoiled? You're one to talk. You've never had to do a thing yourself outside your precious palace."

"You don't even believe in yourself, and you run at the first sign of trouble! Like at the ball!"

"Jamil! What! Why? Never mind. Maybe I should turn around and let you deal with this on your own since you don't need anyone if that's what you think of me!"

"Maybe you should since it must be what you want to do."

"Not a wifferin!" Olug yelled and pushed Jamil to the ground.

"You deserved that!" I yelled at him as he squirmed. "Maybe you are of no use!"

"Hush! All of you." Nontu closed in on the three of us. "Did you hear that?"

"Jamil is stirring up trouble," I said, "and got what was coming."

"Don't act innocent. Besides, I never asked you to come."

"But you needed me, you selfish, stubborn, suffering fool!"

"Don't let them in your head," Nontu said emphatically.

"Maybe he shouldn't have said what he said," I barked at Jamil.

"Heard too!" Olug yelled at Nontu. "Not a cheat! Not a wifferin!"

"He is hearing the whispers," Nontu said almost to herself. Then louder she added, "You all are."

"Ya'i. See. Whispers on me. Talk behind my back," Olug barked.

Something dropped to the ground that sounded like the bags Olug had carried.

"What? It was Lafia who called me a spoiled prince. Nobody said anything about you."

"Now you want to laugh? Which one of you is laughing?" I demanded.

"It's not us. Keep moving," Nontu begged.

"I didn't call you a spoiled prince and no one said anything about Olug either. But you had a lot to say about me."

"Be quiet. All of you. You are feeding it. The energy of the whispers."

"What are you talking about, Nontu?" I yelled.

"I am not. I am not. I am not. I am—" Nontu said over and over to herself until I spoke loud enough to get over her.

"Nontu! What are you talking about?"

"The whispers."

We all fell silent for a moment. "Whispers? What is that?" I asked again.

"They get in your head. They whisper things to weaken you, make you sad or vulnerable. They take your fears and insecurities and repeat them to you. They use whatever they can to get in your head."

"How do you know this, Nontu? Why didn't you warn us?" I demanded.

"I..." she paused and took a deep breath through the mask, exhaling enough to push the fog out from around her face. "I have heard of it before. It is difficult to know what is true. What might have changed."

"You could've told us. At least we could have been prepared for it."

"I am sorry. This journey has been stressful for all of us."

I looked at her as best I could through the obscuring fog. "It's alright. It'll be alright. What do you know about it?"

The sytes travel throughout the Maradobu realm. These are the mugaljana and the lost souls they've collected, convinced by the mugaljana to remain here. The mugaljana are like the haskeals but sinister. It means the Tokahaya is on the other side of this fog."

"Mugaljana? I've never heard of them. How do we not let them get in our heads? They sound like us?"

"Do you really believe Jamil would say those things about you?"

I studied what I could see of Jamil's face, pained and graying. "Ni. I guess not."

327

"And you, Olug. Do you believe any of us would say that about you?"

Olug grunted, "Ni."

"Even if any of those things were said of any of you, does it matter? Do you believe them?" Nontu continued.

"They said something to you too. Didn't they?" I asked.

"Ya'i. None of us are perfect. We all wrestle with some part of ourselves. It does not matter who or what we are," she said with a glance in the direction she knew Olug stood.

"What can we do about it?"

"We must block them out and keep a strong mind. If you hear a whisper, whisper something back about yourself you know is true. Olug, you are strong, prepared, and reliable. I saw that coming here with you. You are good."

"Strong. Prepared. Reliable. Good. Olug," he repeated.

I chuckled softly, wishing I could see his face. "She's right, Olug. You are all of those things."

"Jamil, you are persistent, smart, and a dutiful son of Sparaka. You are also quite brave. There is no one else I would have trusted to help Lafia make this trip. You are the one," Nontu said like a mother reassuring her child.

Jamil cleared his throat emotionally.

"And Lafia, you are special. More special than you know. You are not the same young woman at the Crossing of the Ties ceremony. Ni. You are someone else. You are important in all of this. You are important to me."

"Thank you, Nontu. You are important to me too. Whatever those whispers said about you, it's not true. I wouldn't be who I am or standing here without you."

Nontu leaned in through the fog and peered into my eyes. "We can only be who we are. We all wrestle, do we not?"

"We do. You can't let them get to you either, Nontu," I searched through the fog to find Nontu's hand, my face close to hers.

Nontu nodded briefly and reached her hand out to touch me on my forehead, as she'd done all the years I'd known her. "And you, you must always remember what you know." She leaned back and pulled her hand away before her face faded into the fog. "We must continue."

24

INTO THE TOKAHAYA

The fog, or collection of the mugaljana and lost souls, began to disperse as it drifted downward, towards Narut. Despite the thinning it was difficult to see. A fine mist covered everything.

"Jamil?" I'd finally gotten the courage to speak again.

"What?"

"Nontu is right, you know."

"About what?"

"What she said about you being smart and brave and handsome." I recoiled briefly at my accidental insertion.

"I don't recall her saying that exactly."

"You know what I mean. I just thought you should know. You are a good prince. Even if we're what some people call spoiled it doesn't mean we can't do good and make a difference. Maybe it's precisely because we do have more that we can."

"You're pretty 'n smart too."

"Pretty smart or was that pretty and smart?"

"Both. But I don't know how long these looks of mine or this body are going to hold up," Jamil stumbled, caught only by my holding him up. He resisted my help, propping himself up on his walking stick. He was languid and if he didn't stop soon, I feared this would all be a waste.

"You don't have to do it all on your own. My mother used to say that no one does anything of value completely on their own. Someone came before them and planted some seed, that took root in some fertile ground, that received water and light. No one of us can be the seed, the ground, the water, and the light. Not at the same time."

"She's Clarhugaba, of course she'd say something like that."

"She's right. We are out here together trying to do something important. Trying to secure a future. We must help and support each other."

"Spoken like a true future Clarhugaba." There was a sincere smile in his voice.

"We need water. Drinkable water," I said, turning to Nontu. "Is there some magic we can use on the water or this mist?" I pulled off the goggles and took a long deep breath before coughing several times. "That was too much too soon."

"Only if there is some good water, I can use with it. Cannot have you all falling down after we have gotten this close. Check your water bags. We just need a drop and a dry empty container.

"What's that?" Jamil pointed at a shadowy figure ahead.

Olug waved the map in the air. "Map ends."

"We're at the edge," Jamil whispered.

"Through there is the Tokahaya," Nontu whispered, almost to herself.

"We can't go in there without water. Everyone, check your water bags. One drop, right, Nontu?" I turned again to Nontu who stared at the dark shadow ahead of us. "Nontu?"

"And a dry container," she answered slowly. Her eyes snapped back into focus from whatever had taken her attention.

She then slowly considered me, Jamil, and Olug before checking her own water bag. "I have no water. But I do have a dry container."

"Olug, water? I asked.

He squatted on the ground. "Ni."

"Jamil?"

He shook his head.

"You mean between the four of us we don't have a single drop of water?!" I snapped. "Am I to accept that we are going to perish on this mountain filled with springs, for lack of clean water?"

"We don't have time. We must continue. The dark will be upon us," Jamil said. "I can make it." He slowly rose to his feet. His entire neck and both hands showing gray.

"We're through the fog or that soul mess back there. Ahead is the Tokahaya. If we don't get water now, we risk not making it." I ruffled through my bag again, searching for anything that might have held even a drop of clean water.

Nothing.

"If we don't go now, I'm not going to make it." Jamil's eyes again appeared somewhat unfocused.

I studied his face. "If you think you can make it, I can too. I'm not letting you die. Being one of those things is as good as dead." This time he let me wrap my arm around his waist. Together we began our approach towards the shadowed shape looming ahead.

The mist swirled around us as the wind picked up.

"What is that? Where is it coming from?" I asked.

"It sounds like someone is over there. Are they crying?" Jamil said.

"Sounds hurt." Olug walked faster towards the sounds of soft whimpering, moans, and people in anguish.

"Someone is trapped back there!" I tried to walk faster, forcing Jamil to quicken his pace. "We can help them. Just have to open that door."

"This wind is turning for the worst," Jamil yelled over what was now howling wind and the sounds coming from beyond the shape in front of us.

"I can't hear you." The wind wrestled my twists from the ponytail, allowing them to whip my neck. I tried to put the goggles back on, but a gust of wind snatched them from my fingers.

The moaning grew along with the threat of dangerous weather.

"Something's happening. A storm is coming!" I yelled.

Olug yelled something unintelligible.

"We're in a wind funnel or something. We have to get out." I called out.

The swirl of mist became as thick as the fog we'd come through. Two bright lights flickered above, followed by the sound of booming thunder. The fog was taking on a shape.

"Not wind. Wifferin!" Olug yelled. His voice was angry and loud enough to be heard through the tempest that surrounded us. He held Wyrden firmly in his grasp.

"What's wifferin?" I brought forth Clarod and moved so Jamil stood between me and Olug. Nontu raised her hands, and her eyes narrowed, focused on the wifferin quickly taking shape.

"There's another!" Jamil shouted.

"People-eating beast. All body, no brains." Olug lifted Wyrden towards the beasts.

"They're surrounding us!" My backpack touched Jamil as we turned in circles with him in the center. "What do we do? They can become air! How do we get past them?"

"Wyrden!" Olug planted his feet wide and ripped off the hat holding his mane in place. I took a step back as he stomped the ground and let out a roar. "Not stupid wifferin!" He leapt into the air. Wyrden slashed through the heavy, swirling fog and then something let out a welp before the wifferin that had been lunging toward Jamil vanished into the mist.

"Is it gone?" I searched the thick mass of fog. Three were still there and one was spawning.

Olug swiped and fought the air. "Hurry! Get past," he roared, his eyes flashing gold for an instant.

Nontu continued to hold her hands up, using her magic to help but we needed to move.

"Come, Nontu. We have to get inside. The book said the entrance would be guarded by vanishing beasts. Those are what it was talking about!"

Nontu followed me and Jamil, my arm securely around him. The wind rushed around us, and Jamil was pulled away as our feet left the ground. I swung Clarod but my arms barely grazed the wifferin's striped, amber fur. It whipped me around and let out a roar like the thunder I'd heard. My head shook from the force, making it impossible to tell what I was seeing. I regained control of my eyes and saw my friends, each in the firm grip of a wifferin. Nontu wrestled against the huge beast that had lifted her with as if she were a small haskeal.

I tried again to slice the one holding me trapped by the backpack still on me. I cut through the air as it separated and came back together. I snapped my teeth at the hand holding me but where I thought I'd bitten a wifferin there was nothing, leaving me to close my teeth on themselves. The hand reformed where it had been, unbothered. The wifferin glanced back and forth at each other, their eyes glowing like an orange and red blaze.

Olug struggled with Wyrden slicing through vanishing hands and other body parts. It was doing more damage than Clarod, as the body parts he cut didn't come back the same way as the beasts holding us. But Wyrden could only do so much against four beasts, when the others were out of Olug's reach.

Wifferin eat people, crossed my mind.

"Wait!" I yelled. The beast holding me wiggled my feet above its mouth. My scarf dangled from where it was caught in the hood. Then the wind caught it and it dropped into beast's mouth.

"Ni!" Nontu screamed. "Ni!" The wifferin holding Nontu turned her around and shook her slightly before flipping her upside down.

The wifferin who had me firmly in its grasp opened its mouth and his paw. He waited for me to fall in, but I clung to the fur on the back of his paw. I feared his paw and the fur I clung to would vanish. "Let us live and you can have all you can eat!" I shouted. This time my voice made it to my captor.

It leaned a curious ear to me, and the others turned to listen.

"Ya'i. Just past the fog there are many people who followed us but couldn't get through. They are waiting for us to come back."

"Not people!" Olug cried out angrily.

He would have to be. I was not failing.

"What are you doing, Lafia?" Nontu asked.

You'll see. The book mentions the smoke, crossing back."

"We haven't gotten through and I will not lose you. Not now," Nontu said.

"You can have all the people but if we scream, they'll run. They'll be gone." I was afraid my voice might not hold out much longer.

"Eat!" The largest wifferin said to the others.

Another seemed to argue back, "Eat more!"

"Guard here. Not there!" the large one yelled angrily, shaking the fist that held Nontu while he spoke.

The other two chanted, "Eat more! Eat more!"

"Not safe there!" the largest one challenged.

'You could have ten people each. Never be hungry," I screamed.

The large wifferin pointed at the smoke we'd just come through, "Eat more now!"

"Put us down and get all you can eat," Nontu said. She stared into the eyes of the wifferin holding her sideways in his fist.

He opened his fist and Nontu began falling.

"Ra-ge faduwa, kada a yi cuta!" I shouted without faltering.

Nontu's falling slowed and she landed, tumbling slowly, but unhurt.

"How? It worked?!" Nontu almost seemed afraid. I wondered if I'd done something wrong.

The other wifferin opened their palms, forgetting we'd been their captured prey. Olug and Jamil were about to fall. Then I realized we were all careening with abandon.

"Ra-ge faduwa, kada a yi cuta!" I shouted again, my heart pounding.

We hit the ground as Nontu had, but Jamil writhed, his body too weak for much more.

"Olug, we need to carry him." I started to help Jamil to his feet, searching for the walking stick to no use. "Help me get him up."

Olug took off the backpacks he carried and handed one to me and one to Nontu.

"Carry these. Olug carry Jamil."

Olug heaved Jamil up and across his shoulders with surprising ease and we hurried towards the shadowy shape that now appeared as a door.

Behind us the wifferin plodded and disappeared into the smoke. They'd get lost in there if they were anything like they seemed and like Olug had said, no brains. The mugaljana would have their way with them.

We closed in on what had been a door only to see it evaporate the closer we got. The mist had filled back in and behind that was a visually impenetrable wall of smoke.

"Nontu, remember what the book said about the wall of smoke?"

Nontu shook her head, "We are not there yet. Keep walking. We are entering—"

"The Tokahaya," I finished. "Jamil's cure is here. My magic is here. And how we save Maradobu is here." I was determined and my pace quickened into a jog. "We can't stop now. We can do this."

Olug lumbered beside me with Jamil bouncing uncomfortably.

"Put me down, Olug. I can walk now."

Olug bent down to let Jamil slide off. He stumbled, ashen faced, and caught himself before either of us could offer help again. Holding his hands out in front of him his voice was labored. "Everything is blurry."

"Olug, he's losing his sight!" I yelled.

Olug was already ahead of us, slashing at the air. When he came to check on Jamil I shrieked. Olug was gone, replaced by a person with a wifferin head. He touched his face and pivoted to hide.

"Olug! What happened?" I cried. "Did you get bit by a wifferin?"

Ignoring my question he turned and continued forward, running toward a swirling mass of smoke. This must be the portal the book spoke of. What I'd copied said that it, too, was guarded so that unwanted intruders did not enter their dimension.

Olug charged forward with a great and fearful roar. He held Wyrden extended in front of him. A ring of gray light sparked and Olug flew back into me and Jamil, knocking us both down with him. The force of the shock stunned Nontu.

"Is everyone okay?" Nontu held her head as we attempted to regain our footing.

Olug clambered off of us, still trying to hide his face.

"I'll be alright." I tried to catch my breath from Olug's blow.

Jamil lay writhing on the ground, the area around the wound had soaked through, showing dampness on the coat as he held his head.

I helped him sit up and noticed the wound on the back of his head oozed a metallic liquid. "You hit your head! I think you're bleeding. Can you walk?"

"I will walk."

I reached into the large bag and pulled out another small bag with a geometric design in red and burgundy hues. I pulled out my royal Maradobuan sash and wrapped it around his head to stop the bleeding.

"There may be something I can try." Nontu moved closer to the portal. She picked up a rock and knelt. "Lafia, help me."

"Are you sure?"

"Ya'i. We will see what you can do even if your magic has been siphoned, as you believe. Perhaps through this trip you will demonstrate your magic yet."

Even then, she encouraged and supported me, like no one else.

"What do you mean?"

"You may prove to yourself that your magic works."

"I will try. I will get my magic and I will try, Basi Nontu."

"You do not need to call me that."

"But it is a title of honor and respect. You're trusting me to do this with you and I will not let you down."

"Of course. I know you will do what is needed. Come kneel with me and help me draw a half moon in front of this portal."

I picked up a rock to match Nontu's and started on the other side, moving across the ground until arcs connected.

"Now draw four lines spaced out, from the arc towards the portal."

"What now?"

"Draw another half circle where the lines are, towards us."

"What does that do?"

"It is so we do not get rejected and can remain on the other side." Nontu smiled at what we'd etched into the ground before standing and turning her smile to me. "Very good. You are doing this."

"Ya'i. It's mundane magic. Anyone can do that part."

"The next part is not. You believe your full magic is trapped over there? That his cure is over there? That the answer to protecting your sister is over there?"

"I do."

"Do you remember the spell for breaking through?"

Between me and my sisters, I'd always been the most studious. Even if it was only because that was the one thing I could control when everything had come easily to them.

"I remember."

"Break us through, Lafia."

"Olug help Jamil and come stand in front of one of these lines." I motioned them over as I tried to distract myself from the fluttering in my stomach.

Once we were in place, I closed my eyes and recalled the words I'd committed to memory but never thought I'd put to use. I grabbed Jamil's hand. "Hold hands, everyone and follow my lead." I held up my other hand towards the angry swirling gray mass and took a small step forward. Then I waited for the others to do the same. I moved forward again and again until our toes were at the edge of the lines and the tips of my fingers could feel the warmth that emanated from the portal.

I stared into the grayness and yelled.

"Budemu wuce au!"

The smoke moved side to side as if I'd hit a large drum. Then it spread apart, thinning as if called elsewhere.

"Go now! Stay holding hands!"

I charged forward pulling Jamil, Olug and Nontu through into an eerie darkness. Instinctively, I pulled my hat down again to combat the cool air on the other side. My breath dissipated in front of me and throughout the sky were scattered flashes of light. There was barely a mist or any haze on this side.

Screams and cries cut through the still air. "They need help," I whispered.

"It could be a trick," Jamil warned. "Like the mugaljana."

"You first. How do we find the cure for him?" I looked to Nontu for an answer.

"Lafia, get your magic first. Then maybe you can better face this dark place," Jamil argued.

"But you don't have much time."

"This will all be for naught if you don't get your magic and save your sister."

"Ni. I won't let you die, Jamil."

"I won't let everyone else die, Lafia."

"Olug, help me get him someplace he can be comfortable. If we aren't getting his cure first, we have to hide him."

"There is no guarantee of anything in this place." Nontu searched the darkness.

"Then we need to hurry. You stay with him, Olug. Keep him safe. Promise me, Olug."

"Do as possible. No promise." Olug's words held a finality as if that was all I would get from him.

"Thank you, Olug. I know you will do everything you possibly can. Nontu? Help me find my magic so we can get back here to Jamil."

Nontu nodded but her silence wasn't what I needed.

"Where do we even look?" I asked desperately.

"Inside first."

"The book? There's hardly anything useful in here." I pulled it out and tried to find enough light to see it with.

"Inside yourself, Lafia. You must feel it. Always."

I put the book back inside the bag and closed my eyes. I took a deep breath and opened my eyes.

"This is strange, Nontu. This has never happened. I feel like I connected. I see it. It's like a golden thread weaving in the air. Is this what it's supposed to be like?" I asked excitedly.

"It could be. I have only known one other person who saw the threads that connect as you describe. I would assume you have a very strong connection."

I walked in the direction the thread led me. It curved gently around the few low growing and barren trees and over rocks that jutted from the dirt. The land was like Narut, but as if everything had ceased to live, stuck eternally in the replenishing season.

"What will you do once you get there?" Nontu whispered.

"I don't know. Take it back and figure out how to make it a part of me."

"What made you think it was not a part of you?"

"You might remember this. It wasn't long after you came to us. I had only started coming into my magic and it was going well. Nontu, it really was. Especially when I'd do my solo practice. I was doing better than even Adamma had done at sixteen. Mada was so proud of me. For once, even Abada was proud. Then I choked. I couldn't do anything right and nothing worked like it should. It's been like that since. Do you remember?"

"I do not recall exactly."

"I had it, Nontu. I promise you I did, even if only for a short while. Then it was as if someone put a shade over me and only a little could get out. I've felt like that ever since. I know in my heart someone took it. I never expected to actually be right, but my heart is leading me straight there, Nontu. Finally."

"I will help you get it," Nontu said quietly.

"I couldn't have done this without you, Nontu. None of this. Since you volunteered to be our syte and our mentor you have always been there for me. All the way to the ends of our world. Or should I say past it," I joked.

"Please, do not make so much of it. It is nothing. I am fulfilling my commitments."

"Maybe it's only a commitment to you, but to me, it's always been more. When I couldn't talk to anyone else, even my own parents, I had you."

"Please, Lafia, watch where that string is leading. I do not wish for us to fall into a pit or a trap."

"Like the book mentioned? I don't remember that in the book. But we don't have it all."

"In a place like this, one might well assume there are pits and traps."

"I'll keep a better eye out." I carefully followed the winding ribbon as it led us through the darkness.

Occasionally, my toe hit a rock or elbow grazed a branch, but we were getting closer.

"Nontu. Look!" I pointed ahead.

"Keep your voice down. The watchers could be anywhere."

"Watchers?" I asked, suddenly demure. "I think I see something ahead. They look like haskeal homes. But what are they doing here? Are they trapped?" I was horrified at the idea of the beautiful haskeals being held in that place.

"Not likely haskeal homes since they can travel through dimensions so easily."

"Then I don't know what they are, but my thread," I said eagerly before lowering my voice again, "my thread goes to the tree with the lights." I could barely contain my excitement. I picked up my pace, stumbling over the rough landscape.

"I do not wish to be injured here," Nontu warned.

"I'll run ahead then." I left Nontu to maneuver the terrain at her own pace. There was the shape of a tree with the lights hanging all about it. It was the only thing with life I'd seen since coming through the portal. My breath caught in my chest at its beauty as it lit up the dark sky. Standing in front of the giant tree my golden thread vanished.

Nontu came up behind me and stared at the expanse of the tree. "Do you know what you are looking for?"

"Not specifically. But you were right before. I trusted myself and got us this far." From beneath the branches I reached for a lower hanging metal, glass, and gold box filled with light.

As my hand neared it, the light dimmed. I snatched my hand back and it regained its brilliance. I tried another box, and my approach had the same effect. One after another I reached for the light cubes, only for them to dim when I came near.

"Nontu. This isn't good. I make the boxes dim."

"Perhaps there is another tree."

"I was led to this tree. What if my magic is so broken I..." I took a deep breath. "Ni. Ni. This is my tree. My magic is here. I will find it."

I stood back and focused on the front of my forehead at the space between the eyes. My heart felt full and open as if it were expanding. I raised my hands towards the tree.

"Show me. Guide me."

Tingling crossed my chest and rose into my forehead. My body prickled just below my skin's surface. When I opened my eyes, a faint glow surrounded me.

"Lafia, dear child, surely you do not think you will speak to a tree."

And it was gone. "I was doing it, Nontu. You broke my concentration."

"I have seen you hurt so many times." She looked around as if expecting something to appear and capture us at any moment. "I do not want you to be disappointed."

"I am ready to take the risk. All this time I've been afraid that I'd fail and then I would fail. This time, Nontu. I'm trying something different. I'm going for it."

"You have tried before, and I am concerned for you."

"I have tried, but I'm not the same person I was on the night of the Crossing of the Ties. If I don't do this, even if I get my magic, I'll never use it like I know I need to as Clarhugaba. My mada doesn't doubt her magic. You don't yours. I can't anymore. What I have, I'll use so that I can get what I know is mine and help everyone."

Nontu fell silent, as if deep in thought, yet still scanning the wasteland. I closed my eyes again and patted the stones in my pocket before tuning back in. My forehead tingled, my heart opened and began vibrating. A wave of energy coursed through my entire body. When I opened my eyes again there was a soft glow around me. This time it was more than before.

"Show me. Guide me."

I waited for something to happen. The tree swayed gently in a breeze that cut through the otherwise still air. I began humming, and my body swayed. It wasn't the breeze. It was a rhythm inside.

"I need to sing, Nontu."

"Ni. Not here. You will be caught."

"I feel it, Nontu. If I sing, I'll find it."

"You will be caught. We will be caught."

"Then I'll hum."

I hummed the melody that was desperate to spill out of me. The energy inside me pulsed and grew. I swayed back and forth in front of the tree and one light began to show brighter than the rest.

"Thank you," I whispered to the tree, gently patting the trunk. Now how do I get up there?

"It's okay, Nontu. Don't be scared." I tried to reassure her.

The sound of footsteps approaching caused us to jump into a defensive stance. I placed my hand against Clarod and slowly unsheathed the blade. A large two-headed figure, one with horns, emerged from the darkness. I held Clarod in front of me while Nontu fell to her knees, her head lowered.

"Came over," the two-headed figure said in a familiar voice.

"You two were gone a while. We didn't want to be separated," Jamil said.

"Jamil worried," Olug grunted.

I sighed with relief and put Clarod away. "You almost got yourselves killed and that's not what you do when I am supposed to be trying to save you."

"Sorry," Olug shrugged.

"Did you get it?" Jamil asked. He tried to step towards me and stumbled.

"I found it. I found my magic. Up there. It's the one glowing brightest." The joy in my voice was obvious. "It's too high though."

"Not too high," Olug stated.

"I can't climb that high up. If I fall, I'll die."

"Then fly."

"I am not a haskeal, Olug."

Olug fell silent for a moment while smoothing the fur on his face with his big fingers.

"May as well," Jamil said. "It'll make things go faster."

"May as well what?"

Jamil's skin was ashen and Olug was still in the beastly form. His appearance was now considerably more wifferin than person. He too had been bitten and was changing.

"Father wifferin. Mother half-wifferin. Mother change from person to wifferin. Cast spell to be person in Maradobu. In Tokahaya, no spell."

"I'm sorry, Olug," I said. "I don't understand what that means though."

"Mother changed. Loved people. Father refused. Banished here but mother already with child. Olug. Mother came to Tokahaya after Olug born. Get father. Left Olug with family. Never returned. Olug will save mother."

I grabbed Olug's hand. "I'm so sorry, Olug. I'll help you find your mother. We all will."

"First your magic, Lafia, so we can go get my cure."

"Magic in tree?" Olug asked.

"Ya'i. And still way too high and I still cannot fly."

Olug roared softly and shook himself from his head to his back, revealing a long furry tail. He had long since taken the coat off and now pulled the stretchy shirt off his back, revealing two wings, each as long as the length of his body. Nontu and I both stepped back, my jaw slack.

"You have wings, Olug? You can fly!" I was in awe.

"Get on," Olug said.

"Wait. Where'd it go? It was up there. It was bright."

"How'd you find it before?" Jamil asked. "There are so many."

"I focused and I hummed." I nodded as I began humming again to tune into my light cube.

"Show me. Guide me."

I kept humming quietly, careful not to put us at risk by singing.

The light cube glowed brighter. "There," I whispered excitedly.

Olug leaned down and I climbed awkwardly onto his back, doing my best to avoid his massive wings while wrapping my arms around him. He began flapping the large wings and tried to take off, stumbling several times.

"You can do it, Olug." I stroked the soft fur that reminded me of Saren.

He flapped his wings again, this time, leaving the ground. He bumped the tree, causing branches to shake. I held on tighter, pressing down my fear of the distance growing between us and the ground. There was a giant roar. "You can't roar, Olug, they'll hear."

"Didn't roar," he said back.

"That means there's a wifferin nearby. Hurry. Get me to my magic." This time I didn't try to stay quiet.

Olug's horns leaned in as he rose higher, navigating the branches, and only snagging them a few times as we neared my cube.

"Grab cube," Olug said as we heard a swoosh nearby.

"I can't reach it. Get closer." If I stretched too far, I'd fall and the lightheadedness I was feeling didn't help, especially with only his fur to hold to.

Olug flew around the tree trying to get closer. Instead he collided in the air with something. A wifferin. I screamed as I was flung from Olug's back. I reached towards my magic light cube and stretched as much as I could. Knocking it with my fingers it was free from the tree and careening with me towards the ground.

Olug slammed into the wifferin again as it tried to knock the falling ball and me with its tail. I grabbed onto a branch before crashing into it. The ball kept falling and then it was nearly gone, dim like the others but on the ground.

"Ni!!!!" I cried out and tried climbing down from the branches as Olug battled the wifferin around the tree. I swung my body to get out of the way of Olug and the other wifferin and missed the next branch.

"Help!" I screamed, panicking.

"Ra-ge kada a—"

I stopped, trying to calm my panic and grab hold of another branch, narrowly missing.

"Ra-ge faduka cuta!"

Still wrong. Calm down, Lafia. The ground was getting closer.

Something came under me. Olug. I grabbed his fur as he dove towards the ground and twisted, letting me tumble off. I stopped rolling inches from Jamil. He'd been reaching for the light cube and though his ashen skin blended into the darkness, he held it safely. I reached for it, and it lit back up.

"You saved it," I whispered and took it into my hand.

"What are you going to do with it?" Jamil asked, from where he laid.

"I'm going to get it in me, somehow. But right now Olug needs help, and we have to get you a cure." I stood up and took Clarod out.

"He has Wyrden. Look, he's winning."

Jamil was right. Olug had wrestled the wifferin and held it against the tree, Wyrden drawn. He pulled it back fiercely, roared angrily and then stopped. He flew back a few feet and stared at the other wifferin. Had he wielded Wyrden, and we not even seen?

He moved back to the wifferin and said something that I couldn't hear. Then they hugged. I sought some answer from Jamil and Nontu for why he'd gone from ready to expire the wifferin to hugging it.

Together they came down to the base of the tree where I held Clarod, ready.

"Mother, here," Olug said refusing to let go of the wifferin's hand.

"This is your mother, Olug?" I was shocked.

He nodded. "Found Mother."

The wifferin growled lightly. "Olug here."

"Found Mother," Olug said again gently, and with an underlying warmth that was truly Olug, but so much deeper than I'd seen.

"Found Olug," his mother repeated, hugging him again tightly, even their long tails curled around each other.

"I'm so happy for you, Olug. You found her. You can get her out of here."

"Can't go. Nashwa must stay," Olug's mother said, the sound of fear heavy. "Stay always," she whimpered.

"Are you Nashwa?"

"Nashwa." She pointed at herself.

"Ni," I said emphatically. "We are getting out of here and you're coming with us, right Olug?"

"Ya'i. Save Jamil. Nashwa and Olug go home." Olug's tail swished anxiously.

"I need to get my magic in me. Then I can be of more help."

I held the light cube and tried to open it but couldn't find a way into it. I tried squeezing it between my palms and into my hands. I held the cube up and turned it around, shaking my head in disbelief. Then, I tried pressing the light into my stomach and finally my chest.

"Why isn't it going in?" Jamil asked. His voice was labored and barely audible.

"I don't know. How do I get this in me, Nontu?" I asked in frustration.

"I am inexperienced with this. It likely must be opened first."

"I don't know how. I can't find any latch or lock."

"I am certain if this is your box, you will get into it. However, like anything else, you and your magic must be one."

I huffed and held the light cube out once more. I closed my eyes, trying to let it soak inside. "Nothing! We don't have time for your broken magic now, Lafia," I yelled aloud.

Nashwa's eyes darted fearfully. Jamil lay with his head resting on his bag, watching me struggle.

"No time," Olug said and knelt beside Jamil.

"I'll figure out how to get this to work, but for now, I'm keeping it safe. We need to get Jamil help." I wrapped the cube inside a spare shirt and tucked it deep inside the bag.

"What's wrong?" Nashwa asked.

"He's been bitten by an eper. He doesn't have much time," I answered.

"Eper. Not good." There was a heaviness in Nashwa's voice.

"Nontu said someone here has the remedy. Do you know where we can find them?" I begged.

"She saves. She takes." Nashwa shook her head sorrowfully.

"Who is she? Wait!" A passage from the journal came to mind. "I thought it was the abada of the Tokahaya. Is the Tokahaya a being?"

"This place," Nashwa said and waved her large paw around her.

"It is this place. Everything else we have come through has only been how we arrive. To this part of the Tokahaya," Nontu clarified.

"Who is she then and how do we find her?" I queried.

"Finds you."

"She rules this place. She is likely near, watching. Listening," Nontu whispered.

Nontu had hardly finished her words when a shimmery smoke appeared several yards ahead and began to take shape. The sound of thunder clapped repeatedly around us and streaks of lightning shot across the sky.

Nashwa vanished as the wifferin outside had, leaving Olug turning in circles, looking for her.

"Ni! Mother gone. Again," he whimpered. He searched the shadows unconcerned with what enraptured the rest of us.

The figure of a beautiful woman formed. Her bright silver eyes matched her flowy shimmering gown, her ornately decorated hair, and spiked crown. All were in sharp contrast to her bronze skin. She floated towards us, remaining several feet above the ground.

The woman studied each of us scrupulously, in turn, as we stood motionless under her gaze.

"You look dis eased." She spoke at a leisurely pace in a higher pitch than I'd expected. Her hands moved dramatically as she aimed one long silver nail at Jamil. They reminded me of Ajur Bellrin's, only these were even longer and ended in a deadly tip.

"He...he...he is unwell. He's been bitten by an eper and doesn't have much time," I said after a painful struggle.

"Bitten? So he'll be an eper or dead soon? If nothing is done about it."

"Can you help him?"

"I can," she said, circling us from above.

"Thank you. He's turning and it's bad."

"I said I can. I did not say that I will."

"Will you please help him?" I begged as Jamil dropped to his knees.

"Is he why you've come here?"

"We need to save him."

"Help Jamil," Olug said, sounding timid. His eyes hadn't stopped searching for Nashwa.

She laughed as she examined him again. "It speaks. It's a half-wif or something." She laughed again this time loudly from her stomach.

Olug was becoming more and more upset. A low growl escaped his throat.

"I don't care for wifferin. Much too simple-minded and they can't be trusted around our residents. Which is why all the males are kept out there, guarding. Speaking of which, how did you manage to survive their appetite? Never mind. It's unimportant. You are here now but if any harm came to them, I'm holding you accountable," she smiled and floated down to look him in his eyes. "Do not test me, half-wif. Beasts that growl get put down. And their friends receive none of my assistance. Remember that."

Olug's wide nostrils flared open over and over as she stared at him until he gave in, and cast his eyes elsewhere.

"Very well. And you?" She came to me, resuming her higher floating position. "Who are you and who is he to you?" Her silver eyes brightened, glowing through the darkness.

My mouth lost the little moisture it had left as it went into my palms, despite the cool air.

"Do you not speak? Or did you give your voice to this half-wif? That would be a waste. You look...promising."

I tried to swallow and open my mouth. I'd spoken before. Speak, Lafia! I tried to will my mouth open while it seemed something else was keeping it shut.

"I said SPEAK!" Her voice cackled like quiet thunder. The fearful shrieks and cries began again.

"Lafia of Narut I love him." The words fell from my lips in one breath. I avoided glancing where Jamil lay on the ground. His look of shock was obvious even from the corner of my eye.

"That wasn't so hard, now was it? Narut." She almost spat the word Narut from her mouth. "Ahhh. And I suppose you don't want him to die then or be a freak eper, do you?"

I shook my head trying to ignore the sounds coming through the darkness.

"Do you?" she yelled.

"Ni." My voice held the same chill as the air around us.

"Do you love her?" The shimmering woman floated down and held Jamil's face in her hand so she could look in his dull eyes.

Jamil nodded slowly.

"Speak when spoken to!" she yelled at him.

"Ya'i."

"Ya'i what? She professes her love for you, and you have no words?"

"Ya'i. I love her too." He was barely able to get the words out.

She giggled and then shook her head with pity. "He doesn't have much time. You should've gotten him help before the situation became desperate."

The shimmery woman turned sharply back towards Nontu. Behind her, two figures appeared, one in a gown of dark silver and other in shimmering gray.

"And you? Who are you?"

"I am Nontu."

"Nontu? You are...what are you?" the woman asked curiously, circling close to her.

"I am a venna." Nontu paused and looked at me. "I am a syte for Narut."

The beautiful woman's eyes glowed an even brighter silver. "A venna and a Narutian syte," she spat. She glared at Nontu before moving closer and narrowing her eyes to study Nontu's. Nontu lowered her head. The woman smirked and moved in front of us.

"There is something someone is not saying. You want something daughter of Narut. Not just his remedy. What is it?"

I watched her glide back and forth. "May I ask you something?" I stammered.

She rushed towards me with fury. "I'm asking the questions!"

"My apologies. Sincerest apologies. I only wished to know how to address you."

"Oh," she said, her tone softening. "I am the Tokaya Ru. Tokaya Ru Farsona and it is I who rules these lands now. And if you aren't careful, I'll have three new subjects." She cast a side glance at Olug, "and one new guard."

"Please can you help, will you help him?"

"You think you're smart, don't you? Distraction will not work. I asked you a question, daughter of Narut. What is it you want here?"

"I want him well because I love him."

"What do you think, my lovelies?" Tokaya Ru Farsona asked the women who'd gathered behind her.

"She loves him," they echoed.

"You love him, and?" Farsona prodded.

"And and…one day I wish to be a clarhugaba."

"Now that you know my title, feel free to use it."

"I wish to be a clarhugaba, Tokaya Ru."

"What is that? Some kind of leader of the light? You want to be his leader? Do you think he's looking for someone to lead him? Oh poor girl, you know nothing of men," she cackled.

Farsona turned to Jamil. "Is that what you want, you feeble thing? To be led?" She waved her hand at him as if speaking to him was a waste of her time. "I created all of this! All of it. It was a wasteland."

It still appeared to be a wasteland.

"I'm in control of my destiny now. Everyone here respects me," she smiled. "Clarhugaba. When did this happen?"

"After the first sacrifice," Nontu answered. "Will you please help him? He's going to die."

"He won't die right away. Time is different here. Tell me, how long has it been in your time since that first sacrifice?"

"The next full lavender moon will be one hundred years," Nontu answered quietly.

Behind Farsona the darkness showed little silver lights. Figures began to form. More beautiful women.

"You know your history then? Daughter of Narut? You know how this place came to be?"

"Ni. Only that there was a battle, and the sacrifice means peace."

"Everything requires some type of sacrifice. I remember the first one and each one since. It's almost time for the next," she said to the women behind her.

She extended her hand and motioned into a circle creating a smoky portal. Silvery tendrils extended from her fingertips and reached inside, pulling Nashwa through. Olug's mother didn't struggle or make a sound.

"Nashwa? You would sacrifice your own freedom for someone you care about, wouldn't you?"

Nashwa whimpered before nodding in agreement. She avoided Farsona's eyes. "Oh so much is happening right now," Farsona sighed dramatically. When no one said anything, she threw one hand up and yelled, "Is no one going to ask what I mean?"

Olug started to open his mouth and she pinched her fingers forcing it back shut. "Anyone else?" The floating women laughed in chorus.

"What do you mean?" I asked nervously.

"Well it is convenient that I have a daughter of Narut in my home when it's so close to the next sacrifice. I can probably trade her and get even more than I'd expected."

"And a son of Sparaka," Jamil whispered.

"The near dead speaks willingly! But you failed to address me properly."

"A son of Sparaka, Tokaya Ru Farsona," Jamil gasped.

"Please let Nashwa go, Tokaya Ru Farsona," Olug said, struggling to contain his anger and frustration.

"The beast speaks again. Even the half-wif knows to address me properly. Can the rest of you learn so quickly?"

"Don't hurt Olug, Tokaya Ru Farsona," Nashwa pleaded.

"Nashwa, you know well enough I do not enjoy begging from my subjects. What I say goes. I don't need two of you. I don't want two of you. You already told me you understand my position. You do understand, don't you? And besides he'd be outside."

She nodded slowly, her eyes never leaving Olug.

"Good. You have the opportunity to serve your queen by helping me demonstrate to these guests that I mean what I say from here on out. I promised you I'd spare his life. What do you think that should cost?" Farsona turned to Nashwa and ran one long nail against her fur before flicking the loose hairs from her fingers.

"Nashwa loves Olug," Olug said.

"Nashwa loves you," Farsona said mockingly. "You can thank her for your life."

One of the strands that extended from Farsona's fingers straightened and hardened, ending in a sharp point.

"Make sure you're paying attention, half-wif," she said to Olug. "This reminds me of what I did to another wif, to spare your mother. That was a disgusting full-blooded wif. I could barely stand the sight of him."

Olug entire body heaved up and down with his breath, but he didn't speak. His mouth was encased in webbing, but his eyes were as wide as the rocks beneath our feet.

"You should be grateful you got to see your son again, Nashwa. Take a look at that face. All animal now. Your magic to transform still doesn't work here. Your true nature is revealed. You're an animal."

Olug's eyes were wet. I searched for something, anything that might help.

Jamil tapped my knee and pointed to Farsona then touched his neck. I followed his eyes.

She cackled loudly, her eyes turned completely silver and the razor-sharp nail was as long as Clarod. She swung it across Nashwa's neck, slicing through the fur. Nashwa's eyes filled with terror as she held her neck with one hand and reached towards Olug with the other. He struggled to reach back but before he could a portal opened, and her fading essence was pulled through. The portal closed and Nashwa disappeared.

Olug collapsed, his cries muffled by the webbing over his mouth. I ran to him to help him get free of the binds.

"Don't think about moving or helping that half-wif get free, lest you meet a similar fate," Farsona threatened. "Lest I visit my wrath immediately upon your homes rather than give this little warning I've given."

Olug writhed on the ground as I knelt beside him, feeling every bit of his pain.

"I see he is going to be a distraction." Farsona sighed and pointed to one of her sagals. "Take him to the haison. I don't need him interfering here."

The sagal opened a portal and drew Olug towards it as if he were the size of a small child. As she tossed him into the darkness, Farsona threw a bolt of lightning at him, causing his entire body to illuminate. Within the portal was again cloaked in an impenetrable darkness before it was nothing more than wisps of shimmers in the darkness.

Tapping my chest I tried to force myself to breathe, to keep my heart from beating itself out of my chest. She was going to let Jamil die. I patted my pocket and rocked back and forth on my heels, trying to calm myself. Finally I was able to suck in a cool breath of air through my nose, holding it and letting it become warm from the inside. The hole that had consumed Olug had completely vanished. I let the warm air out through my mouth and watched it cloud in front of me. And then did it again. My eyes finally began to focus, narrowing in on her.

"Alright then. I hope we have an understanding." Farsona smiled sweetly and touched her chest. "Remember this is my world and I hold the power. I also hold power over your world. Do not cross me."

There was something under her dress. That's what Jamil had been pointing at.

"My lovelies, we have a son of Sparaka." She came down to Jamil's level. This time she noticed the bandage around his head. She ripped it off causing him to spin hard and fall from where he kneeled. She pulled it straight before snapping it hard like a whip. "This is a Narutian royal sash! You really are a royal syte. That means I can hold you here until they make good," she told Nontu. "I will have my sacrifice!" Her scream prickled through my entire body like hundreds of tiny pins.

From her long silver nails extended glowing silk threads that wound Nontu from her waist to her chest. Nontu broke the first set of threads and began pointing her own long nails at Farsona before Farsona's team of sagals surrounded her, extending their own threads and wrapping her up like a bug in a web. Farsona lifted Nontu and examined her carefully.

"I don't want to lose this one. Put her somewhere...comfortable," she smirked.

My chest began to heave again. "Ni! Don't! Don't hurt her. Please, Tokaya Ru." I took a step towards Farsona and dropped to my knees. "It's mine. The sash is mine."

"Yours? You are a foolish girl. Delivering yourself up for sacrifice and trying to save this boy you claim to love. Don't be stupid. They don't ever love like we love. Ever! You're better off letting the poison take him and save you the misery. And besides, I don't care for liars."

"I'm not lying. I am a royal daughter of Narut. I must know; will you heal him, Tokaya Ru Farsona?"

"I don't like the way you said that! A daughter of Narut?" she laughed condescendingly. "Am I to believe this is what passes for royalty now?"

The other sagals laughed with Farsona before she raised a hand and silenced them.

"Will you heal him? Ya'i or Ni!? If you will, you can...you can have..." I paused. "I will make sure you have a suitable sacrifice."

"You are nothing to be making promises! Do you think me a fool?!" she cackled thunderously.

"I think you are powerful and wise. I think you are able to heal him and get what you want too." I lowered my eyes, waiting on the response that would either damn him, save him, or be all our ruin.

25

FARSONA

Farsona eclipsed the little light there was as she floated above me, steadily growing. Small strands of silver from her fingers danced towards me, gently caressing my cheeks.

"Tell me, daughter of Narut, who is your father?"

"He is Addeyam Ketonga, Tokaya Ru Farsona."

"Ajur Addeyam Ketonga is your father?"

"Ya'i."

"My messenger was with him recently. He owes me. Maradobu owes me."

"Why must you take a sacrifice? It's been a century of ruining lives. Isn't it time to end this?"

"We must end it," Jamil whispered.

"There is no end!" she boomed. Her body swelled with anger. "There will never be an end until!" Farsona stopped. She was at least two times the size she'd been, and her voice rolled like thunder as the sky lit around her. Even her collection of sagals shrunk back in fear.

"I don't understand why," I said softly.

"What did you say?"

"I don't understand why!"

"It isn't for you to understand, you obstinate child. You dare to come into my dimension, into my world, and question my rule!?"

"It impacts my dimension," I shot back, my hands feeling steady, even without the stone. "Your dimension creeps into Maradobu, like a festering disease without a cure, destroying lives and what we could be."

"I take nothing that has not been given. You know nothing!"

"The storms have already come to parts of Narut and even into northern Emervy and Wallarin."

"Surely, you aren't afraid of water. As I've heard, it is something you need. Consider it a favor."

"We need clean water."

"What do you want, girl? Save this boy? Save Maradobu? Clean water?" She was now back to the size she'd been when she'd first appeared and stood a finger's length from me. "Or is it something else? I do detest liars, cheats, and thieves."

Chalk had replaced the moisture in my mouth and I coughed uncomfortably, trying to clear it and speak.

"You don't know what you want and when you don't know what you want you will chase everything."

I pulled out the pendulum and held it in front of me, asking the question I'd been asking since Sparaka. Show me my heart's deepest desire.

"Hahahahaha! You need that to tell you what you want?"

"Help me, please," Jamil gasped.

"If he turns, can it be reversed?"

"With the right tools and the right level of magic, it is possible. But you should know that."

"I've never seen it before. We didn't know it was possible until he was bitten."

"That is incorrect. Perhaps you didn't know. I'd imagine this decrepit thing there didn't know. I might give that half-wif the benefit of doubt that he didn't know." She turned to Jamil, then me, and finally her silver eyes fell on Nontu. "But you, you knew, didn't you!"

Nontu trembled, horrified. The sagals held the strands firmly even as Nontu tried to cower, forcing her to remain standing.

"I also don't like to wait for my debts to be paid. I've waited longer than promised, but you delivered before the next sacrifice, if only barely. You nearly failed to secure your freedom and hers."

"What is she talking about, Nontu?"

"Nontu? Did you fail to mention our arrangement? I wasn't sure you'd fulfilled it, but I see her father in her and his father and his father." She said father with a scowl filled with history.

"Nontu?! What's going on?"

"I am sorry, Lafia. I did not wish for any harm to come to you. I had hoped you would be more ready. I thought your magic would work. I am—"

"Enough! Don't apologize for something you've been planning for years because she looks at you that way. You promised me a royal daughter of Narut and I have been waiting five years."

"But the sacrifice isn't due!" I yelled.

"This isn't about a sacrifice. This is about me saving her life in exchange for delivering me a bride for my son. You said there was a daughter in Narut but you failed to deliver her before now. She stays as his bride and your debt is paid."

"Ni. Please. There must be something else," Nontu said, awkwardly wobbling towards Farsona.

Farsona's glare sharpened at Nontu. "You were spared from the fate he will suffer and now you want to go back on your word! A soul for a soul. That's the deal! What kind of syte and venna are you?"

"This whole time? You've been planning a way to get me here all this time?" There was a stabbing pain in my chest and my cheeks burned.

"This is bad," Jamil gasped.

I felt the first tear escape through my lashes and then my entire face was wet.

"Don't cry. From what I hear, there's not much for you to miss over there anyway and my son requires a bride and only a royal daughter of Maradobu is acceptable. It's a perfect match."

"I'm not staying in this wasteland where even the light of the dark moon refuses to shine."

"Do not insult your home. You will stay because it's the deal and because you took something from me."

I stopped breathing and pulled the bag tighter on my back."

"I took back what was mine. You stole it from me. You've stolen from many people!"

"Not I. I stole nothing. It was a gift for my tree of magic and power."

"You siphoned magic!" I yelled back.

"I did no such thing."

"That tree is filled with light cubes, and I hear the cries of the people you took too. You can't deny it."

"My hands are clean," she smiled.

"If you didn't steal it then...," my words fell as I turned towards Nontu. "You stole my magic? You trapped it here. You are the reason I started on this journey. You didn't stop those epers and I believe now you could have but you wanted to make sure I came all the way here. That I had enough reasons to come to the gray dimension, the Tokahaya," I said in disbelief. "How could you? Why, Nontu?"

"I was going to die and the baby inside me too. I did what I had to do for us to survive."

"And where is this baby then!"

"My child is here. You stay and she comes with me."

"Perfect," Farsona beamed. "You stay, your soul for Nontu's soul."

"What about him?"

"I'll heal this dying thing in exchange for a soul," Farsona kicked Jamil as he lay on the ground, as if testing the life in him.

Jamil moaned as he tried to prop himself up on his one good arm.

"How long?" I asked angrily.

"Once I give him the treatment he will be healed within moments."

"Ni. How long would I have to stay?"

"You certainly don't seem as bright as Nontu made you daughters out to be. Marriage is supposed to be for life, even if the Maradobuan forefathers didn't honor the institution."

"Life? Til I die?"

"And you'll live a long life here. Just look at me. I don't look a day past forty."

"I won't do it and I won't trade anyone else's soul either," I spat towards Nontu.

"Then he dies." Farsona waved an uncaring hand at Jamil and then instructed the sagal in shimmering gray, saying, "Jantasa, bring out the child."

Nontu stood near the sagals behind Farsona. They'd set her down, one standing close, but the strands no longer binding her. Her eyes opened wide as Janta floated about and began swirling smoke that turned to shimmering silver. A portal opened and on the other side appeared to be daylight and a young girl. Nontu dropped to her knees in tears.

Jantasa took the child's hand and helped her through the opening.

"Catia!" Nontu cried as she ran to her. "Catia! I told you I was coming to bring you home."

The little girl was the image of Nontu, only her ears weren't grown in yet and she only had a few spots. My mouth fell open as I realized it was the same child I'd been dreaming of. The one Nontu would hear of when she asked of my dreams. What was the song?

"You're sentencing me to death for your child, Nontu?"

"I certainly hope you won't always be this dramatic, Lafia. Seriously. Death? We are very much alive. Little Catia is very much alive. He," she said, waving dismissively at Jamil, "is not. I might say his breaths are numbered. And if you decide to try and go, you'll find getting out is even harder than getting in and you won't be leaving with what you've taken from me. However, if you stay, I'll let you keep it."

"You'll let him die anyway. If I stay, I can't bring you a soul and he dies without a soul."

"Not so dense after all," Farsona said thoughtfully.

I considered the light cube in my bag and then what Nontu had done to stop the other attackers. What I'd done at the transport station. We no longer had the haskeal deanimation dust. I still had Clarod and the possibility that I could repeat the spell from the station and slow things again, even if I couldn't stop them.

"Could she have healed him?" I pointed to Nontu angrily.

"Ni. The only treatment and magic is here, through me and the power I wield. His time is short and still you don't know what you want or what you need."

"I do know!"

"Then act like it! These are your choices, daughter of Narut! Listen well. Stay willingly and little Catia goes home, and you keep that light cube you stole. Or, you decide to leave and you either take an eper or a corpse with you and leave your magic behind. That little girl stays here forever as does Nontu. I require her soul or another's. And let's face it, that little girl didn't ask for any of this. What will it be? Don't forget if you decide to leave, you'll have to survive getting out on your own."

"Why? Why make me stay here?"

"Your duty will be to marry my son. He deserves a royal wife."

This couldn't be. "What about the next sacrifice? What is happening with my sister?"

"Who told you something was happening?" she snapped.

"I overheard my father speaking to someone."

"It is due. It always comes due. It is the way it is. A royal sacrifice so that Maradobu can have its peace."

"It's my sister! You can't kill her."

"Why not? Others have sacrificed loved ones to the Tokahaya to save Maradobu from what lies in store if they refuse."

"What happens if they refuse?" I asked, concerned.

"Suffice it to say, I can take out nations!"

"Please, don't kill my sister."

368

"Focus! There is right now! You ask for so much and give so little. My options are available to you. You can stay and be my son's bride. You'll have the chance to ascend to queen, one day. A day far far far away from now, of course."

"This is an insane request. You can't do this!"

"But I can. I am being very reasonable."

"Who agreed to this sacrifice?"

"The ones who needed to. They are wiser than your royal forefathers of Maradobu. Those who agreed know what will come of Maradobu if a sacrifice is not provided, starting with Narut. What is it they say? You sacrifice one to save many?" Her hands waved in the air dramatically.

"Don't take my sister. There must be something else."

Farsona circled me and Jamil. "There might be something else you can do for me. I long not only for a bride for my son, but that we have a royal child."

"And you'd save Jamil and not take my sister?"

"You'd save Jamil or your sister by being his bride and bringing forth a royal child."

I sank to my knees, tears again streaming down my cheeks. The bag fell from my back and the light cube made a gentle thud. I brought the bag around slowly. This was impossible.

"Can you do this?" she asked, expecting my response.

Nontu cleared her throat. "Tokaya Ru Farsona, please help him."

Farsona smirked mockingly, "You do not wish to ask for anything. Remember my costs are high."

Nontu wrapped her arms around Catia even tighter.

"May we leave now?" Nontu asked shakily.

369

"Absolutely...not. You are leverage. She may come to her senses about him but leave a poor innocent child and her beloved Nontu? Unlikely."

Nontu bristled and lowered her gaze again, focusing on the top of Catia's head.

"You wouldn't hurt them," I said, questioningly.

"She's not my child. And she was a bit of a rotten brat. Always complaining about not seeing her mother and whining about not having friends even though the sagals played with her, spent plenty of time with her. I couldn't have her all about the land. Annoying. I'm glad to be rid of her, either way."

"Any other child will be the same," I said. I finally held it, the light cube, at my feet. I slid it behind me and willed it to work.

"What are you doing? Were you trying to distract me again?"

"Nothing." Please go inside me.

"Is that my light cube? The one you've stolen?" Farsona appeared in front of me instantaneously.

I shoved it in my jacket, the glowing light peeking out of the arms and neck.

"Liar! You don't even know how to use it. Hand it over!"

"Ni!"

I clamored to Jamil but before I could get my arms around his neck, the sagals had him lifted above my head and bound in their silver strands. They set him down yards away where he writhed on the ground, a silky cocoon, only his nose free.

Farsona lifted her hand towards him and he slid back even further. "He doesn't need to be a part of this conversation and he certainly doesn't need your help. You are completely helpless for what he needs."

"Please, Tokaya Ru Farsona."

"Take the dying thing to the well, Kesi."

"Jamil. I'm going to save you. I promise!"

"As you wish, Tokaya Ru," a tall full-figured sagal sang.

"Hold onto Catia in case Nontu decides she wants to make use of her magic."

Jantasa shot out silver strands and lifted the girl to her.

"Where are we going?" Catia said.

"You can't travel hungry, dear. Let's eat something and then when your mother is ready, you can go," said the sagal with black and silver hair that twisted around her head.

"Please, please do not take her," Nontu pleaded. "I did everything you asked."

"You delivered a royal daughter of Narut, but she must choose to stay. That or the deal is off, permanently."

Nontu watched Catia vanish through the portal, her spots glowing brightly along with her eyes..

"You will not make me lose her again!" Nontu charged at me, her teeth bared and with a power I didn't know she had.

I hit the ground hard and immediately felt for the light cube. Nontu drew her hand back and the spots on her face glowed even brighter. Her fist came fast, meeting my jaw with a force that shook me. I rolled over and pulled the light cube from inside my jacket where the metal poked my ribs.

"Don't do this, Nontu."

"I will not go back without her. Not for a princess who cannot even do mundane magic. What good is your magic and these dreams of being a clarhugaba when your magic is flawed at the most basic level!" She swung at me again, this time missing, but only barely.

I pulled out Clarod. "Stay back, you liar. My magic would've been fine, but it was you that left me with just enough to give me hope but not enough to be useful."

"Your magic is useless if you have not figured it out yet!" Nontu declared venomously. She patted her pockets and then pulled out the Sparakan pin. She ripped off the metal clip on the back.

"Within my hand
this clip expands
let it grow
into a blade
to give death
so that it saves."

The clip grew, straightening as it did, and the curled part became a rounded handle. I'd never seen Nontu do anything like that. I ducked and the blade grazed my hair. A single twist fell at my feet. Clarod hit the sword hard, but it was strong, as Nontu was. I danced with her, our blades leaning forward and back and from one side to the other.

"I will kill you to save my daughter," Nontu said calmly as she swung her makeshift sword, slashing my jacket and drawing blood.

My eyes widened at the sight of blood on my fingertips. I gripped the firm handle of Clarod and spun around Nontu, slashing her in the back. She crashed, yelping, and reaching instinctively for her wound.

"It's not deadly. Just stop!"

Nontu's response was to swing her blade around from where she now crouched down. I jumped back causing her to screech angrily, narrowly missing my calf.

I fell back, stumbling to get my footing before Nontu found hers. I hit my head with my palm, trying to refocus from the song that found this inopportune moment to infiltrate my thoughts. Despite wanting to remember the lyrics, it wasn't the time.

Nontu's eyes were narrow and unblinking as she placed both hands on the rounded handle. She rolled it in her palms and the blade began to shimmer as she limped painfully towards me.

I stepped back, looking for an exit through the shadows that had begun to burn away. Gathering a handful of rocks, I threw them at Nontu before barreling into her with my shoulder, landing it in her chest. She stumbled back and the shimmering blade flew from her hands clanking on the rocks scattered around us.

I pressed my leg on her chest. Clarod rested at her neck. "Don't make me do this, Nontu."

"I will not lose my child again because of you." Every spot glowed brightly, and her eyes were a brilliant amber.

I averted my eyes from her gaze.

"You are indecisive as always. You never trust yourself and that will be the death of you! I will not let it be the death of me or Catia!"

Something was happening. My thoughts were sluggish. My body lethargic. I glared at her.

"Cancel out the spell she's made
restore my mind
restore my strength."

I muttered the cancellation quickly. My mind cleared and my body returned to normal.

"Even now, with all that lies in the balance, you could've given a spell that weakened her, stopped her, killed her. But ni, you want everyone to be happy."

Farsona laughed from her perch in the tree filled with light cubes where she and her sagals had set up a viewing party.

"Your life and your beloved's life. Even your sister's life all hang in the balance and you still can't do what needs to be done. But she would willingly kill you to save her daughter."

My blade pressed into Nontu's neck. A drop of purple blood rested on the point where it met her skin. Any further and I would slice through and the richly colored blood would begin to leak as it had already done on her back. My breath was shallow. Farsona was right. I grabbed another rock and landed it against Nontu's temple, knocking her unconscious.

"The easy way," Farsona said with an air of disappointment. "Take Nontu to haison with the half-wif."

A sagal bound Nontu with silver threads and lifted her into the air before they both went through a portal leading to the same place they'd taken Olug. Jamil was somewhere else. A place called the well. The well.

And find great power from the well.

There was power in the well? Power that was helping Jamil? The rest of the song continued to elude me.

"Bring Jamil back so you can heal him," I demanded.

I held Clarod out towards Farsona. It had been recently infused with the power of the light of the dark moon by sytes so that it could cut through the darkness. It would be enough. If there ever was a darkness, Farsona was it.

"You haven't learned anything yet," Farsona rumbled, lifting me from the ground. "You don't give orders here and I am not satisfied with the arrangement."

I spotted the ground below. My eyes widened and I stiffened, afraid to make any sudden movements. From there, I would certainly not walk out of the Tokahaya. Ni. I would remember the spell, this time. The light cube lay on the ground, dim like those on the tree.

"Please will you—"

"What is it now? Will I?"

"Will you give me some water please?"

"Water!!!" she screamed and tossed me across the open sky.

Suddenly I was catapulting back towards her, her threads around my back and arms. She stopped me in front of her once again larger self and pointed a finger at me.

"Your friends' lives, your life is in the palm of my hand and you ask for water?!"

"The water is undrinkable. I wish for water I can drink. I wish that all of Maradobu might have water that is drinkable."

"So…reasonable," Farsona snarled, bringing me close to her face. "Why water all of a sudden?"

"We have been without it since we left the last real town, Kanir. We couldn't find clean water."

"Ha! Of course you couldn't! You all don't deserve clean water when your hands are so dirty!"

"We only came for help."

"And you, little princess, came for your magic. Don't think me ignorant."

"You're right, Tokaya Ru Farsona. I did come for my magic, but if we don't have water all of Maradobu will suffer and then what use will my magic be?"

"You aren't so stupid after all. And what of your dying thing. The thing you claim to love?"

"I need water to think."

"What is there to think about? You stay and become my daughter in law, an enviable position here, and deliver me a royal child. In exchange I heal your dying thing. Even that little innocent Catia can leave. Those are your choices."

"May I have water please?" I was lightheaded, either from dehydration or from being so high up in the air feeling unsecured. I thought of Saren and Olug.

"You must really be thirsty. Weak beings." Farsona waved her hand around while looking at something that wasn't there. She reached into the blackness of a hole and pulled out an ill-shapen mug. "Here. Do not ask for more."

I quaffed the wetness. The chain Jamil had tried to show me fell into her dress.

"Which option do you choose?"

"I have a proposition."

Farsona threw me down and I screamed dropping the stone mug before quickly reciting the spell that had saved us before.

"Ra-ge faduwa, kada a yi cuta!"

I hit the ground with more force than I'd hoped, landing on my bottom and scrambling to put Clarod back on my belt before Farsona spotted it.

"How dare you think I am still open to negotiate!" Farsona's voice shook the trees.

"I believe it will be amenable to you."

Farsona was growing larger as she'd done before. The shattered mug lay beneath her. She began turning me around in thick silver threads until I was in front of her oversized face.

"I give the options."

In line with her nose was the chain that ended beneath her dress. The bulge of a stone was evident. That must be it. The wedding gift from her late husband and former ruler of the Tokahaya.

"I can marry your son."

The threads loosened, allowing me to breathe more easily.

"You ask for," she dramatically counted on her fingers, "one, two, three, four things! And only offer yourself? That seems rather unfair, doesn't it?."

"This is for you, Tokaya Ru Farsona. Your son wants a royal wife—"

"Correction! He deserves a royal wife!"

"Your son deserves a royal wife, and I am a royal daughter. I do this and there are no more sacrifices."

"Who do you think you are? You cannot satisfy the demand for a royal sacrifice. Do you think I am unaware of the engagement between your sister and that thing's brother? Do not make me out for a fool! Your sister can satisfy the demands for sacrifice and give me the other thing I want. From what I understand, she's the better option anyway."

"What is that?"

"You don't know what you want and you don't listen. A royal child!" she smacked. "The blood line must be enhanced. I'm being gracious, as it is."

If I gave her what she wanted, she would then kill Adamma. I knew it. I searched for an answer. "Heal Jamil, let me have my magic, accept me as the sacrifice instead of my sister, and stop contaminating the water. In exchange I will marry your son and will bear a child."

"I could kill you now and be done with it. The future eper dies, I keep Nontu and Catia, and soon I'll have the regular sacrifice anyway. Your sister. In fact, I could just as easily make your sister my son's bride. And she is a crown royal who already has magic that works as it should," she smirked.

Farsona lost nothing without me and possibly gained more than she would gain with me.

"I don't understand why you want us to suffer. What happened?"

"You don't question my reasons. I don't need this headache. You offer nothing I need more than the trouble you are. But there is a strong magic in you. Here, in the energy of my realm you somehow got past the wifferin and you kept yourself from falling just now."

"So? It sometimes works and usually doesn't."

"You've seen a Maradobuan do these things then?"

I thought about it. I hadn't seen anyone ever do it. It was in the books I studied. "Ni. Not in practice. Not in real life."

"When you are in your element, it works."

"This isn't my element. It is you who has held my magic all this time."

"If the strength and power of your magic has been siphoned and held in that light cube, how powerful could you be here with all of it? Under the care and tutelage of one as powerful as me?"

"Are you powerful on your own or because you've taken everyone else's magic and keep it in that necklace?"

She rested one graceful hand on her chest and grinned.

"We all pull from the same source of light."

"What light? The light of the dark moon doesn't shine here. The lavender moon doesn't even shine here."

"And where does the dark moon get its light?"

The uncertainty I felt by her simple question wasn't something I could hide.

"There's something even bigger, more expansive, not trapped in any object like a moon as you all have limited yourselves to in Maradobu."

"Even the Zhirians speak of the light of the dark moon," I argued.

"There is power there but even they know the dark moon doesn't create its own light. The power isn't from there. How do you think they do what they do and have the magic they have? They understand what you don't. I understand it too. Lafia, you could have all this and more."

"It's a wasteland here!" I screamed, my voice echoing.

My body began to buzz, from the inside as I imagined what I had to do.

"What are you doing?"

"I'm not doing anything."

I held my hand towards her, focusing on the spot between her brows. My lips moved as I silently said the spell, hoping I'd have the chance to get it out properly.

"Mai rai ni jiki gareni."

I immediately followed those words with the spell in the back of the book I studied. One I'd never seen used, like others within those pages.

"Zomini abinda nakeso."

Farsona glared angrily and the threads that had been a loose air support system, tightened, constricting my breath. It was a gradual tightening as her reactions slowed in response to the spell. Wriggling in the strong fibers was useless and the seething of her eyes was only matched by her size. The stone pulled at her neck, lifting under her dress.

"You dare try to take my wedding gift!" Her words roared like a storm blowing past my head.

I'd failed. I'd failed everyone. Even as she squeezed until my breaths were shallow and I feared I'd lose consciousness, her prior words echoed.

There was something beyond the light of the dark moon? That couldn't be, but here I was, in a magical and powerful land where the dark moon did not shine.

Farsona loosened her grip and I gasped. "You were humming something." One large eye peered into my face. My vision went in and out as I struggled for each breath.

She sat me on a high stump still wrapped. Farsona scanned the lands, now that a new day had broken.

"Never do that again. Or you and everything you hold dear will be destroyed." Her voice was calm and even.

She'd returned to her prior size, which was still at least two of me. She would likely kill me anyway. If that was the case, I needed to know what Jamil had risked his life for.

"As powerful as you are, why do you need that?" I pointed to the necklace protruding from around her neck. The one I'd wanted to destroy.

"This realm is built on stones, all of it. The stones are external amplifiers for the power we can access. You know this."

"But why do you need it when you are so powerful?"

Farsona stepped back, her size expanding as she pulled out the oval shaped stone that rested on her heart.

"Nontu said she had a very special daughter of Narut. I always thought she meant the other one, Adamma. But instead she shows up with you. Yet, you don't even know what or who you are. You have no idea of the power you could wield over this world."

"I don't care about ruling here. I only care about Maradobu."

"Is that why you tried to take my stone?"

My lips stayed shut as she came closer, curious.

"How much do they care about you?"

I sought out the distant barren trees.

"Forget all of them. I know how it feels to be cast aside. Unwanted. But here, we are strong together. We rule this dimension and have created something no one else understands. And we protect it fiercely. We protect our own, with everything we have."

"Yet you are cruel and take souls. You torture them."

"We are misunderstood. How many do you know that have come here and come back to tell their story?"

"The Tokahaya is the path to no return."

"Maligned. That's what we are. You should be here. We need a powerful light wielder such as you."

"I am not what you think. I can't have everything I wanted, I know."

"You can have more, daughter of Narut."

"I only ever wanted one thing. To use my magic to serve Maradobu as Clarhugaba."

The song began again, more powerfully, and I pushed it out but not before I heard, shall walk amongst the other side.

"What is it you keep humming?"

I hadn't realized I'd been humming at all.

"I know that song. Where'd you hear it? Who taught it to you?"

I couldn't tell whether she was angry or truly curious. Her bright silver eyes made me uneasy as she tried to capture my attention.

"I don't know. It just comes to me. I didn't know I was humming." Off to the side, near the backpack on the ground was my light cube. It was brighter but I was still the same distance away.

Farsona noticed too. Then she returned, her face close with an unwavering gaze. Her nostrils released air that tickled the fine hairs on my face. I wanted to grab the necklace from around her neck, but Clarod lay below me and Jamil hadn't returned. Olug was somewhere suffering, or worse. I'd failed once and still breathed. She'd already told me what would happen if I tried again.

"You've lied to me. You've tried to cheat me. You've stolen from me, tried to take my necklace, and now I offer you a home, family, power. Stay and marry my son and deliver a royal child and all currently due will be settled."

"You still want me?" I asked in shock.

"Unlike those where you come from, Lafia, I see your potential and I believe in you."

"You want me to give up everything I know and everyone I love, to live here."

"I said that all currently due will be settled. There is nothing more you need to offer."

"All currently due doesn't include the next sacrifice."

Her skin shimmered in anger and frustration. My absence would hardly be missed but I couldn't leave Adamma to be killed. She was the next light of Narut and Sparaka.

"She is important to you, but the sacrifice is due soon. I will make one final offer for I feel you truly belong here, amongst your own kind."

"My kind?"

"Your kind," she said with no further explanation. "Stay now. You do not leave the Tokahaya. You conceive a child. This will be your home, forever."

"Conceive with Parin?"

"Ya'i. It's what must be done to preserve the line."

"What happens if we don't or can't?"

"We will still have a royal child. If you can't, we will take Adamma to fulfill your promise. And if Adamma is unable to fulfill your promise your younger sister is also an option. "

I gasped audibly.

"After what has been done to us, it is the least that can be given."

My heart raced. No one would care very much about my absence, except Adamma. But my sisters were everything that Maradobu needed. I touched my chest and the monedutse stone Adamma had given me. Inside my pockets were the stones I always carried and the smooth stone that had been a gift from Nontu.

If I could save Jamil and save my sisters, it would be the greatest service I could ever give to Maradobu. I would be the sacrifice.

"And future sacrifices?"

"That will depend on your upholding of your end of the agreement and the kind of daughter in law you are."

"Then can you get Olug and Jamil? You need to heal him."

"Do not speak of that half-wif!" she barked before calming again. "Now, before we do anything, I need to know we have an agreement. Let me see your hand."

I held out my hand, palm side up. She scanned it and then touched the necklace on my neck.

"Hmmm. I will also take this, daughter of Narut." Farsona fingered the Narut ajurdom ring I wore. "It will be a reminder of your promise."

"But I never take this off."

"You've also never been to the Tokahaya and made a deal with the Tokaya Ru. This will be the first of many firsts for you."

I wiggled the ring off my finger and handed it to Farsona who slid several strands of hair through the center and tied it on. Together we slowly drifted to the ground where my feet felt the hard dirt and I sighed with relief.

"There. Now keep your hand out for this deal is one sealed with blood."

I squeezed my hand closed.

"Open up if you want to save the people you claim to love."

My hand unclenched, revealing the fleshy center.

"Do you promise to remain in the Tokahaya as spouse to Parin and produce an heir for our dimension in return for healing your friend, fixing the water in Maradobu, and letting you have your magic light cube?"

As Farsona spoke a scroll materialized and what she said appeared written there for me to read.

"I have not met your son. What is Parin like?"

"He is a good man. Born at the edges of Maradobu and raised here. Royal blood runs through his veins."

I wiped the sweat collecting at my hairline. "And what of my sisters, Adamma and Naeemah?"

"Alright. Alright. And that upon producing a child, your sisters will be released from the threat of sacrifice and replacing you as my son's wife. Now, that's four things you are receiving."

"I thought only untouched royal women could be sacrifices?"

"Who told you that foolishness? I wasn't untouched when I arrived here and my late love and the prior Tokaya Ru found me to be most desirable. Certainly some man must have begun that rumor."

"I understand. As long as I stay and produce an heir, Adamma is safe? Naeemah is safe?"

"Ya'i. And I give you everything else you've asked for. Lafia, you belong here. This is where your power lies."

I stared in disbelief at the words inscribed on the scroll. She read the agreement aloud that had been outlined moments before."

"Why do you want me, Tokaya Ru Farsona? That you'd give me all this?"

"You are the one the seers speak of. We have waited for you."

"The seers are wrong about whatever they think they saw. You need to know that I have failed over and over and I'm not a leader."

"Perhaps not there, but you will see what you can be, here. I don't believe it's a coincidence you've chosen to journey here."

"Tokaya Ru Farsona. What happens if I can't do this?" My stomach knotted as I negotiated the terms of everyone else's freedom, in exchange for my own lifelong captivity and marriage to someone that could be worse than her.

"Are you already planning to break your promise?"

"Ni. I just need to know."

"It's quite simple. Failure to remain, means I visit my wrath on Maradobu and the sacrifices resume. Failure to deliver an heir and we take Adamma. If she fails, then Naeemah. It is quite fair. Another thing, you may not speak of this agreement to anyone or that will be seen as a breach. A breach means I will collect damages in the form of destroying you and everything you know and love. Is that clear?"

The terms inserted before the signature lines.

"Ya'i."

"Do you agree to the terms of this agreement?"

"Ya'i. I agree."

Farsona took one sharp nail and cut into my palm, drawing fresh blood and a wince from my lips. A silver pen with a well appeared in her hand.

"Take this pen, dip it, and sign."

I did as she instructed and then watched Farsona's signature appear on the other line.

"Will you heal Jamil now, please?"

"Jamil, yes. He should be just about ready for you."

"And Olug?"

"He wasn't a part of the agreement."

"What will become of him?"

"Do you want me to heal your Jamil or are you more interested in the beast?"

"I just wanted to know he's okay."

"I do not answer to you. You will do well to remember that."

My blood marked the scroll as it rolled up, and a silver string tied it. My full name, Lafia Rinal Saleera Ketonga, was inscribed on the outside before it was lifted onto a gray leafless tree filled with rolled scrolls like mine. In the darker light the scrolls hung like flowers or blooms. Now in the early light of day, I could see them clearly for what they were.

"What about Nontu and Catia?"

"You concern yourself with the wrong things. She betrayed you."

"Will they be alright?"

"Of course. Nontu kept her promise and delivered a soul." Farsona's smile was cool and calculated.

A portal opened beside Farsona and Duluri, the tall full-figured sagal, came out carrying Jamil. He was still bound in the threads, his body gray and small. His closed eyes were covered in webbing.

"You promised!" I sobbed and touched his loose clothing.

"Back up and give me space. And stop crying. It's not too late. He's already gotten healing waters from my special well and now he just needs me. This is why no one else can do this.," she said arrogantly. "At least not yet."

She raised one hand above her, curving each finger particularly and then placed it on top of his head. The other hand she placed on her heart, over the stone.

The stone. Once he was healed, I would destroy the necklace. Then everything would return to the way it should be. The contract would be unenforceable, and I would destroy all the darkness here that had stolen our royals and others. The voices and cries had been a background chorus through this entire ordeal. Invisible to the eye, but in pocket dimensions.

Clarod would first cut through the stone and then the rest of the darkness.

I had seen many healed this way but nothing as severe as Jamil. I considered something Nontu had told me before shuddering at her betrayal. The power was only one power, how it was used was the difference. Nontu had made me think she'd been helping me and that I had simply been struggling, while all the while she'd been keeping my power away from me. My magic still lay in that light cube.

"Is it working?" I asked.

"It is. My magic works and quickly. You will see." She clapped her hands and waved them over his body slowly from the top of his head and past his feet.

Farsona was right. Jamil's body stretched and the color returned. His features were restored as the webbing fell from his eyes. I dropped to his side, wiping wayward tears away as I hugged him.

"I plan to learn," I whispered.

Jamil moaned in pain under my weight and struggled to sit upright.

"Don't try to get up. Your body is still adjusting," I said.

"Did I die?"

"You turned, but now you're back."

"Where's Olug?"

"He is no longer of your concern," Farsona said coldly.

"Olug?" Jamil cried out and tried to stand, only to stumble back to the ground.

A glimpse of the tree of agreements was a sober reminder of what had to be done.

I smiled and nodded. "You're going to be okay, Jamil. You need to get out of here."

"I can't leave Olug."

"We don't have a choice, right now."

"I'm not leaving him," Jamil said, pushing away from me.

"Would you like to join him?" Farsona asked threateningly.

"Olug." Jamil held his head and cried in his hands. "Can I tell him bye?"

"Sure. Just yell it out. Nothing is ever really gone, right? Even when you can't see it."

"Olug! Olug! It's me, Jamil! I'm going to come back for you. I will. I promise!" he yelled through the tears.

"Satisfied?" Farsona asked, her voice still cool.

Jamil rose to his feet, with me supporting him and his bag. I wish we'd still had dust, enough to make her completely stop, and not simply slow. We only had Clarod, my spotty magic, and a weakened Jamil.

"Lafia, I'm sorry. I'm sorry about Nontu and—"

"It's alright. Save your strength, Jamil. Everything is going to be alright. It's time to get out of here and go home."

"How?"

"You aren't in any shape to worry about that," Farsona said in a motherly voice. "I told you it's easier to get out, when we work together."

"Come on, Lafia," Jamil said.

Farsona's stone fell around her neck, beckoning me, still. I'd have time. "Can I walk with him?"

"To a point. He will be fine." Farsona sounded smug and confident. She'd won and gotten what she'd wanted.

"What do you mean? What about you, Lafia?"

"I need to do something. It's okay," I whispered and winked.

"Don't even think about it, Lafia. Not by yourself. That's ridiculous," he said angrily but was still too weak to do anything.

"It'll be fine. I'll be right behind you. We can walk back together," I smiled, supporting him.

"You can't do this, Lafia. We'll go together and I'll come back to finish this."

"You are special, Jamil. You would make a great Ajur if you let yourself. Maybe now, you can. You aren't irresponsible or selfish or any of those things I thought. Now I understand why you made some of the choices you did, but you should live your life for you and keep your royal genes alive. They are good ones."

I swallowed and pressed down my tears this time.

"Just come with me now." He took pained steps back the way we came.

The first shimmers of light appeared. Farsona was opening a portal. I put the bags down and stood in front of him. I wanted to remember his face, his bright brown eyes that took in the world as only he could, and the lips I would never kiss, but had yearned to for so long. His hands were strong and warm on mine. I let my fingers slide between his, not wanting to let go.

"Jamil. I am sorry if you thought I didn't like you before. But you were never available to me, and my heart couldn't take loving you from a distance. That may have to be enough now."

"Lafia, I love you too and if ever I would rethink my choice, it is because of you."

I lowered my head and slid off the other ring and placed it on his pinky. "Keep this as a reminder of this journey we shared on behalf of Maradobu, a land we love more than anything else, including ourselves."

"You never take these off, Lafia. You've lost the Narutian ring! You should keep this. I will see you again soon for the wedding."

I looked into his eyes and unclasped the necklace Adamma had given to me.

"Will you hold onto this for me? I don't want to lose it. Not here. It was a gift from Adamma."

"Lafia Ketonga, what are you doing?" Jamil squeezed my fingers as he whispered, unable to mask the concern.

"I'm finishing this and making things right because I love you. I love Adamma. I love Naeemah and my parents. But above all else, I love Maradobu. Maradobu is, always."

He put his forehead to mine. "Be careful. I expect to see you at the wedding after you've passed your Demonstration of Magic so I can be the first to officially court you and dance with you."

I smiled weakly and gently kissed his cheek. "You would do that? Court me?"

"It would be my honor. If you would allow me."

"Well, I believe after this trip passing my Demonstration of Magic will seem easy and when I do, I'll hold you to that."

"You've done everything. You've proved it all and I will testify to that. That's the other way to pass, through real life demonstration." He took both of my hands, his fingers grasped around mine.

"May the light of the dark moon be within you, Jamil. Always."

"Lafia," he said his eyes narrowing before nodding, "And may it be—"

The portal was directly behind him. I slung his backpack through. He paused to look. "And may it be within—"

I pushed him through as the word "you" fell from his lips.

It would not be within me again.

***

The shimmering faded as the portal separating me from everyone on the other side disappeared. My palms were damp from the tears that continued to fall.

Farsona floated above me, lingering a moment before holding her hand out and drawing closer. "We have much to do! A wedding to plan and so much to prepare for."

Her smile was different now. "Those from the other side can only see what they choose to see. They don't see the Tokahaya I see; the magic and beauty that exists within. But you will."

"I am completely disconnected," I wept.

"Daughter of Narut you will one day be Queen of the entire Tokahaya, but first you will learn of the inner workings of the Cantulet realm and the Tokahaya, which is separate from your world but connected. You are already connected to us and will never be disconnected."

Farsona spun her hands to reveal another shimmering portal.

"Understand that until you complete your vows the rains will continue. When your commitment is satisfied, I will be as well."

My head ached as I tried to process what she'd said and what I was seeing. The portal was nothing like the one she'd opened for Olug, reminding me instead of where Catia had gone. Beyond the opening was a dazzling brightness and the warmth on my face was inviting as we floated through.

"Let me welcome you, newest daughter and future queen, to the Tokahaya."

Thank you for reading Light of the Dark Moon.
Your review of this novel would be greatly appreciated.

If you enjoyed this book, please check out
Star Jumpers: An Accidental Quest for Freedom.

GLOSSARY

Please note this is my (the author) attempt to provide some helpful context to the reader of people and places, most importantly.

Maradobu, Faduwata and Zhiri

To help you get a lay of the land, Maradobu is a land mass with mountains bordering the north and oceans to the west, south, and east. Zhiri, the island where magical mythical creatures are primarily from is an island to the south, connected to the mainland of Faduwata by a long bridge.

Maradobu is the world containing Faduwata and Zhiri. Maradobu is primarily inhabited by those living in the Faduwatan alliance area and in Zhiri.

The Tokahaya is a realm accessible from Faduwata but within a different dimension. It has a strong connection to Faduwata.

There are four ajurdoms (kingdoms) in the Faduwata alliance, each with a leader and light leader. The ajurdoms are Narut, Sparaka, Emervy, and Wallarin. At the center, in a neutral area is Faduwata Central, where alliance governance is done, and all stations can be accessed by going through it.

GLOSSARY OF PEOPLE AND PLACES

Emervy

Emervy is a forested land with mining resources to the east of Faduwata.

Emervy is led by the Koda royal family consisting of:

Arstut: Ajur and Clarhugaba of Emervy. Father/Adon of Najurvod

Najurvod – Only child and sun of Arstut. Crown prince (ajursun) of Emervy

Royal Stone: The royal stone is the Jerhun stone. This stone is known for its gifts of renewal and restoration of life and energy.

Color: Forest green

Narut

Narut is the northernmost ajurdom. It is led by the Ketonga royal family.

Rufan Ketonga: Ruler of Narut. Spouse and partner to Selifaya. Adon/father of Kyari, Lafia, and Naeemah.

Selifaya Ketonga: Light Leader (Clarhugaba) of Narut. Second in command of Narut. Spouse and partner to Rufan. Mada/mother of Kyari, Lafia, and Naeemah.

Kyari (kee ar ee) Ketonga: Eldest child and daughter of Selifaya and Rufan. Crown princess (ajursun) and future clarhugaba with access to throne of Narut.

Lafia Ketonga: Middle child and daughter of Selifaya and Rufan.

Naeemah Ketonga: Youngest child and daughter of Selifaya and Rufan. Sister of Lafia. Also called Ny.

Helna: Hair, makeup, and nail artist for royal family

Tamki: Transport Operator working on outskirts of Narut

Royal Stone: The royal stone is the Dunha stone. This stone offers Narut and Faduwata courage, motivation, and the renewal of the inner light.

Color: Ruby red

Sparaka

Sparaka is the southernmost ajurdom. It is led by the Ketonga royal family.

Led by the Rityr royal family consisting of:

Orin Rityr: Ruler of Sparaka. Spouse and partner to Kima. Adon/father of Hakur, Jamil, and Asabe.

Clarhugaba – Kima Rityr: Light Leader (Clarhugaba) of Sparaka. Second in command of Sparaka. Spouse and partner to Orin. Mada/mother of Hakur, Jamil, and Asabe.

Hakur: Eldest child and son of Orin and Kima. Crown prince (ajursun).

Jamil: Middle child and son of Orin and Kima.

Asabe: Third child and daughter of Orin and Kima.

Royal Syte: Mareda

Olug: Jamil's friend from Sparaka

Orfil: Orin's twin brother.

Juxi: Transport Operator who took Lafia from Sparaka to Zhiri

Meyrnul: Owner of Maradobuan House of Magic and Mystery

Royal Stone: The royal stone is the Eltris stone. This stone gives the important gifts of patience and forgiveness and the power to remain thoughtful and calm under stress.

Color: Royal Blue

Wallarin

Wallarin sits between Narut and Sparaka, bordering the ocean with ample farmlands and agriculture. It is led by the royal family led by Bellrin Adera.

Bellrin Adera: Ruler and Light Leader (Ajur and Clarhugaba) of Wallarin. Grandmother of Hemole and Bletondu.

Bletondu: Oldest grandchild and crown princess (ajursun).

Hemole: Second grandchild and grandson of Bellrin.

Royal Syte: Femi

Royal Stone: The royal stone is the Clori stone. The clori stone provides abundant energy and a strong will.

Color: Golden yellow

Tokahaya

The Tokahaya is the dimension from which gray smoke appears.
Tokaya Ru Farsona – Ruler of the Tokahaya
Jantasa – One of Farsona's primary sagals, wears shimmering gray.
Catia – Child held in the Tokahaya.
Kesi – One of Farsona's primary sagals, wears dark gray.
Duluri – Tall full-figured sagal

GLOSSARY OF TERMS AND MYTHICAL CREATURES

Ajurdom: A land area united under a leading family (Kingdom)

Ajur: Ruler of an ajurdom

Ajursun: Children of the Ajur

Bintas: Pegasus type, flying animal like a horse and unicorn from Zhiri

Bollak Tree: Grows in Emervy and is extremely strong. Used for building and furniture as well as ships. Takes a tree three hundred primary moons to reach maturity and bear fruit.

Carsos: Horse

Clar: Light

Clar magana: Light communicator

Clarhugaba: Light Leader

Dakruhi: Spiritual practice room

The Dark Moon: The moon of power

Epers: Under grounders. They have no sight and are adapted to colder temperatures. They were placed in Zhiri.

Etawae Moon: Waning phase of their moons

Haskeal: Light fairies

Joju Syrup: Sweetener similar to honey

Kanamu: Dwarves

Monedutse Stone: The sacred stone of the Dark Moon

Mugaljana: The mind and thought whisperers

Ni: No

Reffal: A noisy bird in Maradobu

Ruwatane: Water people

Sagals: Tokahaya women in service to the Tokaya Ru

Syte: One from Zhiri holding the four light gifts and magic.\

Teta Fruit: Grown in Wallarin (Inspired by the soursop fruit grown in Jamaica)

Venna: Elves

Wifferin: Manticore

Ya'i: Yes

PHRASES FROM THE EPERS

Echrugen au?: Who goes there?

Heim: Boy/Man

Oulls: Under Grounders

Ne: No

Su'Heim: Girl/Woman

Weide oulls: Upper grounders

Also by the Author

Fiction

The Story of Ervin James

Star Jumpers: An Accidental Quest for Freedom

Out of the Woods

Crossed: The Karma Crusades

Nonfiction

Heaven is Now: Enough Excuses

Resist Persist

Protect and Clear with the Divine

ABOUT THE AUTHOR

Bernette is a multi-genre writer and creative with a passion for creating and inspiring positive change in people. She lives in the metro Atlanta area with her family.

Creative Works: https://MountHopeMedia.com
Intuitive Services and Books: https://BernetteSherman.com
TikTok: https://TikTok.com/@BernettetheWriter
Instagram: https://Instagram.com/IAmBernette
Instagram: https://Instagram.com/MountHopeMedia
Facebook: https://Facebook.com/IAmBernetteSherman
Facebook: https://Facebook.com/MountHopeMedia

www.ingramcontent.com/pod-product-compliance
Lightning Source LLC
Chambersburg PA
CBHW020930020726
47495CB00002B/423